The Darkening Sea

Also by Alexander Kent

To Glory We Steer
Form Line of Battle!
Enemy in Sight!
The Flag Captain
Sloop of War
Command a King's Ship
Signal – Close Action!
Richard Bolitho, Midshipman
Passage to Mutiny
In Gallant Company
Midshipman Bolitho and the 'Avenger'
The Inshore Squadron
Stand into Danger
A Tradition of Victory
Success to the Brave
Colours Aloft!
Honour This Day
With all Despatch
The Only Victor
Beyond the Reef

The Darkening Sea

Alexander Kent

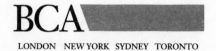

LONDON NEW YORK SYDNEY TORONTO

This edition published in 1993 by BCA
by arrangement with William Heinemann Ltd
an imprint of Reed Consumer Books Ltd

Copyright © Highseas Authors Ltd 1993
The author has asserted his moral rights

CN 2275

Phototypeset by Intype, London
Printed In England by Clays Ltd, St Ives plc

To Mike and Bee Hartree,
with our love

The lights begin to twinkle from the rocks:
The long day wanes: the slow moon climbs: the deep
Moans round with many voices. Come, my friends,
'Tis not too late to seek a newer world.
Push off, and sitting well in order smite
The sounding furrows; for my purpose holds
To sail beyond the sunset, and the baths
Of all the western stars, until I die.

Tennyson, 'Ulysses'

Contents

1

Landfall

The meandering track that ran around the wide curve of Falmouth Bay was just wide enough to allow passage to horse and rider, and only slightly less dangerous than the footpath which was somewhere beneath it. To the stranger or the fool-hardy either could be hazardous.

On this particular dawn the coast appeared abandoned, its sounds confined to the cries of seabirds, the occasional lively trill of an early robin, and the repetitive call of a cuckoo which never seemed to get any closer. In places some of the cliff had fallen away, so that where the track ran closer to the edge it was possible to hear the boom of the sea against the jagged rocks below. Rarely still, it was never to be taken for granted.

There was a damp chill in the air but this was late June, and within hours the horizon would be hard and clear, the sea glittering with a million mirrors. The horse and rider rose slowly above a steep slope and paused like a piece of statuary or, like this bewitched coast, a vision which might suddenly vanish.

Lady Catherine Somervell tried to relax her body as she stared back above the drifting mist. They must have thought her mad at the big grey house below Pendennis Castle, like the stableboy who had snatched up a lantern when she had startled him out of sleep. He had mumbled something about calling the head groom or the coachman, but she had refused. As he had saddled Tamara, the powerful mare Richard Bolitho had found for her, she had felt the same sense of urgency, and a conviction which her rational mind could not dismiss.

She had dressed herself in the big room, their room, with the same driving desperation. Her long dark hair was only loosely pinned about her ears, and she wore her thick riding skirt and one of Richard's old sea-going coats, which she often used on her cliff walks.

She had felt the gorse and bushes dragging at her skirt as Tamara had moved purposefully along the track; had tasted the sea. The enemy as Bolitho had once called it, his voice so bitter in one of those rare, private moments.

She stroked the horse's neck to reassure herself. A fast packet had brought news to Falmouth from the Caribbean. The English fleet and a considerable force of soldiers and marines had attacked Martinique, the main base for French naval operations there. The French had surrendered, and most of their activities in the Caribbean and on the Main had ceased.

Catherine had watched the faces of the people in the square when the news had been read out by a dragoon officer. Most of them would be unaware of the importance of Martinique, a thorn in Britain's side for so many years, or even know where it was. There was little enthusiasm and no cheers either, for this was 1809, and four years had passed since the death of Nelson, the nation's darling, and the battle of Trafalgar which must have seemed to many the final stage of this endless war.

And with the packet had come a letter from Richard. He had written in great haste, with no time for details. The fighting was over and he was quitting his flagship, the ninety-four gun *Black Prince*, and was under orders to return to England with all haste. It did not seem possible even now. He had been absent for little more than nine months. She had steeled herself for a much longer period, two years or even three. She had existed only for his letters, and had thrown herself into helping Bryan Ferguson, Bolitho's one-armed steward. With every young man pressed into the fleet, unless they were lucky enough to hold a protection, it was difficult to keep the farm and estate working. There were several crippled men who had once served with Bolitho, men he now cared for much as he

2

had tried to do at sea. Many landowners would have thrown them on the beach, as Richard called it, left them to beg from those they had fought to protect.

But all that mattered now was that he was coming home. First to Falmouth. She shivered as if it were winter. The rest could wait until he was here, in her arms.

She had read his short letter so many times, trying to guess why he had been required to hand over his command to another flag officer. Valentine Keen had also been replaced, and perhaps was intended for promotion. She thought of Keen's young wife and felt a touch of envy. She was with child; it must be due, born even. But Keen's well-meaning family had taken Zenoria to one of their fine houses in Hampshire. She had been the only girl Catherine had found it easy to talk with. Love, suffering, courage – they had both experienced their extremes in the past.

There had been a very unexpected visitor after she had received Richard's letter. Stephen Jenour, his flag lieutenant and the newly appointed commander of a smart brig, *Orcadia*, had come to see her while his command was taking on stores in Carrick Roads: a different Jenour, not merely because of what he had endured in the open boat after the wreck of the *Golden Plover*, but matured also by a sense of loss. His own command, taken at Richard Bolitho's insistence after returning to England with their captured French prize, had also removed him from daily contact with the superior he respected, loved even, more than any other yet encountered in the course of his young life.

They had talked until the shadows were deep in the room and the candles had been guttering. He had told her of the battle in his own words, as Bolitho had requested. But as he had spoken she had heard only Richard, the men who had fought and died, the huzzas and the suffering, victory and despair.

What would Richard be thinking on his way home? Of his Happy Few, his band of brothers? There were even fewer now with Jenour gone.

She nudged the horse and Tamara moved forward again, her ears twitching towards the sea, the continuous murmur against the rocks. The tide was on the make. She smiled. She had been listening too long to Richard and his friends, and the fishermen who brought their catch up to Flushing or into Falmouth itself.

Always the sea was there. Waiting.

She strained her eyes towards it now but there was still too much mist, and not enough light to see the headland.

She thought of her ride here. The countryside stirring itself, the smell of freshly baked bread, of foxgloves and the wild roses in the hedgerows. She had seen few people about but had sensed their presence: very little was missed by these folk whose families had known the Bolithos from generation to generation, and the men who had gone year after year to die in forgotten campaigns or great sea-battles. Like the portraits on the walls in the old house, watching her when she had gone up alone to bed, measuring her still.

At least Richard would have had his beloved nephew Adam with whom to share the days at sea. He had finished his letter by revealing that he would be sailing independently in Adam's own command. She allowed her mind to stray once more to Zenoria, and then to Zenoria and Adam. Was it merely imagination, or that warning instinct which had been born out of her own early years?

She reined the horse around, her fingers groping for the small carriage pistol she always carried. She had not even seen or heard them. Relief surged through her as she saw the dull glint of their buttons. They were coastguards.

One of them exclaimed, 'Why, Lady Somervell! You gave us a start! Toby here thought some gennelmen were runnin' a cargo up from the beach!'

Catherine tried to smile. 'I am sorry, Tom. I should have known better.'

The light was already strengthening, as if to dispel her hopes, lay bare her foolishness.

Tom the coastguard watched her thoughtfully. The admiral's lady, the one who was the talk of London according to some. But she had called him by his name. As if he mattered.

He said carefully, 'May I ask what you be doing up 'ere at this hour, m'lady? Could be dangerous.'

She faced him directly, and afterwards he was to remember this moment, her fine dark eyes, her high cheekbones, her utter conviction as she said, 'Sir Richard is coming home. In the *Anemone*.'

'I knows that, m'lady. We had word from the navy.'

'Today,' she said. 'This morning.' Her eyes seemed to blur and she turned away.

Tom said kindly, 'There be no way o' knowing, m'lady. Wind, weather, tides . . .'

He broke off as she slipped from the saddle, her stained boots striking the track as one. 'What is it?'

She stared out at the bay as it began to open up, the light spilling above the headland like glass.

'Do you have a telescope, please?' Desperation put an edge to her voice.

The two coastguards dismounted and Tom lifted his glass from a long leather case behind his saddle.

Catherine did not even see them. 'Be easy, Tamara!' She rested the long telescope on the saddle, still warm from her own body. Gulls were swooping around a tiny boat far out towards the point. It seemed much clearer than before, and pink on the sea's face she saw the first sunlight.

Tom's companion had also extended his telescope, and after a few minutes he said, 'There *be* a ship out there, Tom, by God so there be! Beggin' your pardon, m'lady!'

She had not heard him. She watched the sails, misty and unreal like shells, the darker line of the slender hull beneath.

'What is she, Toby? Can you see her rig?'

The man sounded stunned. 'Frigate. No doubt o' that. Seen too many o' they in an' out o' Carrick Roads over th' years!'

'Still, could be anyone. Ride down to the harbour an' see if you can discover anythin' . . .'

They both turned as she said quietly, 'It is he.'

She had extended the telescope to its full length. She waited for the horse to quieten so that she could stare without blinking. Then she said, 'I can see her figurehead in the sunshine.' She handed back the glass, her eyes suddenly blind. '*Anemone* . . .' She saw it in her mind's eye as she had seen it in reality, before the ship had tacked into shadow again: the

5

full-breasted girl with the raised trumpet, her gilt paint so clear in the reflected glare. She repeated as if to herself, '*Anemone* . . . daughter of the wind.'

She leaned her face against the horse. 'Thank God. You came back to me.'

Vice-Admiral Sir Richard Bolitho awoke from a disturbed sleep and stared up at the darkness of the small sleeping-cabin, his mind responding instantly to the sounds and movements around him. His sailor's instinct told him that like the cabin the sea was still dark outside this lithe, graceful hull: a command for which any young officer would give his right arm. He listened to the dull thud of the tiller head as it matched the rudder's strength against the sea and the wind's thrust in the sails, heard the sluice of water alongside as the frigate *Anemone* leaned over on a new tack to a different motion. Gone were the great soaring thrusts of the Western Ocean, through hard sunshine and lashing rain in equal portions. Here the seas were short and steep as the ship ploughed her way nearer to the land. Three weeks from the Caribbean. Adam had driven his *Anemone* like the thoroughbred she was.

Bolitho clambered from the swaying cot and steadied himself with one hand on a deckhead beam until he was accustomed to the lively movements. A frigate: no man could want more. He recalled the ones he had commanded as a youthful captain, younger even than Adam. The ships so different, yet still familiar. Only the faces, the men themselves seemed blurred, if not forgotten.

He felt his heart beat faster as he thought of the nearness of land. After miles of ocean without even sighting another ship, they were almost home. Today they would anchor in Falmouth, and after a brief pause for fresh water Adam would sail again for Portsmouth, from which place he would send the brief details of their return to the new telegraph that linked the senior naval port with the Admiralty in London.

They had sighted the Lizard at dusk the previous evening before losing it again in a sea mist. Bolitho recalled how he and Allday had watched it on another occasion. It had been

6

first light then too, and he had whispered her name, longing for her, as he was now.

Overnight Old Partridge, *Anemone*'s sailing master, had changed tack so that in the darkness, close-hauled and under reefed topsails, they had given the dreaded Manacles a wide berth.

Bolitho knew he could not sleep and toyed with the idea of going on deck, but he was also aware that his presence there might distract the watchkeepers. It had been hard enough for them to get used to a vice-admiral in their midst, and a famous one at that. He gave a grim smile. Notorious, anyway.

He had watched and listened to the way the frigate's cramped company of some two hundred and twenty officers, seamen and marines had worked as a team, quick to respond to storm and screaming gales like the seasoned hands they had become. Adam could be proud of what he and his young wardroom had achieved, with the backing of some excellent warrant officers like Old Partridge. Adam was probably dreading the arrival in Portsmouth, where it was more than likely some of his best hands would be transferred to other vessels that were short of men. Like poor Jenour, Bolitho thought. So eager to do well in the navy, and yet because of his loyalty and friendship, unwilling to leave his admiral and take charge of the French prize, and a captured enemy flag officer for good measure. He thought too of the good-byes when he had left the *Black Prince* for the last time. Julyan the sailing master who had worn Bolitho's hat to deceive the enemy when they had closed for battle with the French flagship after Copenhagen; Old Fitzjames the gunner who could lay and fire a thirty-two pounder as easily as a Royal Marine could aim his musket; Bourchier, major of marines, and so many others who would never see anything again. Men who had died, often horribly, not for King and Country as the *Gazette* would proclaim, but for each other. For their ship.

The keel bit into a deep swell and Bolitho opened the screen door to *Anemone*'s stern cabin. So much more spacious than older frigates, he thought; so unlike *Phalarope*, the first he had commanded. But even here in the captain's private domain the guns were tethered securely behind their sealed ports. The

7

furniture, the small touches of civilized living, could all be rushed below decks, the screens and doors torn down to open this place, this ship, from bow to stern with the long eighteen-pounders on either side. A ship of war.

He thought suddenly of Keen. Perhaps his departure had been the greatest wrench of all. Promotion, and well-deserved, awaited him: to commodore or even to rear-admiral. It would be as big a change of circumstances as it had once been for Bolitho himself.

One night when he had been dining with Adam, while the ship drove blindly on into an Atlantic squall with every shroud and halliard screaming like an insane orchestra, he had mentioned Keen's promotion and the differences it would bring to Zenoria. Catherine had written to him of the impending birth, and he had guessed that she had wanted Zenoria with her at Falmouth. What would become of the child, he wondered. The navy like his father? Keen's record and success as both captain and natural leader would give any boy a good beginning.

Or the law, or the City perhaps? Keen's family came of far wealthier stock than the usual inhabitants of any midshipman's berth in some overcrowded liner.

Adam had not commented immediately. He had been listening to the slap of feet on deck, the sudden bawl of commands as the helm had gone over yet again.

'If I had to begin all over again, Uncle, I'd not ask for a finer tutor.'

He had hesitated, just for an instant the thin, half-starved midshipman who had walked all the way from Penzance to search for his unknown uncle, with only Bolitho's name scrawled on a piece of paper. 'Nor a better friend . . .'

Bolitho had intended to make light of it, but knew that this was far too important to the youthful captain who had been sitting across the table from him. It was something very private, like that other secret which was rarely out of Bolitho's thoughts. They had shared so much, but the time to share that had not yet come.

Then Adam had said quietly, 'Captain Keen is a very lucky man.'

Adam had insisted that the sleeping cabin should be for his guest, while he had been content to take his rest in the stern cabin. That caused Bolitho to recall another incident on this passage, which for the most part had been uneventful. On the day after the ship's company had spread the lighter canvas for the final run in toward the Western Approaches he had found Adam sitting in the stern cabin at his table, an empty goblet in his fingers.

Bolitho had seen his distress, the disgust he obviously felt for himself, and had asked, 'What ails you, Adam? Tell me what you will – I shall do all I can.'

Adam had looked up at him and replied, 'It is my birthday today, Uncle.' He had said it in such a steady, level tone that only Bolitho would have known he had been drinking, and not merely the one goblet. It was something Adam would have punished any of his officers for. He loved this ship, the command he had always wanted.

'I know.' Bolitho had sat down, afraid that the sight of his vice-admiral's gold lace would drop a barrier between them.

'I am twenty-nine.' He had glanced around the cabin, his eyes suddenly wistful.

'Beyond *Anemone*, I have nothing.' He had swung round as his cabin servant had entered. 'What the *hell* do you want, man?'

That too had been unusual, and it had helped to bring him to his senses.

'I am sorry. That was unforgivable when you cannot answer me back for my intolerance.' The servant backed away, hurt and confused.

Then there was another interruption, when the second lieutenant had entered and informed his captain that it was all but time to call both watches and change tack.

Adam had acknowledged him with equal formality. 'I shall come up directly, Mr Martin.' As the door had closed he had reached for his hat, and hesitated before adding, 'On my birthday last year I was kissed by a lady.'

Bolitho had asked, 'Do I know her?'

Adam had already been listening to the trill of calls, the

9

stampede of feet across the deck. 'I think not, Uncle. I don't think anyone does.' Then he had gone.

Bolitho made up his mind, and disdaining a boat cloak he found his way to the quarterdeck.

The smells, the creak of spars and timbers, the stress and strain of all the miles of standing and running rigging – it made him feel very young again. He seemed to hear the admiral's response to his plea for a ship, any ship, when the war had broken out with Revolutionary France.

Still weakened by the fever which had cut him down in the Great South Sea, and with every officer clamouring for re-employment or a command, he had almost begged.

I am a frigate captain . . .

The admiral's cold answer, '*Were* a frigate captain, Bolitho,' had wounded him for a long, long time.

He smiled, the strain dropping away from his face. Instead of a frigate they had given him *Hyperion*. 'The Old Hyperion', about which they still yarned and even sang in the taverns and wherever sailors gathered.

He heard voices and thought he could smell coffee. That would be his mole-like servant Ozzard. Ozzard never seemed surprised by anything, although it was hard to read the man's thoughts. Was he glad to be going home? Or did he even care?

He stepped on to the wet planking and glanced at the dark figures around him. The midshipman of the watch was already whispering to the sailing master that their illustrious passenger was up and about.

Adam stood with Peter Sargeant, his senior lieutenant. Sargeant was probably already ear-marked for his own command, Bolitho thought. Adam would miss him if that happened.

Ozzard moved from the shadows with his coffee pot and presented him with a steaming mug. 'All fresh, Sir Richard, but almost the end of it.'

Adam crossed to his side, his dark hair ruffling in the damp wind.

'Rosemullion Head on the larboard bow, Sir Richard.' The formality was not lost on either of them. 'Mr Partridge assures me we shall be off Pendennis Point by four bells of the forenoon watch.'

Bolitho nodded and sipped the scalding coffee, recalling the shop to which Catherine had taken him in London's St James's Street. She had bought fine coffee and good wines, cheeses, and other small luxuries he would never have troubled about. He watched the sunlight breaking across the rocky coast and the rolling green hills beyond. *Home.*

'That was a fast passage, Captain. A pity you cannot take time to come to the house.'

Adam did not look at him. 'I shall cherish that in my mind, sir.'

The first lieutenant touched his hat. 'I shall hoist our number when we are within range, sir.' He was speaking to his captain, but Bolitho knew it was directed at himself.

He said quietly, 'I think she will already know, Mr Sargeant.'

He saw Allday's powerful shape by one of the gangways. As if he could feel his gaze like something physical the big coxswain turned and glanced up at him, his tanned face breaking into a lazy grin.

We are here, old friend. Like all those other times. Still together.

'Stand by to wear ship! Man the braces! Hands aloft an' loose t'gallants!'

Bolitho stood by the rail. *Anemone* would make a perfect picture as she altered course.

For a perfect landfall.

Captain Adam Bolitho stood at the weather side of the quarterdeck, arms folded, content to leave the final approach to his first lieutenant. He watched the crouching walls and tower of Pendennis Castle as it seemed to swing very slowly through the black criss-cross of tarred rigging as if snared in a net.

Many glasses would be trained from the old castle, which with the fort and battery on the opposite headland had guarded the harbour entrance for centuries. Beyond Pendennis and hidden in the green hillside was the old grey Bolitho house with all its memories, of its sons who had left this very port never to return.

He tried not to think of the night when Zenoria had found

11

him drinking brandy, his eyes burning with tears for his uncle who had been reported lost in the transport *Golden Plover*. Was that only last year?

Bolitho had told him Zenoria was with child. He had dared not consider that it might be his. Only Catherine had been near to discovering the truth, and Bolitho's concern for Adam himself had almost made him confess what he had done. But if he feared the consequences, Adam feared what the truth might do to his uncle far more.

He saw Allday's massive bulk by the larboard guns, lost in his own thoughts; wondering perhaps about the woman he had saved from robbery and worse and who now owned the little inn, the Stag over at Fallowfield. *Home is the sailor*.

Old Partridge's voice intruded.

'Let 'er fall off a point!'

'Nor' by East, sir! Steady she goes!'

The picture of the land shifted again as the frigate pointed her long tapering jib-boom towards the entrance and Carrick Roads.

A fine ship's company. It had taken patience and a few knocks, but Adam was proud of them. His blood still ran like ice-water when he recalled how *Anemone* had been lured into the range of a shore battery firing heated shot by a vessel carrying French soldiers. It had been as near as that. He glanced along the clean length of the maindeck where the men now waited at the braces and halliards for the run up to the anchorage. Heated shot would have turned his beloved *Anemone* into a pillar of fire: the sun-dried sails and tarred rigging, the stores of powder and shot would have been gone in minutes. His jaw tightened as he recalled how they had gone about to pull out of range, but not before he had poured a devastating broadside into the enemy's bait and given her the terrible end intended for his own ship.

He remembered too how Captain Valentine Keen had been ordered to return home in this same ship, but then at the last moment had sailed in a larger frigate accompanying the captured French admiral, Baratte. It had been a near thing. Bolitho had never revealed his innermost thoughts about

Herrick's failure to support him in that engagement when he had so needed help against great odds.

Adam gripped the quarterdeck rail until the pain steadied him. *God damn him to hell.* Herrick's betrayal must have hurt Bolitho so deeply that he could not talk about it.

After all he had done for him – *as he has done for me.*

His mind returned warily to Zenoria. Did she hate him for what had happened?

Would Keen ever discover the truth?

It would be sweet revenge if I ever have to quit the navy as my father once did, if only to protect those I love.

The first lieutenant murmured, 'The admiral's coming up, sir.'

'Thank you, Mr Sargeant.' He was bound to lose him when they reached Portsmouth, and some other valuable men as well. He saw the lieutenant watching him and added quietly, 'I have been hard on you, Peter, over the past months.' He touched his sleeve as Bolitho would have done. 'A captain's life is not all luxury, as you will one day discover!'

They turned and touched their hats as Bolitho walked into the sunlight. He was dressed in his best frock coat, with the glittering silver stars on either epaulette. The vice-admiral again: the image the public, and for that matter most of the navy, cherished and recognised. Not the man in the flapping shirt and shabby old sea-going coat. This was the hero, the youngest vice-admiral on the Navy List. Envied by some, hated by others, the talk and the topic of gossip in the coffee houses and at every smart London reception. The man who had risked everything for the woman he loved: reputation, security. Adam could not begin to measure it.

Bolitho was carrying his cocked hat as if to hold at bay the last trappings of authority, so that his hair was dishevelled by the wind. It was still as black as Adam's own, except for the one rebellious lock above his right eye where a cutlass had almost ended his life. The lock over the scar was greyish white, as if he had been branded.

Lieutenant Sargeant watched them together. It had been a revelation to him when, like the rest of the wardroom, he had overcome his nervousness at the prospect of having a man so

13

famous and so admired by the navy in general amongst them, sharing the intimate life of a fifth-rate, and he had been able to observe his admiral at close quarters. Admiral and captain might have been brothers, so strong was the family resemblance. Sargeant had heard many remark on this. And the warmth of their regard for one another had put the wardroom at ease. Bolitho had gone around the ship, 'feeling his way' as his burly coxswain had described it, but never interfering. Sargeant was aware of Bolitho's reputation as one of the navy's foremost frigate captains, and knew in some way he must have been sharing Adam's joy in *Anemone*.

Adam said gently, 'I shall miss you, Uncle.' His voice was almost lost in the squeal of blocks and the rush of hands to the cathead, ready to let go one of the great anchors. He too was holding on to this moment, willing to share it with nobody.

'I wish you could come to the house, Adam.' He studied Adam's profile as his eyes moved aloft and then to the helmsmen, from the masthead pendant streaming out like a lance to the slope of *Anemone*'s deck as the wheel and rudder took command.

Adam smiled, and it made him look like a boy again. 'I cannot. We must take on fresh water and depart with all despatch. Please convey my warmest greetings to Lady Catherine.' He hesitated. 'And any who care for me.'

Bolitho glanced over and saw Allday watching him, his head on one side like a shaggy, questioning dog.

He said, 'I shall take the gig, Allday. I'll send it back for you and Yovell, and any gear we may have overlooked.'

Allday, who hated to leave his side, did not blink. He understood. Bolitho wanted to meet her alone.

'Ready to come about, sir!'

With her courses already brailed up and under reefed topsails, *Anemone* curtsied around in the freshening breeze. It was the sort of weather she had always relished.

'*Let go!*'

A great burst of spray shot above the beakhead as the anchor plummeted down for the first time since the sun and beaches of the Caribbean. Men, starved of loved ones, homes and perhaps children they had barely known, stared around

14

at the green slopes of Cornwall, the tiny pale dots of sheep on the hillsides. There were few who would be allowed ashore even when they reached Portsmouth, and already there were scarlet-coated marines on the gangways and in the bows, ready to fire on anyone foolish enough to try to swim to the shore.

Afterwards he thought it was like a dream sequence. Bolitho heard the trill of a call as the gig was hoisted out and lowered alongside, its crew very smart in checkered shirts and tarred hats. Adam had learned well. A man-of-war was always judged first by her boats and their crews.

'*Man the side!*'

The Royal Marines fell in by the entry port, a sergeant taking the place of their officer, who had died of his wounds and now lay fathoms deep in that other ocean.

Boatswain's mates moistened their calls with their lips, eyes moving occasionally to the man who was about to leave them, the man who had not only talked with them in the dog watches but also had listened, as if he had really needed to know them, the ordinary men who must follow him even to the cannon's mouth if so ordered. Some had been perplexed by the experience. They had been expecting to find the legend. Instead they had discovered a human being.

Bolitho turned towards them and raised his hat. Allday saw his sudden distress as a probing shaft of sunlight lanced down through the shrouds and neatly furled sails to touch his injured eye.

It was always a bad moment, and Allday had to restrain himself from stepping up to help him over the side where the gig swayed to its lines, a midshipman standing in the stern-sheets to receive their passenger.

Bolitho nodded to them, and turned his face away. 'I wish you all good fortune. I am proud to have been in your midst.'

Vague impressions now, the cloud of pipeclay above the bayonetted muskets as the guard presented arms, the piercing twitter of calls, the fleeting anxiety on Allday's rugged features as he reached the gig in safety. He saw Adam by the rail, his hand half-raised, while behind him his lieutenants and warrant officers sought to be the first to take his attention. A man-of-war at sea or in harbour was never at rest, and already boats

15

were putting off from the harbour wall to conduct, if they could, every kind of business from the sale of tobacco and fruit to the services of women of the town, if a captain would permit them on board.

'Give way all!' The midshipman's voice was a squeak. Bolitho shaded his eyes to see the people on the nearest jetty. Faintly, above the scream of gulls circling some incoming fishing boats, he heard the church clock strike the half-hour. Old Partridge had been right about the time of their arrival. *Anemone* must have anchored exactly at four bells as he had predicted.

More uniforms at the top of the stone stairs, and an old man with a wooden leg who was grinning as if Bolitho were his own son.

Bolitho said, 'Morning, Ned.' He was an old boatswain's mate who had once served with him. What ship? How many years ago?

The man piped after him, 'Did 'ee give they Frenchies a quiltin', zur?'

But Bolitho had hurried away. He had seen her watching him from the narrow lane that led eventually to the house by a less public route.

She stood quite still, only one hand moving as it stroked the horse's neck, her eyes never leaving his face.

He had known she would be here, just as she had been drawn from her bed to be the first, the only one to greet him.

He was home.

Bolitho paused with his arm around Catherine's shoulder, one hand touching her skin. The tall glass doors leading from the library were wide open, and the air was heavy with the fragrance of roses. She glanced at his profile, the white lock of hair etched against his sunburn. She had called it distinguished, to comfort him, although she knew he hated it, as if it were some trick to constantly remind him of the difference in years between them.

She said quietly, 'I have always loved roses. When you took me to see your sister's garden I knew we should have more of them.'

16

He caressed her shoulder, still barely able to believe that he was here, that he had come ashore only an hour ago. All the weeks and the months remembering their time together, her courage and endurance before and after the loss of the *Golden Plover*, when he himself had doubted that they would survive the misery and suffering of an open boat, with the sharks never far away.

A small housemaid hurried past with some linen and looked at Bolitho with astonishment.

'Why, welcome home, Sir Richard! Tes a real joy to see you!'

He smiled. 'I relish being here, my girl.' He saw the servant dart a quick glance at Catherine who was still wearing the old coat, and the riding skirt splashed with dew and marked by the dust of the cliff track.

He asked quietly, 'Have they treated you well, Kate?'

'They have been more than kind. Bryan Ferguson has been a tower of strength.'

'He told me just now when you were sending for coffee that you have put him to shame in the estate office.' He squeezed her. 'I am so *proud* of you.'

She looked across the sloping garden to the low wall and beyond, where the sea's edge shone above the hillside like water in a dam.

'The letters that were waiting for you . . .' She faced him, her fine eyes suddenly anxious. 'Richard – there will be time for us?'

He said, 'They will not even know I am back until Adam sends his despatch on the telegraph from Portsmouth. But nothing has been explained about my recall nor will it be, I suspect, until I visit the Admiralty.'

He searched her face, trying to dispel her fear that they would soon be parted like the last time. 'One thing is certain: Lord Godschale has quit the Admiralty. We shall doubtless have an explanation for *that* before long!'

She seemed satisfied, and with her hand through his arm they walked out into the garden. It was very hot, and the wind seemed to have fallen away to a mere breeze. He wondered if Adam would be able to claw his way out of the harbour.

17

He asked, 'What news of Miles Vincent? You wrote to me that he had been pressed by the *Ipswich*.'

She frowned. 'Roxby wrote to the port admiral when he discovered what had happened. The admiral was going to send a despatch to *Ipswich*'s captain to explain the mistake . . .' She looked at him with surprise as Bolitho said, 'Being pressed into the service he abused with his cruelty and arrogance might do him good! That petty little tyrant needs a lesson, and feeling the justice of the lower deck instead of the gunroom might reap some reward, but I doubt it!'

She paused to shade her eyes. 'I am sorry Adam could not accompany you here.'

The mood left her and she twisted round in his arms and gave him her radiant smile.

'But I lie! I wanted to share you with no one. Oh, dearest of men – you came as I knew you would, and you look so well!'

They walked on in silence until she asked quietly, 'How is your eye?'

He tried to dismiss it. 'Nothing changes, Kate. And sometimes it reminds me of everything we have done . . . that we are so much luckier than those brave ones who will never know a woman's embrace, or smell a new dawn in the hills of Cornwall.'

'I hear people in the yard, Richard.' Her sudden frown faded as she heard Allday's deep laugh.

Bolitho smiled. 'My oak. He stayed behind with Yovell to supervise the landing of some chests, and that splendid wine cooler you gave to me. I would not lose it like the other one.' He spoke calmly but his eyes were faraway.

'It was a brave fight, Kate. We lost some good men that day.' Again the tired shrug. 'But for Captain Rathcullen's initiative I fear things would have gone very much against us.'

She nodded, remembering the intensity on young Stephen Jenour's face when he had visited her, as Richard had requested he should.

'And Thomas Herrick failed you again, in spite of all the danger, and what you had once been to one another . . .'

He stared at the sea and felt his left eye smart slightly. 'Yes.

18

But we won, and now they say that but for our victory our main forces would have had to fall back from Martinique.'

'But for *you*, Richard! You must never forget what you have done for your navy, your country.'

He lowered his head and gently kissed her neck. 'My tiger.'

'Be certain of it!'

Ferguson's wife Grace, the housekeeper, came out to them and stood beaming with a tray of coffee. 'I believed you would like it out here, m'lady.'

She said, 'Yes, that was thoughtful. The house seems extra busy today.'

She reached out suddenly and gripped his hand. 'Too many people, Richard. Demanding to see you, to ask for things, to wish you well. It is difficult to be alone even in our own house.' Then she looked at him, a pulse beating quickly in her neck. 'I have ached for you, wanted you in every way you dare to use me.' She shook her head so that some of her loosely pinned hair fell across her face. 'Is that so wicked?'

He took her hand tightly. 'There *is* a small cove.'

She raised her eyes to his.

'Our special place?' She studied him until her breathing became steadier. 'Now?'

Ferguson found his wife by the stone table in the garden. She was looking at the coffee, which was untouched.

He said, 'I heard horses . . .' He saw her expression and sat down at the table. 'Pity to waste it.' He reached out with his one arm and squeezed his wife's waist. It was hard to remember her as the thin, sickly girl she had been when Bolitho's press gang had caught him and Allday with some others.

'They've gone to find one another again.' She touched his hair, her thoughts, like his, drifting, remembering.

Even down in the town they looked at her ladyship differently now. Once she had been the whore Sir Richard Bolitho had abandoned his wife for, who would turn any man's head with her beauty and her proud defiance. There would always be dislike and contempt from some, but the awe at what she had done and endured aboard the ill-fated *Golden Plover* and the squalor and the fight for survival she had shared with the others in that open boat had changed almost everything.

19

It was said that she had cut down one of the mutineers with her own Spanish comb when Bolitho's plan to retake the vessel had misfired.

Some women had tried to imagine what it would be like to share a small boat with the good and the bad, the desperate and the lustful when everything else seemed lost. The men watched her pass and imagined themselves alone with the vice-admiral's woman.

Grace Ferguson came out of her dreaming with a start. 'It'll be lamb for tonight, Bryan.' She was in charge once more. 'And some of that Frenchie wine they both seem to like.'

He looked at her with amusement. 'Champagne, they call it, my dear.'

As she made to hurry away to begin her preparations she paused and hugged him.

'I'll tell you one thing. They can be no happier than we've been in spite of all th' devils that plagued us!'

Ferguson stared after her. Even now, she could still surprise him.

2

A Very Honourable Man

Bryan Ferguson reined his little trap to a halt and watched his friend as he stared down the lane towards the inn. The Stag's Head was pleasantly situated in the tiny hamlet of Fallowfield on the Helford River. It was almost dusk, but on this balmy June evening he could still see the glint of a stretch of the river through a rank of tall trees, and the air was alive with late birdsong and the buzz of insects.

John Allday was wearing his best blue jacket with the special gilt buttons Bolitho had given him. Each button bore the Bolitho crest, and Allday had been bursting with pride at the gesture: *one of the family*, as he had described himself many times.

Ferguson watched his friend's uncertainty, a nervousness he had not seen in Allday since he had first visited the Stag after saving the life of the woman who now owned it: Unis Polin, the comely widow of a master's mate in the old *Hyperion*. She had been attacked by two footpads even as she had driven her few belongings down to this very place.

Ferguson considered it. With his face tanned like leather, and in his fine blue coat and nankeen breeches, to most people Allday would seem the perfect example of Jack Tar, the sure shield against the French or any other enemy who dared to come against His Britannic Majesty's navy. He had seen and done almost everything. To a privileged few he was also known as more than just Vice-Admiral Sir Richard Bolitho's

21

coxswain. He was his true friend. For some it was hard to picture one without the other.

But on this evening it was difficult for Ferguson to see him as that same confident man. He ventured, 'Losing your nerve, John?'

Allday licked his lips. 'To you an' none other I'll confess that I'm all aback. I've thought of the moment and of her, right enough. When *Anemone* showed her copper as we tacked past Rosemullion Head yonder, my head was packed so full of notions I could barely see straight. But now . . .'

'Afraid of making a fool of yourself?'

'Something like that. Tom Ozzard thinks as much.'

Ferguson shook his head. 'Oh, him! What does he know about women?'

Allday glanced at him. 'Not too sure o' that either.'

Ferguson laid his hand on Allday's arm. It felt like a piece of timber.

'She's a fine woman. Just what you need when you settle down. This damned war can't last much longer.'

'What about Sir Richard?'

Ferguson looked at the darkening river. So that was it. He had guessed as much. The old dog worried about his master. As ever.

Allday took his silence for doubt. 'I'd not leave him. You knows that!'

Ferguson shook the reins very gently and the pony started down the slope. 'You dropped anchor only yesterday, and you've been like a bear with a sore head ever since. You couldn't think of anything else.' He smiled. 'So let's go and see, eh?'

It was St John's Eve, the twenty-third of the month, a feast that dated from pagan times although it was bound up with Christian traditions. Old folk could remember when the celebration was held after sunset and marked by a chain of bonfires right across the county. The fires were blessed with wild flowers and herbs and when all was well alight young couples would often jump hand-in-hand through the flames to ensure good luck, and the blessing was spoken in the old Cornish tongue. A good deal of eating and drinking had accompanied the ceremony, and some doubters maintained that witchcraft rather than religion was paramount.

But this evening was quiet, although they had seen one fire beyond the hamlet, where some farmer or landowner was celebrating with his workers. The chain of bonfires had ceased when the King of France's head had been hacked from his shoulders and the Terror had ripped through that country like a fast fuse. If anyone was indiscreet enough to start up the old custom again here every countryman and the local militia would be drummed to arms, because such a chain of fires would cry invasion.

Ferguson played with the reins. It was almost time. He had to discover something. He had heard all about Allday's old chest wound cutting him down as surely as any enemy ball when he had rescued the woman from the two robbers. Allday could cross blades with anybody, and was like a lion just so long as the wound held its peace. But it was a long walk from the inn to the Bolitho house at Falmouth. A dark track: anything might happen.

He asked bluntly, 'If she takes kindly to you, John – what I mean is . . .'

Surprisingly Allday grinned. 'I'm not staying the night, if that's what you think. It would damage her name hereabouts. She'll still be a foreigner to most.'

Ferguson exclaimed with relief. 'From Devon, you mean!' He looked at him gravely as they turned into the yard. 'I've got to go over and visit old Josiah the mason. He was injured on our land a few days back, so her ladyship bid me take some things to cheer his hours away.'

Allday chuckled. 'Rum, is it?' He became serious again. 'By God, you should have seen Lady Catherine when we were in that bloody longboat, Bryan.' He shook his shaggy head. 'But for her, I don't reckon we'd have come through it alive.'

The little trap swayed over as Allday climbed down. 'I'll see you when you returns, then.' He was still standing staring at the inn door when Ferguson guided the trap on to the road again.

Allday took the heavy iron handle as if he was about to release some raging beast and pushed open the door.

23

His immediate impression was that it had changed since his last visit. The woman's hand, perhaps?

An old farmer sat beside the empty fireplace with his tankard of ale, and a pipe which appeared to have gone out some time ago; a sheep dog lay by the man's chair, only his eyes moving as Allday closed the door behind him. Two well-dressed merchants looked up with sudden alarm at the sight of the blue jacket and buttons, probably imagining he was part of a press gang making a last-minute search for recruits. It was not so common now for innocent traders to be snatched up by the press in their never-ending hunt for men to feed the demands of the fleet: Allday had even heard of a young groom who had been taken from his bride's arms as he had been leaving the church door. Ferguson had been right; most of the local people must be at the St John's celebrations elsewhere. These men were probably on their way to the Falmouth stock sale, and would lodge here overnight.

Everything shone like an individual welcome. A smell of flowers, a table of fine cheeses and the sturdy pints of ale balanced on their trestles completed the picture every countryman cherished when far away from home, the men of the blockading squadrons or in the fast frigates like *Anemone*, who might not set foot ashore for months, or even years.

'And what'll your pleasure be?'

Allday swung round and saw a tall, level-eyed man wearing a green apron watching him from beyond the ale barrels. No doubt he thought him to be a member of the hated press. They were rarely welcome at any inn, where custom would soon become scarce if they visited regularly. There was something vaguely familiar the man, but all Allday could feel was disappointment, a sense of loss. He was being stupid. He should have known. Perhaps even the secretive Ozzard had been trying to save him from the hurt of it.

'There's some good ale from Truro. Fetched it myself.' The man folded his arms and Allday saw the vivid tattoo: crossed flags and the number '31st'. The pain went deeper. Not even a sailor, then.

Almost to himself he said, 'The Thirty-First Foot, the Old Huntingdonshires.'

The man stared at him. 'Fancy you knowing that.'

He made to move around the barrels, and Allday heard the thud of a wooden leg.

He reached out and clasped Allday's hand in his, his face completely changed.

'I'm a fool – I should have guessed! You're John Allday, the one who saved my sister from those bloody hounds.'

Allday studied him. *Sister*. Of course, he should have seen it. The same eyes.

He was saying, 'My name's John too. One-time butcher in the old Thirty-First, 'til I lost this.'

Allday watched the memories flooding across his face. Like Bryan Ferguson and all the other poor Jacks he had seen in every port, and the others he had watched go over the side, stitched up in their hammocks like so much rubbish.

'There's a cottage here, so when she wrote an' asked me . . .' He turned and said quietly, 'An' here she be, God bless her!'

'Welcome back, John Allday.' She was looking very neat and pretty in a new dress, her hair set carefully above her ears.

He said awkwardly, 'You're a real picture – er, Unis.'

She was still watching him. 'I dressed like this for you when I heard Sir Richard was back home. I'd never have spoken to you again if . . .'

Then she ran across the floor and hugged him until he was breathless, although she barely came up to his shoulder. Beyond her he could see the same little parlour, and the model of the old *Hyperion* he had given her.

Two more travellers came in, and she took Allday's arm and guided him into the parlour. Her brother, the other John, grinned and shut the door behind them.

She almost pushed him into a chair and said, 'I want to hear all about you, what you've been doing. I've got some good tobacco for your pipe – one of the revenue officers brought it for me. I thought better than to ask where *he* got it.' She knelt down and looked at him searchingly. 'I've been so worried about you. The war comes ashore here with every packet ship. I prayed for you, you see . . .'

25

He was shocked to see the tears drop on to her breast, which the footpads had tried to uncover that day.

He said, 'When I came in just now, I thought you was tired o' waiting.'

She sniffed and wiped her eyes with her handkerchief. 'And I wanted to look so right for you!' She smiled. 'You thought my brother was something more than that, did you?'

Then she said in a quiet, firm tone, 'I never questioned that Jonas was a sailor, nor will I you. Just say you'll come back to *me* an' none other.'

She moved quickly before Allday could reply and reappeared with a tankard of rum, which she put into his hands, her own around them like small paws.

'Now you just sit there and enjoy your pipe.' She stood back, hands on her hips. 'I'll make you some victuals, which you must surely need after one o' those men-of-war!' She was excited, like a young girl again.

Allday waited until she had turned to a cupboard. 'Mr Ferguson will be calling for me later.'

She turned, and he saw the understanding in her face. 'You are a very honourable man, John Allday.' She went into the kitchen to fetch his 'victuals', but called over her shoulder, 'But you could have stayed. I wanted you to know that.'

It was pitch-dark with only the sliver of a moon to lighten the sky when Ferguson pulled into the inn yard with his pony and trap. He waited until Allday's figure loomed out of the gloom and the trap tilted over on its springs.

Allday glanced back at the inn where only one window showed any light.

'I'd have taken you in for a wet, Bryan. But I'd rather we waited 'til we're back home.'

Bryan was too anxious to smile. It *was* his home, the only one he had.

They clattered along the track in silence, the pony tossing its head when a fox passed briefly through the glow of the lanterns. The bonfires were all out now. There would be plenty of headaches when the dawn called the men back to the fields and the milksheds.

Eventually he could stand it no longer.

'How was it, John? I can tell from your breath she's been stuffing you with food and drink!'

'We talked.' He thought of the touch of her hands on his. The way she looked at him, and how her eyes smiled when she spoke. 'The time went fast. Seemed only a dog-watch.'

He thought too of the catch in her voice when she said over her shoulder, 'But you could have stayed. I wanted you to know that.' *An honourable man.* He had never seen himself in that light.

He turned on his seat and said almost defiantly, 'We're to be wed, an' that's no error!'

The two weeks that followed *Anemone*'s brief visit to Falmouth to land her passengers seemed to pass with the speed of light. For Bolitho and his Catherine it was a world of fantasy and rediscovery, and days and nights of love which left them spent in one another's arms. There had been shyness too, as on the day of Bolitho's return, when like conspirators they had ridden to that cove they called their own, to avoid well-meaning callers at the house, to be with one another and nobody else. It was a small crescent of pale sand wedged between two towering cliffs, and it had been a landing place for any smuggler daring or reckless enough to chance a passage through the jagged reefs until a rock fall had closed the only way out.

Leaving their horses on the cliff path they had climbed down to the hard-packed sand, where she had pulled off her boots and pressed her own prints in the beach. Then they had embraced one another, and she had seen the sudden shyness, the hesitation of a man still unsure, doubting perhaps that the love was his for the asking.

It was their place and always would be. He had watched her throw aside her clothes as she had done aboard the *Golden Plover* at the start of their brutal ordeal, but when she had faced him there had been a wildness and a passion he had not seen before. The sun had touched their nakedness and the sand had been warm beneath them when they had realised that the tide was turning once again; and they had splashed through the hissing, lapping water, the sea's embrace sharp and cleansing as they had laughed together, and waded around the rocks to the safety of another beach.

There had been evenings, too, of formality, with Lewis Roxby's household doing its best to provide lavish banquets and entertainment that would ensure that his nickname, The King of Cornwall, remained unchallenged. Moments of tranquillity, memories shared and reawakened while they had ridden around the estate and surrounding villages. Old faces and some newcomers had greeted them with a warmth Bolitho had never experienced. He was more used to the surprise he saw whenever they were both walking together. It was probably inconceivable that the returned vice-admiral, Falmouth's most famous son, should choose to toil along the lanes and hillsides like any bumpkin. But he knew from long experience that after the confines of a King's ship, the monotonous food and the strain of command, any officer who failed to exercise his mind and body when he could was a fool.

Allday's announcement had caught them by surprise. Bolitho had exclaimed, 'It is the best thing I have heard for a long, long time, old friend!'

Catherine had kissed him on the cheek, but had been bemused by Allday's sudden uncertainty. 'I am a troubled man,' he had proclaimed more than once, as if the pleasure shown by everyone else had dispelled his earlier confidence.

As they lay in their bed, listening to the distant boom of the sea through the open windows, she had said quietly, 'You know what disturbs him, do you not, Richard?'

She had leaned over him, her long hair silvered in the filtered moonlight, and he had held her closer, his hand pressing her naked spine, still damp from their eagerness for each other.

He had nodded. 'He fears that I shall leave him on the beach. Oh, how I would miss him, Kate! My oak. But how much pleasure it would give me to know he was *safe* at long last, able to enjoy his new life with this lady I have yet to meet.'

She had touched his lips with her fingers. 'He will do it all in his own way, Richard, in his own time.'

Then she changed the mood, the touch of reality which had

intruded to remind them both of that other world that was always waiting.

She had kissed him slowly. 'Suppose I took his place? I have worn a seaman's garb before. Who would notice your new coxswain?'

Ferguson, smoking a last pipe in the balmy night air, had heard her familiar laughter. He had been glad for them; sad, too, that it could not last.

There had been news from Valentine Keen at his Hampshire home. Zenoria had given him a son, to be named Perran Augustus. From the tone of the letter Keen was obviously ecstatic with pride and delight. A son: a future admiral in his eyes already.

Bolitho had been curious about the choice of Perran, a very old Cornish name. Zenoria must have insisted upon it, perhaps to assert herself against Keen's rather overwhelming family.

Catherine had said simply, 'It was her father's name.'

Her mood had not lightened and Bolitho had imagined that it was because of the poisoned past. Zenoria's father had been hanged for a crime committed when fighting for farm workers' rights, and Zenoria's own involvement had indirectly caused her to be transported. Keen had rescued her, and had cleared her name. Bolitho still wondered if it was truly love, or gratitude which had given them a son.

'What is it, Kate?' He had held her to him, and she spoke softly.

'I would give everything to bear you a child, our very own. Not one to don the King's coat as soon as he is able, like so many of the names I see in the church where your family is honoured. And not one to be spoiled beyond his or her own good!' He had felt the tension in her body as she had added bitterly, 'But I cannot, and mostly I am content. To have and hold your love, to cherish every moment together no matter how short they might be. Then at other times I have this demon inside me. Because of me you have given so much. Your friends, or those you have believed to be so, your freedom to do as you please without the eyes of envy watching every move—' She leaned back in his arms and studied each feature of his face, the rare tears unheeded on her skin. 'You do so much for others and for your country. How dare they squeak their petty hatreds behind your back? In *Golden Plover* I was often terrified, but I would have shared it with none other. Those qualities you do not even know you have lifted my heart. They talk and sing of you in the taverns – a sailor's sailor they call you, but they can never know what I have seen and done with you.'

And then at the end of the second week the Admiralty messenger rode up to the old grey house below Pendennis Castle, and the orders they had both been expecting were delivered in the usual heavily sealed envelope.

Bolitho sat by the empty grate in the big room where he had heard his first stories of the sea and of distant parts from his father, his grandfather: it was now difficult to distinguish one from another in this house where life for so many of his family had begun, and as each grave portrait on the walls could testify, to which few had ever returned. He turned the envelope over in his hands. How many times, he wondered? *Upon receipt of these orders . . . will proceed with all despatch . . .* To a ship or a squadron, to some unknown part of the expanding power of Majesty, to the cannon's mouth if ordered.

He heard Ferguson's wife talking to the messenger. He would leave here eventually well fed and cheered by some of her homemade cider. Bolitho's acknowledgement would be taken to London, passed from clerk to clerk, to the faces of Admiralty who knew little and cared even less for the countless ships and men who died for King and Country. The scrape of a pen by some Admiralty quill-pusher could leave men dead or horribly disfigured, like the unbreakable James Tyacke. Bolitho could see him now as if it had only just happened, Tyacke's brig *Larne* bearing down on their wretched longboat even in the hour of death. Now Tyacke, whom the slavers he hunted called 'the devil with half a face', drove himself and his ship as only he could, and for a purpose known only to himself. These same clerks of admiralty would turn away in horror if they saw his terrible disfigurement, simply because they could not see beyond it to the pride and courage of the man who wore it like a talisman.

He sensed that Catherine had come in, and when he glanced at her he saw that she was quite composed. She said, 'I am here.'

He slit open the envelope and quickly scanned the fine round handwriting, and did not see her sudden concern when he unconsciously rubbed his damaged eye.

He said slowly, 'We shall be going to London, Kate.' He gazed through the open doors at the trees, the clear sky beyond. *Away from here.*

He recalled suddenly that his father had sat in this same chair many times when he had read to him and to his sisters. You could see the trees and the hillside from here, but not the sea. Was that the reason, even for his father, who had always seemed so stern and courageous?

'Not to a new flagship?'

Her voice was calm: only the rise and fall of her breast made it a lie.

'It seems we are to discuss some new strategy.' He shrugged. 'Whatever that may be.'

She guessed what he was thinking. His mind was rebelling against leaving the peace they had been able to share for these two happy weeks.

'It is not Falmouth, Richard, but my house in Chelsea is always a haven.'

Bolitho tossed the envelope on to a table and stood up. 'It was true about Lord Godschale. He has gone from the Admiralty and the London he so obviously enjoyed, although I suspect for the wrong reasons.'

'Who will you see?' Her voice was level, prepared, as if she already knew.

Bolitho replied, 'Admiral Sir James Hamett-Parker.' In his mind he could clearly see the thin mouth and pale eyes, as if he were intruding into this very room.

One hand went to her breast. 'Was he not the one . . .'

He smiled grimly. 'Yes, dear Kate, the President of Thomas Herrick's court-martial.' Was it only a year ago?

He added, 'So he has the whip-hand now.' He turned as Ozzard entered with a tray and two goblets.

31

Catherine looked at the little man and smiled. 'Your timing is better than that of any sand in a glass!'

Ozzard regarded her impassively. 'Thank you, m'lady.' To Bolitho he said, 'I thought some hock might be suitable, Sir Richard.'

No secrets. The news would be all over the estate soon, then the town. Bolitho was leaving. For glory or to some fresh scandal, it was too soon to predict. Bolitho waited for the inner door to close, and then he placed a goblet in her hand.

'I raise a glass to my lovely Kate.' He did so, and smiled. 'Don't worry too much about Godschale's successor. It is better, I think, to know an enemy than to lose a friend.'

She watched him over the rim of her goblet. 'Must it always be you, Richard? I have said as much in the past, even at the risk of offending you. I know you might hate a position ashore . . . at the Admiralty perhaps, where respected leaders like you are in short supply, it seems . . .'

He took her goblet and stood it beside his own. Then he gripped her hands and looked at her steadily for some time. She could feel his inner struggle like something physical.

'This war cannot last much longer, Kate. Unless things turn against us it *must* end. The enemy will lose heart once English soldiers are in their streets.' She knew it was important to him, too vital to interrupt.

'All my life I have been at sea, as is the way in my family. For over twenty years of my service I have been fighting the French and whatever ally they might have at any one moment – but *always the French*. I have seen too many men and boys torn apart in battle, and I blame myself for many of them.' He gripped her hands more tightly and said, 'It is enough. When the enemy flag comes down . . .'

She stared at him. 'You intend to quit? To abandon the life you have always known?'

He smiled slowly, and afterwards she thought it had been like seeing the real man emerge. The one she had loved and almost lost, the man she shared with none other.

'I want to be with you, Catherine. It will be a new navy when the war ends, with younger officers like Adam to improve the sailor's lot.' He smiled again. 'Like Allday's song that day, "to keep watch for the life of Poor Jack". Our men have earned that reward at least, a thousand times over.'

Later they stood by the open doors, so that she could see the orchard and the hillside, with the rich display of roses she had planted for his return.

Bolitho said quietly, 'There is a moment in every sailor's life.' He looked for the first time at the sea, its hard horizon like a steel blade. 'I think brave Nelson knew it, even before he walked the deck that day off Cape Trafalgar.' He turned and looked at her. 'I am not ready, dear Kate. Fate alone will decide, not the Hamett-Parkers of this world.'

They heard the clatter of a post-horse leaving the stableyard, carrying his brief reply to the lords of Admiralty.

He smiled and held her waist more tightly. *So be it then.*

3

Voice in the Night

It took Bolitho and Catherine all of six days to make the long journey to London. Using their carriage, and with a regular change of horses, they could have done it in less. But the Admiralty had named no particular date for his interview and had merely suggested 'at your earliest convenience'. Flag rank had its privileges after all.

With Matthew the senior coachman up on the box and Allday at his side, they had drawn many stares and quite a few cheers from passers-by and farm workers as they had clattered along the cobbled streets of towns and villages, or churned up the dust of twisting lanes and the King's highway.

When they stopped at inns, either for the night or for some refreshment, it became common for people to crowd around them to wish them well, some timidly, others less so, as if they wanted to be part of the legend.

As expected, Allday had been adamant about not staying in Falmouth. 'Suppose you gets ordered to a new command, Sir Richard? What would they think o' that?' Who *they* were he did not specify. 'Vice-Admiral o' the Red, Knight of th' Bath no less, and yet he's without his coxswain!'

Bolitho had pointed out that Ozzard and Yovell would be remaining at Falmouth until the situation was more definite, and Allday had been as scornful as he dared. 'A servant an' a quill-pusher! The likes o' them would never be missed!' But Catherine had told him that Allday needed to get away, if only to ponder on his new undertaking.

Sometimes Catherine slept, her head on his lap as trees and churches, fields and farms rolled past. Once she clutched his arm, her eyes suddenly wide but seeing nothing, as she lived through a bad dream or worse.

While she slept, Bolitho considered what might await him. Perhaps there would be no familiar faces this time; no ships the names of which conjured up violent memories, or friends lost now forever.

Perhaps he might be sent to hoist his flag in the Mediterranean and so relieve Vice-Admiral Lord Collingwood, Nelson's dearest friend and his second-in-command at Trafalgar. It was well-known that Collingwood was a sick man, some said already on the threshold of death. He had not spared himself, nor had he been spared by the Admiralty, and he had been at sea almost continuously since the battle when Nelson had fallen, to be mourned by the whole country. Collingwood had even overcome his pride enough to plead to be released from command in the Mediterranean, but Bolitho had heard nothing of their lordships' response.

He thought of Catherine's suggestion concerning duty ashore and was almost surprised that he did not regret his decision to quit the sea, nor that he had shared his determination with her. The sea would always be there, and there would always be wars: the Bolitho family had shown their mettle in enough of them in the past, and there was no reason why greed and the search for power should not continue.

He stroked her hair and her neck until she stirred slightly in her sleep, recalling the love they had shared, even on the endless journey from Cornwall. Beaming landlords, curtsying maids, waving customers: it had all blurred together now. Only the nights were real. Their need for one another, and other nights when they had merely lain close, in silence, or shared the cool of an evening at some window in a sleeping village, or a town where wheels rattled through the night and a church clock kept a count of the hours.

Once, when he had confessed how much he was dreading leaving her, she had faced him in the darkness, her long hair loose about her bare shoulders.

'I love you, Richard, more than life itself, for without you

35

there is no life. But after what we endured in *Golden Plover* we can always be together. Wherever you are I shall be with you, and when you need me I will hear your voice.' She had taken his face in her hands and had said, 'You are so many things to me, dearest of men. You are my hand in yours; you are one so unsure sometimes that you cannot see the love others hold for you. You are my lover as I am your mistress, or whatever they choose to call me. And you are also a friend, one I can turn to without fear of rebuff. I would not have you change, nor would I try to change you. But if others attempt to harm you or to force us apart, then . . .'

He had held her very close and had murmured into her hair, 'Then my tiger will show her claws!'

It was dusk when they finally approached the Thames, not far from the tavern where Bolitho had met secretly with Herrick before his court-martial to ask if he might act in his defence. Herrick's refusal had been like a door slammed in his face. Last year, and yet it seemed so long ago. Over the great bridge with the gleam of black water below where ships lay moored like shadows, yards crossed and sails tightly furled, waiting for the next tide perhaps, when they would quit the Pool of London and spread their wings for the open sea and maybe the vast oceans beyond. The lifeblood of commerce and survival, envied and hated by others in equal proportions. The navy was stretched to the limit and could barely maintain the blockade of the enemy's ports and the convoy of vital shipping, but every master down there in those drowsing vessels would expect their protection, and it was right they should have it.

There were a few lights at the water's edge, wherrymen plying for hire as they would throughout the night. Young bloods coming and going from their gambling and their women, and across the river to the pleasure gardens where Catherine had taken him to show him part of her London, of which he knew so little.

Eventually the river ran closer to the road and the horses trotted into the tree-lined street called Cheyne Walk.

Bolitho climbed down, stiff from so many miles, glad there were no curious onlookers this time. Her tall, narrow house with its iron balcony and the room which faced the river had become their other haven. Here people minded their own affairs, and showed no surprise at those who owned or rented such property. General or pauper, artist or mistress, there was privacy here for all.

Sophie, Catherine's half-Spanish maid, had been sent on a day ahead, and had prepared the place and the housekeeper for their arrival.

Allday helped Catherine down from the carriage and said quietly, 'Don't you fret for me, m'lady. I'm just thinking it all out.'

She smiled at him. 'I never doubted it.' She turned away. 'And that's no error either!'

Bolitho touched his arm. 'Strike now, old friend, the battle's already lost!'

Later they stood on the small iron balcony and watched night closing over the city. The glass doors were wide open so that the air from the river was quite cool, but the housekeeper had with the best intentions lit fires in every hearth to drive out the damp in the unused rooms. Catherine shivered as he put his arm around her and kissed one bare shoulder. Together they watched two lurching soldiers, probably officers from the barracks, as they made their way unsteadily back to their quarters. A flowergirl was going past, a huge empty basket on her shoulder. It was likely she would be up and about to gather her wares long before sun-up.

Catherine said quietly, 'I wish we were at home.'

She spoke in the same steady voice as on that terrible day when they had abandoned *Golden Plover*. *Don't leave me.*

How had she had such faith even then that she had truly believed they would see home again?

'Soon, Kate.'

They went inside and undressed before lying down together in the darkening room. Wearied by memories and by the uncertainty of the future, they lay unspeaking. Only once Bolitho seemed to come out of his sleep, and imagined her sitting on the bed beside him, her fingers on his skin. He thought he heard her say very softly, 'Don't leave me.' But it was only part of a dream.

37

Vice-Admiral Sir Richard Bolitho stepped down from the smart carriage while Allday held the door for him. Like Matthew the coachman, his burly coxswain was turned out in his best coat and breeches, and Bolitho had already noticed that the carriage was clean and shining although it had been pitch-dark when they had reached Chelsea the previous night. His glance lingered on the family crest on the door, and thought of it carved above the great stone fireplace at Falmouth. Only days ago. He could not recall ever missing it so much, so soon.

He said, 'I have no way of knowing how long this may take.' He saw Matthew squinting down at him, his face like a red apple in the fresh morning sunshine. He was still known on the estate as Young Matthew, a constant reminder of the years he had worked with the horses since he was a young lad. 'Return to Chelsea and drive Lady Catherine anywhere she wishes.' He looked meaningly at Allday. 'I'd take it as a favour if you would stay in company with her.'

He thought he saw a small crinkle around the man's eyes, as if he were saying privately, 'Told you you couldn't manage without me!'

Allday grunted. 'I'll be there, Sir Richard, an' that's no . . .' He did not finish it but grinned, obviously remembering how Catherine had teased him with his favourite expression.

Bolitho glanced up at the austere Admiralty building. How many times had he come to this place? To receive orders; to beg for a ship, any ship; to be employed again when the clouds of war had spread once more across the Channel. Where he had met Herrick and where they had shaken hands as friends, but parted as strangers in this same building. Bolitho had sent word here by messenger, and wondered if Godschale's successor would keep him waiting, or perhaps delay the meeting altogether. It was strange that even in the navy's private world he should know so little of Sir James Hamett-Parker. He had first heard of him in any depth during the great mutinies throughout the fleet at the Nore and Spithead. All England had been shocked and horrified at that sudden display of defiance, which had incited even the staunchest men into open mutiny, leaving England undefended and at the mercy of the French.

The mutineers had formed themselves into councils with delegates to represent their cause, their plea for better conditions at every level, pay, food, and the harsh routine which had reduced some ships to the level of prison hulks, in which any bad captain could make a seaman's life a living hell. Some of the officers who had become notorious for their cruel and heartless treatment had been put forcibly ashore and their authority overturned. One of those had been Hamett-Parker.

Someone in the Admiralty must have decided against displaying any sympathy or weakness at Herrick's court-martial, and it was obvious that a guilty verdict had been taken for granted. But for his flag captain's change of evidence it was certain that Herrick would have faced disgrace, and very possibly death. Hamett-Parker's rigid ideas of discipline and duty must have made him the obvious choice for President of the Court.

Bolitho loosened the sword at his hip, not the fine presentation one given to him by the good people of Falmouth for his services in the Mediterranean and at the Battle of the Nile, but the old family blade. Forged for his great-grandfather Captain David in 1702, it was lighter than some of the more modern blades, and as straight and keen as ever. A show of defiance? Conceit, some would say. He smiled to himself. There was little margin in between.

'Can I 'elp you, sir?' An Admiralty messenger paused in polishing the big pair of brass dolphins from which a ship's bell was suspended and peered at him. In seconds his watery eye had taken in the bright epaulettes, each with its pair of silver stars, the lace on the sleeves, and above all the gold medal of the Nile about his neck.

'Bolitho.' He knew he had little to add to that. He asked, 'What happened to Pierce?'

The man was still staring. 'I'm afraid 'e slipped 'is cable, Sir Richard.' He shook his head, wondering how this famous officer, beloved by his sailors and all who served him, could even remember the other old porter.

Bolitho said, 'I am sorry. Is there anything I can do?'

The porter shook his head. 'Bin ill fer quite a time, Sir Richard. Often spoke of you, 'e did.'

Bolitho said quietly, 'He taught me many things . . .' He broke off, angry with himself, and saw a lieutenant with a fixed smile of anticipation waiting by the staircase. His arrival had already been signalled, apparently. As he followed the young officer up the stairs he was reminded suddenly of Jenour, and wondered how he was settling down to his new role of command. That new maturity gained after the *Golden Plover*'s loss and his own daring efforts to retake that wretched vessel after the mutiny had convinced him that he was ready to offer his hard-won experience to others. As Keen had said after they had been snatched to safety by Tyacke's brig *Larne*, 'None of us will ever be quite the same again.'

Perhaps Keen was right. Who would have believed it possible that Bolitho himself would have declared his intention of leaving the navy when the war was finally over? He walked along the passageways, past the blank impersonal doors, the line of chairs where captains could sit and wait to see a superior, to be praised, promoted or disciplined. Bolitho was glad to see they were all empty. Every captain, no matter how junior, was beyond price; the war's harvest had made certain of that. He himself had sat here many times, waiting, hoping, dreading.

They paused at the big double doors behind which Godschale had once held court. He had once been a frigate captain like Bolitho, and they had been posted at the same time. There was no other similarity. Godschale loved the good life: receptions and balls, great banquets and state occasions. He had an eye for a pretty face, and a wife so dull he probably considered it a fair distraction.

He had clumsily tried to make Bolitho return to his wife and their daughter Elizabeth, and his other ideas on strategy had, Bolitho thought, often failed to consider the logistics of available ships, supplies, and the great distances of ocean in which the enemy could choose its victims. But despite Godschale's annoying way of brushing obstacles aside, Bolitho knew in some strange way that he would miss him, bombast and all.

40

He turned, aware that the lieutenant had been speaking to him, probably all the way from the entrance hall.

The lieutenant said, 'We were all excitement when we heard of your latest victory over Contre Amiral Baratte. I am honoured to be the one to meet you!'

Bolitho smiled. The young man's French accent was faultless. He would go far.

The doors opened and closed behind him and he saw Admiral Sir James Hamett-Parker facing him across a massive marble-topped table. It was as if he had been seated for some time, staring at the doors, waiting for the first seconds of confrontation. The great wine cabinet, the clock with its cherubs, the model of Godschale's first command had all vanished. Even the air felt different.

Hamett-Parker stood up slowly and shook hands across the vast table.

'Welcome back, Sir Richard.' He gestured to a chair. 'I thought we should meet without further delay. There are many things I wish to discuss.' He had an incisive voice, but spoke unhurriedly as if each word came under scrutiny before being released. 'Your nephew made a fast passage, it seems. Where time is concerned I must be a miser. Too much of it has been wasted here.'

Bolitho listened carefully. Did he imply that Godschale was the culprit? Or was he testing him for his own past loyalty?

Hamett-Parker walked slowly to a window and flicked a curtain aside. 'I observed your entrance, Sir Richard. I see you came alone.'

He had been watching. To see if Catherine had been with him, or if she was waiting now in the carriage.

He said, 'From Chelsea, Sir James.'

'Ah.' He said nothing else, and Bolitho saw the finely cut profile, the slightly hooked nose, the young man still clinging behind the mask. His hair was grey, quite white in some places, so that it looked in the hazy sunshine like a wig; he even wore an old-style queue. He would not have seemed out of place in some fading portrait from a century earlier, although Bolitho knew Hamett-Parker was only about ten years his senior.

41

'There is much speculation as to what the enemy intends if, or rather *when* Sir Arthur Wellesley brings the war in Spain to a victorious conclusion. The despatches from the Peninsula remain encouraging – news is daily expected of some dramatic climax. But the French will not surrender because of Spain. Our forces are fully extended, our yards unable to keep pace with the need for more ships, even if we could find the men to crew them. The enemy is aware of this. With all aggression ended in the Caribbean, we can withdraw certain vessels.' He looked away and added crisply, 'But not enough!'

Bolitho said, 'I believe that the French will intensify their attacks on our supply lines.'

'Do you?' He raised an eyebrow. 'That is most interesting. The Duke of Portland said as much to me quite recently.'

The prime minister. Bolitho felt his lips relax into a smile. He had all but forgotten who it was. Moving from one campaign to another, watching men die and ships torn apart, the final authority beneath His Britannic Majesty too often seemed unimportant.

'It amuses you?'

'I beg your pardon, Sir James. I am out of touch, it seems.'

'No matter. I understand he is of a sickly disposition. There will be a new hand on the tiller before too long, I fear.'

Bolitho winced as a sharp line of sunlight passed over the admiral's shoulder and made him turn his head to one side.

'The light disturbs you?'

Bolitho tensed. Did he know? How could he?

He shook his head. 'It is nothing.'

Hamett-Parker returned slowly to the table, his steps, like his words, measured, unwasted.

'You are wondering why you were withdrawn from your command?'

'Of course, Sir James.' He saw the admiral's eyes for the first time. So pale they were almost colourless.

'Of course? That is strange. However, we need to discuss possible French interference with our shipping routes. One frigate, a privateer even, could tie down men-of-war we could not spare even if we had them. It is widely believed that more attacks are already being planned – they will be hastened if,

42

as we anticipate, Wellesley drubs the French army on the Peninsula. The prime minister will wish to know your thoughts, as will Sir Paul Sillitoe.' He saw Bolitho's surprise and said calmly, 'Something else you did not know, it would appear. Sillitoe is senior advisor to the prime minister and certain others in high places. Even His Majesty is not unaware of him.'

Bolitho looked for some sign of sardonic humour or even sarcasm. There was none. In his mind he could see the man quite clearly: tall and slender with the quick, sure movements of a duellist. A dark, interesting face with deceptively hooded eyes. He was as quick and as sharp as steel, and he had been both charming and gracious to Catherine at one of Godschale's ridiculous receptions when she had been deliberately snubbed by the Duke of Portland. A strange, remote man, but not to be underestimated; perhaps not to be trusted. Bolitho had heard that Sillitoe had travelled all the way to Falmouth for the local memorial service after the loss of the *Golden Plover* and the reported deaths of all those aboard. He did not need to warn Catherine of any other intentions Sillitoe might have.

He thought of her this morning, warm in his arms, holding him, watching him later while Allday shaved him, and sharing a quick breakfast downstairs. In a rough shawl or in gleaming shot-silk like the night they had been reunited at English Harbour, she would never pass unnoticed. No, Catherine would recognise any ploy, subtle or otherwise.

'You were well known for the energy of your performance when you were a frigate captain, Sir Richard.' Hamett-Parker continued in the same curt manner. 'The line of battle has been *my* lot in life.' He changed tack again. 'I seem to recall that you were flag captain to Sir Lucius Broughton in *Euryalus*?'

'I was flag captain to Rear-Admiral Thelwall until he was relieved due to ill-health. Broughton hoisted his flag in *Euryalus* after that.'

'I deduce from your tone that you disliked him. I always thought him to be an excellent flag officer. Like me, he would never allow sentiment to blur the needs of duty and discipline.' He clenched his fist as if he had allowed himself to say too much, and continued, 'You were involved in the Great Mutiny?'

It sounded almost like an accusation.

'We were lucky in *Euryalus*.'

'Luck? What has that to do with it? We were at war with a ruthless enemy as we are now. I commanded *Cydnus*, a two-decker of ninety guns. Well trained, well drilled, she was the envy of the squadron.'

Bolitho saw the hand clench into a tight fist again. Hamett-Parker's one weakness: the incident he could never forget.

'There are always rotten apples in some casks. The plan for mutiny amongst my people was fed to those simpletons and knotheads like poison. They defied me – *me*, their captain.' His pale eyes shone like glass in the reflected light. It was as if he could still not believe it. That ordinary, common seamen could demand their rights even at the risk of death by hanging or a flogging around the fleet, which had been the punishment meted out to more than one delegate.

Bolitho said sharply, 'Admiral Broughton was a fool. If he were one of my officers today I would tell him as much!'

They both became calm again, and Hamett-Parker said, 'My record is one to be proud of.' He glanced meaningly around the room. 'I think others must have appreciated that.'

Bolitho said, 'What is expected of me, Sir James?' He was surprised how calm he sounded. Inwardly he was burning like a fireship, angered by this unreachable man, angry with himself.

'We need a plan, one that can be exercised with simplicity, one that will not antagonise the flags of nations not already drawn into the fight.'

'You mean the Americans, Sir James?'

'I did not say that!' He wagged one finger and gave a stiff smile. Then he said, 'I am glad we met before we meet the others involved.' He pulled some papers towards him. 'My flag lieutenant has the address of your lodgings in London, I assume?'

'I imagine so, Sir James.' Probably half of London knew it. 'May I ask something?'

44

He tugged out a bright gold watch and glanced at it. 'I must not be too long.'

Bolitho thought sadly of Godschale. *One cannot do everything.* 'What is intended for my last flag captain, Valentine Keen?'

Hamett-Parker pouted. 'For an instant I thought you would ask about someone else.' He shrugged, irritated. 'He will hoist a broad pendant when all is decided. If he performs adequately I am certain flag rank will be his privilege, as it is ours.'

Bolitho stood up and saw the other man's glance fall to the old sword. 'May I take my leave, Sir James?' It was over; the rapiers were to be laid in their cases again. For the present.

'Please do.' He leaned back in his great chair, his fingertips pressed together like a village parson. Then he said, 'Vice-Admiral Sir Lucius Broughton, the *fool* you so bluntly described, died doing his duty in the penal settlements of New South Wales.' His pale eyes did not blink as he added, 'His position will, I am certain, be ably filled by your friend, Rear-Admiral Herrick.'

Bolitho turned on his heel and flung open the doors, almost colliding with the hovering lieutenant.

Hamett-Parker had got deep under his skin, out of malice or for some other purpose, he did not know or care. What did he want? He had been careful not to mention Catherine, or 'the scandal' as he would no doubt call it.

He hurried down the stairs, his mind reeling with ideas and memories. Just the mention of the *Euryalus*: Thelwall coughing out his life, Broughton watching the terrible flogging unmoved. But most of all, Catherine. He had commanded *Euryalus* when he had first met her. She had been aboard the merchantman *Navarra*; her husband had been killed by Barbary pirates, and she had cursed Bolitho for causing his death.

'Would the nice sea-officer like a ride in comfort?'

He spun round, half-blinded by the sunlight, and saw her watching him from the carriage window. She was smiling, but her fine dark eyes were all concern.

'How did you know?'

She took his wrist as he climbed into the carriage, and replied quietly, 'I always know.'

Admiral Sir James Hamett-Parker held the curtain aside and looked down as the woman aided Bolitho into the elegant carriage.

'So that is the notorious Lady Catherine.'

Sir Paul Sillitoe, who had just entered by another door, smiled at the admiral's back. 'Never underestimate that lady, Sir James, and do not make her an enemy.' He walked casually to the littered table and added coolly, 'Or you will make one of me. Be assured of it, sir!'

Bolitho sat on a bench in the shade of a solitary tree in the neat little garden behind the house. It was peaceful here, and the clatter of iron-shod wheels and the regular passing of horses were muffled, as if far away. Behind the rear wall were the mews for this row of houses, for horses and a limited number of carriages.

He watched Catherine cutting roses and wondered if she were still missing Falmouth and what must seem the unlimited space of the house there, compared to this small town-house. Her gown was low-cut so that she could feel the benefit of the sun directly overhead, and the darker line on her shoulder where she had been so cruelly burned in the open boat was still visible.

It had been three days since his interview with Hamett-Parker and the uncertainty, the waiting, had unsettled him.

She looked at him and her expression was troubled. 'Is there no way we can learn what is happening, Richard? I know what you are thinking.'

He stood up and crossed to her side. 'I am bad company, dear Kate. I want to be with you and have no senseless burden hanging above me!'

A breeze turned over the pages of *The Times* and blew it on to the grass. There was more news of enemy attacks on shipping heading for home around the Cape of Good Hope. Each vessel had been sailing independently and without escort. It seemed likely that that had been what Hamett-Parker had been hinting at. Suppose he were ordered back to Cape Town, *Golden Plover*'s original destination when mutiny and shipwreck had erupted like a sudden storm? Were the marauding ships which had carried out these attacks French naval vessels or privateers? Whatever they were, they must be based somewhere.

She touched his face. 'You are worrying again. You hate this inaction, don't you?' She moved her hand across his mouth. 'Do not protest, Richard. I know you so well!'

They heard the street bell jangle through the open door and Sophie's merry laugh as she spoke to someone.

Catherine said, 'She is seventeen now, Richard. A good catch for the right man.'

'You treat her more like a daughter than a maid. I've watched you often.'

'Sometimes she reminds me of myself at her age.' She looked away. 'I would not want her to endure such a life as that!'

Bolitho waited. Like Adam, she would tell him one day.

Sophie appeared at the top of the steps. 'A letter, me lady.' She glanced at Bolitho. 'For Sir Richard.'

He tried to imagine Catherine at sixteen, as Sophie had been when she had been taken into the household. Like Jenour she seemed to have matured suddenly after the open boat and their experiences at the hands of the mutineers.

She gave the square envelope to Bolitho. 'Nice young officer it was, me lady. From the Admiralty.'

Catherine recognised the card in Bolitho's sunburned hands. It was a beautifully etched invitation, with a crest at the top.

'From Hamett-Parker. A reception to mark his appointment. His Majesty will be in attendance, apparently.' He felt the anger mounting inside him, and when she took the card from his hand she understood why. She was not invited.

She knelt down by him. 'What do you expect, Richard? Whatever we think or do, others will believe it improper.'

'I'll not go. I'll see them all damned!'

She watched his face and saw something of Adam there, and the others in the portraits at Falmouth. 'You must go. To refuse would be an insult to the King himself. Have you thought of that?'

He sighed. 'I'll lay odds that somebody else has.'

She looked at the address on the card. 'St James's Square. A *very* noble establishment, I believe.'

47

Bolitho barely heard. So it was beginning all over again. A chance to isolate one from the other, or to eagerly condemn them if Bolitho chose to take her with him.

'I wonder if Sillitoe will be there?'

'Probably. He seems to have many irons in the fire.'

'But you quite like him.'

He thought she was teasing him to take his mind off the invitation; but she was not.

'I am not sure, Kate.'

She laid her head on his lap and said softly, 'Then we shall wait and see. But be sure of one thing, dearest of men. He is no rival – nobody could be that.'

He kissed her bare shoulder and felt her shiver. 'Oh, Kate, what should I be without you?'

'You are a man. My man.' She looked up at him, her eyes very bright. 'And I am your woman.' Her mouth puckered and she exclaimed, 'And that's no error!' Then she relented. 'Poor Allday, what must he have thought?'

She recovered her roses and added evenly, 'They may try to discredit me through you, or the other way round. It is a game I know quite well.' She touched her shoulder where he had kissed it and her expression was calm again, faraway. 'I shall accept Zenoria's invitation to visit Hampshire.' She saw the sudden cloud cross his face. 'Only for that day. It will be a wise precaution. Trust me.'

They went into the house, where they heard Sophie talking with the cook in the kitchen.

She looked at him, smiling faintly when she said, 'I think I strained my back.' She saw his understanding and added, 'Perhaps you could be the navigator again and explore it?'

Later as she lay in his arms she whispered, 'Sometimes, dearest of men, you have to be reminded of what is important . . .' She arched her back as he touched her again. 'And what is not . . .' The rest was lost in their embrace.

4

Strategy

Captain Adam Bolitho reined the big grey to a halt and stared across a flint wall towards the great house. The wall was new, probably one of the many being built by French prisoners of war, he thought. He stroked the horse's mane while he gazed at the rolling Hampshire countryside with its air of timeless peace, so different from his home county where the sea was rarely out of sight.

People had glanced at him curiously as he had ridden through villages, following the old coaching road. A sea-officer was obviously rare in these parts, while the military were only too common.

He looked at his hand and extended it in the hot sunshine. It was quite steady, untroubled. He almost laughed at himself. He felt far from either, and doubted more than ever the wisdom of his having come here.

Anemone lay at Spithead awaiting orders, but he was so short of hands after the port admiral had insisted on transferring some of his men 'to more deserving vessels' that the frigate would not move for a few more days. As he had expected he had lost his senior lieutenant Peter Sargeant. It had been a sad parting but Adam had not hesitated, knowing too well how important it was to grasp the chance of promotion, in Sargeant's case the command of a fleet schooner. You rarely got a second opportunity in the navy.

Aubrey Martin, the second lieutenant, had moved up, and they were hourly expecting another junior officer and some midshipmen. Having lost some of his most seasoned warrant officers to the needs of the fleet as well as his first lieutenant and good friend, Adam knew it would be a long haul to regain *Anemone*'s status as a crack frigate with a company to match.

The captain of the dockyard had discovered that he was going for a ride, if only to free himself from the constant stream of orders and requests which were the lot of every captain under the watchful eye of a flag officer. The captain had received two letters for Valentine Keen, which had followed him from the flagship *Black Prince* in the West Indies and had eventually arrived in Portsmouth.

The dockyard captain had commented dryly, 'One is from his tailor, same as mine in London. I'd know that skinflint's scrawl anywhere. But you never know.' He added helpfully, 'Nice canter anyway.'

That at least was true. The powerful grey had been loaned to him by a major of marines at the barracks, an officer who was apparently so well supplied with horses that he would have had to serve for a hundred years in the Corps to pay for them if he depended on his service allowance alone.

Adam studied the house again. About five miles to the east of Winchester at a guess, and not many villages nearby. Five miles – it could be ten times that, he thought.

But why was he here? Suppose Keen suspected something, or Zenoria had blurted out the truth. He made himself face it without embroidering the facts. He had taken her. A moment of despairing passion when each had thought they had lost someone loved in the *Golden Plover*.

He had taken her. Had she refused him he dared not think what might have happened. He would have been ruined, and it would have broken his uncle's heart. Of her they would have said, no smoke without fire. The easy way for the liars and the doubters.

He often remembered his fury when he had heard the stranger at the inn insulting the Bolitho name. Each time he had come to the same desperate conclusion. *I nearly killed him. Another instant and I would have done it.*

You fool. Go back while you can. Even as he thought it his heels dug into the grey's flanks and he was trotting down a

50

slope towards the tall gates, each with a bronze stag on the top. The family was very rich and influential, and Keen's father was known to think his son mad for remaining in the navy when he could have almost any career he wanted.

An old gardener was stooping amongst flower beds, his barrow nearby. Adam touched his hat as he rode up the sweeping drive, and noticed that there was a long fowling piece propped against the barrow. This place must be very isolated, servants or not, he thought. How would an untamed girl like Zenoria settle to this after Cornwall's wild coastline?

The house was even larger and more imposing than he had imagined. Pillars, a magnificent portico adorned with carvings of lions and strange beasts, and steps clean enough to eat from.

He would have smiled but for his inner tension. The old grey house at Falmouth was shabby by comparison. A place that welcomed you. Where you could live.

A small, wizened man darted from somewhere and held the reins while Adam dismounted.

'Give him some water. I shall not be long.' The man nodded, his face completely blank.

He did not turn away from the house as the man led the big horse around the corner of the building. He thought his nerve would break if he did.

One of the paired doors swung inwards even before he could reach it, and a prim-looking woman with keys at her waist stood facing him without warmth.

'Captain Adam Bolitho, ma'am. I have letters for Captain Keen.' Or was he already promoted to flag rank?

'Are you expected, sir?'

'No. Not exactly.' Used to sailors jumping to his every command, he was taken aback by her chilling tone.

She remained firmly in the centre of the doorway. 'Captain Keen is away, sir.' She may have considered telling him where he was, but changed her mind. 'Will you leave a message?'

There were voices and then he heard Zenoria call, 'What is it, Mrs Tombs?'

Adam felt his heart beating faster. The housekeeper was aptly named.

The door opened wide and she was there, staring at him. She wore a simple flowered gown and her dark hair was piled above her ears. Her only adornments were some pearl earrings and a pendant, which he guessed was worth a small fortune. He did not quite know what he had been expecting, but she looked like a child dressing up in adult's clothing. Playing a part.

'I – I am sorry, er, Mrs Keen. I have some letters.' He fumbled for them, but his cuff caught on the short fighting sword he always favoured. 'My ship is still at Portsmouth. I thought—'

The forbidding housekeeper asked, 'Is everything in order, ma'am?'

'Yes.' Zenoria tossed her head as he had seen her do when her hair had hung down like glossy silk. 'Why should it not be?'

'Very well, ma'am.' She stood back to allow the newcomer to enter. 'If you require anything . . .' She glided away soundlessly on the marble floor but her words remained like a warning.

Zenoria stared at him for several seconds. 'You know you are not welcome here, *Captain*.' She glanced around as if afraid someone would hear. But the house was completely silent, as if it were listening. Watching.

'I am so sorry. I shall go directly.' He saw her draw back as he took a pace towards her. 'Please. I didn't mean to offend you. I thought your husband would be here.' He was losing her, even before he had made any contact.

She was very composed, dangerously so. 'He is in London. At the Admiralty. He will be back this evening.' Her eyes blazed. 'You should not have come. You must know that.'

A door opened and closed discreetly and she said, 'Come into the library.'

She walked ahead of him, very erect and small in this great cathedral of a house. *The girl with moonlit eyes*, as her uncle had called her.

There were books piled in little heaps on a table. She said in an almost matter-of-fact voice, 'All mine. Waiting for our new house when it is ready for us.' She stared at the tall

52

windows where a bee was tapping on the glass. 'They are so kind to me here . . . but I have to *ask*. I have no carriage and I am told not to ride alone. There are footpads and they say deserters always close by. It is like the desert!'

Adam thought of the gardener and his musket. 'When will you leave here?' He barely dared to speak.

She shrugged. Even that sent a pain to his heart. 'This year, next year – I am not sure. We will live near Plymouth. Not Cornwall, but close. In truth I find this life daunting. The family is away in London for the most part, and Val's youngest sister never wants to leave the baby alone.'

Adam tried to remember the sister. She was the one who had lost her husband at sea.

'I see nobody. Only when Val comes back can I . . .' She seemed to realise what she was saying and exclaimed, 'And what of you? Still the gallant hero? The scourge of the enemy?' But the fire refused to kindle.

He said, 'I think of you so much I am almost beside myself.' A shadow passed the window and he saw a girl carrying the baby across a neatly trimmed lawn. 'It's so little,' he said.

'You are surprised, are you? You thought perhaps he might be older – even your own son?'

She was taunting him, but when he turned towards her he saw the real tears in her eyes.

'I wish to God he were mine. Ours!'

He heard his horse being led to the front of the house again. The housekeeper would feel happier if he left without further delay. She would likely tell Keen about his visit.

He laid the two letters on the table. 'For your husband. They were my key to your door. But I failed . . .'

'What did you expect? That I would take you to my bed merely because it is you, because you always get what you want?'

He picked up his hat and pushed his unruly hair from his forehead. He did not see her start at the familiar gesture. 'I wanted only you, Zenoria.' It was the first time he had spoken her name here. 'I did not have the right, or the courage to tell you that I loved you.'

She pulled a silk bell-cord. 'Please go.' She watched him

move to the library door, her figure very still. 'Perhaps God will forgive both of us, but I can never forgive you.'

The door closed, and for several minutes she stood quite still until she heard a groom calling out his thanks to the young captain for the coins that had been put into his hand. Only then did she take a small book from one of the piles, and after a further hesitation she opened it. Pressed in the middle were a pair of wild roses, now as flat as silk. He had given them to her on that ride, on his birthday. She said to the silent room, 'And I loved *you*, Adam. I always will.'

Then she dried her eyes and adjusted her gown before going to the double doors and out into the sunshine.

The old gardener was still working unhurriedly. Only his barrow and musket had moved. Along the drive and through the gates she could see the road. It was empty. As if none of it had happened.

She heard the child crying, the placating sounds from Val's sister, who had wanted one of her own.

All was as it had been before. But she knew she had just lost everything.

Bolitho paused by the ballroom's pillared entrance, using the time it took for a bewigged footman to notice him to accustom his own eyes to the light.

The footman had a reedy voice, and he thought it unlikely that anyone heard his announcement above the scrape of violins from an orchestra and the great din of voices. It was certainly a very impressive house in fashionable St James's Square, 'noble' as Catherine had aptly described it, and far too large for Hamett-Parker alone. The admiral had lost his wife in a hunting accident, but had certainly retained a liking for lavish living. Bolitho had also noticed a marble statue of a centurion in the entrance hall, and had realised then that it had been put there by the house's original owner, Admiral Anson, to commemorate his own flagship of that name.

Footmen and some Royal Marines pressed into service to assist them laboured through the throng. There were red coats and the scarlet of the marines, but the navy's blue and white made up the majority of guests: there were very few below the rank of post captain. Of His Majesty there was no sign, and Bolitho had heard that he quite often failed to attend such receptions even though he was reminded of them by his long-suffering staff.

He felt a prickle of annoyance as he saw the large number of women present. Some might be wives: some, with their bold glances and barely-covered bosoms, were unlikely guests. But they did not count because nobody cared. If any ordinary officer were having an affair others would merely ignore it. But if Catherine had been on his arm, looking as she did on these rare occasions, you could have heard a pin drop, and every eye would be staring.

Someone took his hat and was lost amongst the crowd. Another, a Royal Marine, reached him with a tray and turned it carefully towards him. Bolitho glanced at him questioningly and the marine said in a conspiratorial whisper, 'That's the good stuff, Sir Richard.' He nearly winked. 'I'm proud to be servin' you. Wait till I tells the lads!'

Bolitho sipped the wine. It *was* good. Cold too, surprisingly enough. 'Do I know you?'

The man grinned, as if such things were impossible. 'Bless you, no, Sir Richard. I was one o' *Benbow*'s afterguard when you came for us.' His face was suddenly grim. 'I'd bin wounded, y'see, otherwise I'd 'ave bin lyin' dead with all me mates.'

Bolitho heard someone snap his fingers, and turned to see a captain he did not know beckoning to the marine.

This was one of Thomas Herrick's own marines, a man who thought himself lucky to be alive and recovered from his wound, unlike so many on that terrible day.

He snapped, 'Have you no manners, sir?'

The captain stared at him and at his rank and seemed to sink into the throng like a fish in a pond.

He said, 'Rear-Admiral Herrick was my friend.'

The marine nodded gravely. He had seen the captain flush, then cringe at this man's sharp rebuke. Something else to tell the lads in the barracks.

'I knows it, Sir Richard. Beggin' yer pardon, I think it's wrong to send 'im to New South Wales.'

55

Bolitho took another goblet from among *the good stuff* and nodded. Why had he said, '*was* my friend'? Was there no hope? Was friendship really dead between them? Herrick had always been a stubborn man, sometimes beyond sense or reason. He could still not accept Bolitho's love for a woman not his wife, even though Catherine had been the only one to stay with Herrick's own beloved Dulcie when she had been dying so horribly of typhus. It was a miracle that Catherine herself had not fallen to the same fate.

He looked through a gap in the crowd and saw Hamett-Parker watching him intently, his pale eyes reflecting the hundreds of candles like chips of glass.

Bolitho walked towards him. The marine had vanished for another tray. Bolitho had smelt brandy on his breath: he had better watch his step if his officer noticed it.

Hamett-Parker bobbed his head. 'I was aware of the charisma they say you possess, Sir Richard. That common fellow was obviously an admirer.'

'I always draw comfort from such men, Sir James. I saw what he and his comrades endured. He and others like him make me very aware of what we owe them in leadership.'

The admiral grunted. 'I'll not deny that. But we must all take care that popularity does not win more friends than leadership.' He glanced around at the noisy crowd. 'Lord Godschale would have approved, don't you think?'

'What has become of him?' He sensed that Hamett-Parker was trying to goad him.

'He should be well on his way to Bombay by now.' The admiral appeared indifferent, but his voice was sharper. 'A most important position with the Honourable East India Company. Extremely lucrative, I would surmise.'

Bolitho could not imagine Godschale willingly exchanging the pleasures of London for the intense heat and fevers of India. Hamett-Parker remarked, 'I believe it was not unexpected. An indiscretion can often be overlooked. A political scandal cannot.' He gazed at him coldly. 'As I said, one must lead by example!'

'Is Captain Keen to be here tonight, Sir James?'

Hamett-Parker offered a faint smile. 'No. He is not long married, and I can spare him a while.'

'I had hoped that he would be promoted directly to flag rank.'

'Were *you*?'

Bolitho prayed that someone would come and interrupt this verbal fencing match. 'No, I was not. I was commodore first.' Hamett-Parker would know that better than anyone. He contained his anger and added, 'I have known Captain Keen for a long time. He was a midshipman under my command. He is a fine officer and a decent man.'

'And comes from a powerful and influential family, yes? I respect your concern, of course, but you must accept that Captain Keen must be more than a *fine officer* to hoist his flag as rear-admiral. But we shall see. He will have every chance to prove himself, that I promise you.'

A footman came towards them, a single goblet in the centre of his tray. The admiral took it and said, 'Refreshing at times like these.'

Bolitho noticed that he was drinking lime juice. Perhaps so that he could watch the antics of his subordinates and equals as the hock and madeira flowed freely.

Hamett-Parker frowned but instantly contained it as Sir Paul Sillitoe, elegantly dressed in dark grey silk and wearing a slender court sword at his hip, strode across the floor.

'My apologies for my late arrival, Sir James.' Several guests nearby were making a pretence of not listening. They were not to be disappointed. 'I have been with the prime minister – we saw His Majesty together. The King will not be coming here after all.'

Hamett-Parker regarded him balefully. 'What ails him now?'

Sillitoe smiled at Bolitho for the first time, then said, 'We have just received word, Sir James, from Talavera. General Wellesley has won a great victory over Marshal Soult. The war on the Peninsula is all but won.'

There was a stunned silence, then as the word spread across the room and into other parts of the house a great burst of wild cheering made the chandeliers quiver like pieces of ice.

Hamett-Parker nodded. 'Earlier than expected.' He sounded completely unmoved.

Sillitoe took a glass of wine and smiled again. 'A perfect way to celebrate your appointment, Sir James. Congratulations!' He looked at Bolitho. 'A great moment for you also, sir. Without you and your seamen no soldier could have set foot on enemy soil!'

Hamett-Parker said, 'We shall sup very shortly, while some of them can still stand. Pass the word!'

As the admiral turned away to play the host, however ungraciously, Sillitoe said lightly, 'You are alone tonight, Sir Richard?' His hooded eyes gave nothing away.

'I came only because Lady Catherine insisted.'

He nodded impassively. 'Very wise. There are times when discretion is worth more than a squadron.'

Bolitho was suddenly tired of it. 'I'll not wait. I shall make my excuses.'

Sillitoe shrugged. 'We shall meet again very soon. There is work for both of us now that Arthur Wellesley has dished up his old enemy.'

'What is it to be?' He wanted to leave, but needed to know.

Sillitoe took his arm and guided him to an anteroom where the din of cheers and tipsy laughter were muffled, if not quenched completely.

'Advise me, Richard, and I will advise the Duke of Portland. The French intend to strangle our trade – our lifeline, if you like.'

'I read of the latest attacks. If we had not captured the French rear-admiral André Baratte I would see his hand in this.'

Sillitoe smiled gently. 'You are very shrewd. But Baratte was released, exchanged for Lord Derwent who was captured in Spain. You see? So soon back in England and already you are proving your worth.' The smile widened but did not reach his eyes. 'Especially to me!'

He pulled out his watch and yawned. 'My carriage is outside. I will take you to Chelsea, if you like. We can talk in peace.'

In sight of the Thames again, the street deserted in an

unexpected rainfall, Sillitoe lost no time in questioning Bolitho about the threat to merchant shipping.

'I am all ears, Richard, eager for knowledge. I would never make a sailor in five hundred years!'

Bolitho was still pondering the stupidity of those who had chosen to exchange Baratte for some English aristocrat. Baratte had had a high reputation as a frigate captain and then as commodore of a squadron before being promoted to his rank. Several attempts had been made to capture him in battle, all unsuccessful. It had fallen to Bolitho's *Tybalt* to change matters by seizing Baratte's frigate and the man himself when all the odds had decreed otherwise. It was said that Baratte hated the English as much as he loved France; and now he was gone, probably better aware of England's strength or weakness than before his capture.

Sillitoe remarked, 'We hold Good Hope, largely thanks to you. Surely that should be enough?'

Bolitho saw the straggling trade routes in his mind, from India and the East Indies, as far as New South Wales and the expanding colony there. Baratte would have the pick of any ship or cargo he chose to attack. But he would need a base, somewhere to water and provision his ships and unload his prizes. It could be no half-hearted operation like the haphazard killing and plunder practised by common pirates.

He said, 'We would need a small, fast-moving squadron, a flotilla even. Six frigates with a competent captain . . .' He sensed Sillitoe's reaction and said, 'I *know*. It is like asking for the moon. But without a planned and practical strategy the losses will become worse and their lordships will be forced to release more men-of-war, no matter how badly they are needed in home waters.' He glanced out of the window and wished that Sillitoe were sitting on his right. His eye was sore, and he wanted to touch it even though he knew it would not help.

He said, 'Like Baratte, I suppose I have always been a frigate captain at heart. I commanded three. It was like nothing else.'

'Oh? What of *Sparrow*?'

He tensed. 'She was a sloop-of-war, not even as big as a

59

sixth-rate.' Like Hamett-Parker, the mysterious Sillitoe had done his research well.

'I see.'

Bolitho continued. 'There are the anti-slavery patrols that run out of Good Hope and Freetown. Their aid could be useful. They would know all the likely anchorages, if only from interrogating the slavers when they catch them.' He was reminded again of Tyacke. A dedicated seaman, alone because of his terrible disfigurement, and yet able to command respect and a kind of strange affection from the men who served with him. That day when they had been close to death, the sight of *Larne* had made even the hardest survivor gasp out his thanks to heaven.

Sillitoe was saying, 'That is one of the things I like about you. You don't merely toss away ideas without consideration. You think them through, as only a professional officer can. Our new lord of Admiralty is not yet ready to bend. In time he will have to.'

'Why did Godschale leave?'

Sillitoe said coolly, 'You are also very direct. Godschale, as I think you know, was fond of the ladies. But he was neither consistent nor careful. He compromised a lady of quality, then spurned her for another. It was unfortunate that the one he turned his back on was the wife of a certain member of the House of Lords. More I cannot say.'

'He will not like Bombay.'

Sillitoe watched him from the shadows. 'That is an understatement.'

It was very dark when they reached the house but the rain had stopped, and there were stars already showing between the clouds.

'I have a favour to ask you, Richard.'

Bolitho half-turned, one hand on the carriage door. 'Well?'

'You will need a good flag-lieutenant when you take up your next appointment, now that young Jenour has become the amateur captain. I think I have the right one for you.' He sounded as if he were smiling in the darkness. 'My nephew, to be exact. At present serving as lieutenant in the old *Canopus*. The ship is undergoing extensive repairs at the Nore.'

'I would have to see him.'

'Naturally. I will arrange it. He is not one of those pompous little upstarts . . . he is intelligent, better educated than many who wear the King's coat.'

'I cannot promise anything.' It was strange to think of Sillitoe having a nephew, or any relations for that matter. Catherine had told him that Sillitoe had known her dead husband, Viscount Somervell. In what role, he wondered. Gambler, duellist, or cheat? One usually led to the others. But not Sillitoe. He was too clever, too secretive.

He was looking out at the darkened house. 'My regards to Lady Catherine. A pity she is not at home.' He rapped the carriage roof. 'Drive on!'

Bolitho touched his eye. He always trusted Catherine's instincts about people. Wait and see, she had said. Where Sillitoe was concerned it was sound advice.

The housekeeper opened the door and said, 'I've a table laid for you, Sir Richard.'

'Thank you, no, I've no appetite. I shall go to our room.'

Our room. He closed the door behind him and looked around at their other haven. Her perfume was here; the gown she wore so often when she came to bed because he liked it so much, as if she might enter at any moment.

He hurried to the window as a carriage slowed down at the street corner. But it carried on past the house. They had been separated only because she had feared he could be blamed for snubbing the reception. Hamett-Parker would know he had left early; he would also be told that he and Sillitoe had been together. He tossed his heavy dress coat on to a chair, and smiled when he thought how indignant Ozzard would be about it.

He lay staring at the dancing shadows cast by a solitary candle and thought of her kneeling over him, or lying with her dark hair spread out in disorder across the pillows while she waited for him, unashamed, even proud of the body which he would explore until they could delay no longer.

He was soon asleep, and even then she was with him.

5

No Secrets

By mid-August 1809 the general attitude of England's population was one of apathy and disinterest, except for those who had loved ones at sea or in the army abroad. With Wellesley's victories in the Peninsular War and his return home to receive the title of Duke of Wellington from the King, the real enemy, France, seemed suddenly remote. Only in the City of London, in the counting houses and the world of insurance, was the true damage to trade and shipping really understood.

Bolitho had been twice to the Admiralty where he had been welcomed by four of their lordships, two of whom were senior officers and the others civilians. He had come away bemused by the casual fashion in which the Admiralty Board appeared to be run, with hundreds of instructions and orders being despatched every week to squadrons and solitary vessels, many of which were already obsolete by the time they were delivered.

Reunited with Catherine, he had been troubled by her reluctance to discuss her visit to Zenoria. He had gathered that the girl was still overwhelmed by the Keen family, suffocated by kindness; and when they received an invitation to the christening in Hampshire he had sensed that Catherine's mood went even deeper.

He knew she was disturbed by the lack of confirmation of his next appointment: the news of Collingwood's worsening health made the Mediterranean a possibility for the first time, and yet the Admiralty, and some said the King himself, whose mental state was rumoured to be deteriorating, continued to refuse Collingwood's plea for a recall to England.

He discussed the christening with Catherine, and felt even more that something was wrong.

She had come to nestle at his feet, her hair hiding her face as she had said, 'Val is so excited about it. He wants to invite all his friends, all those who are in the country at the time.' He heard the hesitation as she had added, 'Including Adam.'

'That is unlikely, Kate. *Anemone* is very short of hands, I gather. He will likely search further afield for replacements. A frigate captain is at his best when at sea with no admiral to trouble him!'

She had said quietly, 'Then I thank God for it.' She had looked up at him. 'I know you love him like a son, and I feel like a traitor when I tell you these things. But tell you I must. We swore there would be no secrets from the very beginning.'

Bolitho had listened without interruption: what she had seen in Adam's face at the wedding in Zennor; how she had heard of his visits to the house and Falmouth, and of an outburst in some coaching inn when Adam had called out a complete stranger for insulting the Bolitho family, but had satisfied his anger by shooting out the flame of a candle in a room full of witnesses. Zenoria had told her that Adam had even visited her recently, had ridden all the way from Portsmouth where *Anemone* was taking on stores.

Bolitho had stroked her hair to calm her but his mind had been in turmoil. What was the matter with him that he had not noticed something on the long haul back from the Caribbean? Did he see only what he wanted to see? His nephew had always been a restless one, from the very first day he had joined his ship as a skinny midshipman. He had never thought of him as being much like his brother Hugh. And yet . . . Hugh had always had a quick temper and could not hold down a grudge without showing it. Captain James, their father, had referred to it as bad blood, but surely there was more to it than that.

Catherine had exclaimed, 'Zenoria needs to have a house of her own, somewhere she can be herself. She is young, dear

Richard, but her experiences have given her an eagerness for life that Keen's family do not understand.'

The day of the christening arrived, and as promised they had driven down to the great house, where many friends both local and from London came to pay their respects to the child named Perran Augustus, the latter after Keen's father. There was not enough room to accommodate everyone in the small village church but there was food and drink in the grounds of the house to serve a regiment.

Bolitho had promised to give no hint to Zenoria that he knew part of her secret. If Valentine Keen ever discovered the truth, or even some twisted rumour of it, there was no telling where it might end.

There were several incidents, trivial in their separate ways, but enough to make them glad they had decided to drive back to Chelsea on the same day. The first had occurred at the laying-out of the many presents brought by well-wishers, some of great value or handed down in a family, others notable for their warmth, like the fine carved hobby-horse, its card written in Ozzard's pinched hand to show it was a gift from Allday, who with Bolitho had been introduced to the gathering by Keen as 'The two men who saved my life when I thought all was lost.'

It had happened before they had all gone to the church, and the room's door had been ajar so that Bolitho had not been able to ignore the angry voice of Keen's father.

'Sometimes I think you are a damned fool! A King's captain and a brave one you certainly are – but sense? You don't have the sense you were born with!' Catherine had pulled at his arm, but Bolitho had heard the voice continue. 'Why not wait to see how the boy develops, eh? I'd like to think his name might follow mine in the City, or in the profession of law. I don't want to see him on the roll of killed or missing!'

The cause of his anger was Keen's gift to his tiny son: a beautifully fashioned midshipman's dirk 'to wear one day with pride'. When Keen had shown it to them Bolitho had seen the shaft of despair on Zenoria's features, had seen her quick glance at Catherine, perhaps her only true friend.

His disturbing thoughts continued. He recalled when he had

found Adam drinking heavily in the cabin when they had been homeward bound. Was that only two months ago? *I should have known, challenged him myself.*

Another incident, perhaps to be expected. A woman had approached Bolitho and after a defiant glance at Catherine announced loudly, 'I took tea with your wife some days ago in London, Sir Richard. Such an enjoyable occasion!'

Two bright patches of colour had burned on her cheeks as Bolitho had answered quietly, 'For you, I daresay it would be.'

He had seen the expressions and sensed the nudges among the guests, but others from the villages had shown genuine pleasure at meeting them together for the first time.

'Don't you let him go back, my dear! Let some of the others do their dirty work instead!'

An anonymous voice had called from the rear, 'Huzza for our Dick an' 'is lovely lady!'

Obviously a sailor, probably one who had served with Bolitho at some time. It was like a ghost calling out for all the others who would never see his face again.

In the carriage again with Allday sitting opposite, fast asleep and smelling strongly of rum, Catherine asked softly, 'Shall we know soon?'

Bolitho squeezed her arm. She did not have to explain. It was always there like a threat, while they made each hour of every day their own.

He said, 'I think so. Sir Paul Sillitoe has spoken of a new flag lieutenant, so I suspect he knows more than he is prepared to tell.'

'Will you take his nephew?'

'I'm not sure. Sometimes it is better not to know people too well, to care for them in a way which can hurt, even harm.' He hesitated. 'We have discussed the Indian Ocean too much for coincidence. A quick campaign to cut out further attacks on our shipping.'

'That will mean returning to Cape Town?'

They both fell silent, each reliving the nightmare of the shipwreck.

He said, 'It will be in a King's ship this time. We shall stand well clear of the hundred-mile reef!'

She pressed closer and said, 'I wish I could be there, wher-ever they send you.'

He watched the houses passing in the red glow of sunset and wondered how many sailors and would-be admirals had rolled along this very road.

'A friend at the Admiralty told me that Adam's ship will sail under orders very soon. He thinks it will be to Gibraltar.'

He thought of Adam's face when he had remarked, 'On my birthday last year I was kissed by a lady.' He ought to have realised what he had meant, when in response to his question Adam had said that he did not think anyone really knew the lady. It had been tearing him apart even then. How much worse it would become if he could not learn to control his feelings.

He added, 'I will speak with him, Kate. Whenever I think it prudent.'

But she had fallen asleep against his shoulder.

Three days after the christening Bolitho received his expected summons to the Admiralty.

Catherine had insisted that she should accompany him, and he was surprised that he had made no protest. If they were to be parted in the name of duty, he wanted – needed – every possible moment with her.

The day was fine and warm with some of those who walked and loitered in the tree-lined squares wilting in the dusty sun-shine.

Bolitho watched as she descended the staircase with Sophie hovering behind her.

She looked directly into his face. 'Well, dearest of men? Will it suit?' She wore a gown of deep blue which almost matched his own coat, with facings of gold lace. 'The admiral's lady, or his woman in any case!' She flicked open the fan he had brought her from Madeira to hide the lower half of her face, so that her eyes seemed overpowering. Beneath the fan only the shadow between her breasts moved to show her true emotion.

He took her shoulders. 'I have never been more proud.'

At the Admiralty he was conscious of the eyes watching them, and he felt suddenly reckless and defiant.

He bent his head and kissed her on the neck, and spoke only one word. 'Together.' Then he replaced his hat and walked up the steps.

There was no delay and he was met by the same elegant lieutenant. It was pointless to ask why he had not told him about Baratte's release when he had first greeted him here. An oversight, or was someone afraid he might make trouble about it?

The acting Controller of the Navy, a big florid-faced admiral, and two other lords of admiralty with Hamett-Parker and his secretary sat at one end of the table. As he had anticipated, Bolitho saw Sillitoe seated slightly apart from all the others, his face set in an impassive mask.

Hamett-Parker raised his eyebrows questioningly, a habit he had displayed at Herrick's court-martial. 'You are very prompt, Sir Richard.'

One of the other admirals who was unknown to Bolitho said, 'On behalf of the board I must thank you for your patience and your invaluable help since you came to London. Your experience, not merely in the art of war but also in your past dealings with the military, make you an obvious choice for this appointment.' They all nodded soberly except Hamett-Parker. He continued, 'We understand from Sir Paul Sillitoe that you were thinking of a force of perhaps eight frigates? That, of course, would be out of the question.'

Bolitho thought of Godschale. *One cannot do everything.*

He leaned his elbow on one arm of his chair and touched his eye. He had not been to see the surgeon again. Had he accepted that it was hopeless?

'The army is gathering its strength in Cape Town, Sir Richard. You are senior enough to assist but not necessarily conform to their strategy, for it is the intention of His Britannic Majesty's government to invade and overthrow the French island of Mauritius. But before that we must seek out the enemy's naval strength in that ocean and destroy it.'

Bolitho said abruptly, 'Nobody could do that without ships.'

Hamett-Parker commented, 'Frigates, and perhaps some smaller vessels?'

Bolitho looked at him. 'Yes. Otherwise . . .'

Hamett-Parker snapped, 'There is a new frigate, *Valkyrie*. She has been accepted into the fleet and now lies at Plymouth.' He gave a small smile. 'She is captained by one of your fellow Cornishmen, no less!'

Bolitho had heard something of the new frigate. She had been designed originally as an experiment, to compete with the enemy's larger frigates, which in turn had been copied from the latest contenders in the new American Navy. Bigger than any other frigate in the fleet, *Valkyrie* carried forty-two guns, but was said to be faster and more manoeuvrable than even thirty-eight gun ships like *Anemone*.

Hamett-Parker continued, 'Captain Aaron Trevenen, d'you know him?'

'I know *of* him.'

Hamett-Parker pressed his fingertips together. He was enjoying it. 'Another of your curt summings-up of a proud man's achievements?'

Sillitoe said, 'Many, many months ago – it feels like years – we met at Godschale's house by the Thames. You may recall that Lady Catherine Somervell scolded me for . . .'

Hamett-Parker snapped, 'We require no personal references here, Sir Paul!'

Sillitoe ignored him but raised his voice slightly. 'Scolded me for sending you, Sir Richard, to yet another demanding appointment. I protested that we could send no other, there was none better or so qualified for the task. After the terrible experiences she shared after the loss of *Golden Plover*, I am certain that she would not disagree with me again.'

Hamett-Parker swallowed his anger. 'I will send orders to the *Valkyrie*. You and your staff can take passage in her as Trevenen will be the senior officer of our eventual flotilla. I shall let you know what I think will be required when and if . . .'

Bolitho said, 'If I am to command this enterprise against Baratte . . .' He saw two of them start with surprise. Did they really not know what was happening, and what to expect? 'Then I will inform *you*, Sir James.'

He bowed his head to the table and walked to the door. Sillitoe followed him as he knew he would.

Outside the door Bolitho said, 'I appear to have talked myself into something I would have wished to avoid.'

'I meant what I said. The sailors respect you, and you have their hearts. They will know that you will not betray them merely to satisfy some crude craving for glory, nor will you sacrifice their lives for no good purpose.'

He watched Bolitho's profile, the arguments matched only by the sensitivity on his sunburned face.

Sillitoe persisted, 'If it can be done, you will do it. If not, we shall have to think again.' He added indifferently, 'By which time the King will be raving mad and, more to the point, there may be those not afraid to mention it!'

They paused by a tall window on the stairs. Sillitoe looked down and said, 'How I envy you, Richard. For nothing else but her.'

'If anything happens to me . . .'

Bolitho saw her shading her eyes to look at the window, almost as if she had heard his words.

Sillitoe laughed. 'Do not think such thoughts.' The mood left him and he said smoothly, 'Now, the matter of your new flag lieutenant.'

Bolitho barely heard him. 'We are returning to Falmouth.' He shivered. 'How I hate this place, where men's minds are frozen in time.' He looked at him steadily. 'Send him to me at Falmouth with a letter of introduction.'

Sillitoe was watching him curiously. 'Is that all? Then I will attend to it.'

He gazed after Bolitho as he descended the stairs, and he thought he saw him stumble at one shadowed corner.

He called down, 'When you find Baratte again, do not hesitate. *Kill him.*' Then he was gone.

Later, Bolitho thought it had sounded like something personal.

Bolitho stood by the open doors and looked across the garden to the orchard. The breeze from the sea that cooled his face filled the room behind him with the scent of roses.

A few more days, and then he would retrace the way to Plymouth. He could feel Catherine watching him from beside the empty fireplace. She had tried to hide her own preparations for their parting: new shirts from London, another store of wine from the shop in St James's Street, which had been sent directly to Plymouth. Ozzard had been packing chests, checking every item, his features giving nothing away. He was always like that now, Bolitho thought, ever since the old *Hyperion* had gone down. A man haunted by something, and yet in the open boat after the shipwreck he had been surprisingly strong, tending a dying man, rationing out their wretched portions of food and water, his eyes searching secretly for the remaining mutineer who had been hidden amongst them.

'What about John Allday?'

Bolitho turned towards her. It was as if she had been reading his thoughts.

He said, 'He'll not stay ashore. So wedding, if wedding there is to be, must wait until we return.'

'I'm glad. I shall feel you are safer with him close at hand.' Her dark eyes were full of questions, as they had been when she had found him studying his packet of information from the Admiralty.

'Will it be difficult for you?'

Bolitho sat beside her and held her hand, the one on which she wore his beautiful ring of rubies and diamonds. He had slipped it on to her finger immediately after Keen's wedding at Zennor in the little mermaid's church.

'I shall have *Valkyrie*. I am being given *Triton* too.'

'That was Baratte's ship?'

'Aye. It might drive him to do something foolish.' He touched the ring on her finger where she had once worn Somervell's.

'I must ask, Richard. Do you dislike this Captain Trevenen? You may have to rely on him so much.'

He shrugged. 'Our paths have crossed a few times. His father once served with mine – I suspect that has the makings of something. He is the kind of captain I might have expected

Hamett-Parker to approve.' He looked up at her eyes, her mouth. 'I will get *Anemone* also, if their lordships are good to me.' He saw her relief.

'He needs you, Richard.'

He smiled. 'We shall see.'

There was a sound of voices and Grace Ferguson entered, unwilling as ever to disturb them.

'There is an officer to see you, Sir Richard.'

He saw Catherine's hand go to her breast as she whispered, 'From the Admiralty?'

Mrs Ferguson said, 'A Lieutenant George Avery.'

Bolitho released her hand and stood up. 'Sillitoe's nephew.'

She asked, 'Is it wise? May it not be a ruse to have an aide who will know all your secrets?'

He smiled at her. 'Not all, dearest Kate. If he does not fit, I shall send him back to the Nore.' He added to the house-keeper, 'March him in.'

Catherine said, 'They will all miss you, Richard. They love you so.'

He turned away as the eye smarted again. 'I cannot bear to think on it.'

The lieutenant came in and stared at them. He had obviously travelled by a series of coaches, and looked crumpled and dusty.

Bolitho saw his surprise as he said, 'I am Richard Bolitho. This is Lady Catherine Somervell.' It must be rather a shock, he thought, they were probably far from what Avery was used to. The much-talked of flag officer dressed in an old shirt and breeches, looking more like a gardener than a vice-admiral, and a Knight of the Bath at that. 'Please be seated, Mr Avery. I will see that you are given refreshment.' He did not even glance at her but heard her go to the door.

'I will arrange it,' she said.

'Sit down.' He turned slightly so that the bars of the after-noon sunlight should not irritate his eye.

Avery was not quite what he had expected, either. Tall, with thick dark hair which was touched with grey, he seemed old for his rank, older than Adam certainly. Sillitoe had sent the promised letter of introduction, but as was his custom

71

Bolitho had left it to read after this interview. He would draw his own conclusions first.

'Tell me something of yourself.' He watched the lieutenant's eyes move around the room, absorbing the history of the place, the portraits, the old books through the library door. His face was deeply lined, like that of a man who had suffered and not been able to forget.

'I have been serving as second lieutenant of the *Canopus*, Sir Richard.' He had a low resonant voice with only a faint accent. West Country, probably Dorset.

He was trying to relax, muscle by muscle, but could not restrain his curiosity, as if he were still surprised to be here.

'*Canopus* needs a good deal of refitting, Sir Richard. Rot and blockade have taken a toll of the old lady.'

'And before that?'

Bolitho recognised the pain, the sudden look of hopelessness as Avery answered, 'I was in the schooner *Jolie*, a prize taken from the French two years earlier. We were serving off Biscay when we came upon a Dutch trader working right inshore. We had often used those tactics because she was French-built and usually roused no suspicion.' He said bitterly, 'With our little pop-guns what could we do anyway?' He seemed to recall where he was, and went on quietly, 'I was second-in-command, and the captain was another lieutenant. I liked him but . . .'

'But?'

Avery looked directly at him and Bolitho saw that his eyes were tawny, very clear like a wild cat's.

'I thought him reckless, Sir Richard.'

Bolitho touched his eye without noticing it. *Jolie*. It did not mean anything. Perhaps he should have read Sillitoe's letter after all.

Avery had paused, expecting an interruption, a rebuke even, for criticising his commanding officer no matter how junior at the time.

He said, 'We put two shots across the Dutchman and he came up into the wind. The master probably imagined that there was more than one of us.' His face stiffened. 'There was. The other one was a French corvette. She came around a headland under full sail. We had no chance. We were already close-hauled and on a lee shore, but all my captain said was, "Two for the price of one." They were the last words he uttered on this earth. A ball cut him in half even as he waved defiance to the enemy.' He was silent for a moment, then he continued. 'The corvette raked us from bow to stern. Men were falling and dying. I still hear the screams, the pleas for mercy. Then I was hit. As I lay on the deck I could see our people pulling down the flag. If they had fought on, they would all have been killed.'

Bolitho said, 'If you had not been wounded, would you have ordered them to fight on?' Again he watched the pain. It was probably a question Avery had asked himself many times.

Avery said, 'It was about the time of the Peace of Amiens, Sir Richard, when I was taken prisoner. As I was wounded I think the French were glad to release me.' He paused. 'Then I had to face a court-martial.'

Bolitho could see it as if he had been there. The Peace of Amiens had been an excuse for the old enemies to re-arm and lick their wounds. Nobody had expected it to last. So, to prepare the fleet for whatever lay ahead, a scapegoat, no matter how lowly, had to be found.

Avery said, 'I was found not guilty of cowardice or hazarding the ship. But *Jolie* had struck her colours, so wounded or not, I was reprimanded.' He began to rise from his seat. 'I knew it would be hopeless. I am only sorry that I had to waste your time.'

Not guilty, but condemned to be a lieutenant until he was discharged or killed.

Bolitho asked quietly, 'Do you have any family?'

He did not seem to hear for a moment. Then he said, 'There is nobody. Apart from my uncle, whom I barely know.'

Bolitho saw Catherine's shadow beyond the open door.

He said, 'Falmouth is not London, but there is a highly respected tailor here, Joshua Miller, who has served my family through several generations. See to it that you obtain the necessary clothing as befits a flag lieutenant.' He could not bear to see Avery's expression. Astonishment, gratitude, disbelief: it was all and none of them.

He added, 'My own nephew was once in the same

demanding role. It will not be an easy one for you. You will see my secretary, Mr Yovell, and he will drill you in your duties. Where is your gear?'

Avery tried to control his thoughts. 'In the inn yard, Sir Richard. I would have taken a room there, but I never thought—'

Bolitho said, 'Have someone bring it to the house. It will be easier for you to find your feet here, and to know the little crew who work with me.'

'I do not know what to say, Sir Richard! I can only promise . . .'

'Promise nothing! It is wiser in the long run.' He hesitated and said, 'If it helps, I once threw down my sword to save the life of one very dear to me.' He thought of Allday falling to the Spanish blade, the terrible wound which still rendered him helpless if he was unprepared for it. 'I hope I would be strong enough to do it again.'

When he turned again the tall, gaunt lieutenant with the streaks of prematurely greying hair had gone, as if he had been the spirit of someone past.

Catherine was in the room, her arms outstretched until she had thrown them around his shoulders.

He kissed her neck. 'Did I do right, Kate?'

She could barely speak for a few moments. 'He is a good man. I will never forget his face when he left you.'

He hugged her, wanting to make light of it. But all the time the lieutenant had been blurting out his story he had seen only himself. *It might have been me.*

Later in the evening light, with a faint mist coming in from the sea, they walked together along the track to the stile, beyond which was the cliff path. They watched the sea as it hissed among the rocks where a few gulls bobbed up and down on the swell, but they could have had the world to themselves.

She said suddenly, 'I want to come with you to Plymouth, and be at your side. Until the last moment.'

He held her against him, her loose hair blowing into his eyes. That day when *Anemone* had sighted the shores of Cornwall their time together had seemed infinite, reaching out ahead of them with so much promise. Now, in days perhaps, they would be parted, and her letters and his memories would have to sustain him.

'If you wish it, Kate. I am as greedy as you are persuasive.'

They returned to the old house, and Bolitho was surprised to see his secretary Yovell working on some books in the library.

She frowned at him. 'I'll not have you overtaxing yourself, Mr Yovell!' Then she laughed. 'I shall go up.' Her gaze lingered on Bolitho as he watched her mount the stairs. 'There will be no regrets, Richard.'

Bolitho was not certain what she meant. To Yovell he said, 'How did you get along with Mr Avery?'

Yovell breathed on his little gold-rimmed spectacles and polished them vigorously with his handkerchief.

'A man of many parts, Sir Richard. Understands Latin too. He will suit.'

There could be no higher praise from him.

Bolitho went upstairs, past each watching portrait with its background of some forgotten battle or campaign. The house was still hot from the day: there might even be thunder in the air.

He went into the room and saw her standing by a window, which was opened wide. It was airless and even the candles shone unmoving, the shadows around the room quite still.

As he put his arms around her she turned towards the tall cheval glass, which was surrounded by hundreds of carved thistles. It had belonged to Bolitho's Scottish mother, a gift from Captain James. She watched his face as he looked at her reflection in the mirror. She wore the favourite robe with its fine gold cord, her body clearly etched against his own shadow.

'Remember, no regrets. Do with me as you will. Use me, take me, for I am yours – and always have been, although we did not know it.'

He saw her body move against him as he played with the cord about her throat. It was like watching her being taken by someone else, a stranger.

'Slowly.' Her eyes were watching the mirror, her mouth moist as he pulled the cord and began to lower the gown until her breasts were revealed, his hand dark around them until she was suddenly completely naked, her hair falling across her bare shoulders as if to protect her.

He took her to the bed and lay with her, touching her, kissing her breasts, her body, her legs, until delay was unbearable.

Only a moment more while he threw off his clothes, and she pretended to hold him away, then she murmured, 'But I surrender . . .' The rest was stifled as he came down and entered her, holding her wrists, taking her like the stranger in the mirror.

There was thunder, lightning too. But in the room there was only peace.

6

The 'Valkyrie'

The long stretch of water named The Hamoaze which separated Plymouth Dockyard from the neighbouring county of Cornwall shone like burnished pewter in the forenoon sunlight. The last day of August, and yet there was already a chill in the air, a hint of misty rain across the Devon countryside.

The waterway was alive with shipping of every kind and size, from two lordly ships-of-the-line tugging at their cables in a brisk off-shore breeze to collier brigs, deep in the water with their cargoes for the towns on the River Tamar and the dockyard itself. A masting vessel towing a great tangle of spars was following them, using the tide to make a safe passage from the Sound through the narrow strait that guarded the final approach.

To any ignorant landman one man-of-war was much the same as another, size being the only comparison, but in any true sailor the frigate anchored closest to the dockyard would rouse an immediate interest. From her tapering jib-boom to her finely-raked counter with her name, *Valkyrie*, below the stern cabin windows, she was obviously much larger than any other ship classed as a fifth-rate, and but for her long main gun-deck she might have passed for a ship-of-the-line.

Men moved quietly about her gangways and high above the decks on rigging and yards. A last full inspection: who could tell for how long? She was a new ship, built at the famous Bucklers Hard to an advanced design, and she had been with the fleet for less than two months. The strain on officers and seamen alike had been considerable.

Extra officers and experienced hands had been poached from other vessels in Plymouth with the aid of the port admiral, who was better aware than most of *Valkyrie*'s importance. Properly used, she could out-fight any other man-of-war below the line of battle, and had been so designed that she could be used as a squadron commander of almost any number of vessels.

Right aft in the great cabin, Captain Aaron Trevenen was considering this very possibility as he glanced into the adjoining quarters, which were already prepared for Vice-Admiral Sir Richard Bolitho's use for as long as the situation dictated.

The quarters were spacious by any standard, he thought, for *Valkyrie* boasted a beam of just over forty feet with head-room, aft at least, to make every movement comfortable. Trevenen had spent almost all of his life at sea in frigates or similar vessels. This would probably be the last, he thought. A fine ship, and as a senior post-captain he had every chance of promotion to flag rank when *Valkyrie* had completed her commission. It had not been a definite promise, but Trevenen had been in the navy long enough to recognise the unwritten parts of his orders.

He was thickset rather than heavily-built, with a strong jaw and crows' feet to mark the years of standing watch under all conditions. His hair was a gingery chestnut colour, cut short, but not short enough to conceal the streaks of grey. He was forty but looked much older. He stood now, hands clasped behind him as if he could penetrate the full length of his command. *Valkyrie* was a true reward, when properly handled, for any captain. One hundred and eighty tons displacement, she could still respond like a four-in-hand. The sailing master had been astonished when the ship had logged over eighteen knots, despite her size and her forty-two guns and carronades.

Trevenen closed the door as if to shut the coming vice-admiral from his thoughts. He could not allow him to intrude. It was too dangerous. He heard the marine sentry tap his musket on the deck outside the screen door and prepared himself for his visitor.

It was Lieutenant Urquhart, his senior, an alert, quietly spoken man who had already been a first lieutenant in another frigate. Trevenen knew that, like some of the others, Urquhart had not yet got his captain's measure on so short an acquaintance.

Nor would he, he thought. He almost smiled. Almost.

He heard the tap at the door and said, 'Come!'

Urquhart glanced round the day cabin as he strode aft, his cocked hat pressed under one arm. It was as if he expected to discover some identity here, a clue to the man who next to God would hold the lives of two hundred and twenty souls in his hands.

Trevenen did not miss it. 'You are early, Mr Urquhart. Is something amiss?'

The lieutenant said, 'It is the surgeon, sir. He wishes to have an interview with you.' He flushed as Trevenen's eyes came to rest on him. They were dark and deepset, yet managed to dominate even his strong features. Urquhart added awkwardly, 'About the punishment, sir.'

'I see. Tell him I do not wish to discuss it. I want it over and done with before the admiral comes aboard.' He turned to the great stern windows as a yawl, tilting deeply as she tacked, passed dangerously close to the frigate's counter, then he snapped his fingers even as the first lieutenant turned to leave. 'No! Belay that, Mr Urquhart! I *shall* see him!'

Urquhart closed the screen door and found that his hand was shaking. In his previous ship the captain had called him by his first name when it was an informal occasion. If Trevenen ever did it to him, he would likely die of shock.

He found the surgeon waiting by the wardroom, his battered hat gripped in both hands. An untidy man, with sprouting grey hair and a face ruined by an excess of drinking. But they said he was a good surgeon; it was to be hoped they would not discover otherwise.

'It's no use. The punishment goes ahead.' He shrugged helplessly. 'But he will see you.'

The surgeon stood his ground, his eyes angry. 'The cap'n insists on the bosun's mates using the lash with the heavier knots! No man can stand up to that!'

Urquhart said, 'I can do nothing.' Secretly he agreed with him, but to show what amounted to disloyalty at the beginning of a commission was nothing short of madness. This ship was luckier than many, and the captain must know it. She had fewer pressed men than most, and had been fortunate in collecting some twenty new hands who, although not seamen, were tough and fearless Cornish tin miners who had been thrown out of work by a pit collapse.

The sentry brought his heels together and called, 'Surgeon, sir!'

The door was opened by the cabin servant and closed instantly.

'You wish to see me?' Trevenen was standing with his broad shoulders towards the windows and the glistening panorama of water and shipping beyond.

'Aye, sir. About the landman, Jacobs. I'll not vouch for his surviving punishment. It's his second flogging in two weeks, sir.'

'I am aware of it. The man is an ignorant lout. I'll not tolerate insubordination nor will I see my subordinates' authority undermined.' The servant padded over the black and white checkered deck covering and placed a tall glass of wine within reach of his captain.

The surgeon said, 'He *is* an ignorant lout, sir, I'm not defending his . . .'

The captain held up one hand. 'I have something to ask you.' He saw the surgeon's raddled face watching the tall glass and added, 'You were surgeon at one time in the *Hyperion*, Sir Richard Bolitho's flagship, I believe?'

George Minchin stared at him, caught completely off balance by the question.

'Well, yes, sir. I was in *Hyperion* when she went down.' Some of his weary despair seemed to vanish as he said with a certain pride, 'I was one of the last to leave the old lady.'

'It is confidential, of course, but we shall weigh anchor once our passengers are on board. To suit the purpose of admiralty this will no longer be a private ship. Your Sir Richard Bolitho is hoisting his flag over us.'

He saw the emotions chasing each other across the surgeon's face. How could a man allow himself to decay like this?

Trevenen asked, 'How did you find him?'

Minchin looked into the distance, so far now beyond the cabin and the ship. The thundering roar and recoil of the old seventy-four's artillery, the unending stream of wounded and dying who had been dragged down to him on the orlop deck, the 'wings and limbs' tubs as the Jacks termed them overflowing with grisly relics of saw and knife. Arms, legs, pieces of men Minchin had once known, and all the while the deck had shivered to the fury of the battle above and around them.

'The finest man I ever met. A gentleman, but only in the true sense. I've seen him shed a tear when some poor lad lay dying. He was not too proud to stoop and hold his hand for his last minutes.' He glared at the captain with sudden dislike. 'Not like some!'

'Very commendable. But the punishment will be carried out at four bells this forenoon and you will attend it, sir. I have long discovered that authority and severity must often go hand in hand!'

He waited for the door to close after Minchin's shabby figure. The man was a fool. As soon as possible he would try to have him replaced, although surgeons with experience and the stomach for their butcher's work were difficult to find.

He touched the wine with his tongue. His hardest task would be to conceal and suppress the old animosity born when his father and Captain James Bolitho had become enemies. Trevenen came from Truro and he resented hearing Bolitho proclaimed Cornwall's greatest son. He frowned, his mouth setting in a thin line.

We shall see about that.

At exactly four bells the calls trilled between decks and along *Valkyrie*'s gangways while the marines took up their station across the quarterdeck.

'All hands! All hands! Hands lay aft to witness punishment!'

The first lieutenant came to the cabin again but Trevenen said calmly, 'I heard, Mr Urquhart. This is a quiet ship and I intend it should remain so!'

81

Then he picked up the folder that contained the Articles of War, and after a slow scrutiny of his quarters walked out.

Unmoved? Urquhart sighed. It was not that. There was no sign of feeling at all.

Lady Catherine Somervell stood by the tall windows of the room they had shared for only one night. The windows opened on to a small balcony and faced south across Plymouth Sound. It looked as if it might remain fine for her journey to Falmouth. She felt a shiver run through her. Perhaps she should have returned to London, the city she had once known so well. In the same breath she knew she needed to go to the old grey house below Pendennis Castle. She could keep busy amongst people who, for the most part, kept to themselves and did not stare at her wherever she went. She would always be a foreigner in Cornwall; even Yovell was, and he came from no further than Devon. But they respected her now, and she found that it mattered. Most folk probably thought she was above it, that she was used to the gossip and the lies, but she was not. And the man she loved more than life itself, who was prepared to risk everything for her and because of her, would soon be gone. Back to that other world which she had shared for a while at the mercy of the sea's cruelty, and the danger which had drawn them even closer, if that were possible.

A carriage had been sent from the dockyard with some porters to carry Bolitho's chests and cases to the ship. The wine-cooler she had given him to replace the other that lay on the sea bed in his old *Hyperion* would remain at Falmouth until the future had made itself clear. It would be a ready reminder whenever she saw it. Something of his.

Allday had gone with Ozzard and Yovell to make sure that nothing was stolen in the dockyard on its way to the ship, as he had bluntly put it. The serious-faced flag lieutenant, Avery, was somewhere downstairs in this inn, The Golden Lion, the best in Plymouth.

She had said good-bye to Bolitho's *little crew* as he called them, but Allday had lingered to say his own piece.

'I'll take good care o' Sir Richard, m'lady. Have no fear o' that.' He had seemed subdued, even sad.

She had said, 'Is it harder this time?'

He had given her his steady stare. 'Aye, it is. When we gets home again, will you come an' see us wed?'

She had almost broken at his use of the word *home*.

'Nothing will keep us away.' She had hugged him. The true sailor with his special scent of rum, tobacco and tar: the smells of the sea. 'And take care of yourself, John. You are very dear to me.'

She had seen his surprise at her emotion, the easy use of his name. She could read his thoughts. The woman who had been married to the lowest and the highest, who had stripped naked to don a man's clothing while the ship had been bearing down on the reef, who had half-killed a mutineer with a Spanish comb: how could she feel like weaker souls?

She heard Bolitho coming in now from the adjoining room, patting his pockets as she had seen him do so many times.

He was watching her gravely, his uniform and gleaming epaulettes like a barrier between them. He was wearing the beautiful presentation sword, and she knew Allday had been entrusted with the old family blade.

When they had arrived they had stood by this same window and he had remarked, 'They used to have a telescope mounted here so guests could see the shipping in the Sound.' He had tried to make light of it but there was something in his voice, some indefinable sadness. 'I expect some rogue stole it.'

'Secrets?' she had said.

'I was leaving then. I was captain of *Hyperion*. So long ago, it seems now. Nearly fifteen years.'

She had thought of the portrait of his first wife, Cheney, found dusty and forgotten where Belinda had hidden it. She had had it cleaned and replaced on the wall.

Bolitho had said quietly, 'It was the last time I saw her. She died when I was at sea.'

It had been a precious moment. She knew she would study the portrait again when she returned to Falmouth: the young bride who, but for a tragic accident, would have given him a child.

A servant appeared at the door. 'Beggin' yer pardon, Sir Richard, but th' carriage is 'ere.'

83

'Thank you.' He faced her again and she saw the pain in his grey eyes.

'I wish you were coming with me but I shall go directly to the dockyard. It hurts me so much to part with you, to become entangled again with the affairs of others.' He crossed to the open window and said softly, 'In God's name, there is a crowd outside!'

Catherine watched his dismay. Why was he always so surprised that wherever he went people wanted to see him? To ordinary men and women he was their protection, the hero who stood between them and the hated enemy.

He said, 'We must say good-bye, dearest Kate. It should be a tumbril out there, not a carriage.'

They stood quite motionless in one another's arms, and they kissed, clinging to the last minutes.

She whispered, 'I shall take the locket from you when you are with me again. Go down to them, Richard. I will watch from here.'

'*No*. Not from up here.' He forced a smile. 'Come to the door. They will adore it.'

She nodded, understanding. The window where the telescope had once been mounted was the last place where he had seen Cheney, when he had gone to join his ship.

'Very well. Afterwards I shall send for Matthew, and never fear, we will have a guard with us.' She touched his mouth, her fingers very cool. A last contact. She thought of the night. Unable to love, each thinking of the dawn, of today. Now.

'I love you so much, darling Kate. I feel I am leaving so much of me behind.'

Then they were on the staircase and Bolitho saw Avery standing below with the Golden Lion's landlord. The latter was all smiles at the attention his famous guest was attracting. He had probably spread the word himself.

Bolitho had noticed that Avery stood and walked with one shoulder slightly raised, because of the wound he had suffered when the schooner's men had struck to the French corvette. But the old tailor at Falmouth had done well, and Avery looked quite different in his new coat with its white lapels, his cocked hat bedecked with gleaming gold lace. The tailors could stitch a uniform together in less than four days; with the comings and goings of sea officers they would work twenty-four hours a day if need be. Bolitho had thought more than once that they would make a fortune in London.

Avery doffed his hat to Catherine. 'Good-bye, my lady.'

She held out her hand and he put it to his lips.

She said, 'We have had no time to become acquainted, Mr Avery. We shall put that to rights when we meet again.'

Avery replied awkwardly, 'You are most kind, my lady.'

It was obvious he had been badly hurt, far more than by his wound.

The landlord threw open the door and the roar of voices swept over them. People were cheering and calling out he knew not what in the confused din of excitement.

'You drum them Frenchies to perdition! Just like our own Drake!'

Another yelled, 'God bless you, Dick, an' yer ladyship too!'

They fell strangely silent as Avery opened the carriage door with the crest of the fouled anchor on it. Bolitho looked at her and knew her mouth trembled, but only he would have seen it. Her fine dark eyes were very steady, too much so; but he knew that as far as she was concerned they were quite alone.

'Dearest of men.' She could not continue. Even when they kissed there was absolute silence, as if the crowd were too awed, perhaps too sad to make a sound. When he climbed into the carriage beside Avery the whole street erupted in cheering. Civilian hats flew into the air, and two passing marines doffed their own in salute.

She watched the coachman touch the two horses with his whip and the wheels began to clatter across the cobbles. Even then they cheered, and small boys ran alongside the carriage until it gathered speed. All the while he kept his eyes on hers, locked together until the carriage had vanished around a corner. Not once had he glanced up at the window with the balcony, and she was deeply moved.

She returned to the room, and without going close to the window, watched the crowd disperse, the sound dying away like a receding tide.

Sophie was waiting for her, her eyes filling her face.

'I was that proud, me lady. All them people!'

She nodded, her hand pressed beneath her breast, afraid almost to breathe, unable to believe he had gone.

'They used to do it to poor Nelson.' Then she said abruptly, 'Tell Matthew to fetch our things.'

'All done, me lady.' Sophie was puzzled. Lady Catherine should have been excited, or burst into tears. She did not understand that the tall, lovely woman with the dark hair and high cheekbones did not want to share it, not even with her.

Catherine said quietly, 'Go down, Sophie. There is something I must do.'

Alone she stood in the room and looked at the window where another woman had watched him go.

'May love always protect you.' She spoke aloud, momentarily unconscious that what she had just said was part of the engraving on his locket.

She walked slowly down the same staircase, holding her skirt with one hand, her eyes looking directly ahead.

The landlord bowed to her. 'God be with 'ee, m'lady!'

She smiled, and then froze as a carriage rolled to a halt behind the one with the Bolitho crest.

'What is it, m'lady?' Matthew made to take her arm, his round apple-face full of concern.

She stared at the other carriage as a figure climbed down.

The familiar frock coat and epaulettes, one hand reaching up for his lady's even as the inn servants ran to fetch their bags.

'It's nothing, Matthew.' She shook her head as the street and the carriage misted over. She added with sudden despair, 'Take me home.'

As Matthew climbed up to his box and kicked off the brake, with the hard-faced guard sitting beside him, she turned at last and allowed herself to look up at their window. There were no ghosts; or were there? Was someone there, watching her depart, still waiting for the ship which had come too late?

Sophie was holding her hand, like a child. 'Better now, me lady?'

She said, 'Yes,' suddenly glad the girl was with her for the long journey to Falmouth.

She attempted to reassure her. 'If Allday were here I think I would ask him for a wet.' But the remark only saddened her.

Don't leave me. . .

Lieutenant George Avery paused as Bolitho left his side and walked to the edge of one of the many dockyard basins. Ships being repaired, re-rigged, and in some cases new vessels still under construction: Plymouth was always a busy place, and the air was filled with the din of hammers and the scrape of saws. Teams of horses dragged miles of cordage towards a ship bereft of rigging, where more men waited to transform the apparent tangle of meaningless rope into a pattern of stays and shrouds: a thing of beauty to some, an endless tyranny to those who would eventually control it in every sort of sea and weather.

But Bolitho was looking at this one dock in particular. His old *Hyperion* had been berthed here after her terrible battle, when he had been her young captain. A proud ship which even the stains of death, the torn planking and smashed hull, could not destroy. They had made her into a stores hulk, like the one he saw now in this same dock. Nelson's words seemed to ring in his mind, when due to the shortages and the losses in the fleet *Hyperion* had been brought out of her humble role to be reborn, ready to stand once more in the line of battle which was her rightful place. When the choice of a new flagship had been Bolitho's, he had astounded many at the Admiralty by asking for his old command. Nelson had silenced the doubters by saying, 'Give him any ship he wants!'

Hyperion had been old, but the little admiral's own choice for what was to be his last flagship, the *Victory*, had been forty years old when she had broken the enemy line at Trafalgar, and Nelson had paid the price for his courage.

Then, in this dockyard, Bolitho had been returning to an empty house, with nothing to believe in and nobody to care for. Now he had everything to sustain him: his lovely Catherine and a love he would never have believed possible.

Avery watched him curiously. 'Sir?'

Bolitho looked at him. 'Memories. I left an old ship here. But she came back to me. Until that day in October six days before Trafalgar. Some say we tilted the scales for Nelson . . . only Fate can be certain. I often think of it, and the fact that only my nephew ever met Nelson himself. I'm glad. It is something he'll never forget.'

He thought suddenly of what Catherine had told him, how she had felt like a traitor. Only she had noticed it at first. Now others must never see it, or know that it must have been inevitable. The girl with the moonlit eyes, and the young captain. Perhaps that, too, was Fate.

He turned away. His new flag lieutenant probably thought him mad. He was very likely regretting his decision to leave the tired old *Canopus* at Chatham. They walked on, and some dockyard labourers who were hoisting a spar by tackle up the foremast of a frigate waved, and one shouted, 'Good luck, Sir Richard! You burn them buggers!'

Bolitho raised his cocked hat and called, 'You give us the ships, my lads! We'll do the rest!' They all laughed and nudged one another as if it was one huge jest.

But Avery saw Bolitho's face as he turned away from them. His eyes were bitter like his voice. 'It is quite all right if you don't have to go out and do it!'

'I expect they meant well, Sir Richard.'

Bolitho said coldly, 'Is that what you think? Then I am sorry for you.' Then he took Avery's arm and exclaimed, 'That was unforgivable of me! It is not how I want it to be.'

They reached the main jetty and Bolitho stood looking at the moored ships, the endless bustle of small harbour craft. His nerves were on edge. *I need you, Kate.* In her uncanny fashion she might hear his unspoken words. He could feel the sun burning into his back, her locket clinging to the damp skin beneath his shirt, one of the new ones she had bought for him. It helped to calm him in some way, and when he recalled how he had only owned one undarned pair of stockings as a youthful lieutenant, he almost smiled. *Bless you, Kate . . . you heard me.*

Avery said quietly, 'Boat's coming, Sir Richard.' He seemed

afraid to disturb his thoughts. He was not shy or so easy to read as Jenour had been: he was withdrawn, biding his time.

Bolitho faced the water as a smart gig appeared around a moored hulk and veered sharply towards the jetty, her oars rising and falling like white bones. He touched his eye and Avery said immediately, 'Is there something I can do, Sir Richard?'

He said, 'Something in my eye, I think.' The lie came easily enough. But how long before Avery, like Jenour, realised the truth? 'Who is in the boat?'

Avery seemed satisfied. 'A lieutenant, sir.'

It was strange not to have Allday beside him at this moment, critically measuring up the boat's crew and anything else that took his attention. He was not in the gig either.

Avery commented, 'Smart boat, Sir Richard.'

The bowman was already standing with his boathook poised: the lieutenant was beside the coxswain, gauging the moment.

'Oars, *up!*' The boat's crew tossed their oars, each blade in perfect line with the next. It said a lot for their training, when *Valkyrie* had been commissioned for so short a time.

The gig glided alongside the weed-covered stairs and the bowman hooked on to a mooring ring.

The lieutenant scrambled ashore, his hat already in his hand as he snapped stiffly to attention with a flourish.

'Finlay, Sir Richard, fourth lieutenant!'

Bolitho saw the young officer's eyes flicker between them, from the famous vice-admiral to the lieutenant with the twist of gold cord at his shoulder to mark him as Bolitho's aide.

'Very well, Mr Finlay. You have an impressive crew.' He saw the lieutenant blink, as if he were unused to praise.

'Thank you, Sir Richard!'

Avery climbed down into the sternsheets and looked up to watch his new master as he turned, shading his eye to look at the land, the green hump of Mount Edgcumbe, the tiny cottages huddled together in the sunshine.

Bolitho knew the two lieutenants were observing him. Only the gig's crew remained motionless on their thwarts, although the nearness of dry land was usually enough to relax even the tightness of any discipline.

Good-bye, my dearest Kate. Though distance separates us, you are always with me.

Then, holding the presentation sword against his hip, he climbed down into the boat.

The lieutenant jumped down and called, 'Cast off! Bear off forrard!' And as the stream carried them clear he added, 'Out oars! Give way all!'

There was a breeze on the water and Bolitho could feel it stinging his eyes, as if to mock his formality. He glanced at the oarsmen, well turned out in their checkered shirts and tarred hats. There was something different, something wrong. Their eyes were fixed on the stroke oar, their bodies pushing the looms, then leaning back as the blades bit into the water as one. He tried to put it from his mind. A new ship, a different captain to most of them, a future as yet unknown; it was to be expected. He turned to watch a passing guard boat, oars tossed and an officer standing in the sternsheets, his hat raised in salute as he saw the flag officer in the gig. They would probably all know by now, he thought. He glanced at the seamen again. Not hostile, not indifferent. Cowed. It was the only description.

So Trevenen had not changed. On matters of discipline and performance he had been described as a fanatic.

Finlay the fourth lieutenant ventured hesitantly, 'There she lies, Sir Richard.'

Bolitho shaded his eyes. *Valkyrie* was big, right enough. From a distance she looked almost as large as *Hyperion* had been, and she had been a two-decked seventy-four.

Finlay was shifting nervously on his seat. 'Watch her, Cox'n! You have the current under your coat-tails!'

The man at the tiller nodded, his eyes measuring the boat's speed through the water.

Bolitho saw the scarlet coats of the marines already in position and had the impression they had been there for a long time. Sunlight flashed on several telescopes, and even at this distance he thought he heard the trill of calls. It had taken him years to get used to these moments, steeling himself for the first encounter. He had always tried to put it in proper

90

perspective, telling himself that they would be more worried about him than he should be about them.

Another boat was leaving the frigate from the opposite side, moving fast, two armed marines in the stern.

Avery said quietly, 'There's a body in that cutter, sir.'

Bolitho had already seen it. Covered in a piece of canvas, one arm outflung as if the man was asleep.

Bolitho asked, 'What has happened?' When Finlay remained silent he snapped, 'That was a *question*, Mr Finlay!'

The lieutenant stared ahead of the boat and answered unhappily, 'A defaulter, Sir Richard.' He swallowed hard. 'He died under punishment this forenoon.'

Bolitho saw the stroke oarsman watching him for just a few seconds before he stared fixedly aft again. He had been looking at him, trying to find something. As if he were pleading.

Bolitho pulled down his hat more tightly as the breeze dashed spray over the gunwale.

'What had he done?'

Finlay had gone pale, as if he was revealing something improper which might rebound on him.

'He – he swore at a midshipman, Sir Richard.'

'And?'

'Three dozen lashes, Sir Richard.' He was biting his lip so hard it was a wonder it did not bleed.

Bolitho was aware that his flag lieutenant was listening, learning, trying perhaps to understand why someone so well-placed in the navy should care about a common seaman. Men were flogged every day: one more would make no difference. There were always the hard men who could withstand three dozen and many more and live to boast about the scars left by the infamous cat. The discipline of the lower deck was often worse when one of their own was caught stealing from a shipmate's meagre possessions. It was something that happened and everyone knew about it, and that crude justice separated them from the wardroom and warrant officers as surely as the afterguard and the ship's marines.

Bolitho looked at the frigate, closer now, her mastheads towering to the sky and the Red Ensign streaming above her taffrail, the Union Flag in the bows. He studied *Valkyrie's*

91

impressive figurehead: a maiden in horned helmet and breast-plate, one of Odin's faithful attendants, one hand raised as if to beckon a dead hero to Valhalla. He was surprised that the beautifully carved figure was decorated only with dull yellow dockyard paint. That was strange. Most captains would pay out of their own pockets to adorn their ships' figureheads and the 'gingerbread' around the stern, as Adam had paid for the seductive nymph on *Anemone*, all gold apart from her eyes. Apart from anything else the gesture showed that the ship had a successful captain, who was not unwilling to spend some of his own prize money. A small thing in its way: but there was more to Trevenen than he had thought.

He still did not know why his father had disliked the Trevenen family, and his grandfather had apparently loathed them. Land, property, or some other conflict – it could be anything.

He looked at the main battery of guns as the gig swept beneath the tapering jib-boom. They were powerful eighteen-pounders, whereas many of the older frigates still mounted twelve-pounders, as his own had done.

He had heard that the new American navy had gone even further, and their larger frigates carried twenty-four-pounders. Less manoeuvrable perhaps, but with a broadside like that they could dismast any enemy before she could get within range.

The gig turned in a tight arc and Bolitho saw the figures at the entry port, the neatly packed hammocks in the nettings, the fresh black and buff paint, which made the hull reflect the current alongside as if it were glass.

'Boat ahoy!' The age-old challenge echoed across the water, although the telescopes would have revealed much earlier that their expected flag officer had arrived.

The lieutenant raised a speaking trumpet and replied, 'Flag, *Valkyrie!*'

Bolitho thought of Allday. He would have used just one hand to make his voice carry.

Avery saw Bolitho's fingers adjusting the gleaming presentation sword. It was a steep climb up the frigate's side, slippery too. No officer, let alone an admiral, would want to pitch headlong into the water after tripping over his sword.

Bolitho was also thinking as much. Allday had always been there to offer his hand if need be: he was even more protective now that he knew about the damaged eye, and carried the secret like some special award, shared only with the trusted few.

With oars tossed again the gig hooked on to the main chains and Bolitho reached out to the guide-ropes, waited for the boat to rise on the swell, and then climbed quickly up the ship's tumblehome. He thought of Catherine, the many walks they had enjoyed, the rides across country at full gallop. It had worked wonders. As he stepped into the entry port he was not even breathless.

Then, as the Royal Marines presented arms, a cloud of pipeclay lifting above their glinting bayonets, and the calls twittered and shrilled, a small band of boy drummers and fifers struck up *Heart of Oak*. After the quietness of the gig it was deafening.

Bolitho doffed his hat to the quarterdeck and the ensign, while from the foremast truck his own flag broke out into the wind.

He saw Captain Aaron Trevenen stepping forward from his officers, his lined face grave and unsmiling as he said, 'Welcome aboard, Sir Richard. You honour me by hoisting your flag above my command, no matter how temporarily.'

Bolitho was equally formal. 'A fine ship, Captain Trevenen.' He heard Avery coming aboard behind him, probably wondering how *Valkyrie* would suit him after a ponderous ship-of-the-line.

He glanced around at the crowded figures on the gangways and clinging in the shrouds, the mass of blue and white on the quarterdeck where the lieutenants and warrant officers waited in respectful silence.

Trevenen said, 'Your quarters are ready, Sir Richard. If there is anything you need, I shall do my best to provide it.' His deepset eyes flickered across Bolitho's frocked coat and the Nile medal around his neck. The presentation sword was not missed, either.

'Perhaps you would wish to meet my officers at your convenience?'

Bolitho looked at him calmly. 'It is a long passage to Cape Town, Captain Trevenen. I hope I shall meet every man-Jack before that.' He spoke without raising his voice, but he saw the deepset eyes spark as if he had shouted an insult.

The captain removed his hat and called, 'A cheer for Sir Richard Bolitho! *Huzza! Huzza!*'

The watching sailors and petty officers responded loudly. But there was no life in it, no warmth, and as the cheers died away he was reminded of the gig's crew.

It was then that he saw Allday for the first time. He was standing beside a long eighteen-pounder, somehow managing to look apart from everyone else in his smart gilt-buttoned coat.

Across the frigate's wide deck their eyes met and held. Only then did Allday give a barely perceptible shake of the head.

It was all he needed.

7

Confrontations

Bolitho was standing in the cabin's quarter gallery, shading his eyes from the reflected glare while he studied the impressive slab of the Rock of Gibraltar. *Valkyrie* had made a fast passage despite her size, only five days, and could have done it faster but for the need to stay in company with the captured French frigate, now renamed *Laertes*. He could just make her out through a lazy haze that floated above the busy anchorage like an artist's impression of gunsmoke. If he had been right about Baratte, would he already know of his old ship's departure from England under her new name? It seemed quite likely, he thought. Their lordships would probably have retained her original name but there was already a *Triton* on the Navy List, so that had settled it.

Bare feet moved about the deck above, and occasionally an authoritative voice called out an order which was always obeyed instantly. It was uncanny after the frigates he had known. Everything was done at the double and in silence. Failure to respond immediately, or walking rather than running to the call even of a lowly midshipman invited a starting at the hands of any boatswain's mate or petty officer on duty.

They had been at Gibraltar swinging to their anchor for seven days, the new hands staring longingly at the Rock's grim outline or at the passing throng of colourful traders, who were never allowed to venture alongside. The water casks had been refilled, the mail bags had gone ashore. He could not order Captain Trevenen to delay any further.

Bolitho knew him no better than when he had greeted him on board, and he wondered what his flag lieutenant thought of him. Even on the matter of discipline when Bolitho had mentioned the seaman who had died under the lash, he had not been able to read the man.

Trevenen had answered almost indifferently, 'I reported his death in my despatches to the Admiralty.' He had allowed a small hint of triumph into his voice. 'I am the senior officer of this squadron, and was authorised to act accordingly. You were not here, Sir Richard, and in any case it was hardly a major crisis.'

'A man's life, for instance?'

It had been a strange experience to meet *Hyperion*'s old surgeon, still as defiantly independent, and obviously ill at ease under Trevenen's command. Bolitho had avoided mentioning the flogging, but had said, 'I thought you might have quit the sea after we lost *Hyperion*.'

'I pondered on it, Sir Richard. But they don't want me at home.' Minchin had waved one powerful hand around the deck. 'Besides, the rum's better in a King's ship!'

The man who had lived through the battle, unable to see what was happening while the timbers shook and cracked around him, had even proved a match for Sir Piers Blachford, the great surgeon from London who had been in *Hyperion* throughout the battle. A more unlikely pair it was hard to imagine.

Bolitho left the thick windows, their sills hot from the afternoon sun, and crossed to the small desk which had been provided for his and Yovell's use. Not like a ship-of-the-line but sufficient. In his mind's eye he could picture their weaving passage, first to Freetown then south again along the coast of Africa to Cape Town and Good Hope, where he had done and seen so much.

At Freetown there might be more information available, which he could digest before the Cape. If they still intended to invade Mauritius they would need many soldiers, horses, guns and supplies. As in the Caribbean these essentials had to be protected, and if he could not root out the island that was being used as a base for French vessels then their lordships would have to support him with more men-of-war, whether they liked it or not. And every mile of the way, through each change of watch and Trevenen's continuous drills, he was being carried further and further away from Catherine. In the past he had expected it and had been prepared for parting. It was his life, as it had been for every sea-officer past and present.

But with Catherine everything had changed. There had once been moments, up until the very day they had been reunited at Antigua, when he had cared very little if he lived or died. Only the reliance of the many men who had depended upon his skills, or lack of them, had held empty recklessness at bay.

Unlike Jenour, Avery was little help beyond their daily routine and duty. Bolitho had known officers like him before, able to stay remote even in a crowded man-of-war. He messed in the wardroom but spent most of his time either in his hutch-like cabin, or on deck right aft by the taffrail watching the sea's change of moods.

Bolitho had been invited to the wardroom just before they had left Plymouth: a pleasant collection of men, mostly young with the exception of the angry-eyed surgeon, the sailing master and the purser. An average wardroom in any such vessel: only a captain would know the strength and the weakness of these men and all the midshipmen and warrant ranks who supported them. They had been very curious about a vice-admiral being in their midst, but had been too polite to say much. If there were rebels against Trevenen's severity, apart from Minchin, they did not reveal themselves.

There had been another flogging this forenoon. The process had seemed so slow and relentless, the rattle of the drums broken only by the crack of the lash across the man's naked back. Even after Ozzard had closed the cabin skylight he had been unable to shut it out. The defaulter had apparently been found drinking rum in the hold when he should have been painting.

Two dozen lashes. The man had broken towards the end and had begun to whimper like a beaten animal.

He is the captain, with all the authority, including mine, to support him. I can do nothing. Trevenen must know exactly

97

what he was doing, how far he could go without criticism from above.

But also he must surely know that Bolitho could ruin any hope of promotion to flag rank with only a few words in the right place. *He must understand me better than I do him.*

Bolitho heard the boats being hoisted up and over the gangway to be swayed down on to their tier. The same would be happening aboard *Laertes*. The French prize was a command any young officer would cherish. Originally of thirty-six guns and built in the renowned naval dockyard at Toulon, her main armament was reinforced by some heavy bow-chasers, which would prove invaluable if they ever ran the marauders to earth. Her captain was young and had been posted about the same time as Adam. His name was Peter Dawes, and as the son of an admiral he would seize any opportunity to prove his worth.

The thought of Adam troubled him greatly. *Anemone* had been due here at Gibraltar just after them, two days at the most, with a complete ship's company or not. Trevenen had hinted at it, but seemed to be watching and waiting for Bolitho's final decision. He had made it shortly after the latest flogging. They would sail in company with *Laertes* and continue on passage to Freetown.

Calls trilled, feet pattered along gangways and down ladders. *Valkyrie* stirred herself like an awakening beast.

He could hear the clink of the capstan pawls, the scrape of a fiddle as the seamen threw themselves on the bars to drag the big frigate slowly towards her anchor.

So many times. Leaving harbour had always roused him, enlivened his young mind as a midshipman or lieutenant. A ship coming to life, the hands ready to dash to their stations where every yard and mile of cordage had its proper place and use. *An equal strain on all parts* as one old sailing master had explained to him many times.

He heard feet in the passageway, heavy, authoritative steps. As expected, it was the captain.

'Ready to proceed, Sir Richard.' His deepset eyes were questioning, bleak.

'I shall come up.' It occurred to him that he had hardly been on deck since *Valkyrie* had weighed at Plymouth.

He glanced around the cabin and saw Ozzard's small shadow beyond the pantry door. 'I hope that *Anemone* can make up some time along the way.' It was only a thought spoken aloud as he might have done to Keen or Jenour.

'I expect he will have an explanation of sorts, Sir Richard. *Anemone*'s captain *is* your nephew, I believe?'

'That is so.' He met Trevenen's cold stare. 'Just as my flag lieutenant is the nephew of Sir Paul Sillitoe, the prime minister's adviser. I am constantly surprised by such connections.'

He brushed past him, feeling stupidly childish that he had used Trevenen's own tactics against him. A challenge then? So be it.

'Hands aloft! Loose tops'ls!'

Bolitho saw Allday by the nettings, his face grim as he watched the bare-backed seamen swarming up the ratlines like monkeys. Many of them had scars on their skin, some pale with age, others still livid from the cat.

'Anchor's hove short, sir!'

Trevenen said abruptly, 'Start those laggards on the capstan bars, Mr Urquhart! They are like old women today!'

As a boatswain's mate moved towards them with his rope starter, the men at the bars used every ounce of strength, their naked feet digging into the grips like claws.

'Anchor's aweigh, sir!'

Bolitho saw the first lieutenant's obvious relief. The men had been saved further beatings. This time.

Topsails and jib, then her great forecourse filling out and hardening to the wind, *Valkyrie* turned her stern towards the Rock, her high lee side comfortably clear of the water.

Before she was out of the anchorage her pyramid of fair-weather canvas towered above her busy deck as an indication of the power which drove her through the water. Bolitho saw the other frigate tacking round to follow in their wake, a creature of beauty and challenge.

He stared across the taffrail and made out a low shadow of land. Spain. Some there were at peace under English protection; others would still be too terrified of Napoleon's regiments

99

to surrender. Bolitho recalled those optimistic words at Hamett-Parker's reception: 'The war is all but won.' How many times had he seen these shores, knowing that many telescopes were trained on the ships leaving this great natural fortress. Fast horses ready to take their messengers at top speed to lookouts and coastal batteries. *The English ships are out.* He had known the Spanish as reluctant allies and then as enemies. He had felt safer with the latter.

He said to Allday, 'Come aft with me.' He knew that the watchkeepers on the quarterdeck were listening with astonishment and perhaps disbelief. Another part of the legend. The vice-admiral who could at the snap of his fingers sail them all to hell if he wished, a man so well-known in the navy, and yet there were few who had ever seen him, let alone served with him. Now he was going down the companion ladder with his burly coxswain as if they were old friends, shipmates like themselves.

They reached the comparatively cool air between decks and walked aft to where the marine sentry stood between the two doors of Trevenen's and his own quarters. A blank, ordinary face, a bayonetted musket at his side, his eyes looking straight past them.

Inside the cabin Ozzard was ready and waiting. Hock for the vice-admiral, rum for his coxswain.

Bolitho sat on the bench seat and stared at the creaming water bubbling up from the rudder.

'What is the *matter* with them, old friend?'

Allday held up the tankard and blinked in the sunlight. 'I seen an old dog once, the way it cowered when its drunken master raised a stick to it.' His voice was faraway, reliving it. 'Then one day it went for him. That bugger never laid a hand on him again!' He swallowed a mouthful of rum and added reflectively, 'An' there's more'n one dog in this ship!'

Captain Adam Bolitho came on deck and glanced first at the compass and then at the set of each individual sail. *Anemone* was making full use of a fine north-westerly wind that had whipped the blue-grey water into a million cruising white horses, and now filled the sails to the hardness of white metal.

The deck was a scene of busy activity, for although it was not long after dawn the hands were washing down the main deck on the lee side where seas occasionally dashed through the open gunports to gurgle around their bare legs before surging into the scuppers. On the quarterdeck other seamen were busy with the heavy holystones, cleaning and smoothing the pale planking before the sun gained height and softened the seams to make such work impossible.

To the new men Adam probably did not look much like a successful frigate captain. Hatless and without even his faded sea-going coat, his dark hair flying in the wind, he might appear more like a pirate.

It had taken longer than he had anticipated to clear Spithead and put a small press-gang ashore. They returned with only three men, none of whom had ever been to sea. Off Portsmouth Point he had been more fortunate, when quite by chance *Anemone* had run down on a topsail cutter under the command of a notorious lieutenant who controlled the press-gangs there. The lieutenant had been so resourceful that he often followed home-bound merchant ships making for the Solent or Southampton Water. He had long ago discovered that the meaner ship masters often paid off all but the minimum of hands required, to save themselves money. Once paid off – and the lieutenant usually watched the proceedings through a huge signals telescope – the cutter would swoop alongside and the luckless sailors, some almost within sight of home, were snatched up by the press and taken to the guardship.

Adam had obtained twelve hands, all seamen: still not enough, but it had eased the lot of his lieutenants and warrant officers. The delay had taken him off course, however, and when he had reached Gibraltar he discovered that his uncle and the other frigate had already sailed.

The first lieutenant approached him and touched his forehead.

'Sou' west by south, sir. Steady as she goes.'

Adam thought of his sealed orders, which he would eventually deliver to his uncle. Over six thousand miles, with a call at Freetown on the west coast of the African continent. It could have been to the moon: one small ship, *his* ship, free to act as she pleased and without anyone to say otherwise.

Lieutenant Martin watched him anxiously. The captain had never been an easy one to serve when things went wrong. But his predecessor Sargeant, who had been sent to his own command, had managed very well despite his youth. He had stood between captain and company as any first lieutenant should, and out of it had come a friendship which Martin accepted was not yet his privilege to be offered.

He said, 'I was wondering, sir . . . shall we set the stuns'ls when the people have had their breakfast?'

Adam glanced up at the tapering studding-sail booms, which were lashed beneath the yards. Once extended, with the extra sails giving even more power to the ship, *Anemone* might gain a few more knots.

He noticed the greasy smell of cooking from the galley funnel and was suddenly aware of the uncertainty of his second-in-command. To Martin's astonishment he clapped him on the arm and smiled. 'I am bad company, Aubrey. Stand by me, for I am in irons at the moment.'

Martin's face flooded with relief but he was sensible enough not to ask the reason for his captain's despair.

Adam remarked, 'I am in no hurry to catch up with the others, and that is the truth of it.'

'But your uncle, sir?'

Adam showed his teeth in a grin. 'He is still the flag officer, and I never allow myself to forget it.' He swung round as the sailing master appeared from the companion hatch. 'Ah, Mr Partridge, I have a task for you.'

The old master grunted. 'I be ready, sir.'

'If you lay a course to Madeira, allowing for the wind holding, what time will we anchor at Funchal?'

Partridge did not even blink. 'Why, sir, I thought it was to be a tiresome difficult question!' He beamed at his captain, who was less than half his age, although nobody was quite sure how old Partridge himself was.

He said, 'The masthead should be sighting land presently, sir. I'll go and work on the chart.'

He shambled away and Adam shook his head in admiration.

'What a man. If I ordered him to take us to the Barrier Reef he would not flinch.'

The first lieutenant, who had seen nothing in the sailing orders or Admiralty Instructions about calling at Madeira, asked, 'May I ask why that place, sir?'

Adam walked to the quarterdeck rail and watched the two helmsmen at the big double wheel. At times like these he could forget that his company was still short of hands, and all the other problems of command. But for the girl who haunted his thoughts he might even be happy.

He said, 'Madeira is an oasis, Aubrey, a water-hole for brave merchant captains as well as the predators like us. Where vessels of all flags pause to do repairs, to take on stores, to replenish their wine. Also, there are usually a few seasoned sailors who because of one mistake or t'other have been left behind by their ships!' He grinned, and was a boy again. 'So send the watch below to their breakfast, the smell of which has already turned my stomach. After that, we will alter course for Funchal, the last land we shall touch until Sierra Leone.' They both looked up as the hail came down from the main-mast. 'Deck there! Land on the larboard bow!'

Old Partridge reappeared, containing his satisfaction. 'There, sir, what did I say?'

His lieutenant ventured, 'Suppose the authorities there object to our search for men?'

Adam smiled. 'We shall *ask*, for volunteers naturally!'

They both laughed and some of the seamen glanced at each other as the pipe came for the watch below to dismiss to their messes.

As Adam strode to the companion-way the old master grunted, 'That's more like it, Mr Martin. It's put the sparkle back in his eye. Better for us too!'

'What has been troubling him, do you think?'

Old Partridge puffed out his weathered cheeks and answered scornfully, 'A woman, o' course! Officers should know about them things!'

In his cabin where his servant waited to serve him breakfast, Adam thought suddenly of his uncle, and the great love he had envied so much. Bolitho had been in Madeira and had

103

taken a fan and some lace to Catherine. Perhaps if he himself went ashore he might find a piece of silver, some jewellery maybe . . . He swung to the stern windows so that the servant should not see his face. She would never wear it, nor would she take it from him. After her stinging rebuff he was a madman even to consider it.

From somewhere in the length of his command someone was playing a lively jig on a fiddle, and another was keeping him company on a whistle. They would be crossing the equator soon after Freetown, when King Neptune and his court would be welcomed aboard, and the uninitiated would be roughly handled in a ceremony that had been held in every King's ship for as long as anybody could remember.

Adam sat down and stared at the greasy pork on his plate as it moved with a life of its own to the ship's steep motion.

Officers were not exempt. He could recall when as a lieutenant he had been stripped naked and almost choked with the mess they had used to 'shave' him. It was a simple thing, but sailors were simple men. It might help to draw his untried company together. He knew Old Partridge was to be Neptune. He pushed the food aside. He could not keep the girl out of his mind.

Under shortened sail, the frigate *Anemone* changed tack yet again for the final approach. The island of Madeira was shining in afternoon sunlight, its towering, flower-covered hills like a place in a fable.

'Deck there!' Some of the off-duty men looked up, but most of them stared hungrily at the land.

The lookout sounded surprised even from his dizzy perch in the crosstrees.

'Man-o'-war, sir! Ship-o'-th'-line!'

Lieutenant Martin asked, 'One of ours, sir?'

Adam stared at the distant island. 'I can't think what a liner would be doing here. I've no information about it. Where would she be from? The blockading squadron, on passage from the Caribbean? Most unlikely.' He picked up a telescope. 'I'll go aloft myself, Aubrey. You keep the ship on course unless I say otherwise.'

He swung himself out and on to the ratlines, the telescope slung around his shoulder. Then he looked down at his first lieutenant and said quietly, 'At least it will show the people they are not commanded by a cripple!'

Heights had never troubled him, not even as a young midshipman, unlike his beloved uncle who had confided his youthful fears of being ordered aloft. Once he glanced down and saw the pale wave creaming back from the bows, the tiny figures on the quarterdeck and along the gangway nearest the island. Volunteers and pressed men, the good and the bad, and some who had barely escaped the hangman's halter. There was only one thing to weld them together: they had to be tested, to make the ship the thing most worthwhile in their lives.

He reached the main crosstrees and nodded to the lookout, an older seaman named Betts who had eyes like a skua.

Adam said, 'You are troubled, Betts?' He opened the telescope and locked one leg around a stay.

'I dunno, sir. She's the *look* of a two-decker, but . . .'

Adam levelled the telescope and waited for *Anemone* to rise from a lazy trough.

'She's a frigate, Betts. You were right to be confused.' He blinked to clear his vision. Perhaps she was the *Valkyrie*, of which he had heard so much. He dismissed it immediately. His uncle would have left word of any change of plans at Gibraltar. French, then? They would not dare; it would be as dangerous as lying on a lee shore if an English ship like *Anemone* hove into sight. He extended the glass once again and caught his breath as a small gust of wind lifted the flag at the other ship's poop, the starred and striped colours of the new American navy.

He snapped the glass shut and watched the scene that had been so clear fall into the distance. And yet this old seaman Betts had seen everything with his eyes alone, but for the flag.

He slid down a backstay and joined his officers aft, aware of the curious stares of men who for the most part he barely knew. Yet.

He faced the others. 'She's a Yankee. Big too.'

105

Jervis Lewis, the newly-appointed third lieutenant, fresh from another ship's gunroom, asked, 'Shall we run out, sir?'

Martin looked at him with scorn. 'We're not at war, you idiot!'

The master mumbled unhelpfully, 'Far as we knows, sir.'

Adam smiled grimly. 'There was no activity aboard her. She's a visitor.' To the first lieutenant he added, 'Remember? Predators.'

He walked to the rail and glanced along the main deck at the long eighteen-pounders, so jet-black beneath each gangway. 'Have the ship prepared to enter harbour, Mr Martin.' He looked round for the signals midshipman. 'And, Mr Dunwoody, bend on a new ensign to show our good intentions and prepare your crew. Be ready to make and receive any formal signals!'

The officers hurried away, glad to be doing something. Adam considered it. Glad to be told what to do.

Lieutenant Martin watched his captain. *She*, whoever she was, if the master was right, would be proud to see her man like this.

Adam said, 'I shall go below and change. Tell that servant to find me a clean shirt.' He took a last glance at the island and thought he could smell flowers amongst the drift of salt. It was probably nothing, but some inner warning had roused him from his brooding thoughts like the touch of steel.

The great anchor splashed into the clear water exactly as two bells chimed out from the forecastle.

With the sun high over the spiralling mastheads Adam was soon aware of his heavy dress coat. His shirt, found by the servant who was certainly no Ozzard, was already moulded to his skin.

There were plenty of ships at anchor and alongside the jetties. Flags of every kind, vessels as mixed as the men who served them.

The American frigate towered above all of them. Across her broad counter and below the curling striped flag was her name in gold letters, *Unity*. When *Anemone* took the strain on her cable and swung sedately above her reflection Adam saw the ship's beakhead, painted blue and decorated with

106

bright gold stars. The figurehead was a citizen with a folded scroll in his outflung hand, probably a hero or a martyr of their revolt against King George.

Lieutenant Martin lowered his speaking trumpet as the last sail was furled and lashed tightly to its yard. They were getting better and faster, he thought, but not much.

He said, 'I've not heard of her, sir.'

'Nor I. Very new by the cut of her, and look at her teeth. Twenty-four-pounders if I'm any judge!'

Lewis the new third lieutenant said importantly, 'I'd not want to tangle with her!' But he fell silent when Adam looked at him.

'Ship secured, sir!'

'Very well. Send away a guardboat in case some reckless Jack tries to desert to our big friend over there, and to the land of the free!'

He spoke bitterly and Martin wondered why.

A boatswain's mate called, 'They're sending a boat, sir! Officer on board!'

'Man the side!'

A tall lieutenant climbed up through the entry port, and after raising his hat casually to the quarterdeck said, 'Do I have the honour of addressing the captain?'

'Captain Adam Bolitho of His Britannic Majesty's Ship *Anemone*.'

'Captain Nathan Beer of the *Unity* sends his compliments, and has ordered me to extend an invitation to you to visit him at dusk, sir. A boat will be sent for your convenience.' His eyes moved briefly across the deck. 'I see that you do not carry too many yourself, sir.'

'My compliments to your captain . . .' He hesitated. He should perhaps have said *respects*, but that would imply that he thought himself subordinate to the American. 'I will be honoured.' He smiled. 'But I will attend in my own boat.'

More salutes, and the American was gone. Adam said, 'I will go ashore to make peace with the authorities. Lower another boat for the surgeon, and the purser's convenience. Medicine for the one maybe, and fresh fruit for the sick-bay.'

But his mind was on his visitor. So it was to be captain to

107

captain and nothing less formal. Nathan Beer – his name if not his ship seemed familiar. He saw his gig being warped around to the side. Smart enough, but the American lieutenant might have noticed their strength or lack of it. He turned to his first lieutenant. 'Take charge in my absence. Any doubts, and send someone for me.' He let his words sink in. 'But I have every faith in you.' He walked to the entry port, where a side party had re-formed. 'If a deserter tries to swim from the ship, signal the guardboat. But no shooting if he does not give up. I'd rather have him drowned than shot.' He nodded his head toward the big frigate. 'They will be watching. Enemy or not, they will never be our friends, so do not forget it!'

Captain Nathan Beer was a big man in every way, and met Adam at the entry port of his frigate with a jovial informality to match. With his broad, weathered face and unruly hair barely touched by grey, and twinkling blue eyes, in England he would have passed easily for a gentleman farmer. Amongst frigate captains Adam was more used to younger men, although some had been on the ladder for far longer.

Adam glanced along the broad gundeck. They were indeed twenty-four-pounders, and he was reminded of the new lieutenant's tactless remark when they had entered the anchorage. *Unity* would be a formidable opponent. He knew Beer was watching him but was making no attempt to prevent his professional scrutiny. Perhaps it was meant as a warning.

'Come below and share some madeira. I thought I should taste the stuff, but it's a mite sweet for me.'

The after part of the ship was very spacious too. Even so, Beer had to duck his head between some of the deckhead beams.

A cabin servant took Adam's hat and studied him with open curiosity as he was pouring the wine.

Beer was much older than Adam had expected. Despite his glowing health he was close to sixty, maybe more. In his fist, the glass looked like a child's toy.

'May I ask your business here, Captain Bolitho?'

'You may, sir. I came to collect stores, and of course to see what ship had caught my eye.'

108

Beer grinned, his eyes almost disappearing into the crinkles. 'An honest answer!'

Adam swallowed some of the wine. A glance around told him quite a lot. The fittings were expensive, and there was a portrait of a woman and two girls on the bulkhead beside Beer's dress sword.

'Have you been in command long, sir?'

Beer eyed him keenly. 'Since she first tasted salt water at Boston. It was very exciting to see her grow, even for an old sailor like me. My home is in Newburyport, not too far away . . .' He broke off. 'You know it?'

'I have been there.'

Beer did not press him. 'I'm very proud to be *Unity*'s captain. There's not a ship that can stand up to her, not a frigate anyway. To the rest I can show a clean pair of heels if needs be!'

Adam heard a voice call something, which was followed by a gust of laughter. A happy ship then. He could well imagine it under this remarkable captain.

Beer was saying, 'Ours is a small navy as yet. We are feeling our way forward. Our officers must be men of zeal and conviction. I was privileged to visit France recently – how things change. Like my country, France was reborn out of revolution, but the tyranny there remains. Your successes on the Peninsula may bring back the old spirit perhaps.'

Adam said, 'They will be beaten as they have been at sea and are now being trounced in Spain.'

Beer regarded him gravely. 'Heavy thoughts for one so young, if I dare to say as much?' He picked up a refilled glass and did not look at Adam as he said, 'You will be sailing with despatches for your Sir Richard Bolitho. It is common knowledge around here, ships coming and going, only too glad to share information after months at sea. Are you his son, by any chance? The name is not familiar to me, except for one other.'

'I am his nephew, sir.'

'I see. The man I knew was a renegade who joined with us against the British to win our independence.'

'Did he command a frigate named *Andiron*?'

'He was your father? I *knew* it! The same eyes, his manner. I did not know him well but I knew his reputation enough to be saddened by news of his death.'

'Then you have a privilege which I did not share.' A warning voice was telling him to say nothing. Perhaps the secret had been bottled up too long, but the truth of how his father had really died he would never release.

Beer said, 'He was not a happy man, I think. The trouble with renegades is that nobody ever trusts them.' He forced a grin. 'Take John Paul Jones, for instance!' But the humour would not come.

Adam asked, 'And what of you? Is it your mission to carry despatches also?'

Beer answered levelly, 'We are spreading our wings. The British Navy commands the high seas, but such awesome power has taken a heavy toll. The French could still have another trick to play. Napoleon has too much to lose to bow down in submission.'

'So have we, sir.'

Beer went off at a tangent. 'This news about American ships being stopped by your patrols and searched for contraband – in my view it is to seize seamen for your fleet. Our President has twice made his strong displeasure known and has received promises of a sort from His Majesty's government. I hope it is true.'

Adam smiled for the first time. 'Would you join with France against us again?'

Beer stared at him and then grinned hugely. 'You are much as I was at your age!'

'We speak the same language, sir. I think it is the only similarity.'

Beer tugged out his watch. 'I am sailing on the tide, Captain Bolitho. Next time we meet I hope we can sup together.'

As if to a signal they both picked up their hats and went out into the cool gloom of the upper deck.

Adam thought of the crowded anchorage and twisting course Beer would have to steer. No one but the best captain and seamen could do it in the dark.

'Give my regards to your uncle, Captain. Now he is a man I would gladly meet!'

The side lanterns were playing across *Anemone*'s gig as it loitered on the swell, its hull outlined by twisting streamers of phosphorescence. Dunwoody, the senior midshipman at sixteen years old, was at the tiller.

Beer rested one big hand on the breech of the nearest gun.

'Let that meeting not be over the muzzle of those beauties!'

They doffed their hats and Adam climbed down into the boat. He could hear the capstan working busily, and some of the sails had been freed from their yards and were billowing and cracking against the great ceiling of stars.

The boat pulled clear and *Unity* became an anonymous shadow like the others. Another coincidence? Or had Beer kept him aboard so that *Anemone* would have no time to up anchor and go after him? He gave an unexpected smile. Just as well with such a new company.

He asked, 'What news, Mr Dunwoody?'

The boy was smart and alert, an obvious choice for the important world of fleet signals. If the war dragged on he might be a lieutenant in a year. Dunwoody would be more than aware of that.

'The boats brought ten more seamen on board, sir. They all have protection, as they are of the Honourable East India Company.' The boy leaned forward to watch a passing fishing boat. 'The first lieutenant says they are all prime seamen, sir.'

They would be. John Company prided itself on its sailors. Good conditions, fair pay, and the ships were well-armed enough to drive off even a man-of-war. Everything the navy should be. Could be. These ten extra hands were a godsend. They had probably been drunk and had missed their ship's departure.

Adam asked, 'Did they think we are sailing for England?'

The boy frowned, recalling Lieutenant Martin's wry smile, and repeated what he had said. 'He told them we were, but that they would work ship until we got there.'

Adam smiled in the darkness. Martin was learning fast.

'Well, we *are* returning to England. Eventually!'

111

He heard shouts from the big American frigate and thought about her impressive captain.

And he knew my father. He glanced at the midshipman, afraid for an instant that he had spoken out loud. But the boy was peering across the glittering black water at *Anemone*'s riding light floating above it.

'Boat ahoy!'

The midshipman cupped his hands. '*Anemone!*'

For his dead father or for his ship he did not know, but all Adam could feel was pride.

Back aboard the big frigate men were spread out on the yards, while others worked steadily at the capstan as the cable grew tighter and steeper. The senior lieutenant watched his massive captain.

He asked quietly, 'That Cap'n Bolitho. He going to give us any trouble?'

Beer smiled. 'His uncle maybe, but not him, I think.'

'Anchor's aweigh, sir!'

All else was forgotten as the ship heeled to the wind's thrust. Free of the ground, away from the land to her proper element.

Once clear of the anchorage the same lieutenant made his report to the quarterdeck.

'Man the braces.' Beer looked at the swinging compass. 'We'll alter course again in about ten minutes. Pass the word.'

The lieutenant hesitated. 'And you knew his father in the war, sir?'

'Yes.' He thought of the young captain's grave features, driven by something he could barely suppress. How could he tell him the truth? It no longer mattered. *The war*, as his second-in-command had called it, was over long ago. 'Yes, I knew him. He was a bastard – but that is between us alone.'

The lieutenant strode away, surprised and yet pleased that his formidable captain had taken him into his confidence.

By midnight under all plain sail, *Unity* was steering due south, with the ocean to herself.

8

Friends and Enemies

A week after leaving Gibraltar the frigate *Valkyrie* and her consort anchored at Freetown in Sierra Leone. After a swift passage, the final day was the longest Bolitho could remember. Searing heat that drove the bare-backed seamen from one patch of shadow to the next, and a glare so fierce it was almost impossible to discern the dividing line between sea and sky.

At one point the light airs deserted them completely, and Captain Trevenen immediately lowered boats to take the great frigate in tow in the search for a wind to carry them towards the unending span of green coastline.

Bolitho knew from hard experience that the tides and currents and the perversity of the winds off these shores could make even the most experienced sailor lose his patience. It did not help Trevenen's temper when *Laertes*, although only some two miles off the starboard quarter, filled her sails and began to overhaul the senior ship without difficulty.

Monteith, the fifth lieutenant, clambered into the beakhead beneath the flat, listless jibs and with a speaking trumpet shouted to the three towing longboats.

'Use your starters! Mr Gulliver, get them to put their backs into it!' As if he could sense the anger around him he added hastily, 'Captain's orders!'

Bolitho heard it from the cabin and saw Allday look up as he was giving a ritual polish to the old sword.

It was like a furnace on deck. Out there in the unprotected

boats it would be far worse. No boat could offer more than steerage way, especially with a ship as big as *Valkyrie*.

He stared astern at the undulating swell, and at the sky which was without colour, as if it had been burned out of it.

'Send for my flag lieutenant.' He heard Ozzard leave the cabin. It had been a difficult passage. *Valkyrie* was not a proper flagship, and yet he was more than a passenger.

He had lurched from his sleep one airless night, trapped in his cot as the nightmare came at him again. The hundred-mile reef, *Golden Plover* rearing on to its jagged spines with her masts torn from her, then the sea boiling around the wreck, the foam suddenly blood-red as the sharks drove in amongst the drowning seamen, most of whom had been too dazed and drunk to know what was happening.

In the nightmare he had been trying to reach Catherine, but another held her, had been laughing as the sea had closed over him.

It was the first time he had really got to know something of George Avery, his new flag lieutenant. He had woken to see him sitting near him in the cabin's darkness, while the rudder-head had thudded dully like a funeral drum.

'I heard you cry out, Sir Richard. I brought you something.'

It had been brandy and he had drained it in two swallows, ashamed that Avery should see him like this. He had been shivering so badly that for one terrible instant he had believed the old fever was returning, the one which had all but killed him in the Great South Sea.

Avery had said, 'I thought it were better me than another.' He had obviously been observing Trevenen very closely, something that made his apparent remoteness a lie.

After some time Avery told him that he himself had been dogged by nightmares after losing his schooner to the French. As a prisoner of war, and badly wounded at that, he was more of a nuisance to his captors than a triumph. He had been held in a small village, and been visited by a local doctor who had done little to help him. It was not that the French had been cruel or full of hatred towards one of the enemy, but simply that they had believed his death was inevitable. And after the Terror, death no longer had much power to frighten them.

114

Eventually, when he had begun to recover, some of the villagers had taken pity on him, and when he was released following the Peace of Amiens they had supplied him with warm clothing and fresh bread and cheese for the journey home.

As Bolitho had regained his own composure and shared some of the brandy with this quiet-spoken lieutenant, Avery had told him of his distress when he had been court-martialled. Even aboard the old *Canopus* some of his fellow officers had shunned him, as if by a closer contact with him they might somehow become tainted, their own hopes of advancement dashed.

Bolitho had heard of many lieutenants who had served in several campaigns, some with distinction, who had never been selected for promotion. Perhaps Avery would be one of those, and the little armed schooner *Jolie* had been the nearest he would ever come to a command of his own.

Of Sillitoe he had said, 'My mother was his sister. I think he felt obliged to do something for her memory. He did little enough when she needed him. Too proud, too stubborn . . . those were characteristics they shared.'

'And your father?'

He might have shrugged: it had been too dark to see.

'He was at Copenhagen, Sir Richard, the first battle. He was serving in the *Ganges*, seventy-four.'

Bolitho had nodded. 'I knew her well. Captain Fremantle.'

Avery had said quietly, 'I know there were many killed. My father was one.'

The following day after he had been conferring with Yovell over some signals, Avery had spoken to him again. He had said suddenly, 'When my uncle told me of this possible appointment I wanted to laugh. Or cry. With respect, Sir Richard, I could hardly imagine you accepting me no matter what you thought of my record, when so many dozens of lieutenants would kill for the chance!'

Now, with the last order still hanging in the airless heat of the cabin, Bolitho reached for his coat but changed his mind. Nobody seemed to know much of Trevenen's background, but it was more obvious than ever that he owed this command to

115

Sir James Hamett-Parker. Why? A favour for some service in the past?

He said curtly to Avery, 'Please ask the Captain to come aft.'

While he waited he continued his assessment of Trevenen. He was older than expected for a frigate captain, especially for a ship like this, which was the first of her kind.

And there was a certain meanness about the man. He seemed to spend a lot of time going over the lists and books of ship's stores and victuals with Tatlock, the anxious-looking purser. Like the matter of the dockyard paint for the figure-head. Trevenen was known to have made a lot of prize money from attacks on the enemy's supply ships, so it was not lack of funds. A man who gave nothing away about his feelings, his hopes, even his background . . .

The marine sentry bawled, 'Captain, *sir!*'

Trevenen entered, hat in hand, frowning slightly as he tried to see Bolitho after the blinding sunlight on deck.

'I want you to belay that last order, Captain Trevenen. It can do nothing but harm. Apart from the sixth lieutenant, Mr Gulliver, who was a midshipman himself just a few months ago, the other midshipmen in the boats are too inexperienced to understand anything but the need to obey orders.'

Trevenen regarded him calmly. 'I have always regarded that as . . .'

Bolitho held up his hand. 'Hear me. I have not asked you here to discuss varying ideas of loyalty and discipline. I am *telling* you to belay that order. Further, I would wish you to impress upon your officers, through the first lieutenant, that petty bullying must not be tolerated. The man Jacobs, who died because of a second flogging a few days after the first, was being taunted by a midshipman who is no more than a child, and who acted like one!'

He was angry. It went against everything he knew to interfere with his captain's authority. If the situation developed into a full-scale operation against French privateers under skilled leadership, Trevenen as the flag captain would be in a vital role. Was this animosity then a continuation of the old family feud? Or could it be something less obvious, and if so more sinister?

Either way, he had committed himself now.

Trevenen said heavily, 'I hope I know my duty, Sir Richard.'

Bolitho looked at him, feeling his resentment like a blow. 'For all our sakes, Captain, so do I!'

As the door closed a ruler rolled from the desk and across the black and white painted canvas deck.

Bolitho felt the hull shiver, the sudden clatter of blocks and halliards as the uncooperative wind ruffled the sea's face and brought life to the empty sails.

'Hands aloft there!'

'Stand by to recover boats!' A call shrilled and feet padded overhead.

He leaned back in a chair and plucked the shirt from his chest. He felt the locket under his fingers and thought of Catherine in Falmouth, three thousand miles astern. When would her first letter catch up with him? He had suggested that she should write directly to Cape Town, but even then . . .

Avery entered from the adjoining cabin and gazed at him searchingly, his tawny eyes bright in the reflected sunlight from the stern windows. *He must know exactly what happened just now.* Bolitho heard more shouts, the squeal of tackles as the boats were hoisted inboard once again. The boats' crews might never know about his intervention. They were probably too worn out to care.

He stood up as Ozzard came out of the sleeping cabin with a clean shirt.

Avery asked, 'Will there be a salute, Sir Richard?'

Bolitho nodded. Feeling his way. 'There is a captain in command of the anti-slavery patrol here. I think I know him.' He smiled, despite the lingering anger at his conflict with Trevenen. There was usually a familiar face before very long in the family that was the navy.

The deck tilted again and he said, 'Make a signal to *Laertes*. Take station astern.' He pulled on the clean shirt.

Avery looked at him but said nothing, well aware that the order had been given to prevent Trevenen from being humiliated by the other ship's superior performance.

Ozzard held out the dress coat and waited patiently for Bolitho to slip his arms into it. He did so with a faint, rueful smile. He had seen the expression in Trevenen's eyes when he had found his admiral in a crumpled shirt and little else. If they ever went into a fight, Trevenen at least would be dressed for the part, he thought.

As Avery turned to leave Bolitho called, 'Let me know if the brig *Larne* is at anchor.'

He walked to the stern windows and winced as he rested his palms on the sill. It would be good if Tyacke were here. There were bitter memories in this place, but not where that bravest of men was concerned.

On deck there seemed to be no air, and yet every sail was filling and slackening as if the ship herself were breathing. *Laertes* was already tacking obediently astern, her ensign and masthead pendant very bright against the misty backdrop.

Allday stood near him, his hat tilted over his eyes, his thick arms folded across his chest.

Some seamen were making the final lashings fast on the boats on the tier, although the whole drill would have to be repeated once the anchor was dropped. They were getting very brown-skinned, and some were cruelly burned by a climate and a life they were not yet used to.

One young sailor had a red mark like a new scar on his shoulder, a cut from a starter while he had been pulling at his oar. He seemed to feel that someone was watching him, and turned to look over his bare shoulder toward the place where Bolitho stood at the quarterdeck rail. As their eyes met, Bolitho gave just the slightest nod.

The sailor stared round as if afraid of being seen, then almost shyly gave a quick smile before turning back to his lashings.

Allday murmured, 'It's a beginning.' He missed nothing.

Bolitho felt his eye stinging badly and turned away, in case Allday should see that too.

The first bang of the salute echoed and re-echoed across the water from a small hillside battery, and gun for gun *Valkyrie* responded, fifteen in all for the man whose flag fluttered from the foremast truck. Allday watched Bolitho's stiff shoulders

118

and could guess what he was thinking. Few others would understand; could even begin to, he decided. All this, the salute, the honour and the power, and to him it meant nothing. Yet a frightened grin from an unknown, pressed landman had touched his heart. No wonder she loved him.

'*Hands aloft! Reef tops'ls! Stand by to take in the main course!*'

A lieutenant called, 'Bosun! Move those men! Come *along*, Mr Jones!'

But the barrel-chested boatswain shrugged and did nothing.

Urquhart the first lieutenant touched his hat. 'Guardboat in position, sir!'

Trevenen stared past him, his hands gripped behind his back. 'Stand by starboard anchor, if you please.' He did not look at Bolitho. 'Take in the driver and t'gan'sls. Prepare to come about.'

Avery said, 'No sign of *Larne*, Sir Richard.'

'Man the braces!'

Bolitho shaded his eyes and studied the scattered array of shipping. Large and small with a collection of moored vessels, obviously prizes, slavers brought here by captains like Tyacke.

An elderly sixty-four was anchored close to the shore, the headquarters and accommodation ship for the man who commanded the patrols and fought a private war against fever and sudden death.

Despite the new laws against it slavery was still rampant. The risks the slavers took were greater, but so were the profits for the successful. Some of the ships in the trade were as well armed as the brigs and schooners that hunted for them. Most sea officers thought it was all a waste of time, except for those involved in the long-reaching patrols who were making huge sums in prize money. It should be left until the war was over and won, then they could be as pious as all those others who did not have to fight. The need for fighting ships, no matter how small, far outweighed the tongue-in-cheek display of humanity.

'Lee braces there!'

'Helm a-lee, sir!'

Valkyrie pivotted round, and as her great anchor flung spray

119

high over the beakhead she came slowly to rest on her cable. Trevenen glared up at the yards where men were fisting and lashing the furled sails into place.

Bolitho said, 'I should like the gig, Captain Trevenen. I intend to visit the captain yonder.' He glanced around the quarterdeck. 'The ship must have made a splendid sight as she came in.'

There was no response, and Bolitho made for the companion-way. It was obvious that there would be none.

Lieutenant Avery said, 'Mr Guest, you may go below. I shall need you again shortly.' He saw the midshipman's face stiffen as the captain snapped, 'I will give the orders here, *Mister* Avery, and I will trouble you not to interfere! Be content with your grace-and-favour appointment!'

'I resent that, sir.'

Trevenen gave a cold smile. 'Do you indeed?'

Avery stood his ground. 'It is the only thing we have in common, *sir*.'

The midshipman swallowed hard. 'What shall I do, sir?'

Trevenen swung away. 'Do as he asks, and damn your impertinence!'

Avery found that his hands were clenched so tightly that he was in pain.

You damned, bloody fool. You vowed to control your feelings, to do nothing that might hurt you more . . .

He saw Allday watching, just the hint of a smile in his eyes. The big man said quietly, 'Right on the waterline, sir. Well done!'

Avery stared at him. Nobody had ever addressed him like that before. Then he found that he was smiling, the sudden pain of despair already gone. The vice-admiral and his coxswain. Remarkable.

Bolitho's voice came from the open skylight.

'*Mr Avery!* When you have quite finished up there I would be obliged to you for your assistance!'

Allday chuckled as Avery hurried to the companionway. He had a lot to learn, as had young Jenour. That like the old family sword, Sir Richard had two edges.

Captain Edgar Sampson, the senior naval officer at Freetown, watched as Bolitho and Avery made themselves comfortable in two leather chairs that had seen better days. His ship, a small fourth-rate with the once-proud name of *Marathon*, was now accommodation vessel, headquarters, and supply vessel for the anti-slavery flotilla. It was hard to picture her in the line of battle, or in any other active role for that matter. There were tubs of flowers on the old-fashioned sternwalk, and the gunports did not even have quakers to disguise their emptiness. The ship might never move again, and when her useful life was ended their lordships would probably direct that she become a humble stores hulk, or if too late even for that, would order that she be broken up here in Freetown.

Sampson was speaking fast and excitedly as he waved his black servant to lay out goblets and fetch the wine. The servant did not speak but looked at the captain as if he were a god.

Sampson said, 'I knew you were coming, Sir Richard, but even when I saw a frigate with a vice-admiral's flag at the fore I could scarce believe it! I would that I could have prepared a guard of honour to mark the occasion!' He gestured vaguely to the open stern windows. 'Most of my Royal Marines are on guard duty until the *Prince Henry* weighs tomorrow.'

Bolitho had seen the ship in question while the gig had pulled steadily across the anchorage. Big, old and neglected-looking. Even before a guardboat had raced towards them he had recognised her for what she was: a convict transport. He was thankful that Keen was not here. It would remind him of Zenoria as he had first seen her. Seized up like a common felon, her clothes torn from her back while the crowds of on-lookers, prisoners, guards and seamen alike had watched in savage anticipation. She had received just one blow across her naked back, and the wound had opened her skin from shoulder to hip. She would never lose the scar. Like a brand.

Seeing Bolitho's rank, the officer of the guard had saluted and the oars had been tossed as a mark of respect.

Sampson was saying, 'She was caught in a storm and put in for repairs. I'll be glad to see the back of her, I can tell you!'

The black servant returned and solemnly poured wine for them.

'Thank you. You learn quickly!'

The man smiled with equal solemnity and backed away.

Sampson said, 'Took him from a slaver. He works hard, but I think he comes from better stock than most.'

He saw Avery's questioning glance and went on sadly, 'The slavers tore out his tongue. But he has survived, long enough to see his tormentors kicking from those trees on the point.'

Avery asked, 'What is the *Prince Henry* like, sir?'

Sampson raised his glass. 'To you, Sir Richard! I feel cut off from the world out here in this stinking hole, but not so far away that I do not hear of your exploits, your brave deeds!' He downed the wine, which was very warm. 'If I miss anything then Commander Tyacke of the *Larne* will tell me. A strange man, though hardly surprising!' He seemed to recall Avery's question. 'Transports in this kind of work are as good only as their masters, Mr Avery. Captain Williams is a hard man, but fair enough, I believe. The ship will be a living hell for some, a narrow escape from the hangman for others. Williams knows all the risks. His hull will be full of felons, murderers, and wronged men for good measure. *All* will want to escape, and he must be ever-mindful of it.'

Bolitho saw Avery's expression, taking it all in. A strong face, and there was sadness too.

He thought about the transport. It was a long, long haul to the penal colony, the other end of the world. He recalled Admiral Broughton's curt summing-up when he had left the Admiralty. 'Oblivion!'

'I take it that no mail preceded us, Captain Sampson?'

Sampson shook his head. He was not old, but had allowed himself to become a character, the kind you might find in one of James Gillray's cruel cartoons. Sprouting hair, wrinkled stockings and a paunch which made his waistcoat buttons strain to the limit. Like the old *Marathon*, he knew he would end his days here.

'No, Sir Richard. Next week maybe.' He slapped his thigh so that some wine slopped unheeded down his coat.

'Damn me, I almost forgot! The new officer commanding naval vessels at Sydney is also aboard the *Prince Henry*. I think you know him, Sir Richard.'

Bolitho gripped the arm of his chair. It was not possible, just as he knew it was inevitable. Fate.

He said quietly, 'Rear-Admiral Herrick.'

Sampson beamed. 'My memory is going too, I'm afraid. I heard that you were acquainted, but I did not mention it when he came ashore.' He hesitated. 'I mean no disrespect to your friend, Sir Richard, but he discouraged my conversation, and asked that he be shown where the recovered slaves are kept until they can be directed to safety.'

Avery put down his glass, very aware that something important was happening. He knew about the court-martial, and how a change of evidence had saved Herrick from a verdict of guilty. It was too close to his own experience to forget it. There had also been talk of Herrick's failure to support Vice-Admiral Bolitho before the capture of Martinique. Were they still friends?

Bolitho asked, 'If I visit the *Prince Henry* would it . . .' He broke off as he saw the embarrassment on Sampson's red face. 'I see that it would not!'

'I cannot stop you, Sir Richard. You are the senior officer here, probably the most senior one anywhere south of the fifteenth parallel!'

'But my presence on board the transport with the passage stretching ahead like eternity might do serious damage to Captain Williams' authority.'

'As I said, Sir Richard. Williams is a hard man, but no tyrant, nor would he wish to be forced by circumstances to become one.'

'That was well said, and unfair of me to put you in such a position.'

Sampson stared at him. He might have expected any flag-officer, let alone one so famous, to tear him apart and tell him to mind his manners.

An officer hovered by the door and Sampson said awkwardly, 'If you will excuse me, Sir Richard, I have to deal with an accident.' He shrugged. 'Until the relief arrives, I am the healer too. My surgeon died of snakebite some weeks back.'

Bolitho said, 'I shall not detain you further.'

123

Sampson's face fell. 'I dared to hope we might dine together.' He looked at Avery. 'And you too, of course.'

'We shall be delighted.'

He turned to Avery as the captain hurried away. His gratitude had been terrible to see.

'It will likely be a meal to remember, Mr Avery, but if I were here in charge, I too would welcome any arrival and loathe its departure.'

Avery watched him as he moved from his chair, his dark hair brushing the deckhead between the massive beams. He was touching things as if he did not see them; seeing another old ship perhaps. Remembering her.

He was learning more every day. Sillitoe must have known what he was offering him. Here was a man without conceit, who could waste his time merely to help a naval castaway like Captain Sampson. He obviously cared about the man who was or had been his friend, and his question about a mail packet told Avery even more. He thought of the way Bolitho had striped off his soiled shirt without arrogance or shyness in his presence: he had seen the locket too. Bolitho must always wear it. The woman's face came into his thoughts, her throat, and the strong cheekbones. Bolitho's love for her more than made up for the hatred of others, and protected her from those who might want to wrong her. Gossip had told Avery that it would not be the first time in her life.

Allday would know all about her, and might even share some, if not all of his store of memories. Avery smiled. He was still not used to conversing so openly with an ordinary Jack.

He said, 'Tell me I am speaking out of place, Sir Richard, and I will ask for your forgiveness, and tolerance of my ignorance.'

Bolitho watched him calmly. 'I have not yet found you one to ingratiate yourself or to probe. Speak on.'

'Your rank, your position alone would be recognised instantly on board the *Prince Henry*.' He faltered under Bolitho's grey stare. 'They may not know you by name or reputation . . .' He was floundering.

Bolitho said quietly, 'But to them I would represent

124

authority of the highest kind, am I right? In one man they would see every judge, magistrate and law officer who ever ran them to ground.'

'That is what I was trying to say, Sir Richard.'

Bolitho turned and put his hand on his shoulder. 'You spoke only the truth.'

Avery looked down at the strong, sun-burned hand resting on his coat. It was like being someone else, not himself at all. Even when he replied it was like hearing a stranger's voice.

'A lieutenant would mean very little, Sir Richard. I could go. I could carry a letter to the rear-admiral if you wish it.'

He felt Bolitho's fingers tighten on his shoulder as he said quietly, 'He will not come. I know it.'

Avery waited. There was pain in his voice.

Bolitho said, 'But it was well said.' The hand was withdrawn.

Avery said tentatively, 'Captain Sampson might care to invite him to dine also.'

At that moment the captain entered and strode straight to his wine cabinet. He pulled out a bottle of cognac and said huskily, 'I beg your pardon, Sir Richard.' He downed the glass quickly and refilled it. 'Gangrene is a nasty thing. Too late anyway.' He looked at them wearily. 'This is not what I intended for your visit, Sir Richard!'

Avery cleared his throat noisily. 'Sir Richard was wondering if you might extend your invitation to Rear-Admiral Herrick, sir?'

Sampson stared at them, like a drowning man who sees the unexpected arrival of aid.

'I would be *delighted*, Sir Richard! I shall inform my servant immediately and send word to the *Prince Henry* in my launch.'

Bolitho studied his flag lieutenant. 'You take many chances, sir.' He saw him look down in embarrassment. 'But as Our Nel was known to have said, standing orders will never replace a zealous officer's initiative!' He smiled. 'He still may not come.' A small inner voice seemed to say, *You may never see him again. Never.* Like Sampson, like the ships that pass and remain only in memory.

Sampson's personal steward bustled in, almost another Ozzard but with the accent of the East London slums. He poured more wine and remarked, 'Beggin' yer pardon, Sir Richard, but me old dad served under you in th' frigate *Undine*. Begs many a tot o' rum from anyone oo'll listen to 'is yarns abaht it!'

He left the cabin and Bolitho looked at the warm wine. The family again. And yet he had not even told him his name.

As dusk closed in across the moored ships and the riding lights twinkled on the water like fireflies, Bolitho heard a boat hooking on to the chains. The handful of available marines stamped to attention, and there were muffled voices as Sampson greeted the second flag officer to visit him in days.

Bolitho found he was watching the screen door, while Avery stood by the stern windows, barely more than a shadow in the flickering candlelight. Why had he doubted that Herrick would come? Not curiosity, or because of friendship, but because he was and always had been a stickler for duty and correct procedures. He would never show disrespect for Captain Sampson's invitation, no matter what he might think.

That was the worse part, Bolitho thought. He knew him so well, too well perhaps.

A marine sentry opened the door and they came into the candlelight.

Bolitho had two immediate surprises. He could not recall ever seeing Herrick out of uniform, even of the more casual order at sea, and he was shocked to see how he seemed to have aged in so short a time.

Herrick wore a dark frock coat; it could have been black, with only his shirt to break the sombreness of his appearance. He was a little more stooped, probably because of the wound taken aboard his flagship *Benbow*. His face was drawn, with deep lines at the mouth, but as he stepped into the dancing lights his eyes were unaltered, as clear and blue as the day Bolitho had met him as a lieutenant.

They shook hands, Herrick's grip still hard and firm like tanned leather.

Bolitho said, 'It is *good* to see you, Thomas. I never thought we should meet like this.'

Herrick glanced at the tray of glasses, which the black servant was holding out for his inspection.

He asked curtly, 'Ginger beer?'

Sampson shook his head and began to worry. 'I regret, no, sir.'

'No matter.' Herrick took a glass of red wine and said, 'I never thought it either, Sir Richard. But we must do what we must and I have no desire to remain in England,' his blue eyes steadied, 'unemployed.'

Surprisingly Bolitho recalled the tall marine who had pointed out 'the good stuff' at Hamett-Parker's reception in London. How he had said it was wrong that Herrick should be sent to New South Wales.

Herrick glanced at Avery and then at the gold cord on his shoulder. 'The other one was appointed elsewhere, I believe?'

'Yes. Stephen Jenour has a command now.'

'Another lucky young man.'

'He deserved it.'

Herrick watched the glass being refilled as if he did not recall drinking from it.

Then he turned to Captain Sampson. 'Your health, sir, but I do not envy your task here.' To the cabin at large he continued, 'It is strange, is it not, that on one hand we are weakening our defences and deploying men and ships when they are sorely needed elsewhere simply to find and free a lot of savages who sold each other to the slavers in the first place!' He smiled suddenly and for only a second Bolitho saw the stubborn, caring lieutenant he had known. Herrick said, 'While on the other hand we ship our own people like animals, nay, less than beasts, in vessels which can only degrade and brutalise every man and woman amongst them!'

He changed tack and asked, 'And how is her ladyship, Sir Richard, and the child Elizabeth – is she well also?'

'Lady Catherine is in good health, Thomas.' Even calling him by his title had been like a slap in the face.

Herrick nodded gravely. 'Forgive me. I forgot.'

The meal Sampson provided was surprisingly appetising, with some sort of game bird as the main course, and succulent fish which had also been caught by local boats.

Sampson noticed none of the tension between his two principal guests, or pretended not to. By the time they reached the fruit and some excellent cheese left by a visiting Indiaman, he was barely able to speak without slurring his words.

Bolitho looked over at him. Sampson was happy nonetheless.

Herrick asked, 'Do you have big matters arising, Sir Richard? They seem to use you hardly. Perhaps I shall be better off in the colony.'

A lieutenant peered into the cabin. 'Mr Harrison's respects, sir, and the rear-admiral's boat is alongside.'

Herrick stood up abruptly and looked at his watch. 'On time anyway.' He glanced at the captain but he was fast asleep, snoring gently, with wine on his bulging waistcoat like the work of an enemy marksman.

'Good-bye, Mr Avery. I wish you well. I am sure your future will be as illustrious as your breeding.' Bolitho followed him through the door, but not before he had seen the bitterness in those tawny eyes.

In the comparative coldness of the dark quarterdeck, he said to Herrick, 'In his case that is not true. He has had his share of damaging treatment.'

'I see.' Herrick sounded disinterested. 'Well, I am sure you will set the right example for him.'

Bolitho said, 'Can we not be friends, Thomas?'

'And have you remind me later how I abandoned you, left you to fight against the odds as I once did?' He paused, and then said quite calmly, 'And to think of it, I lost everything I cared about when Dulcie died. While you threw it all away for . . .'

'For Catherine?'

Herrick stared at him in the light of the gangway lantern.

Bolitho said harshly, 'She risked everything for your wife, and last year she endured things which have left her scarred like the sun-burns on her body.'

'It changes nothing, Sir Richard.' He raised his hat to the side-party. 'We have both lost too much to cry salvage!'

Then he was gone, and seconds later the boat was pulling strongly from the chains until only the trailing wake could be seen.

'Just as well I came across, Sir Richard.'

Bolitho swung round and saw Allday by the quarterdeck ladder. 'What made you come?' He already knew.

'I heard things. 'Bout Rear-Admiral Herrick going over to the *Marathon*. Thought you might need me.' He was watching him through the darkness. Bolitho could feel it.

Bolitho touched his arm. 'Never more, old friend.' He almost stumbled, and a scarlet arm reached out as a marine made to help him.

'Thank you.' Bolitho sighed. *Probably thinks I'm drunk.* His eye blurred painfully and he waited for Allday to lead the way. Herrick had not even asked him about his injury, although he knew of it.

If only there were a letter from Catherine. Short or long: merely to see it, to read and re-read it, to imagine her with her hair hanging down over her shoulders in their room that faced the sea. Her expression as she paused and touched her lips with the pen as he had seen her do when working with Ferguson on the accounts. *I am your woman.*

He said abruptly, 'Come aft. We will take a wet, as you term it!'

'The Cap'n won't welcome that, Sir Richard!'

'He is beyond caring, old friend.'

Allday grinned with relief, glad he had come. Just in time by the look of it.

They sat at the littered table, where Avery said uncertainly, 'Quite a feast, Sir Richard.' He seemed nervous, disquieted.

Bolitho reached for one of the bottles.

He said, 'Be easy, Mr Avery. There are no officers here tonight, only men. Friends.'

They solemnly raised their glasses.

Avery said, 'To friends then! No matter where they are!'

Bolitho clinked his glass against the others. 'So be it!'

He drank, recalling Herrick in his black coat. When he wrote to Catherine again he would not mention the fiasco of their meeting. She would have already known, while he had continued to hope.

It was over.

129

9

Intrigue

Lewis Roxby, squire, landowner and magistrate, nicknamed with some justification the King of Cornwall, stood at the foot of the bell-tower of the Church of King Charles the Martyr, his eyes watering in the chill breeze from Carrick Roads. Beside him the curate of Falmouth's famous church was droning on about the need for further alteration to the interior so that the new Sunday Schools which he had helped to found could be extended to the opening of a day school. But first more work was needed on the roof, and something had to be done to prevent the spread of rot in the bell-chamber.

Roxby was well aware of the importance of helping the church and the community, or rather to be seen doing it. Richard Hawkin Hitchens was a good enough clergyman, he supposed, and he took a great interest in the education of local children under the church's influence. The actual Rector of Falmouth only rarely visited the place, and his last appearance had in fact been at the memorial service for Sir Richard Bolitho, then believed lost at sea in the *Golden Plover*.

Roxby remembered the wild excitement when two of Adam's lieutenants had galloped into the square with the news that Bolitho was safe. The unfortunate Rector's words had been lost in the bedlam as people had surged outside to the various inns to celebrate.

He realised that the curate had stopped speaking and was looking at him earnestly.

Roxby cleared his throat. 'Well, yes, there is some value in it.' He saw the man's bewilderment and knew he had got it wrong. 'I shall look into it. It does appear necessary, I suppose.'

It seemed to work and the curate beamed at him. Roxby turned on his heel, angry with himself, knowing it would cost him more money. He saw his horse waiting beside the groom's and summoned up happier thoughts, of the next hunt ball he would give.

The groom said, 'She be comin', zur.'

Roxby watched as Lady Catherine Somervell on her big mare cantered round a corner by The King's Head and moved across the square. It was a tasteless name for an inn when you thought about it, Roxby reflected, considering the fate of King Charles.

He doffed his hat and tried not to stare. She was dressed from head to toe in dark green velvet, with a hood partly drawn over her hair, accenting the beauty of her features.

He made to help her down but she withdrew one booted foot from its stirrup and landed beside him without effort. He kissed her hand and could smell the perfume she wore, even through her thick riding glove.

'It is good of you to come, Lewis.'

Even her easy use of his name made him shiver. No wonder his brother-in-law had fallen in love with her.

'I can think of nothing more pleasant, my dear.' He took her elbow and guided her around the corner of a grocer's shop. He apologised for his haste and added, 'The curate has a hungry look. I fear he may think of something more he needs!'

She walked easily beside him and barely hesitated when they left the shelter of the houses and the keen air blew the hood down on to her shoulders. Roxby was already short of breath and made every effort to hide it from her as he did from his beloved wife, Nancy. It never occurred to him that as he drank heavily and consumed far too much rich food, it was not surprising.

Roxby said, 'I must warn you, my dear, that what you intend could be an expensive failure.'

She looked at him, a faint smile on her mouth. 'I know.

131

And I am grateful for your advice and concern. But I want to help the estate. What use are crops if the prices are controlled by the markets? There are plenty of places where they need every kind of grain, where bad harvests have been commonplace to a point of poverty.'

Roxby watched her, still baffled by her involvement. He knew she had recovered a lot of money from the estate of her dead husband, but he would have thought it better if she had spent it on clothes, jewels, property and the like. But he knew she was very determined, and said, 'I've found the vessel you wanted. She's the *Maria José* and she lies at Fowey. I have had a friend look her over. He is well used to the prize courts.'

'Prize?'

Roxby continued to hurry beside her, pacing himself to her stride. 'She was taken by the revenue cutters. A smuggler. You could change the name, if you wanted to.'

She shook her head so that some of her dark hair tugged free of her combs and whipped out in the wind. 'Richard says it is bad luck to change a vessel's name.' She looked at him directly. 'I suppose I need not ask what happened to her crew?'

He shrugged. 'They'll not be smuggling, m'dear, ever again.'

'Are we close to Fowey?'

''Bout thirty miles by the main coach roads. But if the weather breaks . . .' He paused doubtfully. 'I would not let you go unguarded. I'd go with you myself but . . .'

She smiled. 'It would do very little for your reputation, I think.'

He flushed. 'I would be honoured, Catherine, proud to take you. But I am needed here until the winter sets in. You could break the journey at St Austell – I have friends there. I will arrange it.' His tone implied *if you must go*.

She looked past him at the cruising white cats'paws around the anchored merchantmen, at the boats under oars pitching and tossing while they went about their business. She could feel the cold even through her cloak. There were leaves floating on the water, and the bare trees were shining and black from the night's rain. And yet it was still only October, for a few more days anyway.

She had discussed the proposed purchase of a vessel with a

132

lawyer who had come all the way from London upon confirmation of her plans. He had been as doubtful as Roxby. Only Ferguson, the one-armed steward, had shown excitement when she had explained it to him.

'A fine, sound boat, Lady Catherine, one able to take passage to Scottish harbours or across to Ireland if need be. They're no strangers to famine. It will make good sense to them, right enough!'

Roxby exclaimed, 'There's one!' He pointed with his riding crop, his face even redder than usual in the bitter air.

'Two masts?' She looked at him, her dark eyes questioning. 'A brig?'

He hid his surprise that she should know such things. 'Not just a brig but a collier brig, broad in the beam, and deep holds that make them reliable craft for any cargo.'

She shaded her eyes and watched the collier brig tack and head slowly towards the harbour entrance, her heavy tanned sails framed against the headland and the St Mawes hillside battery.

'Two thousand pounds, you say?'

Roxby replied glumly, 'Guineas, I'm afraid.'

He saw the same mischievous smile he had watched at his own dinner table. She said quietly, 'We shall see.'

Seeing her determination Roxby said, 'I will arrange it. But it is hardly the work for a lady, and my Nancy will scold me for allowing it!'

She recalled the young midshipman who had been Richard's closest friend, the one who had given his heart to the girl who had eventually married Roxby. Did Roxby know anything about it? Did Richard's sister still grieve for the boy who had died so young?

It made her think of Adam, and she wondered if Richard had yet been able to speak with him.

Roxby said, 'I'll ride with you. It's on my way.' He beckoned to his groom, but she had already pulled herself into the saddle.

They rode almost in silence until the roof of the Bolitho house showed through the ragged, windswept trees. Solid, reliable, timeless, Roxby thought. He had imagined that one

133

day he might make an offer for it, when things had been bad here.

He glanced sideways at the woman in green. That was in the past. With a woman like her, his brother-in-law could do anything.

'You must sup with us again soon,' he said affably.

She tightened the reins as Tamara quickened her pace at the sight of home.

'That is kind of you. But later on, yes? Please convey my love to Nancy.'

Roxby watched her until she had gone through the weathered gates. She would not come. Not until she knew, until she had heard something of Richard.

He sighed and turned his horse back on to the track, his groom trotting behind him at a respectful distance.

He kept his mind busy and away from the lovely woman who had just left him. His morning would be full tomorrow. Two men had been caught stealing chickens and had beaten the keeper who had challenged them. He would have to be present when they were hanged. It always drew a crowd, although not as large as for a highwayman or pirate.

The thought of pirates made him reflect again on the collier brig. He would provide a letter of introduction for Lady Catherine to give to his friends, as well as one for their eyes only. He was honoured that he could afford her some protection, even if he did not agree with her mission to Fowey.

He was tired and vaguely depressed when he reached his own grand house. The drive and outbuildings were well tended, the walls and gardens in good condition. French prisoners of war had done much of it, for the most part glad to be free of the jails or even worse, the hulks. It made him feel charitable again, and he was in better spirits when his wife met him in the hall brimming with news. It seemed Valentine Keen, who had been made commodore, and his young bride would be calling to see them before Keen took up some new appointment.

Roxby was pleased but he scowled as he said, 'If they bring that brat with them, keep him away from me!' Then he laughed. It would be good for Nancy to have some company. He thought of Catherine. And for her too.

'We'll invite a few people, Nancy.'

She asked gently, 'How is Catherine?'

Roxby sat down and waited for a servant to drag off his boots, while another approached with a goblet of brandy. As a magistrate he believed it wiser not to enquire too closely into its origins.

He thought about her question.

'Missing him, m'dear. Drives herself hard to make the days pass.'

'You admire her, don't you, Lewis?'

He looked into her pretty face and the eyes which, in his ardent youth, he had fancied were the colour of summer lavender. 'Never seen a love like theirs,' he said. As she moved to his chair he slipped his arm around her substantial waist, which had once been so slender. 'Except for ours, of course!'

She laughed. 'Of course!'

She turned as rain rattled suddenly against the windows. Roxby, earthy landowner that he was, could ignore it. But she was a sailor's daughter, and the sister of the most respected officer in the navy now that Nelson was no more, and she found herself murmuring, 'Lord, to be at sea on a day like this . . .'

But when she looked at him Roxby had fallen into a doze by the fire.

She had everything, she told herself. A gracious house, a prominent position in society, two fine children and a husband who loved her dearly.

But she had never forgotten the young man who had offered his heart to her all those years ago, and in her dreams sometimes she still saw him in his blue coat with its white patches on the collar, his open face and fair hair like Valentine Keen's. But she thought of him now as if he were still out there somewhere, braving the seas and the storms, as if one day he might stride up to the house, and neither of them would have aged or changed.

She felt a lump in her throat and whispered, 'Oh, Martyn, where are you?'

But only the rain answered.

*

135

Lady Catherine Somervell walked into the bedroom and paused to listen to the heavy rain drumming against the roof and pouring down from the overflowing gutters.

There was a cheerful fire in the grate and despite the bitter cold outside the house, in here it was warm and welcoming. She had had a hot bath and her body still tingled from the rubbing Sophie had given her back and shoulders. It was as well she had not waited longer in Fowey or with Roxby's friends at St Austell: every road, even the high coaching way, would be flooded or a muddy trap for horse and carriage alike.

Everyone had been kind to her, and even the prize agent at the harbour had eventually been able to overcome his surprise at dealing with a woman.

She poured some of Grace Ferguson's coffee, beside which someone had discreetly placed a glass of cognac.

It was good to be back, especially when she discovered that Valentine Keen and his young wife had arrived at the house just before her.

She imagined them now in the large room at the end of the corridor. In one another's arms perhaps, already spent with lovemaking. Or quiet, as they had been at dinner, unable to think of anything but that they were soon to be parted. Commodore Keen, as he was now, was full of news about his tiny son whom they had left in Hampshire. One of Keen's sisters had insisted on taking care of the baby so that they could make this journey together.

Catherine had wondered if the real reason was to spare her feelings, because she had once told Zenoria that she was unable to bear children. She had not told her why, nor would she.

Whenever she had encouraged Keen to talk of his new appointment she had seen the pain in Zenoria's eyes. Separation so soon after the *Golden Plover*'s dreadful end and their discovery of one another again, their joy at the birth of their son; it might all be lost once Keen had joined his squadron.

She had felt a dagger of jealousy when Keen had mentioned the likelihood of meeting with Richard, before or after he had led his ships to Cape Town. There would be an invasion of

Mauritius, Keen had seemed certain, to stop the attacks on the trade routes once and for all.

'Will it be difficult, Val?'

Keen had seemed almost remote. 'It is always easier to defend an island than to capture it. But if enough soldiers can be spared, and with Sir Richard at the helm, it should be possible.'

Catherine had not dared to look at the girl when Keen had exclaimed with sudden enthusiasm, 'It will be like a family again with Adam there!'

Perhaps that, too, had blown over. Sailors had to go to sea: even poor Allday had had to make a difficult choice.

She thought of the letter which had been waiting for her upon her return from Fowey. Richard had written it at Gibraltar. She looked suddenly at the window as the rain lessened, and a great shaft of moonlight probed against the house. November, and his first letter. It might mark the arrival of many more.

It was a letter of love and tenderness, which with so many miles between them was all the more moving. He had written little of *Valkyrie* and her captain, not even much about Adam except to say that they would be leaving the Rock without waiting for *Anemone* to catch up.

Every day is an obstacle without you, dear Kate, and if you do not come to me in the night watches my whole being aches for you. Some nights ago when we were weathering Cape Finisterre and the winds sought to put us ashore, you did come to me. The cabin was as black as tar, but you stood by the stern windows, your hair waving in the wind although the place was sealed against it. You smiled at me and I ran to hold you. But when I kissed you, your lips were like ice. Then I was alone, a complete man again because of the strength your visit had given me.

She sat on their bed and opened the letters once more. Shy, sometimes over-sensitive, he was a man who gave so much while others demanded more. *It is easier to defend an island than to capture it.* How strange it had been to hear Keen's opinion. Something he had learned from Richard. Like others she had come to know. Oliver Browne, Jenour, and soon perhaps his new flag lieutenant, George Avery.

Next month they would all be preparing for Christmas. How quickly it had come around again. And all the while she would be craving news, waiting for the post-boy; writing to him and wondering how each letter would reach him.

She stroked the bed with her hand. Where she had given herself, again and again. The bed was turned down, and Sophie had laid out a gown for her as she always did.

How would Zenoria accept this latest parting? She could barely have recovered from the last one, when the devastating news had broken about the shipwreck.

Adam had taken her that news himself. Was that when it had happened?

She got up and walked to the window. Most of the clouds had gone, and those still moving to a wet south-westerly glided from the moon's path like solid things.

Catherine picked up the gown and for a few moments stood naked while she threw her heavy robe on to a chair.

She stared at the tall cheval glass where she had stood with Richard, watching his hand uncover her with exquisite slowness. The strong hand had moved over her body, exploring her as she had heard herself beg him to do.

Then she stood at the window again and flung it open, gasping as the bitter air attacked her nakedness.

'I am here, Richard. Wherever you are, I am with you!'

And in the sudden stillness she thought she heard him call her name.

Sir Paul Sillitoe paused beside one of the tall windows in the Admiralty building and watched the carriages shining like polished metal in the persistent drizzle, and wondered how or why he should tolerate such an existence. He had two estates in England and plantations in Jamaica, where he could soon drive the chill from his bones.

He knew exactly why he did it, and even this momentary dissatisfaction was merely a facet of his own impatient nature.

November and barely three o'clock in the afternoon, and

already he could not see clearly across the road. London was wet, cold and miserable.

He heard Admiral Sir James Hamett-Parker re-enter the room and said, 'Is the squadron ready to sail, Sir James?' He turned lightly and saw the weight of worry on the admiral's face. Hamett-Parker was finding this project more difficult than he had believed, perhaps. He thought suddenly of Godschale, who was now in Bombay. Even *he* had been better in some ways; he would certainly have found a woman somewhere to ease his burden. Sillitoe knew that Hamett-Parker's wife had died. He smiled to himself. Of boredom, probably.

'I have sent word today. As soon as Commodore Keen is satisfied, I will tell him to prepare for sea.'

He looked at Sillitoe, barely able to hide his dislike. 'And what of the Prime Minister?'

Sillitoe shrugged. 'When the Duke of Portland decided to resign that illustrious position, owing, he claimed, to ill health, we were prepared to accept changes, in strategy at least. Next month we are to be blessed with another Tory, Spencer Perceval, who given time may make a stronger mark than the Duke.'

Hamett-Parker was astonished that Sillitoe found it easy to display his contempt so openly. It was dangerous, even amongst friends. There was worse to come.

'You realise, Sir James, that without proper leadership we have been laid open to all manner of dangers.'

'The French?'

Sillitoe's hooded eyes gleamed as he answered, 'For once, the French are not the enemy. This time the rot is from within.' He became impatient again. 'I speak of His Majesty. Can nobody see that he is a raving lunatic? Every order of command, at sea or on land, has to be laid out before him.'

Hamett-Parker glanced at the closed doors and replied uneasily, 'He is the King. It is everyone's loyal duty to . . .'

Sillitoe seemed to spring at him. 'Then you are a fool, sir! If this Mauritius campaign is ruined because of his prevarication, do you imagine that he will shoulder the blame?' He watched the sudden anxiety on the admiral's severe features. '*By the Grace of God*, remember? How can a monarch be held responsible?' He tapped the table with his fingers. 'He is mad. But you will be the scapegoat. But then you know all about courts-martial. You will not need reminding.'

Hamett-Parker snapped, 'I'll have no more of your impertinence, damn it! What you describe is treason!'

Sillitoe looked down at the road again as a troop of dragoons cantered past, their cloaks black with rain.

'His eldest son will be crowned one day. Pray that it is not too late.'

Hamett-Parker forced himself to sit upright in his chair. No matter who had the prime minister's ear, or even the attention of royalty, Sillitoe appeared to be at ease with them. He tried not to think of his grand house, which had been Anson's. Like Godschale, he could lose everything. Even the lords of Admiralty were no longer immune to penalties.

'Are you saying that the people do not like their King?'

Sillitoe did not smile. It had cost the admiral a great deal to ask something so indiscreet.

'It would be fairer to say that the King does not know or care about *them*!'

He waited a moment. 'Suppose you were to hold a very splendid reception at your London address?' He knew that Hamett-Parker had no other address, but this was the moment for flattery.

The admiral said, 'What good would it do?'

'For you, d'you mean?' He hurried on before Hamett-Parker could rise to his casual insult. 'Invite guests who are known, cared about, hated even, but not merely the King's officers and officials who have favours to offer.'

'But next year . . .'

'Next year, Sir James, the King will be beyond help or manipulation. His son will take responsibility.' He waited and saw the doubts and fears of a man who was said to be little short of a tyrant.

'Invite him, is that what you imply?'

Sillitoe shrugged. 'It is a suggestion. I am certain that the prime minister would favour it.' He saw the shot go home, like watching a duellist fall when you had believed that your ball had missed the target.

'I will have to give it a good deal of thought.'

Sillitoe smiled. The battle was almost won. He said gently, 'You have reached as high a position in the navy as any officer might hope. Others would have thought it impossible from the start.' He counted the seconds. 'It would help nobody, least of all yourself, to lose it.'

'I have never sought favours from anybody!'

Sillitoe regarded him impassively. *He sounds just like Thomas Herrick.* But all he said was, 'Admirable.'

The same lieutenant entered the room and said, 'Sir Paul's carriage is here, Sir James.'

Hamett-Parker waved him away and wondered how long he had been listening outside.

Sillitoe picked up his cloak and turned towards the doors.

'I shall walk. It keeps my head clear.' He gave a slight bow. 'I bid you good-day, Sir James.'

He descended the elegant staircase and went briskly out past the porter's chair into the drizzle.

His coachman acknowledged him with his whip. He knew where to find him. He was reliable, otherwise he would not be in Sillitoe's employment.

There were few people in the streets. As he walked, ignoring them, Sillitoe was deep in thought. He was still surprised that Hamett-Parker had not put up any fight.

His thoughts ranged on to Catherine Somervell and what he would say to her. She was not on this earth to be hidden away in Cornwall with fishermen and labourers. Nor was she meant to spend her life conducting a hopeless liaison in a little house in Chelsea. Sometimes she must recall her previous marriage to the Viscount Somervell, the grand occasions, being presented as she should be. She would be aware of Sillitoe's influence at the Admiralty and with Parliament. A few words, spoken or written, could bring Bolitho from his constant campaigning, and its ever-present fear of death. She would also be well aware that he could persuade a bigot like Hamett-Parker to prevent Bolitho's return, as they were doing to Nelson's best friend, Lord Collingwood.

The reception he had suggested to the admiral had been the first step.

He thought of the latest piece of news his spies had brought him, that Catherine had purchased an old collier brig from a Cornish prize-court. To impress the man she could never marry, any more than she could reach out and touch him whenever she chose? He doubted if it were only for that reason. Perhaps it was her personal mystery that excited and taunted him like none other.

He stopped at the door of a house in the quiet street, and after a quick glance in either direction dragged the bell-pull.

For a while he would lose himself in a flippant, bawdy world where even the power of politics had no place. He smiled as the door opened slightly. Perhaps whores were the only honest people left after all.

The woman almost curtsied. 'Oh, Sir Paul! A real pleasure! She's waitin' for you upstairs!'

He glanced at the gloomy stairway. He would think of Catherine while he was here. Of how it would be.

10

Exchange of Fire

John Allday sat as comfortably as he could on an upturned dory and stared at the assembled shipping and sluggishly moving boats. If he turned his head he could see the great spread of Table Mountain that dwarfed Cape Town and all else in sight. But every movement was torture in the relentless heat. He was surprised he was not sweating: it was too hot even for that. There was a steady enough breeze from the sea, but it had no life, and reminded him of a village smithy he had once known.

His stomach rumbled and he knew it was time for something to eat and a wet, but not until Sir Richard and his flag lieutenant had returned from meeting the governor and some of the military commanders.

He stared across the shimmering water to *Valkyrie* and the ex-prize ship *Laertes*. Quivering like a phantom vessel, Captain Adam Bolitho's *Anemone* swung at her anchor, and Allday wondered what would happen when he met his uncle again. Captain Trevenen had reported that *Anemone*, the third frigate in their small group, had been sighted at dawn, her arrival reported by one of the army's mountain lookout posts. But she had still not entered harbour when Sir Richard had left *Valkyrie*, and Allday knew enough about signals to realise that as senior officer of the flotilla Trevenen had hoisted *Captain repair on board* almost before *Anemone*'s anchor had hit the bottom.

Allday turned his attention to the gig that had carried them ashore. It was made fast to a small mooring buoy and the crew was smartly turned out, but they were sitting with their arms folded and straight-backed despite the heat and discomfort, as they had been since Sir Richard had stepped ashore. It was as if the boat must not make contact with the land, he thought. As if one might become infected by the other.

There was a lieutenant in the boat. Even he did not have the authority, or the concern for the crew, to let them find some shade ashore. Then there was the captain. Trevenen was respected by his officers, although it showed in the sailors' eyes as something worse. *Fear.*

Some soldiers tramped past, a solitary drum beating out the step. Several were barely sunburned, unsure of themselves, ungainly under full packs and weapons, their red coats adding to the burden of heat. They were only a few of the men gathered here, and there were ships in plenty to carry them when required.

But fighting their way on to a heavily defended cluster of islands? Allday could not see the point of it at all. Why should he care? He had seen enough of it in the Caribbean, on the islands of death as the soldiers called them. Men plucked from the English countryside or the Scottish garrisons, from the Welsh valleys and anywhere else where they could be persuaded to take the King's shilling and go for a soldier.

But he did care. He grinned to himself. It must have rubbed off Sir Richard. Allday had seen many men thrown away, fighting over islands nobody in England had heard of. Like as not they would be handed back to the enemy once the damned war was over and done with.

He tried not to worry about Unis Polin, but to think of their last quiet moments together in the parlour of the Stag's Head at Fallowfield. He had always had an eye for the women, in more ports and harbours than he could remember. But this was very different, and he was almost afraid to touch her until she had looked up at him, with her fresh skin and laughing eyes, and had said, 'I'll not break, John Allday! Hold me like you mean it!'

But even her brightness, which he now understood had been for his sake, could not hold out. She had pressed her face against his chest and had whispered, 'Just you come back to me! You promise, eh?'

She understood about the sea, and things like loyalty. She must have had enough of that from her dead husband, Jonas Polin, master's mate in the old *Hyperion*.

Time moved on, and in his heart, although he knew it was stupid even to make a comparison, he knew Sir Richard had felt the same about leaving.

This time. Why then? It had troubled him. It still did.

He heard footsteps behind him and got to his feet. It was Lieutenant Avery, looking tired and hot from his walk. Another North Sea officer, Allday thought. Rain, wind and more rain. Even as the thought touched his mind, he realised how much he was missing it.

Avery said, 'Call the boat, Allday. Sir Richard will be here presently.'

Allday's bellow made the boat's crew come to life and the oars appear in the rowlocks like magic.

'Everything all right, sir?' He gestured towards the eye-blinding buildings, above which the Union Flag made the only visible movement.

Avery said, 'I expect so.' He thought of Bolitho's face when a staff officer had handed him some letters. He plunged his hand into his coat. 'There's a letter for *you*, Allday.'

He watched the big coxswain take it, with hands so strong and scarred that he could only imagine the life he had led.

Allday turned it over very carefully as if it might break. He knew it was from her. If he raised it to his nose there would be some of her there too. The sweet smell of the countryside and flowers, of the Helford riverbank and the little parlour.

He recalled her face when he had touched on the gold he had given her for safe-keeping, the 'booty' as Ozzard had called it, which he had taken from one of the *Golden Plover*'s mutineers.

He had said, 'It's yours, Unis. I want you to have it.' He had seen the shock in her eyes and had added, 'It'll be yours anyway when we're wed.'

She had answered with the same gravity, 'But not until then, John Allday!'

145

Avery watched him now and wondered if he should risk offending the man.

Allday said suddenly, 'I can't read, y'see, sir. Never got down to it.' He was thinking of Ozzard and his barely contained scorn for what he intended with Unis Polin. Sir Richard's secretary Yovell was a good man, but if he read somebody's letter aloud it always came out like a sermon.

'I'll do it . . . if you like, Allday.' They looked at each other warily until Avery said, 'I'll get none myself.'

An officer, Allday thought. One he did not really know, yet. But the poignancy of that last remark made him answer, 'I'd take it kindly, sir.'

The boat came alongside the jetty and the bowman scrambled ashore with the painter. The lieutenant followed, straightening his hat and pulling his shirt from his skin.

Avery said, 'Seems a pleasant place, Mr Finlay.'

He had mixed very little with the ship's officers and they had seemed ready enough to remain isolated from him. Avery knew the reason well enough; he was used to it by now. But one thing he still possessed was an excellent memory for names.

The fourth lieutenant said irritably, 'You wouldn't say that if you'd been out there in this damned boat!'

Avery faced him so that his eyes glowed in the fierce light. 'I have been in good company.'

The lieutenant glared at Allday. 'And what are *you* doing?'

Allday replied calmly, 'Listening, sir.'

'Why, you insolent . . .'

Avery took his arm and pulled him aside. 'Stow it. Unless you would like a *personal* introduction to Sir Richard Bolitho?'

'Is that a threat, sir?' But the irritation was giving away to caution like sand slipping from an hour-glass.

'Rather, a promise!'

The lieutenant stiffened as Bolitho and two army officers came into sight. Avery saw immediately that there was dirt on the vice-admiral's sleeve.

'Are you well, Sir Richard?'

Bolitho smiled. 'Of course. The military provided too much

146

hospitality. I should have watched my step in more ways than one!' The army officers grinned.

Avery turned and saw Allday staring at Bolitho, the anxiety like pain in his eyes. It was like a cold hand on the spine – but why? There was something else here he still knew nothing about.

But he had observed the exchange of glances before. As strong as steel. What bond did they share on top of all else, he wondered?

Bolitho said, 'I see that *Anemone* is in her rightful berth.' He looked at Allday. It was like an unasked question.

Allday nodded, and tilted his hat further to cut out the glare.

'*Captain repair on board* was hoisted, Sir Richard.'

'Good. I want to see him myself.' He glanced idly at the anchored army transports, the rigging decorated with newly washed shirts and blankets. Almost to himself he said, 'I do not think we have an army of professionals. Not yet in any case.' He seemed to change his mind about something. 'Two brigs are arriving to complete our little squadron. The *Thruster* and the *Orcadia*.'

Avery stared, as did the lieutenant in charge of the boat, even more as Allday exclaimed, 'Can't get rid of Mr Jenour, sir!'

Avery understood: for once he could share it. Jenour had been his predecessor. He had heard that even when promoted to commander and given a ship after that last battle with the French rear-admiral, Baratte, he had not wanted to leave Bolitho. Promotion was something every officer dreamed of, and he had been prepared to throw it all away.

If they fell in with Baratte again out here where one great ocean met another, might he himself be offered the same choice? He looked at the bottom-boards to hide his bitterness. If the chance did come his way, he would take it with both hands.

Allday muttered, '*Anemone*'s gig is still alongside, Sir Richard.'

Bolitho's jaw tightened. What had the two captains been finding to discuss throughout the forenoon?

'Watch your stroke, man!'

Bolitho saw the oarsman in question blink, afraid of spoiling the final approach in case the captain was watching.

The fourth lieutenant was probably just as worried, but determined not to be found wanting.

Bolitho touched his waistcoat pocket and felt the two letters there from Catherine. Now she would join him through her words, and the six thousand miles between them might seem like nothing, if only for a while.

He heard the stamp of feet and the clink of weapons as the marines joined the waiting side-party.

He glanced up at the tapering masts and furled sails. How different from any other frigate, he thought. With a company of two hundred and seventy officers, seamen and marines, she would be a formidable weapon if properly used.

In the first frigate he had ever commanded there had been only three lieutenants, as was usually the case today. He frowned. One of them had been Thomas Herrick.

He looked at his coat and wondered if anyone had guessed about his failing vision. He had not seen the step, just like the time in Antigua when he had slipped and would have fallen, but for a lady who was waiting with her husband to greet him. Catherine.

Allday whispered, 'Ozzard'll soon have that cleaned off, Sir Richard.'

Their eyes met and Bolitho answered simply, 'It is nothing.' So he knew.

On the frigate's deck seamen barely paused in their work to look at the vice-admiral who had come amongst them. The marine guard waited to be dismissed, and Bolitho saw some men swabbing the deck below the larboard gangway. Blood, by the look of it. Another flogging then.

Captain Aaron Trevenen wasted no time. 'I have logged *Anemone*'s time of arrival. Having sent for her captain, I rebuked him for his failure to comply with his orders and make all haste to join us.'

There was more than anger in his voice and eyes. Was it triumph, perhaps?

148

Trevenen said loudly, 'As the senior officer in your absence, Sir Richard . . .'

Bolitho met his stare and said, 'A lot seems to happen when I am not present, Captain Trevenen.' He glanced briefly at the seamen with their swabs. 'I am all ears to hear my nephew's explanation – perhaps more than you realise.' His tone hardened, and later Avery was to remember it. 'We will discuss it in my quarters, not here in the market-place!'

The marine sentry stamped to attention and Ozzard opened the screen door for them. Every window, gunport and skylight was open but with little effect. Adam stood beneath a skylight, his dress coat with its gleaming epaulettes making him look even younger, rather than more mature.

Bolitho gestured to Ozzard. 'Some refreshment.' He knew Trevenen would make an excuse to withdraw after he had said his piece. 'Be seated, the pair of you. We will fight the Frenchies if need be, but not, I pray, each other.'

They sat down, the one avoiding the other. Bolitho studied his nephew and thought of what Catherine had told him. Sitting here, with an incipient crisis to deal with, he marvelled that he had not seen it for himself.

Trevenen said abruptly, 'Captain Bolitho entered Funchal in Madeira without orders, Sir Richard. So he sailed out of company, and our progress would have been curtailed had a strong enemy force come upon us!' He glared at the young captain. 'I reprimanded him.'

Bolitho looked at his nephew. The wildness was still there, defiance too. He could well imagine Adam provoking somebody into a duel regardless of the consequences, just as he could easily see him with Zenoria. He tried not to think of Valentine Keen, so proud and happy, a dear friend who must never know.

He asked, 'Why did you make for Funchal?'

Adam faced him openly for the first time since he had come aboard.

'I believed we might discover some shipping, vessels which perhaps might not be all they seemed.'

Trevenen exploded, 'A likely story, sir!'

149

Bolitho felt vaguely troubled. Adam was lying. *Because of me, or Trevenen?*

Trevenen took his silence for doubt.

He said, 'That island is always a place for loose tongues! By God, I expect that all France knows what we are about by now!'

Bolitho said, 'Well?'

Adam shrugged, his eyes hidden in shadow. 'Maybe not all France, but the Americans are certainly interested in us. I was entertained by a certain Captain Nathan Beer, of the United States frigate *Unity*.'

Bolitho took a glass of wine from Ozzard, surprised that he could remain so calm.

'I know of him.'

'And he of you.'

Trevenen snapped, 'Why was I not told? And if it's true . . .'

Adam retorted, 'With respect, sir, you seemed more concerned with upbraiding me in front of as many of the people as possible!'

Bolitho said, 'Easy, gentlemen.' To Adam he asked, 'Was the *Unity* a new ship? For I have surely never heard of her.' It gave Adam time to control his sudden anger.

'She is the biggest frigate afloat.'

Trevenen scoffed, 'And what do you imagine *Valkyrie* to be?'

Adam glanced around the cabin. 'She is larger even than this ship. She mounts at least forty-four guns.' He looked at the other captain. 'I am aware that that is only two more than this ship, but she carries twenty-four-pounders, and a sizeable ship's company, perhaps to act as prize-crews.'

Bolitho took another glass of wine. Despite his joke about the army's hospitality he had drunk nothing ashore. That might come later, but it was still too soon to lower his guard.

He said, 'I will send word in the next courier brig.' He looked hard at the glass in his fingers. 'That is far too big a vessel to lose, even in an ocean.'

It had to be Baratte. It was not much, but it was like a piece of codline to a drowning man. In the past Baratte had used neutrals, even one against the other to disguise or aid his motives.

Feet thudded on deck, and calls squealed as a lighter came alongside for unloading.

Adam said, 'May I return to my ship, Sir Richard?'

Bolitho nodded. He knew Adam hated the formality of addressing him as he would any other flag officer.

He said, 'Perhaps you will join me one evening before we leave Cape Town?'

Adam grinned, the boy again. 'It would be an honour!'

Captain Trevenen too, as expected, made his own excuses and left.

Bolitho heard Ozzard bustling about in the pantry and wondered how long it would be before he was disturbed again.

He took out the first letter and opened it with great care. There was a small lock of her hair inside, tied with a piece of green ribbon.

My darling Richard. Outside the birds are still singing and the flowers are bright in the sunshine. I can only try to guess where you are, and I have used the globe in the library to ride in your wake like a creature of the ocean . . . Today I went to Falmouth, but I felt like a stranger. Even my lovely Tamara was looking for you . . . I miss you so, dearest of men . . .

He heard the bark of commands and knew Adam was leaving the ship. At least he had been made aware of Trevenen's hostility, part of the old feud which he could not remember.

Ozzard entered with a tray and Bolitho placed the letter with its mate on the table beside him.

On deck Adam turned towards the other captain, his hand to his gold-laced hat as he prepared to leave.

Trevenen said in a fierce whisper, 'Don't you dare abuse your authority with *me*, sir!'

Anybody watching would have seen only Adam's smile, his teeth very white in his sunburned face. But they would have been too far away to hear his response.

'And do not try to humiliate me in front of *anyone*, sir. I

151

had to put up with it when I was younger, but not any more. I think you know what I mean!'

Then, to the trill of calls, he was down the side and into his gig.

The first lieutenant crossed the deck. 'They say he has quite a reputation in the field, sir. Sword *or* pistol, I'm told.'

Trevenen stared at him. 'You can hold your tongue, damn your eyes! Be about your business!'

Much later, as the cooler air of evening moved through the ship and her rigging alike, Bolitho allowed himself to re-read the first letter. Only once did he pause when he heard someone's voice, uninterrupted as if he were reading aloud. Prayers, perhaps. It came from Avery's little cabin, which separated his own quarters from the wardroom.

He turned back to the letter, all else forgotten.

My darling Richard . . .

Captain Robert Williams of the convict transport ship *Prince Henry* took a well-thumbed copy of the prayer book from his pocket, and waited as some of his men prepared a corpse for burial. The fourth since leaving England, and under these conditions there would be more before they reached Botany Bay.

He glanced around his ship, along the decks and gangways where watchful guards stood beside the loaded swivel-guns, and aloft where more seamen were working on the yards or hung from the rigging like primitive apes. It never stopped. The ship was too old for this kind of work, with weeks and sometimes months at sea. He heard the clank of pumps and was grateful that the prisoners could be used for that back-breaking work if nothing else.

There were two hundred convicts in the ship, and because of their numbers they could only be allowed up from the foul-smelling holds a few at a time, some of them in manacles. Separated from them there were a few women, whores and petty thieves for the most part, deported by magistrates who merely wanted them out of their jurisdiction. The women at least would find no hardship in the colony, but many of the others would not survive.

152

His mate called, 'Ready, sir!' Their eyes met. Each was thinking of the waste of time, when the corpse in question was that of a man who had killed another in a brawl and only escaped the gallows because of his skill as a cooper. But he had been a violent, dangerous prisoner, and it would be more fitting if they merely pitched his body outboard like so much rubbish.

But rules were rules and the *Prince Henry* sailed under 'warrant, and was to all other purposes a government vessel.

'He's coming, sir.'

Williams sighed. *He* was their only passenger, Rear-Admiral Thomas Herrick, who had kept very much to himself during every dragging week. Williams had been looking forward to sharing his quarters with an officer of rank, one who had served his country well until his superiors had decided to offer him this appointment in New South Wales. To Williams it made very little sense. Even a junior admiral should be wealthy, by his simple reasoning, and Herrick could have refused the appointment and lived the rest of his life in ease and comfort. Williams himself had been at sea from the age of eight, and his had been a hard climb to his present command.

His lip curled. A rotten, stinking convict ship, with hull and rigging so worn that she could rarely manage more than six knots. Before this, the old *Prince Henry* had been carrying livestock to the many army outposts and garrisons in the Caribbean. Even the army's quartermasters and butchers had complained about the conditions the animals had been forced to endure on these long passages. But they were good enough apparently for humans, albeit the scum of the jails.

He touched his hat. 'Morning, sir.'

Herrick joined him by the rail, his eyes moving without conscious thought from the helmsman's compass to the set of every limply flapping sail. It was habit, as it had become since he had stood his first watch as a lieutenant.

'Not much wind.'

Herrick shifted his gaze to the burial party. They were staring aft, waiting for the signal.

'Who was he?'

153

Williams shrugged. 'A felon, a murderer.' He did not hide his contempt.

Herrick's blue eyes fixed on his. 'A man, nonetheless. Would you wish me to read something?'

'I can manage, sir. I've done it a few times.'

Herrick thought of Bolitho when they had met at Freetown. He still did not really know what had made him react as he had. *Because I cannot pretend.* He was suddenly impatient with himself. He knew that Williams, the ship's master, had thought him mad for taking passage in a convict ship, with men he might have to discipline in places where the navy was the only mark of law and order. He could have chosen a fast packet, or been a passenger among his own kind in a man-of-war. A simple seafarer like Williams could never understand that it was because there had been a choice that Herrick had come aboard the *Prince Henry*.

Williams opened his little book. He was angry, but naval officers often made him feel stupid.

'The days of man are but as grass: for he flourisheth as a flower of the field . . .'

He looked up, caught off guard as the masthead lookout yelled, 'Deck there! Sail on the larboard quarter!'

Herrick glanced at the men around him and down on the gangway. Thinking much the same as their captain.

Prince Henry had the Indian Ocean to herself. The Cape of Good Hope was about three hundred miles astern, and there were nearly six thousand miles stretching away into infinity before they could reach land again and their final destination.

Williams cupped his hands. 'What ship?'

The lookout shouted down, 'Small, sir. Two masts mebbe!'

Williams said, 'Perhaps she's one of yours, sir?'

Herrick thought of the beautiful telescope in his cabin, Dulcie's last present to him.

He tightened his jaw and tried to shut it out. He often held it before he turned in, just to imagine her finding it for him. He felt a lump in his throat. He would not interfere. Anyway, Williams was probably right.

If she were an enemy she was well off any station where she

might be expected. He looked at the seamen who were still standing with the canvas-sewn corpse.

Williams came out of his thoughts. 'Get the royals on her, Mr Spry! I think she'll stand it!' He seemed to see the burial party for the first time. 'What the hell are you waiting for? Tip the bugger over!'

Herrick heard the splash and pictured the bundle twisting and turning, sinking eventually into total darkness. But how did they know that? Many strange things had been witnessed at sea. Maybe there was another world down there beyond the depths.

Calls shrilled and men scampered to halliards and braces as the yards were trimmed until the wind was trapped and the deck tilted slightly to the extra pressure.

Williams said, 'Get aloft, Mr Spry, and take a glass. The lookout is a good hand, but he'll see only what he wants to.'

Herrick turned to watch a great fish leap from the gentle water, only to fall again into the waiting jaws of a hunter.

He had heard Williams' remark. The voice of a true sailor. Take nothing for granted.

Some guards appeared from a hatchway and twenty or so prisoners were pushed roughly into the sunshine.

Herrick saw one of the swivels move slightly, its gunner waiting to drag the lanyard which could turn a group of men into bloody gruel. They were a poor-looking lot, he thought. Dirty, unshaven, blinking like old men in the blinding sunlight. One wore leg-irons and lay down by the scuppers, his pallid face turned away from the others.

He heard someone say, 'Save yer pity, Silas! They'd spit you soon as look at you!'

Herrick thought of Bolitho again. *I should have remembered to ask about his eye.* How was he managing? Did the others notice that something was wrong?

The mate arrived on deck with a thud. He had slithered down a backstay, something which would have torn any landman's palms like a knife-blade.

He said, 'Brigantine, sir. Small enough.' He glanced astern as if he expected to see her sails on the horizon. 'She's overhauling us.'

155

Williams looked thoughtful. 'Well, she can't be a slaver out here. Nowhere for her to go.'

The mate hesitated. 'Suppose she be a pirate?'

Williams grinned hugely and clapped him on the shoulder. 'Even a pirate wouldn't be fool enough to want two hundred extra bellies to fill, an' we've precious little else.'

Herrick said, 'If she is an enemy you can still drive her off.'

Williams looked worried again. 'It's not that, sir. It's the prisoners. If they ran wild we'd never be able to hold them.' He looked at his mate. 'Fetch the gunner and tell him to stand by. We've six twelve-pounders, but they've never had to fight since I took command.'

The mate said unhelpfully, 'Nor before that neither, by the looks of 'em!'

A seaman who was splicing near the companionway stood up and pointed astern. 'There she be, sir!'

Herrick took a telescope from the rack by the compass-box and walked aft with it in both hands.

The other vessel was overhauling them fast. With the extended telescope he soon found her bulging forecourse and jibs, her topsails completely hiding the other mast from view. End on, making full use of the same wind which was helpless to move the *Prince Henry* fast enough to maintain her distance away.

'She wears Brazilian colours, sir!'

Herrick grunted. Flags meant very little. His professional eye built up a picture in the telescope's lens. Fast and handy, a maid for all work. But Brazilian, out here? It seemed unlikely.

Spry asked, 'Will we fight if she tries her chances, sir?'

Williams licked his dry lips. 'Maybe they want stores, water even.' Then he said, 'We've barely enough for ourselves.' He made up his mind. 'All prisoners below. Tell the gunner to open the weapons chest, then arm yourselves.' He turned to speak to the sea-officer with the greying hair, but Herrick had gone.

A seaman said, 'She's a smart 'un!' A sailor's respect for a well-handled vessel, hostile or not.

In his cabin Herrick stood by one of his sea-chests, and after some hesitation opened it, so that his rear-admiral's dress coat

156

shone in the reflected sunshine as if it were coming to life. He pulled out the metal box that contained his best epaulettes, the ones Dulcie had loved to see him wear. He grimaced. The same ones he had worn at his court-martial. He threw his plain black coat and breeches aside and dressed slowly and methodically, the pursuing brigantine still fixed in his mind. He thought of having another shave, but his sense of discipline and what was right made him reject the idea. The water ration was the same for everyone in this pitiful relic, from captain to the lowest felon, even the one who by now might have reached the end of his journey to the seabed.

He sat down and wrote a few words in a letter and sealed it, and then he placed it carefully inside the long leather telescope case. His hand touched it, and the gold-stamped address in London of the people who had made it. He glanced at himself in the mirror, at the undreamed-of epaulettes, each with its silver star. He even smiled without bitterness. A surprising journey it had been for the son of a poor clerk in Kent.

Something moved in the thick glass windows and he saw the other vessel flying up into the wind, the manoeuvre perfectly timed even as she shortened sail.

He heard shouts on deck as the green Brazilian flag was hauled down from the peak, and replaced instantly by the Tricolour.

Herrick picked up his sword and slipped it into his belt. Unhurriedly he took a last glance around the cabin and then made his way to the companion ladder.

'*She's a Frenchie!*'

Williams' jaw dropped as he stared at Herrick, so calm in his uniform.

'I know.'

Williams was suddenly enraged. 'Give the bastards a ball, Mr Gunner!'

The crash of a twelve-pounder brought shouts of alarm from between decks and screams from the women.

Herrick snapped, 'Belay that!'

Two flashes spurted from the brigantine's low hull and a mixture of grape and cannister exploded into the poop, bringing down the two helmsmen. Spry the first mate was on his

157

knees, staring with disbelief at the blood pumping out of his stomach even as he fell over and died.

'They're heaving-to! Repel boarders, sir?'

Williams shouted at Herrick, 'What shall I do?'

Herrick watched the boat being cast off, the rough-looking oarsmen already pulling lustily towards the convict transport. As the brigantine pitched up and down, her sails aback, he saw the guns, their crews already sponging out in readiness for another attack.

He said, 'Heave-to, Captain. You made your point, but men have died for it.'

The captain's hand was on his pistol. 'They'll not take me, God damn them!'

Herrick saw a white flag being held up by one of the boat's crew. He could even see the other vessel's name in gold letters on her counter, *Tridente*.

He said, 'Stay your hand, Captain. Do as they ask and I think they'll not harm you.'

The boat hooked on, and after a few seconds some ragged figures swarmed up the side and on to the deck. They were armed to the teeth and could have been of any nationality.

Herrick watched impassively and heard someone call, 'All ready, lieutenant!' An American or colonial accent.

But the one man in uniform who came last on to the *Prince Henry*'s deck was as French as anyone could be.

He nodded curtly to Williams, then strode straight to Herrick. Long afterwards Williams remembered that Herrick had already been unclipping his sword, as if he had been expecting this.

The lieutenant touched his hat. 'M'sieur Herrick?' He studied him gravely. 'The misfortune of war. You are my prisoner.'

The brigantine was already making sail even as the boat went alongside. It seemed to have taken just minutes, and it was only when Williams saw his dead mate and the whimpering men near the wheel that he understood.

'Call Mr Prior. He can take his place!' He looked at the pistol, still in his belt. Most naval officers would have ordered him to fight to the finish and to hell with the consequences.

But for Herrick he knew he would have done just that. He said heavily, 'We'll put about for Cape Town.'

Herrick had even made a point of putting on full uniform, he thought. When he looked again the *Tridente*, or whatever her real name was, was already standing away, her big fore-and-aft sail already making her show her copper.

Even the prisoners were quiet, as if they knew how close it had been.

He seemed to hear Herrick's last words. *I think they'll not harm you.*

It was like an epitaph.

11

The Cutlass

The house now employed as army headquarters for the growing military strength at Cape Town had once been the property of a wealthy Dutch trader. It nestled below the uncompromising barrier of Table Mountain and drew what breeze it could from the bay where the ships, like the soldiers, waited for orders.

Fans swung back and forth in the biggest room, which overlooked the sea, moved by hidden servants so that they should not disturb anyone. There were blinds at the long windows, but even so the reflected light from the sea was blinding, the sky salmon-pink like an early sunset. In fact it was noon, and Bolitho shifted in a cane chair while the general finished reading the report an orderly had just presented to him.

Major-General Sir Patrick Drummond was tall and solidly built, with a face almost as red as his coat. A successful officer in the early part of the Peninsular War and in many lesser campaigns, he had the reputation of being a 'soldier's soldier': prepared to listen, equally ready to discipline anyone who failed to meet his standards.

Bolitho had already seen some of the military Drummond was expected to mould into a team capable enough to land on enemy islands and take them, no matter what it cost. It was not an enviable task.

Drummond himself was in a half-lying position with his feet on a small table. Bolitho noted that his boots were like black glass, and the splendid spurs that adorned them could have been the work of a famous silversmith.

Drummond looked up as a servant padded into the room and began to pour wine for the general and his visitor.

Bolitho said, 'As you know, I have all my ships at sea, and I am expecting the arrival of two brigs.'

The general waited for the servant to move the goblet so that he could reach it without any effort, and said, 'I am only afraid that we may be in danger of over-reacting.' He scratched one of his long grey sideburns and added, 'You are a famous and successful sea-officer, Sir Richard. It is something to get such praise from a soldier, eh? But one so notable surprises me. I would have thought a senior captain, a commodore even, could perform this work. It is like hiring ten porters to carry a musket!'

Bolitho sipped the wine. It was perfect, and seemed to spark off another memory: the cellars in St James's Street, and Catherine seeking assurances that the wine she was buying for him was as good as the shop claimed.

He said, 'I do not think this campaign will proceed easily if we cannot dispose of the enemy's sea forces. They have to be based in Mauritius, and we must be prepared for other bases in the smaller islands. We could have failed at Martinique had the enemy been able to grapple with our military transports.'

Drummond gave a wry smile. 'Thanks to you, I gather, the enemy got a bloody nose instead!'

'We were ready, Sir Patrick. Today we are not.'

Drummond thought about it, frowning slightly as his world intruded into this long, shadowed room. Marching feet and the clatter of horses and harness, sergeants bellowing orders, probably half-blinded by sweat as they drilled in the relentless glare.

He said, 'I should like to enjoy Christmas here. After that, we'll have to see.'

Bolitho thought of England. It would be cold, perhaps with snow, although they did not get much in Cornwall. The sea off Pendennis Point would be angry and grey with surf along that line of well-remembered rocks. And Catherine . . . would she be missing London? *Missing me?*

161

Drummond said, 'If you had more ships . . .'

Bolitho smiled. 'It is always so, Sir Patrick. A squadron should be on its way here by now, with more soldiers and supplies.'

He wondered at Keen's feelings when he had been parted from Zenoria. Flying his own broad pendant as commodore would seem easy to him after his years of command and having been Bolitho's flag captain.

How different from Trevenen. He was out on the ocean in his powerful *Valkyrie*, the other frigates sailing on either beam to offer their lookouts the maximum range in their search for any vessel of ill-intent. Patriot or pirate, it made little difference to a ponderous merchantman.

Drummond rang a small bell and waited for the servant to reappear and fill the goblets. He looked past him to the door and barked, 'Come *in*, Rupert! Don't stand there hovering about!'

Rupert was a major whom Bolitho had already met. He seemed to be Drummond's right hand, a mixture of Keen and Avery rolled into one.

'What is it?' Drummond gestured to the servant. 'Another bottle, man! Jump about!'

The major glanced at Bolitho and gave a brief smile. 'The lookout station has reported another vessel, sir.'

Drummond paused with his goblet in mid-air. 'Well? Spit it out! I'm not a mind-reader, and Sir Richard here is no enemy spy!'

Bolitho contained a grin. Drummond could not be an easy man to serve.

'She is the *Prince Henry*, sir.'

Drummond stared. 'That damned convict transport? She is not expected in Cape Town. I would have been informed.'

Bolitho said quietly, 'I was in Freetown when she weighed anchor. She should be well on her way across the Indian Ocean by now.'

The others looked at him uncertainly. Bolitho said, 'Please ask my flag lieutenant to investigate and report to me. This wine is too good to leave.' He hoped that his casual comment would conceal his sudden anxiety. What could be wrong? The

162

transports never wasted any time. Packed with people being deported for one crime or another, no master could be certain of anything.

Drummond stood up and unrolled some charts on his table. 'I can pass the time by showing you what we intend to do in Mauritius. But I must have some good foot soldiers – most of my men are barely trained. The Iron Duke makes sure he has the pick of the regiments on the Peninsula, blast his eyes!' But there was admiration there too.

It was close to an hour before Avery and the hard-pressed major came to report.

Avery said, 'She's the *Prince Henry* right enough, Sir Richard. She has made a signal requesting medical assistance.'

The major added, 'I have informed the field-surgeon, sir.'

Avery looked at Bolitho. 'The captain-in-charge has also been told, and the guardboats are already under way.'

His face was quite calm but Bolitho could guess what he was thinking. Medical assistance might mean that some terrible fever or plague had broken out. It was not unknown. If it reached the overcrowded army garrison and camps it would run through them like a forest fire.

The general walked to the window and dragged away the blind as he groped for a brass telescope nearby.

He said, 'She's coming about. The officer-of-the-guard has ordered her to anchor.' He extended the telescope very carefully. 'She's been raked, by the look of her!'

He handed it to Bolitho and said sharply, 'Get down there, Rupert, at the double. Use my horse if you like. Send out some men if there's any trouble.'

As the door closed Drummond said angrily, 'I've got the Fifty-Eighth Regiment of Foot here, but the rest? Yeomanry and the York Fusiliers, so your convoy had better make haste!'

When he looked from the window Bolitho saw that the transport had anchored and was already hemmed in by guardboats and water lighters, while other harbour craft idled about at a safe distance.

Why would any privateer or man-of-war interfere with an old transport and a cargo of convicts? It would be like putting your hand into a ferret's lair.

He touched his eye as the savage glare probed at it like a hot ember.

It was late afternoon by the time Avery returned to the headquarters building.

He placed the leather telescope case on the table and said, 'This was found in the cabin, Sir Richard.'

Bolitho picked it up and thought of Herrick's dying wife, and Catherine, who had nursed her.

Avery watched him. 'The master of the *Prince Henry* was boarded by armed men under the command of a French lieutenant. They took Rear-Admiral Herrick prisoner, then allowed the ship to proceed. Captain Williams decided to turn back, so that we should know what happened. His mate was killed and some of his men badly injured.'

The room was quite silent, as if not even the distant soldiers wanted to intrude on Bolitho's thoughts. Afterwards Avery realised that Bolitho had already guessed what had happened, had known the reason for the attack.

Bolitho opened the leather case and found the piece of paper inside. He held it to the sunlight and saw Herrick's familiar sloping handwriting. *She is the Tridente, brigantine, under Brazilian colours. But she is an American privateer. I have seen her before.* Herrick had not signed it or made any other comment. He must have known, too, that they were coming for him. Baratte's hand again: to make the conflict as personal as it was deadly.

Drummond asked, 'What will you do?'

'There is little enough I can do until my ships discover something that might lead us to the enemy.'

Drummond said, 'Rear-Admiral Herrick was once a friend of yours, I believe.'

'Baratte obviously believes it too.' He smiled, and his face seemed suddenly more grave because of it. 'He *is* my friend, Sir Patrick.'

Drummond glared at his charts. 'It means they know more of our intentions than I would have wished.'

Bolitho recalled Adam's information concerning the big American frigate *Unity*. A coincidence? Unlikely. Involvement then? If so, it could erupt into open war at a time when the

164

French needed more than anything for England's blockade to be broken, and her victorious armies divided by an unexpected ally.

Bolitho looked up, his mind suddenly clear.

'Find Yovell and direct him to be ready to draft some orders for me.' He was seeing it in his mind like a chart. 'I want *Valkyrie* and *Laertes* to return here at once, and *Anemone* to remain on patrol and search duties. I shall order one of the schooners to find Trevenen with all haste. Jenour's *Orcadia* and the other brig are due any day now.' He looked around the room as though he felt trapped. 'I must get to sea.' He paused as if surprised by something, perhaps himself. 'We will send word to Freetown by the first available packet. I want James Tyacke with me. And as someone observed recently, I *am* the senior naval officer here.' He looked into the shadows as if he expected to see all those other lost faces watching him. 'We may no longer be a band of brothers, or *We Happy Few*, but we'll show Baratte something this time, and there will be no exchange at the end of it!'

After Bolitho and his flag lieutenant had departed the major-general thought of what he had just witnessed.

He was a soldier, and a good one, not only in his own opinion. He had never had many dealings with the King's navy, and when he had he had usually found them to be unsatisfactory. There was no better thing than the army's tradition and discipline, no matter what scum you were expected to train and lead for the honour of the regiment.

He had heard of Bolitho's behaviour in England where his blatant affair with the Somervell woman had turned society against him. He had heard too of that lady's courage when the *Golden Plover* had been lost on the reef.

The charisma had been here in this room and he had seen and felt it for himself. Watched the fire in the man, the anguish over his friend, who had perhaps been one of his *happy few*.

Later that day when Yovell had at last laid down his pen, and Avery had been allowed to carry the orders to the schooner, and Ozzard could be heard humming quietly as he laid the table for supper, Bolitho considered his course of action. Impetuous, yes. Dangerous, probably. But there was no other option. He looked around. Gleaming brightly in the candlelight, Herrick's telescope lay near the window of his borrowed quarters as a reminder, if one were needed.

Aloud he said, 'Do not fret, Thomas. I shall find you, and there will be no bad blood between us.'

Close-hauled under topsails and jib His Britannic Majesty's frigate *Anemone* appeared to drift easily on the deep blue water, her reflection hardly marred by the long ocean swells.

In his cabin, Captain Adam Bolitho had spread a chart on his table beside the litter of a late midday meal, and as he studied it his ear was following the muted shipboard noises.

It had been just a week since the courier schooner from Cape Town and the other frigates *Valkyrie* and *Laertes* had parted company with him. It seemed much longer, and Adam had pondered several times on the reason for his uncle's brief letter, written in his own hand and attached to the orders separating *Anemone* from the others. Perhaps he did not trust Trevenen. Adam's face stiffened with dislike. Whenever his ship had sailed in close company with the senior frigate there had always been a stream of signals, and even when within earshot it had been all he could do to hold his temper as Trevenen had bellowed across the clear water through his speaking trumpet. Dissatisfaction about a lack of reports and sightings, complaints about his station-keeping: almost anything. The schooner's arrival had seemed like a blessing. *Then.*

He stared hard at the chart. To the north lay the great island of Madagascar, and to the north-east the French islands of Mauritius and Bourbon. They were certainly well-placed to prey on the busy trade-routes. And nobody knew how many ships the enemy was using, let alone where they were based.

He heard shouts on deck and knew the watch was preparing to lay the ship on her next tack. And so it had been since their arrival in this area: each day the same, with nothing to break the monotony but drills and more drills. But no floggings. That had been the only reward for the patience his officers had shown.

Unlike Trevenen's command, he thought. In retrospect it seemed that each time the ships had moved closer together he had seen somebody being punished at the gratings. Without Bolitho aboard it was as if Trevenen was making up for lost opportunities.

He thought about Herrick's capture by the enemy privateer, as related in his uncle's message. Letters of marque meant very little in these waters. Mercenaries were only a short step from pirates.

He was surprised that he had few feelings about what had happened. He had always respected Herrick but they had never been close, and Adam could never forgive him for his treatment of Bolitho, although he could imagine what anguish his uncle was still suffering for the sake of one who had once been his friend.

His thoughts strayed back to the courier schooner, although he had tried to put it from his mind. He had done wrong, very wrong, and no good could come of it. *But I did do it*. The words seemed to mock him. He had written the letter much earlier, as *Anemone* had left the African mainland astern and the oceans had changed from one to another.

It had been like talking to her, or so he had thought at the time. Reliving the moment when they had loved one another despite the grief and despair of what had happened. Even her anger, her hatred perhaps, had not deterred him in any way. With thousands of miles between them, and the very real possibility that he would never see her again, the memory of their last hostile encounter had softened. When the schooner's commander had asked for any letters to be passed across, he had sent the letter over. He could not accept that such passion as they had shared could end as it had.

It had been madness; and night after night in the humid darkness of his quarters he had been tortured by what his impetuous action might do to her and to the happiness she shared with Keen.

He reached for the coffee, but it was without taste.

Where would it end? What should he do?

Perhaps she would destroy the letter when it eventually reached her. Surely she would not keep it, even to show to her husband . . .

There was a tap at the door and his first lieutenant looked

167

in at him warily. Martin had proved to be far better at his duties than Adam had dared to hope. With Christmas drawing near he had managed to arouse interest even among some of the hard men. In the cool of the evening watches he had organised all kinds of contests from wrestling, which he surprisingly seemed to know a lot about, to races between the various divisions at sail and boat drill. With extra tots of rum as an inducement there had been hornpipes, watched by the majority of the company and eventually cheered when the winners had been decided.

Adam always avoided over-confidence with a cautiousness he had learned from his uncle, but he had seen pressed and rebellious men slowly being welded into a team, a part of the ship he loved.

'What is it, Aubrey?'

The lieutenant relaxed slightly. The use of his first name told him more than anything of his young captain's mood. He had seen him being tormented by something ever since leaving England. Trevenen's goading, the lack of the trained men he had lost to other ships, the endless ocean itself perhaps, all had played their part.

The captain had often been sharp with him, embarrassingly so, but in his heart Martin knew he wanted to serve no other.

'Masthead reports a sail, sir. He thinks.' He saw Adam's eyes flash and added hastily, 'Bad sea mist to the north, sir.'

Surprisingly Adam smiled. 'Thank you.' It was not the vague report that had brought the frown to his face but the fact that he had not heard the lookout's cry through the open cabin skylight. A year ago he would not have believed such a thing possible.

'How goes the wind?'

'Much as before, sir. South-by-west. A fair breeze, it seems.'

Adam returned to his chart and cradled the islands between his fingers as he had seen his uncle do many times.

'What could a ship be doing out here?'

'Mr Partridge thinks she may be a trader.'

Adam rubbed his chin. 'Bound for where, I wonder?' He pointed at the chart with his brass dividers. 'She has a choice. Mauritius or Bourbon – the other islands are nothing of interest. Unless . . .' He looked at the lieutenant, his eyes suddenly very alive.

'Call all hands, Aubrey. Set the courses and get the t'gallants on her! Let's take a look at this *stranger!*'

Martin thought of the quick changes of mood and said cautiously, 'It may be nothing, sir.'

Adam grinned at him. 'On the other hand, you old misery, she might make a nice Christmas present for my uncle, have you thought of that?'

He went on deck and watched the men already spread out on the yards, the released sails booming and cracking as they filled to the wind across the quarter.

He watched from the quarterdeck rail as sail after sail was sheeted home and the deck tilted to the pressure. Spray dashed over the figurehead, and through the rigging and hurrying bare-backed seamen he saw the nymph's gold shoulders glistening as if she had been roused by their thrust through the water.

'Lookout reported that she has two masts, sir.'

That was Dunwoody, the signals midshipman. 'But the mist is bad despite the wind.'

Partridge the grizzled sailing-master looked at him scornfully.

'Proper little Cap'n Cook you are!'

Adam walked a few paces this way and that, his feet so used to the ring bolts and gun tackles in his path that he avoided them without effort.

A two-masted vessel. Could she be the unknown *Tridente* Herrick had described in his hidden message? His heart quickened at the thought. It seemed quite likely. Sailing alone with every sighting a probable enemy.

'Another pull on the weather forebrace, there!' Dacre, the second lieutenant, was striding about the maindeck, his eyes uplifted as the sails emptied and filled again with the sound of musket fire.

'Deck there!' A forgotten lookout's voice was almost lost in the surge of the sea into the scuppers and the whine of stays and shrouds. The conditions which *Anemone* used to full advantage.

169

The lookout tried again. 'Brig, sir!'

Adam looked at the horizon. So it was not *Tridente*.

Several telescopes were trained on the mist-shrouded division between sky and ocean as they waited to see what the masthead had reported.

'Deck, sir! She's spreadin' more sail an' standin' away to the nor'east!'

Adam clapped his hands together. 'The fool's made a mistake. This soldier's wind can't help him now!' He punched the first lieutenant's arm. 'Get the royals on her, Mr Martin, and alter course two points to starboard! We'll be up to that rascal within the hour!'

Martin glanced at him only briefly before he started to shout his orders to the waiting seamen and marines. It was like seeing someone else emerging from a mask.

'Mr Gwynne, more hands aloft! Lively there!'

The new third lieutenant Lewis said casually, 'A bit of prize money, eh?' He flinched as the captain's eyes passed over him. He need not have worried. Adam had not even heard him.

Adam wedged himself against the rail and levelled his telescope. Like a great pink curtain the mist was already rolling away. The brig, and it surely was not a brigantine, was almost stern-on, her mainsail standing out above the sea on either beam, the foam thrown up from her rudder clearly visible as she took the wind under her coat-tails.

'She flies no colours, sir.'

Adam moistened his lips and tasted the salt. 'Soon she will. Of one sort or another.'

He looked sharply at Martin. 'They'll be able to see who we are soon, Aubrey.'

The lieutenant almost held his breath under his stare.

Then Adam said, 'You are about my build, eh?' He smiled as if it was all a great joke. 'We will change coats. You shall be captain for a while.'

Mystified, Martin slipped into the proffered coat with its pair of sea-tarnished epaulettes.

Adam took the lieutenant's coat with its white lapels and grinned.

'Very good.'

Around them the men at the wheel and standing to the mizzen braces paused to watch.

Adam touched his sleeve. 'I trust you, Aubrey, but I need to get amongst them, to see for myself.' He became formal again, even curt. 'I intend to board her. Detail a good party, some marines amongst them. Sergeant Deacon will be useful.' He turned as his coxswain George Starr padded across the deck with his short fighting sword. 'I'll take this with me.' He glanced at Starr's impassive features. Not an Allday, but he was good.

Later, as they bore down on the brig, Adam said, 'Hoist the signal for her to heave-to, Mr Dunwoody. She will do no such thing, so pass my compliments to the gunner and tell him to lay a bow-chaser with his own hands!'

Martin was back again, his young face screwed up with worry.

'But suppose they try to repel boarders, sir?'

'Then you will fire on them, sir!'

'With you on board, sir?' He was shocked.

Adam watched him seriously and then patted one of the epaulettes on his shoulder. 'Then who knows? You may become a real captain earlier than expected!'

'No acknowledgement, sir!'

'Let her fall off a point, Mr Partridge.' Adam watched the other vessel as she appeared to edge into the criss-cross of rigging when the helm went over. It would give the bow-chaser a clearer shot. Even so, it would be a difficult one. He saw sunlight flashing on the brig's stern windows, and from trained telescopes above the creaming water. A fast little ship. He smiled. *Not fast enough.*

'As you bear!' Ayres, the grey-haired master gunner, could not hear him from the forecastle, but he had seen his young captain's hand slice down.

The bang of the long eighteen-pounder made the frames quiver like a body-blow.

Ayres got up with some difficulty from the smoking cannon and shaded his eyes as the ball slapped through the brig's driver, leaving a round charred hole. He was too old for this sort of work, but not even his officers would dare to tell him.

171

There was a muffled cheer and Adam watched as a flag broke out stiffly from the other vessel's gaff.

One of the lieutenants gave a groan. 'Damned Yankee! Of all the luck!'

'She's shortening sail an' coming about, sir!'

Adam said coolly, 'Wouldn't you?'

He gestured with his fist. 'Heave-to, if you please, and call away the cutter.' He looked at Martin meaningly. 'You know what to do. Just watch everything with a glass.' He beckoned to the signals midshipman. 'You come with me.' He did not see the youth's surprise and pleasure as he touched his hat to the '*captain*', and the frigate began to labour round into the wind, her yards alive with men as they shortened sail, as fast and as cleanly as any company could. Adam recalled the *Unity*'s captain's comments about the slowness he had watched in *Anemone*'s half-trained company. He would not say it again if they should meet.

As the boat was cast off from the chains, he saw several of his men peering down from the shrouds or gangway while the oarsmen fought to bring the boat under command. Most of them were still unaware of what was happening, least of all why their captain wore a subordinate's coat.

With the wind assisting them and the seamen pulling hard back on their oars they were soon close enough to see the brig more clearly, her name, *Eaglet*, across her stern.

'They've lowered a ladder, sir!' Dunwoody was leaning forward, his dirk clutched between his knees. He sounded hoarse but not frightened. He was thinking much like Martin. That once aboard they could seize him as a hostage.

Adam stood in the swaying boat and cupped his hands. 'I demand to come aboard! In the King's name!'

He heard some muffled shouts, jeers perhaps, and thought he saw the gleam of sunlight on weapons.

A man without hat or coat stood at the bulwark and stared down at the pitching cutter with anger and contempt.

'Stand away there! This is an American vessel! How dare you fire on us?'

Starr, the coxswain, muttered, 'What d'you think, sir?'

Adam remained standing. 'Bluff.' He hoped it sounded

172

convincing. He cupped his hands again and noticed how cold they were in spite of the sun.

He could almost feel Martin and the others watching him across the tossing strip of water. Very deliberately he raised his hand.

All eyes above him on the brig's deck stared as *Anemone*'s gunports opened as one, and all the weapons which would bear were hauled squeaking and rumbling into the sunlight.

'*You mad bastards!*' The brig's master waved to his men and an entry port was hauled open above the dangling ladder.

Between his teeth Adam said, 'When we hook on, follow me, one at a time up the ladder.' He looked at the midshipman's upturned face. 'If things go wrong get them back to the ship. You're doing well.'

He looked up and waited for the cutter to lift heavily against the brig's weatherworn hull.

Why had he said that to the midshipman? They might both be killed within minutes if the *Eaglet*'s master was foolish enough to condemn himself to death under *Anemone*'s broadside. Pride? Arrogance? How would *she* see him if she were here?

He gripped the entry port and dragged himself inboard.

The deck seemed to be packed with men, most of whom were armed. The vessel's master blocked his way, seaboots astride and arms folded, every fibre blazing with fury. 'I'm Joshua Tobias. Who the hell are you?'

Adam touched his hat. 'His Britannic Majesty's frigate *Anemone*.' He gave a curt nod and thought he heard the infamous Sergeant Deacon clambering from the ladder. Deacon had been broken from sergeant more than once, mostly for brawling ashore: he had even suffered the lash for his behaviour, but as a sergeant there was none to touch him. He had rarely been known to discipline one of his marines. A quick punch from one of his ham-like fists was usually more than sufficient.

'Why have you dared to stop my vessel? Your government will hear of this when I reach port, Lieutenant. I wouldn't be in your bloody shoes!'

173

There were growls from the watching seamen. It just needed one hot-head. Like a spark in a powder keg.

Adam said quietly, 'It is my duty to warn you, sir, that any resistance to a King's ship will be treated as piracy. By the powers vested in me I am required to search your vessel. I would like to see your papers also.'

Someone yelled from the back of the crowd, 'Pitch the bugger overboard! We drubbed his kind afore! Let's be done with 'em!'

The master held up one hand. 'I'll deal with this!'

To Adam he said harshly, 'Do you expect me to believe that your captain would fire on his own men?'

Adam kept his face stiff. 'You do not know my captain.'

Midshipman Dunwoody called, 'Boarding party in position, sir!'

Adam felt sweat on his spine. It was all taking too long.

He snapped, 'Where bound?'

The master replied indifferently, 'The island of Rodriguez, general cargo. You can see my bills of lading if it amuses you! This is a neutral vessel. I'll see you broken for this, an' your damned captain too!'

Adam said, 'Quite.' He looked at the Royal Marines sergeant. 'Take charge on deck, Deacon. Any trouble and you have your orders.' He turned to his coxswain. 'Take four men.' Starr had hand-picked them himself, all from *Anemone*'s first ship's company.

Suppose the master spoke the truth? They would have to release the brig.

Trevenen would make a big case against him. Even his uncle would be helpless.

The thought made him angry. 'Show me the chart.'

They clattered down a short pitching ladder to the tiny chart-room. He studied the calculations, sparse and even casual when compared with the navy's standards. Old Partridge would fall dead if he saw it.

The *Eaglet* was no slaver. There were not even any man-acles, which under the slavery act could condemn any ship's master who carried them.

Starr stood by the ladder and shook his head.

174

On deck again Adam considered it. Provisions, flour, oil, even gunpowder; but the latter was no crime.

The master was grinning at him and there were catcalls from some of his crew. He shouted, 'Bosun! Tell that damn boat to come alongside for their friends!'

Dunwoody stared around. He felt hurt, enraged that his captain should be humiliated, and suffer some punishment later that he could only guess.

The boatswain was a great hulk of a man with thick black hair in an old-fashioned pigtail that all but reached his belt.

Adam looked at his men. This was the moment to retreat, when danger was very real.

He swung round as Dunwoody exclaimed, 'The bosun, sir! He wears a new cutlass!'

Adam stared from him to the burly pigtailed sailor.

Dunwoody was almost squeaking. 'Before we left England, sir, I helped to load and re-arm the schooner . . .' He fell silent as understanding flooded Adam's face.

He said, 'How long have you owned that cutlass?'

The master barked, 'Stop wasting my time, Lieutenant! Talk won't save you now!'

Adam's eyes flashed. 'Nor you, I think, *sir*!'

The boatswain gave a shrug. 'I bin an American citizen for three years!' He tapped his cutlass, which was thrust through his belt. 'A souvenir from my days under another flag, *sir*!' He spat out each word, his eyes never leaving Adam's face.

'Well, then.' Adam's fingers touched the hilt of his sword and he felt the marines stir at his back. 'My midshipman reminded me of something. It was the schooner *Maid of Rye*. She had just been taken into naval service and sailed for the Cape ahead of me. She was never heard of again, and was presumed lost in a storm.' How could he stay so calm when every nerve was screaming at him to cut this man down?

The master interrupted hotly, 'So we're wreckers now, are we?' But he sounded less confident.

Adam ignored him. 'I heard my men talking about the schooner, and my armourer remarked that she was to be the first of His Majesty's ships to be supplied with the new cutlass.' His hand shot out and plucked the naked blade from his belt.

'Not *three years ago*, it would seem!' He snapped, 'Take him, Sergeant!' The astonished seaman fell back, confused by the swift change of fortune. Adam added, 'I would not resist. My sergeant of marines is known for his hasty temper!'

The boatswain yelled, '*Do something!* What the hell's the matter with you?'

Adam said, 'This man will be removed to my ship, and when we reach Cape Town I am sure he will be punished. He could only have got the cutlass from the *Maid of Rye*. At best mutiny, at worst piracy – take your choice. If, as you claim, you have served in the King's Navy, you will know the punishment.'

He turned to Deacon. 'Strip him!'

Two marines tore off the man's coat and shirt. His back was a mass of deep, ugly scars, like one of Trevenen's victims, Adam thought bitterly.

The master said, 'This is a neutral vessel, Lieutenant!'

The boatswain was on his knees as Starr drove the cutlass into the deck so that it stood quivering like something alive.

'You bastard! What did you do to some poor Jack, I wonder?'

The boatswain was pleading, 'It weren't my fault, sir!' Even his colonial accent seemed to have gone. 'You gotta believe me!'

Adam looked at him. It was little enough, and but for Dunwoody he would have missed it completely.

He was surprised how unruffled he sounded. 'Captain Tobias, your vessel is detained for further investigation. If you are carrying deserters amongst your company they will be returned to the fleet and pressed into service. For harbouring that grovelling object you could also be charged with concealment of a felony on the high seas.'

He was to remember the subdued master's words for a long time to come. He looked around the brig's deck and said quietly, 'This ship is all I have.'

What Adam would have thought if they had taken *Anemone* from him after a court-martial for his actions. The thought drove away all sympathy, and he said, 'Signal the ship, Mr Dunwoody. I want a prize crew. Mr Lewis can carry word to

176

the vice-admiral.' He looked at the master. 'After that? We shall see.' He watched another boat pulling from *Anemone*'s shadow. It gave him time to think, phase by phase as his uncle had taught him to do.

Sergeant Deacon jabbed the crouching boatswain with his boot. 'What about this thing, sir?'

'Put him in irons and send him over in the cutter.'

The American master said, 'You take a lot of authority on yourself for a mere lieutenant!'

'I lied. I command *Anemone*. Captain Adam Bolitho, at your service!'

He saw the desperation in the man's eyes and said coldly, 'Tell me your true destination, Captain Tobias. If you were an enemy I would respect you. But any one who tries to harm my country under the guise of neutrality can expect no mercy from me.'

He heard shouts from the other longboat and watched the struggle on the other man's face.

The boatswain shouted at him, 'Tell him, you cowardly bastard! I'll not dance a hangman's jig for you!' He struggled round as the marines pinioned his legs with irons. 'An island called Lorraine! That's where!'

Adam looked at the master and saw him sag. 'You see, Captain Tobias, you lost your chance. A pity.' As more men swarmed aboard he snapped, 'Take him too!'

Adam saw Lewis, his hat awry, pushing through the throng of people.

He said, 'Disarm these men, and have the marines cover them at all times.'

He looked at the departing boat and turned away. He found he could not bear to watch Tobias staring astern at his lost command.

He continued, 'Sail to Cape Town and find my uncle. I will give you some written orders. Can you manage that?'

He saw Starr nudge the sergeant. They probably knew Lewis was to be prize-master simply because he was the least competent of the frigate's three lieutenants.

'Aye, *aye*, sir!'

'Take Deacon's advice. He was once in a slave uprising. He knows how to deal with things like this.'

He put his hand on the midshipman's shoulder. It felt as hot as a raging fever.

'Lorraine Island, Mr Dunwoody. A barren place, and not too far from Bourbon or Mauritius. I should have guessed. But for you . . .' He shook him gently. 'Well, we'll not think of that. We shall rejoin the ship.' He saw the brig's crew being disarmed and sorted into watches. There was no resistance now.

Once back aboard the *Anemone* Adam wasted no time in explaining to Martin and the second lieutenant, Dacre, and of course the sailing master, Old Partridge.

'The brig carries stores enough for a much larger vessel, maybe other evidence if we had had the time to carry out a thorough search. My clerk can write orders for Mr Lewis. Then it's up to us.'

Martin exclaimed, 'It might take weeks for him to find our ships, sir!'

Adam looked at their intent faces and smiled gently.

'Really, Aubrey, I do not think I said anything about *waiting*.'

He saw Starr walking aft, the cutlass grasped in his hand.

He said quietly, 'But for that simple blade and Dunwoody's quick observation . . .' He grinned suddenly. 'But we have troubles enough, eh? So let's be about it!'

Partridge hid a smirk. It was like hearing his uncle amongst them.

12

Trust

Old Partridge leaned against the white-painted timbers and watched his captain and lieutenants studying the charts on his table. It was pitch black outside, the sky filled from horizon to horizon with a million stars. Some were huge, as if they were just above the spiralling mastheads, the others so faint and extended they could have been encircling another earth as yet unknown.

The ship was sailing under close-reefed topsails, jib and driver, the motion lively but regular as they continued towards the north-east. Tomorrow would make it two days since the prize *Eaglet* had left them. Already it seemed that it could not really have happened, but for the brig's master and boatswain, and the cutlass Dunwoody had seen, and about which he had not been afraid to speak out when they had been ready to fall back to the ship.

Adam bent right over the chart and peered at the destination the prisoner had revealed. Partridge had already told him that the island called Lorraine was hardly known, and the charts were unreliable. There was a big lagoon, but no fresh water, nor even any trees for fuel or repairs. It sounded like one of the islands Catherine had described after the escape from the shipwreck.

Partridge had contended that it was unsafe for the unwary. Adam smiled. Everything was, in the great Indian Ocean. Like almost all the other islands in this area it must have changed hands many times as a pawn in strategy, and out of necessity, as a port for trade and a place for ships to shelter when the great storms came; like Mauritius itself, which lay some hundred and fifty miles to the west, ruled by the Arabs and the Portuguese and then the first true settlers, the Dutch, who had claimed it and named it after Prince Maurice of Nassau. After the Dutch had quit the islands the English trading companies had come, but unable to make the place prosper they had withdrawn. The French had occupied Mauritius and all the island group ever since. But the fact uppermost in Adam's mind was this one flaw in the pattern. Lorraine.

An island was always easier to defend than to capture. He had heard his uncle say as much many times. Even so, when the attack was finally launched against the main islands, the captains of the men-of-war and the army transports would have updated charts. Knowing nothing of Lorraine was like being blind, tapping with a stick in some unknown alley.

The new Royal Marines officer who had joined the ship at Portsmouth as a replacement for his unfortunate predecessor, a Lieutenant Montague Baldwin, remarked in his somewhat affected drawl, 'If there is an enemy vessel there, sir, she will soon know we are coming.' His coat shone like blood in the deckhead lanterns as he stared at the chart. 'If I could land a squad of men under cover of darkness we might be able to signal to you when you begin a final approach.'

Lieutenant Martin frowned. 'There are reefs a-plenty, soldier. You'd probably make more noise than we would!'

Lieutenant Dacre said, 'We should sight the island the day after tomorrow.' He flashed his cheeky grin at the sailing master. 'Or so we are led to believe!'

Adam looked at them. The stimulus of danger was like being reborn. The challenge he had come to understand, respect, and sometimes fear. He was their captain: on his skill, or lack of it, their reputations and very lives depended.

He felt the old surge of pride, which had even pushed the letter he had sent to Zenoria out of his mind. This was what he had dreamed about even as a midshipman. He had learned well from those who, knowingly or not, had set him on the path to this ship, his *Anemone*: his uncle and Valentine Keen, and even Herrick with his stolid backbone of experience. He

180

almost smiled. He would never forget Allday's part in it. The man of the sea. A true friend.

Martin offered, 'What about the prisoners, sir? Can we obtain new intelligence from them?'

Adam looked up, his eyes distant. 'Captain Tobias? I could ask him for advice and local knowledge and then do the opposite, I suppose. For he'd surely guide us on to a reef rather than help us, even if we shut him in the cable tier where he would be the first to strike!'

Martin agreed. 'The bosun, then?'

Adam felt his ship tremble as if she had lost her way, then saw the lanterns circle about when she plunged forward again into another long trough.

'It is a thought.' Like most sailors the man probably knew little beyond his own duties. They were usually able to perform such things as daily navigation, and take noon-sights with sextants. But the charts themselves were something beyond their immediate duties.

Much worse was the real possibility that the man, already terrified for his own life because of the accusation that he had been involved in the loss of the schooner *Maid of Rye*, might say anything that came into his head simply to ingratiate himself with his captors.

Adam said, 'The brig was certainly carrying enough supplies to keep a larger vessel at sea for a long while. There would be no need to enter one of the main ports and risk detection by one of our patrols.' He gave a wry grin. 'Even if we had any!'

'Could it be the Yankee, *Unity*, sir?'

'I think not. She has no need to hide, except behind her "neutrality"! Her presence out here, her ability to flaunt her flag openly in the midst of a war, is far more effective. Her captain is too shrewd a dog to miss that!'

Suppose it was Baratte? Adam felt his blood pound. Another frigate maybe? No ponderous fleets and endless signals and counter-orders. Ship to ship, man to man. Like his uncle. He shied away from the thought. *Like my father*.

He made up his mind. 'Mr Partridge has laid off two possible approaches, and just as important, an escape route if the

181

enemy is there and attempts to gain open water, where he can fight or run as the mood takes him.' He watched their intent expressions, each seeing the unknown foe as something real now and not merely a piece of speculation. 'We were short-handed even before we put a prize crew into the brig. We cannot afford to board or be boarded if our adversary is anything like our rate.' He glanced at the two lieutenants. 'Go around the divisions and speak with their gun captains. Each of our three midshipmen must be instructed as to what to expect.' He brought out a few chuckles as he added, 'Except young Dunwoody, perhaps. He appears to be more alert than his captain!'

A bell chimed out from the forecastle, the sound almost buried in sea-noises like an underwater chapel. He said, 'This time tomorrow . . .' he glanced at the chart as if he could see the island and its lagoon, its lack of proper soundings and bearings ' . . . we shall beat to quarters, and I will go round the ship myself.' In his mind he saw his uncle, then a captain, doing just that aboard his old *Hyperion*, showing no trace of his inner doubts and fears as he walked amongst his men. *I must be like that. I must never forget.* 'And then at first light we will begin our final approach . . .'

The marine lieutenant said soberly, 'Christmas Day, sir!'

Martin said, 'The people will be looking to you, sir!'

It fell to Old Partridge to say what was in all their thoughts. 'An' to God, I 'ope!'

Captain Adam Bolitho lay on his back below the tall stern windows of the cabin and stared unwinkingly at the skylight. It was still dark on deck and there was too much caked salt on the glass to know if there were even any stars.

From without *Anemone* would appear to be in shadow. Gunports sealed, hatchways and skylights covered and lanterns reduced to a minimum. Even the ship seemed quieter, he thought vaguely. There was an occasional shuffle of bare feet overhead, or the crisper step of a lieutenant or warrant officer. His cabin groaned as the rudder lifted towards the surface and was then followed by the gurgle of spray when the ship ploughed forward again.

182

He sat up and pushed his fingers through his unruly hair. What did his officers think about it, *really* think? How did they see his proposed attack? The lagoon might be empty when they got there anyway, and he guessed that many of his men prayed that would be so. In his heart he felt there *was* an enemy. It was the obvious choice of a rendezvous for anyone competent enough to grope his way through the reefs and hidden sand bars.

Some might see his intention as pure vanity, the search for glory. He tried to reassure himself with a smile. Precious little of either if his ship came to grief.

Partridge had suggested there were two passages into the lagoon, but even he had no experience of this dismal place. Which was the right one?

He had spoken with the *Eaglet*'s master, Joshua Tobias, but without result. If Tobias survived it was unlikely that American pressure would release him and his ship. To become involved, even if he only wanted to save himself, would only condemn him.

He felt suddenly angry. Why risk *Anemone* and men's lives on a whim? If he stood offshore the enemy would see him and perhaps remain safely at anchor. If she ran for it they could fight in the open. The alternative was to blockade the approaches until help arrived. It might take weeks before Lieutenant Lewis found his uncle or one of the patrols.

And what if another enemy arrived in the meantime, perhaps even Baratte himself? His head throbbed as his mind grappled in every direction.

He got to his feet and moved about the cabin, seeing as others might the set of her reduced canvas, the glow of the compass light, the watchkeepers, all of whom would be thinking of the dawn.

He strode to the screen door, feeling his ship beneath his bare feet, rising and dipping and tilting slightly to starboard under the pressure in her sails. The marine sentry almost dropped his musket as he pulled open one of the slatted doors. He had probably been asleep on his feet.

'Sir?' The whites of his eyes seemed to glow in the solitary watch lantern.

183

'Fetch the . . .' He hesitated and saw the first lieutenant leaving the empty wardroom.

They greeted each other like old friends rather than men who had been sharing the watches with barely a break.

Adam asked, 'Can't you sleep either, Aubrey?'

Martin tried to contain a yawn. 'I have the morning watch, sir.' He too listened to the ship around and above them.

Then he followed Adam aft into the cabin and the sentry lapsed into a doze once more.

Adam held out his hand. 'Happy Christmas, Aubrey.' It sounded so solemn that he wanted to laugh.

Martin sat down. 'I cannot believe it.'

Adam took a bottle from his cupboard and then two glasses. It gave him more time to think. There was nobody he could ask. If he revealed even a hint of uncertainty he would lose their confidence. The margin between life and death.

It was claret but it could have been anything.

Martin looked at him. 'Sweethearts and wives, sir!'

They both drank and Adam thought of the letter again. *If only you knew.*

He said, 'I want a good hand at the masthead, Aubrey. Tell Jorston to do it when we start the final approach. He's a first-class seaman, due for sailing-master whenever he can be spared. Knows the state of the sea-bed, the run of the tide just by looking at it.'

Martin watched the captain refilling the glasses, fascinated. It was like seeing his mind at work.

Adam said, 'Both anchors catted and ready to let go.'

Martin waited, then asked, 'You really think we'll fight, sir?'

Adam seemed far away. 'I know it.'

He was suddenly wide awake. 'Fetch the prisoner, the boatswain – Richie, isn't it?'

Martin stared at him. How could he remember such details?

Adam smiled. 'Send for the master-at-arms and tell him. I want you here with me.' He should have said *need*, he thought.

They said little as they drank their wine and listened to the ship and the sea, each one of them elsewhere in his thoughts, each with somebody else.

The doors were opened and the bosun, accompanied by

the master-at-arms and the ship's corporal, lurched across the tilting deck. Richie wore leg-irons and each step was slow and painful.

He stood quite still, staring down at the young captain he had once thought to be a mere lieutenant.

'I've nothin' more to say.'

The master-at-arms snapped, '*Sir!*'

Adam said, 'A chair, Corporal.' As the man struggled into it he added, 'Wait outside, Master-at-Arms.' The two representatives of the ship's discipline left, obviously mystified.

Adam said, 'I have to know certain things. First, what part did you play in the loss of the *Maid of Rye?*'

The man seemed taken aback, as if he had been expecting something else.

'Nothin', sir!' He saw Adam turn as if to call the master-at-arms back into the cabin and said vehemently, 'I swear to God, sir, it's the truth!'

Adam watched him. 'I'm listening.'

Richie looked at Martin as if to gain his support. 'She was already run ashore, sir, in the Gulf of Guinea it was. There was a terrible blow o' wind and we lost some of our canvas before we could claw clear!'

'Why did you call your captain a coward? Was it because he did not stand up for you when we boarded *Eaglet?*'

Richie looked at his leg-irons as if shocked at what he saw.

'He wouldn't go to the schooner's rescue. Some of 'er people had managed to get ashore – not many, I think. We didn't know she were a man-o'-war at that time. The men who managed to reach the beach were set upon by natives. Hacked 'em to pieces. Even above the wind we could hear 'em screamin'!' He gave a great shudder. 'Probably thought she was a bloody blackbirder!'

Adam reached down and gripped the cutlass, the new short-bladed one which Dunwoody had helped load into the ill-fated schooner. Richie stared at it dully. 'We picked up just the one man, sir. He'd gone outboard when the vessel struck. I went over the side after him even though the Cap'n was shoutin' for me to stop! He was afraid he'd follow the schooner on to the beach!'

185

Adam found time to wonder how many of *Anemone*'s company could swim. Very few probably.

He looked at the cutlass. The man could be lying. Some of the others from *Eaglet* might confirm or refute his story. But that would take too long. They might never know now.

Richie said thickly, 'The man lived for an hour or so. It was then that we knew she was a King's ship. He was a seaman, like I was once.' He sounded beaten, as if he had already seen the sentence of death.

'Where you got those scars on your back? A striped shirt at the gangway?'

'Yessir.'

Adam stood up and crossed to the cabinet again. He could feel the man's eyes following every move, as if he expected to be taunted, despised.

He said slowly, 'You know this island of Lorraine, Richie.' He saw him watching the cognac as it mounted the side of the glass while the deck went down again. 'You've visited it many times?'

'Once, sir. Just the once.'

Adam glanced at Martin's anxious face. 'Once.' He held out the glass. 'Get this into you, man.'

Richie almost choked on it and did not stop until it was empty.

Adam said, 'This is not a game of cards, Richie. My ship and your life are too high for mere stakes. You deserted from the navy?' He saw him give a despairing nod. 'Helping the enemy, being in possession of a cutlass which may or may not have come your way by accident.' He poured some more cognac. 'Not just a hanging, is it?' He forced himself to add, 'Have you ever seen a flogging through the fleet? The rope is a relief after that!' He said sharply so that even Martin jumped, 'What ship were you in? And I want the truth.'

Richie's red-rimmed eyes looked down. 'Last one was the *Linnet*, sloop-of-war. I was a maintopman, sir. I ran from her, I couldn't take no more of it.'

Adam watched him. The man's scars spoke for themselves. Perhaps he deserved them. He held his breath as the man

186

lifted his chin and looked him straight in the eyes. It was like seeing somebody else.

He said quietly, 'Afore that I was in the old *Superb*, sir. Cap'n Keats. Now *there* was a man.'

Adam glanced at Martin. 'Yes, I know.'

Feet moved overhead and somebody laughed. Adam looked around the cabin, soon to be stripped and laid bare like the rest of the ship. Ready for battle, and battle there was going to be. He knew it: could feel it like a sickness. And yet someone had laughed. It was Christmas.

He said, 'Will you trust *me*, Richie, as you once did Captain Keats? I promise I will do my best for you afterwards.' The word seemed to hang in the air.

The man looked at him gravely. He seemed stronger because of it, and not merely because of a promise that might not be honoured.

'Yes, sir.' He nodded slowly, then asked, 'The irons, sir?'

Adam looked at Martin. *He probably thinks me insane.* 'Have them struck off.'

The escort re-entered and Richie was led away.

Did I do right to trust him? But all he said was, 'Leave me, Aubrey.' As Martin turned to go he added, 'I shall see you at dawn.'

As the door was closed he sat and looked at the empty chair. It was strange to accept that he knew more about the man called Richie than he did about most of his ship's company.

He was surging forward through the darkness on the word of a deserter, reliant upon the skills of seamen many of whom had never set foot aboard ship until the press gangs had dragged them from their streets and farms. It was little enough.

He was surprised that he could feel no misgivings or doubts. They were committed. *I have committed them.*

He dragged some paper on to his table and after a moment began to write.

My dear Zenoria. On this Christmas day 1809 we are sailing into a battle. I know not what outcome we may expect, but my heart is brave because of you . . .

187

He stood up and crushed the paper into a ball before pushing it out of the quarter window.

An hour later he climbed to the quarterdeck and saw them watching him. His shirt was clean, and in the gloom his breeches and stockings were like snow.

To the deck at large he said, 'May Christmas be good to us all!' He turned to the first lieutenant. 'Send the hands to breakfast early and tell the purser I am expecting some generosity from his stores!'

A few of them laughed. Adam peered at the horizon, or where it should be.

'I shall go around the ship, Aubrey.' He snapped his mind shut to the letter that she would never see. 'Then you may beat to quarters and clear for action!'

The cards were down.

'Ship cleared for action, sir.' Martin watched his captain standing by the tightly packed hammock nettings.

'Very well.' Adam stared up at the sky. It was paler now, and the sea's face was showing itself beyond the bows, with the occasional hump of an unending roller lifting the deck very slightly before passing away into the remaining shadows.

Faces took on shapes and identities: the men at the nearest eighteen-pounders already stripped to the waist, the gun captains and older hands quietly explaining the workings of their particular division, as if all the others were unimportant.

Lieutenant Baldwin's marines were settling into place at the nettings, while others were already aloft in the fighting-tops, ready to shoot down on an enemy with their muskets or the deadly swivel guns mounted on each barricade. Almost everybody would soon be visible except for two men in the sickbay who were too ill even to work the pumps if required.

The marines' coats looked very dark in the poor light. It seemed quiet, unusual not to hear Sergeant Deacon's rasping voice chasing them, making certain that nothing was amiss.

Old Partridge glanced suspiciously at the released prisoner, Richie, who was standing beside the captain's coxswain.

Adam knew the sailing-master did not approve but had decided to ignore him. It was little enough, perhaps all they had. Jorston, a master's mate due for promotion, was up in the crosstrees with a telescope, although his instinct, his sailor's cunning, was far more valuable.

It was getting brighter much faster now, and Adam saw several seamen at their guns peeking out to see what was happening.

He searched his mind for last-minute faults, or obstacles he had overlooked. But his thoughts were empty now; his limbs felt loose and relaxed. It had often been like that for him before a sea-fight.

He almost smiled. How they would all laugh if there was no enemy ship here, or they found only some innocent trader who had put in for repairs. Unlikely, he told himself. Mauritius was only a day's sailing away for an average vessel. He thought of the powerful *Unity*. Beer would be very wary of risking her in such a dangerous place.

He saw Partridge murmuring with his other master's mate, Bond. They looked like a pair of conspirators.

'Who have you put in the chains, Mr Martin?' Only the clipped formality gave any hint of his awareness, the scent of peril.

'Rowlatt, sir.'

A face came into Adam's mind. Another one who had been aboard since the beginning.

'Good man.'

He crossed to the chart-table, which Partridge had brought up from below, and beckoned to Richie. 'Show me again.'

The tall bosun leaned over the chart and touched it gingerly with his finger.

'It looks about right, sir. The lagoon is on the sou'-eastern corner, an' the reef runs out for about two miles. The other side of the entrance has more rocks.' Surprisingly, he looked up at the great red ensign streaming from the gaff.

A true seaman, Adam thought. To sail clear of the long reef would mean that he would have to tack repeatedly to enter the lagoon, which appeared to be shaped like a great flask. Richie had not been studying the flag itself but was gauging the wind that was lifting it towards the mizzen mast. It would be easier for any ship to quit the lagoon with the south-westerly wind holding so steady. To tack back and forth to get inside would be a lengthy, not to say hazardous, business.

He looked at Richie's strong profile. A man with a history, but there was no time to think about that.

He asked sharply, 'On this course you say we could pass through the reef with barely a change of tack?' He could feel Martin and Dunwoody watching him and knew that Partridge was frowning with doubt.

'That's what we done when we came afore, sir. There's a gap in the reef, and a cluster of rocks on the far side.' He shrugged. It was all he knew. 'The cap'n used to keep them in line, on the same bearing he called it.'

It was not the kind of thing he could invent, Adam thought. But everything he had learned since he had first joined his uncle's ship as a midshipman had given him this inner wariness. As a watchkeeping officer and now as a post captain he had always mistrusted a reef, especially with the wind astern and fewer chances by the minute to avoid running aground.

Richie was staring at him, anxiety, hope, even fear returning to his eyes.

It would be useless to threaten him. Dangerous even.

He thought of the *Eaglet*'s master down below under guard. He had made this same approach, probably more times than Richie knew. He would be listening, wondering, perhaps even hoping that Adam would see his beautiful *Anemone* transformed into a wreck, mastless, with her keel broken on a reef.

He said, 'Begin sounding, if you please!'

He watched the leadsman in the forechains begin to heave on the heavy lead and line, until it lifted high above the creaming bow-wave and began to swing over and down again in one great circle. The seaman was a good leadsman and looked unconcerned as the apron took the whole weight of his body.

It was still too poor a light to see the lead leave his control and fly away ahead of the beakhead and the raked hull below.

'No bottom, sir!'

Partridge said gloomily, 'It'll soon shelve, sir!' To his mate he whispered, 'I'll gut that bastard if he's leadin' us on to the reef!'

Adam walked away from the others and recalled his tour around the mess-decks before the hands had been called to quarters. There had been several familiar faces, but most of them were strangers still. Perhaps he should have tried harder to bridge the gap instead of making them perfect their sail and gun drill? He had dismissed the idea. His uncle had always said that teamwork alone could bring the respect of one man for another. But loyalty had to be earned.

He saw the youngest midshipman, Frazer, who had joined the ship at Portsmouth, full of eagerness and excitement. Now he was thirteen, but looked younger than ever. He was staring at the sea, his hands opening and closing around his puny dirk, lost in thought.

'Here comes the sun!' But nobody answered.

Adam saw it pushing the last shadows from the deeper troughs, making them shimmer like molten glass. Hereabouts the ocean had undergone a sea-change, the surface pale green, with a mist lingering above it, moving with the wind so that the ship seemed to be stationary.

The first sunlight laid bare the deck, the gun crews with their rammers and sponges, and the tubs of sand that contained slow-matches in case the flintlocks failed. There was more sand on the deck below the gangways, so that men should not slip if water came inboard. Adam tightened his jaw. *Or blood.* It seemed bare overhead with the big courses brailed up to give a clearer vision and to reduce the risk of fire. In a ship like this, with tar and tinder-dry planking, even a burning wad from one of the guns could be dangerous.

Colour came seeping through the rigging: the marines' coats were scarlet again, their fixed bayonets glinting like ice.

He looked narrowly along his waiting gun crews, and at the others who would trim the yards, men and boys of all ages and from every background. He had asked some of them about themselves when he had done his rounds before dawn. Some had been shy, then eager to talk; others had crowded closer to listen. Many had just watched him: their captain, the symbol of their hardship, their captivity as they might see it. Men mostly from the south and western counties of England, from

191

farms and villages, and a few who had been unlucky enough to be caught by the press gangs in a sea-port.

The cry from the master's mate from the crosstrees was loud and clear.

'Breakers ahead!'

From the chains the leadsman cried, 'No bottom, sir!'

Adam said, 'Keep your eyes open, lads.' He saw Martin looking at him. 'Put a good bosun's mate at each cathead, Mr Martin. If we have to anchor we will have to shift ourselves!'

'By the mark ten!'

Adam kept his face composed. Partridge was right; it had begun to shelve. From no bottom, where the lead would not even reach, to sixty feet.

He tore his mind from the picture of *Anemone*'s keel cruising relentlessly toward the shallows.

Richie suddenly broke away and ran to the mizzen shrouds before anyone could move, and for a moment longer Adam thought he was casting himself to his death without even waiting to see their destruction.

But he pointed wildly as he clung to the tarred ratlines with his other hand.

'Lee bow, sir!' He seemed all excitement. 'There's the place yonder!'

Adam snatched up a telescope and realised that his fingers were suddenly slippery with sweat.

He saw the gap in the reef immediately, spray bursting on either side and hanging in the air like a shimmering curtain. He felt his heart pounding. It looked about as wide as a farm gate.

The leadsman cried, 'Deep eight!'

Adam looked at Richie. He wanted to ask him if he was certain but knew he could not. If his trust was proved false, it would have the same result as if Richie were mistaken.

The masthead called, 'Let her fall off a point, sir!' He repeated it and Adam realised he had been unable to think or move.

He called, 'Have the braces manned, Mr Martin. We will steer nor' east by east!'

'By the mark seven!' The seaman sounded completely

absorbed, as if he were unaware of or disinterested in the approaching shallows.

'Steady as she goes, sir! Nor' east by east!'

Some men were staring at the island now, suddenly so near. Flat and undulating for the most part but with one hill clearly visible, leaning over like a broken cliff. A good place for a lookout.

Adam clenched his fists. What did it matter? They would never get through. *Anemone* was not like a brig: she drew nearly three fathoms.

As if to mock him the voice floated aft. 'An' deep six!'

Adam said sharply, 'Take in the stays'ls, Mr Martin!'

Their eyes met across the bare-backed seamen. It was already too late. 'By th' mark ten!'

Adam stared at his first lieutenant, then shouted, 'Belay that order!'

He raised his telescope again and saw the reef tumbling away on either bow. There was spray and spindrift everywhere so that the sailors' bodies, the guns and the sails shone as if in a tropical downpour.

For the first time Adam heard the reef, the roar and quivering thunder as each wave crashed across it.

He saw Richie clasping his hands together as if in prayer, the spray soaking his face and hair. But he seemed to need to watch, and when he saw Adam he called brokenly, 'I was right, sir! *Right!*'

Adam nodded, barely trusting himself. 'Prepare to wear ship, Mr Martin!'

'Man the braces there, lively now!'

Men seemed to come out of their stricken postures and ran wildly to the dripping, salt-hardened cordage.

The hull pitched and buffeted, and a great backwash from the reef's undertow gripped the rudder like some underwater monster so that Partridge had to put three more men on the wheel.

The sun swept down on them, the sails releasing clouds of steam as the day's warmth began.

'Stand by to come about! Steer nor' west by north!' It was

as close as they could come up into the wind. But it was enough.

Adam stared until his mind throbbed at the two vessels that lay quietly to their anchors in water so calm that it was hard to believe what they had just gone through. One was a brig. Adam felt his mouth tighten. The other was a brigantine, her decks already alive with men as the frigate thrust through the falling spray, her masts steeply angled on her new tack.

Even before the sharp-eyed master's mate called down from his precarious perch, from which he had helplessly watched what he had thought was oncoming disaster, Adam knew it was the ship in his uncle's letter, the privateer *Tridente*.

'We will engage on both sides at once, Mr Martin. There will be no time and little room for a second chance. Double-shotted, if you please, so load and run out!'

A moment longer and then he called out loudly, 'A guinea to the first gun captain to bring down a spar!'

Martin lingered despite the bustle on every hand, the rammers tamping down the balls and the wads, racing one another as the captain had made them do.

'You never doubted it, did you, sir?'

Then he hurried away without hearing a reply, if there had been one. As the gun trucks squealed up to each open port Martin drew his hanger and glanced aft to the quarterdeck rail. He saw two things. He saw the captain fling the new cutlass over the side; and then he slapped the man Richie on the shoulder.

'As you bear!'

The gun captains were bent double behind the black breeches, each with his trigger-line pulled taut.

Like an avenger *Anemone* swept between the two vessels, neither of which had found time to up-anchor. They passed the brig at half a cable, and the brigantine *Tridente* was barely fifty yards abeam when Adam sliced down with his sword.

Trapped by the lagoon, the roar of the controlled broadside seemed to engulf them. Here and there a man fell, probably to musket fire, but the marines' response was swift and savage.

Tridente lost her foretopmast and her deck was littered with wreckage and fallen rigging.

'Stand by to come about!'

Martin forgot himself enough to grip his captain's arm as he yelled, 'Look! They've struck! The bastards have surrendered!'

But Adam did not hear him. All he could hear was cheering. His own men were cheering him for the first time.

He was suddenly drained. 'Anchor when you are ready and send away the boats.' Rear-Admiral Herrick might still be aboard the brigantine, but in his heart Adam knew he was not.

As the anchor splashed down he left the quarterdeck and walked amongst his men. Startled at what they had done, surprised that they were still alive, they nodded and grinned at him as he passed.

He found Lieutenant Dacre having his head bound with a bandage, where a splinter had narrowly missed his eye.

Adam touched his shoulder. 'You did well, Robert.' He looked around at the peering faces. 'You all did, and I'm proud of you, as England will be!'

Dacre winced as a surgeon's mate tightened the bandage.

He said, 'There was a moment . . .'

Adam grinned, feeling the elation sweeping through him like a different madness.

'There are always those, Robert, as you will one day discover!'

Rum was being brought on deck. A seaman hesitated and then handed a full mug to the man Richie.

As he watched him drinking it he asked simply, 'How was it done, mate?'

Richie smiled for the first time that he could remember.

'It's called trust,' he said.

13

Just Like Us

By late January 1810 Vice-Admiral Sir Richard Bolitho's little squadron was complete, and as far as the Admiralty was concerned no further reinforcements could be expected.

Bolitho was disappointed but hardly surprised. He had been heartened by the arrival at Cape Town of the last army transports, which had been escorted all the way from Portsmouth and the Downs by Commodore Keen's own ships. Fate had decreed that the two seventy-fours that had been the convoy's main protection had both served under Bolitho's flag in the Caribbean campaign, which had culminated in the capture of Martinique. One, the elderly *Matchless*, was commanded by the testy Irish earl, Lord Rathcullen, a difficult man at the best of times; but it had been he who had disobeyed orders and sailed in support of Bolitho's small force, which had been under attack and hopelessly out-numbered. By hoisting a rear-admiral's flag, Rathcullen had forced the enemy to believe that Herrick was also at sea with a much stronger squadron, when he had in fact remained ashore. Rathcullen's voice often twisted in Bolitho's mind, repeating what Herrick had said. *I'll not be blamed twice.* Only at Freetown, when he had dined with Herrick for the last time, had Bolitho truly known the strength of his bitterness.

The other two-decker was the *Glorious*. Keen had been wise to choose her for his flagship, Bolitho thought. Her captain, John Crowfoot, who had the appearance of a stooping village clergyman, would be easier to deal with on day-to-day matters than Rathcullen.

Keen's other escorts had returned with obvious haste to England. Perhaps their lordships had been afraid that Bolitho might overstep his authority and gather them under his flag.

Aboard the *Valkyrie*, his relations with Trevenen had not improved. When Adam arrived triumphantly with his captures, the American privateer *Tridente* as well as a useful French merchant brig which he had cut out at Lorraine Island, Trevenen had scarcely been able to contain his anger and envy.

Bolitho had sent the two prizes, along with the U.S. brig *Eaglet* to Freetown where a court would decide their eventual fate. The brig H.M.S. *Thruster*, which arrived eventually at the Cape in company with Jenour's *Orcadia*, had been sent with them. She would not be much use as a fighting escort but would serve as a daily reminder to the vessel's crews of the King's authority.

Bolitho had moved aboard *Valkyrie*, even though most flag officers would have preferred more comfortable quarters ashore with the garrison. He felt that his place was at sea, or to at least be able to up-anchor if any further news was received concerning Baratte's whereabouts. Of Herrick there had been no word at all. Did Baratte think that an attack would be launched to release him? Or was he being held as hostage for some other reason?

He looked at Yovell who was hunched over the small desk, his pen busily scraping out a fresh set of orders for the various captains. The ship was as quiet as usual, and yet he imagined he could feel a difference. A ship was said to be as good as her captain and no better. Trevenen had gone over to Keen's *Glorious*, where he would soon be joined by all the other captains.

He picked up his hat and said, 'I shall go on deck. Come across with me when they call away my boat.'

He found Avery on the quarterdeck talking quietly with Allday. The barrier was down, it seemed, and Bolitho was thankful for both their sakes.

He shaded his eyes to stare at his little array of ships, dominated by the two seventy-fours. *Valkyrie* would seem as big as themselves to their lookouts and idlers, he thought. It was strange how old ships parted and eventually joined up together again. *The family.* In his last squadron, when he had flown his flag in *Black Prince*, there had been a seventy-four named *Valkyrie*. What had happened to her, he wondered? Wrecked, blown up in some unknown fight, or paid off into rotting old age like the ship at Freetown . . . ? He glanced along the frigate's wide deck and at the men who were working at the hundred and one tasks which daily needed doing.

Some of them looked up, and he thought one was the young sailor who had smiled at him.

Loyalty went from the top downwards. It was not merely Trevenen's fault that this was an unhappy ship. *It begins with me.*

He looked towards the shore and the white-painted buildings and imagined the soldiers drilling in their constant cloud of dust.

They could not wait much longer. A regiment would eventually sail from India, while this force would approach the French islands from the south-west.

He began to pace slowly up and down, barely conscious of the heat across his shoulders.

The enemy must know of their preparations. With so many merchantmen and coastal traders coming and going it would be impossible to keep anything a secret for long. And what of the big U.S. frigate, *Unity*? Was she snug in harbour at Bourbon or Mauritius? She would certainly raise the enemy's hopes if she were.

He knew Allday had stopped talking to watch him. His concern both warmed and troubled Bolitho, and he wondered how soon it would be before Avery found out about his eye. Then what would he do? Write to Sillitoe perhaps to reveal a weakness in Bolitho he had known nothing about?

He thought of the letters he had received from Catherine. Vivid descriptions of the countryside, the preparations for Christmas, and her unexpected and personal venture into commerce with the purchase of the collier brig, *Maria José*. Poor Roxby must have been horrified at the idea, a woman's place being, in his view, very much in the home.

198

When he had first boarded Keen's flagship upon her arrival here, Bolitho had been astonished by the change in him. Still outwardly youthful, Keen had shown a new maturity, a pride in his promotion and all that it represented. When Bolitho had told him of Adam's successes and the taking of three prizes, he had felt his genuine pleasure.

'I told Lady Catherine before I left that he would do well. The scope of a whole ocean rather than clawing around Brest or Biscay is exactly what he needs!'

So far, so good, Bolitho thought. Adam would be over there right now with the others. Their first meeting since . . . since what?

Allday moved from the shadow of the hammock nettings. 'The gig's coming alongside, Sir Richard.' He still sounded disgusted that Bolitho should have to make do with the captain's gig rather than a proper barge like the one in *Black Prince*.

Avery joined him by the quarterdeck and watched Urquhart, the first lieutenant, speaking with the captain of marines while the side-party mustered by the entry port.

'I was wondering, sir. Will the prizes that were sent to Freetown cause any friction with the Americans?'

Bolitho watched him. Avery was managing to drop the use of his title on these informal occasions, and Bolitho himself felt less distanced because of it, more approachable. Allday, of course, still refused to call him anything but Sir Richard.

He considered the question. Avery had been giving it some serious thought. Few others had, apparently. Theirs had been an 'It's a knock at the Frenchies and to hell with all those who help them' attitude. Avery had weighed the possible consequences, and Bolitho was glad of his involvement.

'*Tridente* fired on and boarded a British vessel before removing Rear-Admiral Herrick as a prisoner. That is an act of war, with or without the presence of the French lieutenant who led the boarders. *Eaglet* was, or was not, about her lawful occasions, but she fired on *Anemone* and she was carrying English deserters or the like.' He smiled at the lieutenant's intent expression. 'Doubtful? It will be up to the courts to decide the rights and wrongs of it. My nephew did well, and

I will stand by his actions before the very highest authority. As for the French brig, she will raise a few guineas in prize money or she may become an addition to the fleet.' He clapped his arm. 'I do not think our countries will go to war over it.' He paused. 'Not yet, in any case.'

They walked down to the entry port and Bolitho saw Yovell, complete with his weighty satchel of papers, already in the swaying boat.

He glanced at Urquhart. He was a good lieutenant, or could be. Bolitho hesitated and made certain that the captain of marines was out of earshot.

'A word, Mr Urquhart.' He saw him stiffen and stare at a point above his admiral's shoulder. 'I understand that you have made it known that you would be prepared to act as prize-master in any future successes?'

Urquhart swallowed hard. 'I – I did not speak with the captain, Sir Richard, I . . .'

Bolitho studied him. Young, experienced; it would be a waste as well as a loss to the fleet.

'I hear far more than people give me credit for.' He eyed him impassively. 'It would mean the end of your hopes. To throw away a position on this proud new vessel would be seen as something more, I think.' He recalled Avery's bitterness at their first meeting. 'You are a lieutenant, Mr Urquhart, and a lieutenant you would remain. You could be inviting oblivion.'

'It is only that . . .'

'*I do not wish to hear*, Mr Urquhart. You are committed: I am not. Whatever you may disagree with or find disagreeable, you must consider your part in it, *in this ship*. D'you understand what I am saying, man?'

'I think so, Sir Richard.' His eyes moved to meet Bolitho's. 'I will take the matter no further.'

Bolitho nodded. 'There is the brig *Orcadia* out yonder. She is commanded by a man who was once a lieutenant, and then a prize-master, but there was a difference. I ordered it, and now he holds a command. As a matter of fact, I got my first command after being given a prize to navigate. But remember: *it is so ordered*. You do not choose as you please.' He watched his uncertainty and wondered how Allday had discovered the lieutenant's secret.

Bolitho stepped away, and immediately the Royal Marines and side-party sprang into action.

Allday knew what had just happened. Equally, he knew that the flag lieutenant did not. He followed Avery down into the gig and squeezed against the plump secretary. He did not even glance at the stiff-backed, wooden-faced crew. Allday was thankful he did not have to serve under someone like Trevenen. The first lieutenant had looked stunned by Bolitho's words: not advice this time, but a warning. He was a fool if he ignored it, Allday thought. But then, most lieutenants were.

He watched like a hawk as Bolitho descended into the gig, and almost raised one hand to his aid.

Avery saw it. He had noticed it before. He saw Yovell watching him, his eyes glinting behind his spectacles. He shared this unknown secret too, as did the uncommunicative servant, Ozzard.

'Bear off forrard! Out oars, give way all!'

Allday watched the lieutenant in charge of the boat, here out of necessity because there was a senior officer aboard, and as nervous as a cat because of it.

Bolitho shaded his eyes again to watch the *Anemone* as the boat pulled swiftly abeam. There were men on cradles over the tumblehome busy with paint and brushes where the *Tridente*'s marksmen had fired on Adam's ship until *Anemone*'s measured broadside had completely disabled her. She had left here towed by the captured *Eaglet*. Nobody could criticise Adam for risking an unsupported attack through a barely-known reef. There had been no other ship available. Bolitho smiled grimly. Had things gone against him, however, Adam more than anyone must have known what it would have cost him.

He studied the other vessels of his small command, the scarlet coats already assembled on *Glorious*'s deck to receive him.

Not a fleet, but properly and aggressively used it might be enough. When *Thruster* returned and Tyacke arrived from his patrol, if he was free from other orders, they would be ready.

Allday murmured, 'Fine-looking ship, Sir Richard.' He

201

sounded wistful. Remembering how they had first met, Bolitho guessed, aboard the *Phalarope*. At first commanded by a tyrant like Trevenen, she had become a legend. Herrick had played a large part in it. The thought saddened him.

'Stand by, bowman!'

Bolitho was grateful for the ship's shadow as it towered above him. It was strange how he had never got used to this part of it. As a junior captain and now as a vice-admiral, he was always troubled by what those who now stood motionless in the sunlight might see in him, might find wanting. As ever, he had to insist to himself that they would be far more uncertain than he was.

Avery watched Bolitho clamber lightly up the seventy-four's weathered side. He asked quietly so that only Yovell should hear, 'In all the years, has Sir Richard changed much?'

Yovell picked up his satchel. 'In a few ways, sir.' He looked at him curiously. 'But mostly, he changed all of us!'

Allday grinned. 'I think you are wanted on deck, sir!'

He watched the lieutenant almost fall as he hurried to catch up with his superior.

Yovell said, 'I'm not too sure about him, John.'

'An' I'm not too certain about *you*, matey!'

They chuckled like conspirators and the lieutenant in charge of the gig stared after them without understanding what he saw.

His Britannic Majesty's brig *Larne* of fourteen guns pitched and swayed in a steep swell, her slack sails and clattering rigging clear evidence of her becalmed state.

A few figures moved about her deck, some staggering like drunks as the sturdy hull dipped and slithered into yet another trough. Somewhere to larboard but visible only occasionally to the masthead lookout was the African mainland, Molembo, where many a slaver had been run to ground by vessels like *Larne*.

Most countries had outlawed slavery and the traffic that had cost so many lives, but it still went on where the price was right.

In the brig's cabin Commander James Tyacke tried to

concentrate on his chart, and was cursing the perverse wind that had failed him after such a speedy departure from Freetown after the receipt of Sir Richard Bolitho's orders. It would be good to see him again. Tyacke was still surprised that he could think so when he had always had very little respect for senior officers. Bolitho had changed all that when the Good Hope campaign had been mounting. He had even endured the crowded discomfort of the little schooner *Miranda*, which Tyacke had then commanded, and when she had been destroyed by an enemy frigate Bolitho had given him the *Larne*.

The seclusion and the independence of the anti-slavery patrols had suited Tyacke very well. Most of his company were prime seamen who shared his need to get away from the greater authority of the fleet. Few sailors cared much about the slave-trade; it was something that happened, or had done until the new laws were approved. But to be free from a flag officer's demands, with the prospect of prize money, was to every man's taste.

Tyacke leaned back and frowned as he listened to his little ship rolling and groaning in the arms of the South Atlantic. He often thought of how he had searched for Bolitho and his lady after *Golden Plover*'s loss on the hundred-mile reef. His disbelief had changed to prayer, which was rare for him, when he had confirmed who had survived in that sun-blistered longboat.

He thought of the gown he had kept in a chest in this cabin, the one he had bought in Lisbon for the girl who had promised to be his wife. He had given it to Lady Somervell to cover herself from the sailors' stares. Later, after Keen's marriage, which Tyacke had sat in deep shadow to watch, she had returned it to him, beautifully cleaned and packed in a lined box.

She had written in a little note, 'For you, James Tyacke, and for a girl who shall deserve it.'

Tyacke stood up and steadied himself against the motion by gripping a deckhead beam. The cabin was very small, like that of a miniature frigate, but after a schooner it had seemed like a palace.

He made himself look at his reflection in the hanging mirror. A face which could have been handsome, caring and strong until that day at the Battle of the Nile, as it was now called. The left side of his face was unmarked; the other side was not human. How the eye had survived was a miracle: it seemed to glare out above the melted flesh like an angry, defiant light. Everyone around that gun had died, and Tyacke could remember nothing about it.

For a girl who shall deserve it.

Tyacke turned away, the old bitterness returning. What woman could be expected to live with that? To wake up and see that terrible, mutilated face beside her?

He listened to the sea. Here was the only escape. Where he had won the respect of his men and of the man he was sailing to meet.

He shook himself and decided to go on deck. Most of his men could look at him now without showing pity or horror. He was lucky in that, he thought. He had three lieutenants and more experienced hands than most frigates. *Larne* even carried a dedicated surgeon, one who used his interest in tropical medicine and the various fevers that plagued these coasts to compile a mass of notes that might one day take him to the College of Surgeons in London.

The sea air was abrasive, like hot sand off a desert. He squinted in the hard glare and glanced at the watch around him: men he had come to know better and more intimately than he would have believed possible. Ozanne, the first lieutenant, a Channel Islander who had once been a merchant sailor. He had come up the hard way and was five years older than his commander. Pitcairn, the sailing master, was another veteran who shunned the ways and the manners of a big man-of-war although his skills would have taken him anywhere. Livett, the surgeon, was sketching by one of the swivel guns. He had a youthful appearance until he removed his hat, when his head was like a brown egg.

Tyacke walked to the taffrail and peered astern. The vessel was lifting and dropping into every trough, inert, making no way at all.

Tyacke knew he should accept it, but he had an impatient

204

nature and hated to feel his command failing to respond to sail or rudder.

The sailing master judged his mood before saying, 'Can't hold, sir. Visibility's so bad to the east'rd I think there may be a storm blowing up.'

Tyacke took a telescope and wedged his buttocks against the compass box. Pitcairn was not very often wrong. The glass swept over the writhing sea-mist to where the land should lie.

Ozanne said, 'Rain too, I shouldn't wonder, sir.'

Tyacke grunted. 'We could do with it. The timbers are like kindling.'

The glass moved on, over the swells and troughs and across a group of drifting gulls. They seemed held together, like a pale wreath cast down by someone as a memorial.

Ozanne watched him and his emotions. A handsome man who would turn any lass's head, he thought. Once. There had been times when it had been hard for Ozanne to accept the horrible disfigurement and find the man beneath. The one the Arab slavers feared most of all. *The devil with half a face.* A fine seaman, and a just one to his small company. The two did not always make good bedfellows in the King's navy.

Tyacke felt the sweat running down his face and wiped the skin with his fingers, hating what he felt. Who was it who had told him that it could have been worse?

'I don't see that at all.' With a start he realised he had spoken aloud, but managed to grin as Ozanne asked, 'Sir?'

Tyacke was about to return the glass to its rack when something made him stiffen. As if he had heard something, or some awful memory had sent a shiver up his spine.

The deck quivered slightly, and when he looked up he saw the trailing masthead pendant flick out like a whip. Loose gear rattled and groaned, and the watch on deck seemed to come alive again from their sun-dulled torpor.

'Stand to, hands to the braces!'

The brig swung slightly and the two helmsmen who had been standing motionless, their arms resting on the wheel, gripped the spokes as the rudder gave in to a sudden pressure.

Tyacke looked at the sailing master. 'You were right about

205

a storm, Mr Pitcairn! Well, we're ready for any help we can get!'

He realised that none of them had moved, and cursed suddenly as he heard again the sound he had taken for thunder. His hearing had never been the same since the explosion.

Ozanne said, 'Gunfire!'

The deck tilted more steeply and the big forecourse filled iron-hard with a mind of its own.

'Turn up the watch below! I want all the sail she can carry! Bring her back on course, Mr Manley!'

Tyacke watched the sudden rush of men as the call shrilled between decks. The topmen were already clambering out along the upper yards, and others were loosening halliards and braces ready for the next order. A few found time to stare aft at their formidable captain, questioning, uncertain, but trusting him completely.

Ozanne said, 'A fair size by the sound of it, sir.' He did not even flinch as *Larne* was sheeted home on the starboard tack.

The helmsman yelled, 'South by east, sir! Steady she goes!'

Tyacke rubbed his chin but did not see the others exchange glances. He did not even realise that it was something he always did in the face of danger.

Too heavy for another anti-slavery vessel: Ozanne was right about that. He saw the spray burst over the beakhead and soak the seamen there. In the angry glare it looked almost gold.

Two frigates then? He glanced at each sail in turn. *Larne* was beginning to lean forward into every line of troughs, the sea pattering inboard and swilling into the scuppers. One of their own then, perhaps outgunned or outnumbered?

He snapped, 'Clear for action as the mood takes you, Mr Ozanne.' He looked around and beckoned to a seaman. 'Cabin, Thomas – fetch my sword and lively so!'

As suddenly as the returning wind it began to rain, a downpour which advanced across the water so heavily and thickly that it was like being hemmed in by a giant fence. As it reached the ship the men were held breathless and gasping where they stood, some using it to wash themselves, others just standing amidst the onslaught and spluttering with pleasure. There were

206

more heavy crashes through the rain. The same sound, as if only the one vessel was firing.

Then there was one great explosion which seemed to go on for minutes. Tyacke could even feel it against the *Larne*'s hull like something out of the deep.

Then the distant gunfire ceased and only the sound of the deluge continued. The rain was moving away, and the sun came through as if it had been in hiding. Sails, decks and taut rigging were steaming, and seamen looked for one another as if after a battle.

But the wind was holding, laying bare the distant coastline and the movement of the current.

The lookout yelled, 'Deck there! Sail to the south-east! Hull down!'

As the wind continued to drive away the mist Tyacke realised that much of it was smoke. The other ship or ships were already far away if only the lookout could see them. The assassins.

Some of his men were standing away from their guns or caught in their various attitudes of working ship and trimming the sails. They were staring at something.

It could have been a reef, except that out here there were none. It might have been some old and forgotten hulk left to the mercy of the ocean. But it was not. It was the capsized hull of a vessel about the size of this one, his *Larne*. There were huge obscene bubbles exploding from the opposite side, probably from that one great explosion. In a moment she would be gone.

Tyacke said harshly, 'Heave-to, Mr Ozanne! Bosun, clear away the boats!'

Men ran to the tackles and braces as *Larne* wallowed heavily into the wind, her sails all in confusion.

Tyacke had never seen the boats get away so quickly. The experience gained at boarding suspected slavers was proving itself. Not that these men, his men, would need any incentive.

Tyacke levelled his telescope and stared at the pathetic little figures struggling to pull themselves to safety, others limp and trapped in the trailing weed of rigging alongside.

Not strangers this time. It was like looking at themselves.

207

An officer dressed in the same uniform as Ozanne and the others, seamen in checkered shirts like some of those beside him. There was blood in the water too, clinging to the up-ended bilge as if the vessel herself were being bled to death.

The boats were hurling themselves across the water, and Tyacke saw the third lieutenant, Robyns, pointing to something for his coxswain to identify.

Without looking Tyacke knew the surgeon and his mate were already down on deck to help the first survivors. There could not be many of them.

More big bubbles were bursting and Tyacke had to look away as a figure obviously blinded by the explosion appeared, arms outstretched, his mouth opened in unheard cries.

Tyacke clenched his fists. *It could be me.*

He looked away and saw a young seaman crossing himself, another sobbing quietly, heedless of his companions.

Ozanne lowered his telescope. 'She's going, sir. I just saw her name. She's the *Thruster*.' He seemed to stare around with disbelief. 'Just like us!'

Tyacke turned again to watch the boats standing as near as they dared, oars and lines flung out for anyone who could swim.

The brig began to dip under the sea, a few figures still trying to get away even as she took her last dive.

For a long time, or so it seemed, the boats pitched and rolled in the whirlpool that remained until corpses, rigging, and burned sailcloth were sucked down.

Tyacke said, 'One of Sir Richard's ships, Paul.' He thought of the lieutenant's outrage. *Just like us.* And the blinded man who cried for help when there was none.

Pitcairn the master asked huskily, 'What does it mean?'

Tyacke walked away to greet the few who had been plucked from death. But he paused with one foot on the ladder, his terrible scars laid bare in the sunshine.

'It *means* war, my friends. Without mercy and without quarter until it is finally settled.'

Someone cried out in agony and Tyacke turned away.

Nobody spoke. Perhaps they had all watched themselves die.

208

14

Catherine

Sir Paul Sillitoe sat at a small table by one of his bedroom windows, and frowned as another gust of wind made the rain dash against the glass like hail. Breakfast, a frugal but leisurely affair, was mainly a time for him to prepare himself for the day. Newsheets and papers were arranged in their special order by his valet Guthrie, who then left his master to prop them one by one on a little wooden stand which had once been used for music.

He glanced at the river Thames that curved directly past the house, which was built on this elegant part of Chiswick Reach. It was higher, and might well flood before the day was out.

He returned his attention to a page on foreign affairs, the small paragraph about the proposed military campaigns in the Indian Ocean. They could not wait another year to begin. Napoleon might still hold his defences so that Wellington would have to withstand another year of conflict. It would not do at all. He reached for a biscuit which Guthrie had already spread with treacle, a childish fancy of his.

Then there was the Prince of Wales. Eager to rule in his father's place, but still in need of assurances from those in power who might see the King's insanity more as a protection than a threat to themselves.

Sillitoe wiped his fingers and poured some fresh coffee. This was the best part of the day. Alone, able to think and plan.

He looked up from the paper with irritation as he heard carriage wheels in his drive. Nobody who knew him well would dare to interrupt this sacred hour. He rang a small bell and instantly one of his burly footmen appeared in the doorway.

'Send him away, whoever it is!'

The man nodded and strode from the room.

Sillitoe resumed reading, and wondered briefly how Richard Bolitho was dealing with the military. How could any man give his very life to the sea? Like poor Collingwood, who had been employed on the demanding Mediterranean station without a break since 1803. Why did the King dislike him enough to deny him the chance to come home? He had even prevented Collingwood's promotion to full admiral, although he was ten years older than his friend and commander, Horatio Nelson. It was said that he was dying. No reward for all those years.

The footman reappeared.

Sillitoe said abruptly, 'I did not hear the carriage leave!' It sounded like an accusation.

The man watched him impassively, used to his master's tongue, which could be merciless if the occasion suited.

The footman cleared his throat. 'It is a lady, Sir Paul. She insists that you will see her.'

Sillitoe pushed the papers away. The morning was spoiled. 'Does she indeed? We shall see about that!'

'It is Lady Somervell, Sir Paul.' It was the first time he had seen his master completely taken aback.

Sillitoe held out his arms as his valet hurried forward with his coat, his mind still grappling with the news. 'Show her to a room with a good fire. My respects to her ladyship, and tell her I shall be down without delay.'

It made no sense. She had never given him the slightest encouragement, something which had aroused him more than ever. It must be trouble of some kind. It was nothing to do with Bolitho, he was sure of that: someone would have suffered for it if he had not been informed first.

He glanced at himself in a mirror and tried to be calm. She was here. She wanted to see him. Needed to see him. He watched himself smile. A delusion.

She was sitting near a newly-lighted fire in one of the rooms that adjoined Sillitoe's considerable library.

In seconds Sillitoe took it all in. She wore a long green cloak, a fur-lined hood thrown back on her shoulders, her piled hair shining in the firelight as she held out one hand to the flames.

'My dear Lady Catherine!' He took her hand and held it to his lips. It was like ice. 'I thought you to be in Cornwall, but you honour me greatly by calling.'

She faced him, her dark eyes seeking something. 'I came to London. For some things from my Chelsea house.'

Sillitoe waited. He had often thought of her in that house. It was just around the next great bend in the river towards Westminster and Southwark.

It might have been ten thousand miles. Until now.

'Is something wrong?' He turned to hide a frown as a maid-servant pattered into the room with fresh coffee, which she placed beside the woman in green.

'You once said I could come to you if I needed help.'

He waited, almost holding his breath. 'My lady, I would be honoured.'

'You see, there was a letter for me in Chelsea. Nobody had thought to send it on. It was a week old, probably too late.' She looked at him very directly. 'I have to go to Whitechapel . . . I had no one else to ask.'

He nodded gravely. A secret then. 'That is hardly the place for a lady to wander unescorted, not in these hard times. Must you go?' All the time his mind was reaching out in every direction. Parts of Whitechapel were very respectable. The rest did not bear thinking about.

'When do you wish to go?' He expected a protest as he added, 'I shall come with you, of course . . .'

He glared at the door as a small, round-faced man in spectacles, his arms loaded with papers in long canvas envelopes, peered in at them.

'Not *now*, Marlow. I am going out!'

His secretary began to protest and remind Sillitoe about his appointments. He might as well have said nothing.

He said, 'Tell Guthrie to get two good men.' He looked at the secretary calmly. 'He will know what I mean.'

211

When they were alone again, he said, 'We may leave at any time you wish.' His eyes moved over her, missing nothing.

Guthrie was well-trained, and had summoned two of Sillitoe's men who wore the same gilt-buttoned livery. They looked more like prize-fighters than footmen. They both stared at the tall woman with the dark hair and high cheekbones. They might even have guessed who she was.

A plain carriage came around from the mews and Sillitoe said, 'Less noticeable than yours, I think.'

Young Matthew, who was standing by the Bolitho carriage, looked apprehensive. 'Will you be all right, m'lady?' His strong Cornish accent sounded so alien here.

'I will.' She walked to the horses and patted them. 'This will be between us, Matthew. Yes?'

He removed his hat and fumbled with it. 'To th' grave if so ordered, m'lady!'

He was so serious that she almost smiled. What had she begun? Where might it end?

She heard a savage panting and saw one of the men pushing a broad-shouldered mastiff up onto the box with the coachman.

He said, 'Don't you jump too much, Ben, 'e'll 'ave your leg off else!'

She handed the address on a card to the coachman and saw his eyebrows rise slightly.

Sillitoe said, 'Come, my dear, before the rain gets heavier.' He glanced over his shoulder to the other carriage with the crest on its door. 'Wait at Chelsea, ah, Matthew. I shall ensure her ladyship's safety until then.'

She leaned back against the damp leather cushions and pretended to watch the scenery as the carriage moved briskly along the river road. She was very conscious of his nearness and of his obvious determination not to provoke her.

Sillitoe spoke only occasionally, usually questions about her life at Falmouth. He mentioned the collier brig *Maria José* which was now being refitted, but he never disclosed his sources of information.

Only once did he touch on Bolitho, when he had mentioned his nephew George Avery.

'I think he must be doing well as Sir Richard's flag lieutenant. He has a way with people, lame ducks most of all.'

She turned and looked at him, her eyes in shadow as the
carriage rolled past a line of bedraggled trees. 'How long will
it be before . . . ?'

'Before Sir Richard comes home?' He seemed to consider
it. 'You must know the ways and the prevarications of Admiralty, my dear. It will be a difficult campaign, and now of course
the Americans seem intent on interfering. It is very hard to
say at this stage.'

'I need him so . . .' She did not go on.

As the carriage swayed through rain-filled ruts and over
fallen branches, Sillitoe could feel the pressure of her body
against his own. What would she do, right at this moment
when for some reason she needed his aid, if he took her in his
arms and forced her into submission? Who would she turn to?
Who would believe her? Perhaps only Bolitho, and he might
not come home for years. And when he did, would she tell
him? He wiped his forehead with his hand. He felt as if he
had a fever.

The coachman called down, 'Not far now, Sir Paul.'

He glanced at her, one hand clinging to the strap as the
wheel grated onto cobbles and small houses appeared on either
side. A few shapeless figures huddled over against the rain, a
carrier's cart or two, and to his surprise a smart carriage with
grooms who looked very much like his own.

She said almost to herself, 'I can scarcely remember it. It
was so long ago.'

Sillitoe dragged his mind from the carriage. A brothel perhaps, where respectable but none-too-rich clients could lose
themselves. He thought of his own, safe house. Money could
buy you anything and anyone.

He tried to keep his mind clear. Why was she here in this
awful place?

She dragged at the window. 'There it is!' She was agitated,
distressed.

The carriage rolled to a halt and the driver called, 'Can't
get through there, Sir Paul! Too narrer!'

She climbed down and heard the savage-looking mastiff give

a warning snarl. Sillitoe followed her, and read a decaying sign which said *Quaker's Passage*. Despite her own uncertainty she seemed to sense his confusion and turned towards him, heedless of the rain that ran from her hair and on to her cloak.

'It was not always like this!' It was as if she were speaking to the whole street. 'There were children here.' She gripped an iron railing. 'We played here!'

Sillitoe licked his lips. 'What number do we seek?'

'Three.' Only a word, but it was torn from her.

Sillitoe said, 'Jakes, stay with the coach and driver.' Then to the one with the dog, 'You keep with us.' He put one hand into his coat and felt the pistol. *I must be mad to be here.*

The door of the house was ajar and there was rubbish strewn about the path. Even before they reached it someone screamed, 'It's them bailiffs again! The bloody bastards!'

Sillitoe stood with one hand on the door. 'Hold your noise, woman!'

The man with the dog showed himself, his face eager and intent, ready to set his charge on to anyone who challenged him.

When Catherine spoke her voice was quite calm and steady.

'I've come to see Mr Edmund Brooke.' She hesitated as the woman peered at her more closely. She gestured with one hand like a claw. 'Upstairs.'

Catherine held a rickety rail and climbed slowly to the next floor. The place stank of decay and dirt, and a despair which was like something physical.

She rapped on a door but it swung open, the lock apparently missing. A woman who had been sitting on a chair, her face in her hands, looked up sharply with hostile eyes as she exclaimed, 'What the hell d'you want?'

Catherine looked at her for several seconds. 'It's me, Chrissie. Kate. Remember me?'

Sillitoe was shocked as the other woman threw her arms around Catherine and embraced her. Once she must have been pretty, he thought, even beautiful. But the beauty had all gone, and she could have been almost any age. He wanted to pull out his handkerchief, then plunged his hand into his coat as he saw a man watching him from the bed.

Catherine moved to the bed and stared at the face, but the eyes did not move.

The other woman said thickly, 'He died two days ago. I did what I could.'

Sillitoe said in a fierce whisper, 'Who was he? Was he trying to get money from you?' The stench was vile and he wanted to run from this place. But her complete composure defeated even that.

She looked at the dead, stubbled face, the eyes which were still fired with anger as she had seen them so often.

She seemed to hear Sillitoe's question and answered, 'He was my father.'

'I'll have things done.' He did not know what to say. 'My men will take care of the arrangements.'

'I am sure of that.' She was still looking at the bed when her foot scraped against some empty bottles beneath it.

She wanted to scream at him, curse him. It was too late now even for that. Then she turned and said quietly to Sillitoe, 'Do you have any money?'

'Of course.' He pulled out a purse and gave it to her, glad to be doing something.

She did not hesitate but took a handful of gold coins from the purse and pressed them into the other woman's hands.

The woman stared at her and then screamed, 'One whore to another, eh?' Then she flung the gold at the wall.

Sillitoe guided her to the door and heard the woman's voice break into sobs behind them, and the sound of her scrabbling about the floor to recover the money. Outside he spoke rapidly to one of his men, who was nodding abruptly in agreement with his instructions.

Catherine stared up at the house, the rain running down her throat and soaking through her clothing.

Sillitoe took her elbow and guided her away along the narrow passage. It had been terrible. It must be far worse for her. But how could it be true? He looked at her piercingly in the grey light and saw her still staring back at the little houses.

In turn she was asking herself why she had come. Duty, curiosity? It was certainly not pity.

215

She paused with one foot on the carriage step and said, 'Thank you for coming with me, Sir Paul.'

He slumped down beside her. 'I – I don't understand.'

She watched the street moving away, as it had always done for so many years.

'He killed my child,' she said.

The carriage wheels scraped over the cobbles, and through the rain-soaked windows everything was blurred and unreal.

Sillitoe could feel her tension, but knew if he even laid a hand on her arm she would turn against him. To break the silence he murmured, 'My men will deal with everything. You must not be involved.'

It was as if he had not spoken. She said, 'It was all so long ago. There are times when I can hardly believe it, and others when I see it like yesterday.' She was holding the strap against the uneven motion, her eyes on the street but seeing nothing.

They passed a rough piece of open ground and as though in a dream she saw some children gathering up broken branches for kindling. It had often been like that for her. But there had been laughter too until her mother had fallen sick and died, in that same sordid room.

She heard Sillitoe ask, 'What was his work, his profession?' *Why should I talk about it?* But she answered him. 'He was an actor, a performer. He could do most things.'

Sillitoe thought she sounded as if she were speaking of somebody else. It was hard to imagine that angry, lifeless face as anything but snarling in death.

'I met a young man.' She did not see Sillitoe either. She was thinking of Zenoria and Adam. 'I was fifteen.' She gave what might have been a shrug, the most despairing thing he had seen her do. 'It happened. I was with child.'

'And you told your father, were compelled to, with your mother gone?'

She said, 'Yes. I told him.'

'Perhaps he was too upset to know what he was doing.'

She leaned her head against the cushion and said, 'He was drunk, and he knew *exactly* what he was doing.' *You do not owe this man explanation. Only one, and he is on the other side of the world.* 'He hit me and knocked me down those stairs you saw today. I lost my baby . . .'

Then he did grip her wrist. 'Perhaps it was . . .'

'All for the best? Yes, there were several who said as much, including my young man.' She touched her eyes with her fingers. 'It is not that. I nearly died. I think I wanted to . . . then.' She looked at him, and even in the carriage's gloomy interior he could feel the intensity of her stare. 'I cannot ever bear a child, not even for the man I love above everything.'

Disconcerted, he said, 'When we reach Chiswick I shall have a meal prepared for you.'

She laughed without making a sound. 'You will please leave me at Chelsea. I would not wish to compromise you, nor do I desire to create more scandal. You do not ask me why I was so certain about my father's anger and his true motives.' She could feel the strong grip on her wrist, but the contact did not seem to matter. She continued, 'That man, my own father, wanted to take me to his bed. He tried several times. Perhaps I was too distressed to deal with it properly. Today, I would kill any such man.'

She watched the passing houses, more expensive properties now, with the glint of water beyond. Ships, unloading or waiting to make sail to every quarter of the globe. Richard's world, which they shared even when they were parted.

Sillitoe asked quietly, 'That woman we found there?'

'Chrissie? She was a friend. We used to mime to my father's reading in the market when things were bad, before he finally gave in to drink. She was faithful to him when I left home.' She turned away, her eyes filled with angry tears. '*Home.* Was it ever really that?' She contained her emotion and said, 'You saw her reward. He put her on the streets.'

They did not converse again for some while, and then she said, 'You always speak so highly of Richard, and yet in my heart I know you would use him to make me surrender to your desires, which are unworthy of you. Do you really believe I would betray the man I love, and risk losing him for that same reason?'

217

Sillitoe exclaimed, 'You do me an injustice, Lady Catherine!'

'Do I? I would not answer for your safety if you wronged me.'

Some of his confidence seemed to return as he retorted, 'I am well enough protected!'

She released her wrist very carefully. 'From yourself? I think not.'

Sillitoe felt entirely confused by her calm frankness. It was as if he had been disarmed in a duel, and was having to fall upon his opponent's mercy.

She was speaking again, her eyes on the streaming window as if she were trying to recognise something.

'I have done things in my life which I would tell nobody. I have known warmth and friendship too, and I have learned many things since I danced and mimed on the streets of this great city. But love? I have shared it with only one man. You know him well enough.' She shook her head as if she were refuting something. 'We lost one another once. We will not do so again.' She laid her hand on his sleeve. 'Strangely enough, I feel better for telling you these things. You could leave me in Chelsea and share your discoveries with your friends, if you have any. But nobody can hurt me any more. I am beyond it, even though they call me a whore.'

She gripped his arm and spoke very slowly. 'But do not harm Richard. I beg only that from you.'

She saw the river again, the bare trees like scarecrows in the fading light.

'Chelsea, Sir Paul!' The coachman sounded untroubled, perhaps because the mastiff had stayed with Sillitoe's two prize-fighters.

Then she saw Young Matthew peering out at the coach from the doorway of the basement kitchen, his coat black with rain. How long he had been waiting for her safe return she could only guess. She found that she was crying, something she rarely did. Perhaps because his simple loyalty was the cleanest thing she had seen since their return to London.

'You all right, me lady?' That was Sophie, holding the door wide to reveal the bright lights within.

As if from faraway she heard Sillitoe speak her name as he lowered the carriage step for her. She had not even seen him leave her side.

He gazed at her for what seemed a long time. Then he shrugged elegantly, and, stooping, kissed her hand.

He said suddenly, 'I shall never feel differently about you. Do not humiliate me by denying me that at least.' He did not release her hand. 'I will always be at your service if you need me.' He turned to climb into the carriage and hesitated. 'I will do what I can. You have my word on it.' He was looking at her as if he was seeing her for the last time. 'I will get your man back for you.' Then he was gone, the carriage turning the corner, the horses already aware perhaps of the nearness of home.

She felt Sophie's arm about her waist, hugging her. They stood together in the rain, which had not stopped since she had left here for Chiswick.

She was still holding on to Sillitoe's last words, almost afraid to believe what she had heard.

Then she said, 'Let us go inside.' She wiped her eyes, and Sophie did not know if it was because of rain or tears.

Catherine said, 'Tomorrow we will leave for Falmouth.' Together they climbed the steps, then she turned and looked back into the deepening shadows. 'There is no place here for me any more.'

But stark and clear in her mind she could see the little street and the two young girls at play there.

15

A Feeling

Lieutenant George Avery walked away past the sentry and into the cabin, grateful for the cooler air between decks although he knew that it was little more than an illusion.

'You wanted me, sir?' He glanced round and tried to adjust his eyes to the searing brightness of the sea astern, and another bright shaft of sun that shone down from a skylight. Yovell was sitting on the bench below the stern windows, using some of his papers to fan his streaming face. Bolitho stood by the table, as if he had not moved since their last meeting.

When he looked up, Avery could see the dark shadows around his eyes, the lines of strain by his mouth. It troubled Avery to see him like this. And there had been weeks of it, the endless search of an apparently empty ocean. He could still feel it throughout the ship as it had been felt in the rest of the little squadron when Tyacke's brig *Larne* had arrived in Cape Town with the handful of dazed and wounded survivors whom his boats had managed to snatch from death. None of the *Thruster*'s officers had lived, and of the rest only a surgeon's mate had been articulate enough to offer some description of the disaster. Two frigates, one obviously the big American *Unity*, had fallen on the brig and her convoy of prizes. The surgeon's mate had been below in his sickbay and had been spared the first horrific broadside. Fired at extreme range, the weight of iron had smashed the brig almost onto her beam-ends. Masts, spars, rigging and canvas had thundered on

220

to the crouching gun crews, trapping them amidst the wreckage before they could return a shot.

As the surgeon's mate had said, his voice broken with emotion, 'We could do nothing. The people were dying. What could we have done?' He had rallied for only a moment. 'But our captain refused to surrender. I never saw him after the next broadside. There was an explosion, a magazine I think, and then I was in the water. After that, the boats came. I never really believed in God . . . until then.'

Bolitho said, 'No more ships reported attacked or seized. They know every move we make. I've spoken with the man Richie but he had nothing to offer. Where is Baratte? How much does he know of our plans to invade?' He imagined their extended forces as though on a chart, as he had been doing for weeks. 'Major-General Abercromby and his army will be sailing from India. Our Major-General Drummond will complete the pincers and sail from Good Hope to Rodriguez, where we will re-form if necessary, and then on to Ile de France.' He stared at the chart until his eye stung like fire. 'Then Mauritius. The end of French power across our trade routes.'

Avery said, 'We know Baratte's one weakness, sir.'

Bolitho looked at him, remembering. On the day that *Thruster* had been totally destroyed, the enemy had also fired on the privateer *Tridente* until she had shared *Thruster*'s fate. It could only mean that Baratte did not yet have full facilities for docking or careening any of his vessels. To do so in Mauritius would be inviting an attack, even a cutting-out expedition. He would not risk that. Secrecy and timing were everything. For both sides. They were grasping at straws, and all the while with each turn of the glass the two armies would be completing their preparations for attack.

Avery asked warily, 'How much are the Americans involved, sir?'

'I believe, very much.' He glanced round as Allday, carrying his usual cloth, moved silently across the cabin to begin his daily ritual of polishing the old sword.

As he reached up for it Bolitho saw him stiffen, his arms in mid-air while the old pain lanced through him. It was never far away. He stooped slightly now, which he had never done before that terrible day when he had received a Spanish sword blade in his chest. It would have killed anyone but Allday. Bolitho saw him move his arms more slowly until the sword was safely in his grasp; he would know that he had seen it, just as he always knew when Bolitho was half-blinded by some harsh light. They both knew, and each pretended not to show it.

How long was it now? It had happened during the false Peace of Amiens: difficult to believe it had been all of eight years ago. The two deadly enemies resting briefly to lick their wounds and prepare for their next conflict. It was a wonder they had both survived. Too many familiar faces had not. How much would *Unity* be prepared to interfere to 'defend' American shipping and the rights of her sailors on the high seas? As Adam had commented, she would make a formidable adversary if used against his small mixed squadron.

Bolitho snatched a magnifying glass, and in his mind saw Tyacke's strong profile as he had described these waters he had come to know so well. 'My compliments to the captain. Ask him to step aft.' His voice was quite even, casual. Only the fact that Allday's polishing cloth had suddenly stilled showed that he recognised what was happening.

On the tilting quarterdeck, Captain Trevenen paused in his heavy pacing and regarded the flag lieutenant suspiciously.

Avery was careful not to rouse his temper. 'Sir Richard wishes to discuss a matter with you, sir.'

'Another whim to act upon, is it? My ship is getting short of water, of everything. All we do is waste time!'

Avery knew that the men on watch could hear every word, just as he understood what would happen if he drew Trevenen's attention to the fact.

Trevenen strode past the first lieutenant and barked, 'Keep an eye on these idlers, Mr Urquhart! There'll be extra work for every laggard if I catch them!'

As they passed Avery saw the other lieutenant's mouth form a silent curse. Their eyes met and Avery smiled. Urquhart was human after all.

In the cabin again Trevenen's head seemed to brush the deckhead as he strode to the table.

He sounded incredulous, as if it had been an insult even to ask him. 'What? This place?'

Bolitho watched him, his face like a mask. What was the matter with Trevenen, the real reason for his foul temper?

'This place, Captain. It is called San Antonio.'

Trevenen seemed vaguely relieved. 'It's nothing, sir. A wretched pile of rock in the middle of the ocean!' He sounded contemptuous, or as close to it as he dared.

'You met Commander James Tyacke, I believe?'

'I've *seen* him.'

Bolitho nodded slowly. 'You are quite correct. One does not necessarily mean the other. And to know that fine officer is something even rarer and more valued because of it.'

Bolitho looked at the chart again if only to hide his anger.

'James Tyacke is a very experienced navigator and knows these waters well. He once mentioned San Antonio to me. A bleak place, uninhabited except for a small monastery and occasionally a fishing community, when the season is right. A rare order of monks, I understand, with a code of poverty and devotion. What better place to observe our shipping movements? Hardly *nothing*, I'd have thought!'

He looked at Allday's homely face, the sudden pain in his eyes as he remembered that day at San Felipe. Another island, another ocean; and they had been ordered to hand back the place to the French because of the Peace of Amiens.

He saw Allday nod very slowly. There had been a mission there too, and Allday had all but paid with his life.

He swung aft towards Yovell and said, 'Prepare to copy out some orders.' He put his hand to his eye as the endless panorama of glittering mirrors mocked him.

'I want you to signal *Larne* to close on us. Light a flare if need be, but I think James Tyacke will understand.'

'That is more than I do, sir.' Trevenen stared at him. 'If you value my word, I must tell you I am against wasting more time.'

'It is my responsibility, Captain. I should not need to remind you.'

223

He heard Trevenen's heavy feet crossing the quarterdeck, and the sudden activity as *Larne*'s number was bent on to the halliards.

In his mind's eye Bolitho saw his little command: *Larne* leading the invisible line with Jenour's *Orcadia* well up to windward, her topsails visible to the masthead lookout.

Far, far astern was the other frigate *Laertes*, the prize that had once been Baratte's own flagship.

He thought of Adam when they had last met at Cape Town, the rebellion in his eyes when he had been ordered to remain with Keen's convoy and escort. He was the vital link between them and their flag officer in *Valkyrie*.

Adam had argued that his place was in the van, not with the slow-moving transports. *Not with Valentine Keen*, he had really meant.

Bolitho had been as honest as was possible.

He had said, 'You are arguably one of the best young frigate captains in the fleet. You have more than proved it on this station. The recapture of your prizes and *Thruster*'s loss must not deflect your aim. Your true worth will be at my right hand when I call for it.' He had watched Adam's resistance soften as he had added, 'If I keep you with me all the while, which I am sorely tempted to do, it will reek of favouritism to the others, will it not?'

But it had proved that Catherine's worst fear about Adam and Zenoria must be justified.

He looked at Yovell's fat hand holding his pen, Avery making a few notes from the chart.

Whatever it was, it would have to wait. He saw Allday give his lazy grin as he said, 'Thought I'd forgotten, did you, Sir Richard? When we was together in Old Katie?' Even the affectionate nickname for Bolitho's little two-decker *Achates* brought it all back. 'Strange to see how things slide along. Commodore was the captain, an' young Cap'n Adam was your flag lieutenant.' He smiled almost shyly. 'An' then there was me.'

Bolitho touched his thick arm as he walked back to the table. 'I thought I'd lost you that day, old friend.' He spoke with such emotion that Avery and Yovell stopped to listen. Bolitho did not notice.

A midshipman tapped at the door and he saw the marine sentry's scarlet arm out-thrust, as if the boy was not important enough to be admitted.

'Beg pardon, Sir Richard. The captain's respects, and *Larne* has acknowledged.'

Bolitho smiled at him. 'Quite a mouthful, Mr Rees. Thank you.'

Allday murmured, 'That'll go through the young gentlemen's berth, an' that's no error.'

Yovell said, 'I'm ready, Sir Richard.'

Bolitho touched Avery's shoulder. 'I am going to put a landing party ashore. I want you to go with it.'

Avery replied calmly, 'For the experience, sir?'

Bolitho smiled. 'Don't take offence at everything I say!' He shook his head. 'Mr Urquhart is a good officer.' He almost added, *if he is allowed to be*. 'But beneath his lieutenant's coat there is still only a boy.' He glanced at Allday, but not before he had seen the surprise on Avery's face. 'I would take it a favour if you would accompany my flag lieutenant, Allday.'

He turned, but Bolitho was already standing behind Yovell's round shoulder, his face unusually stern with concentration.

To all captains and officers-in-charge of such vessels under my command . . .

He thought suddenly of the last courier schooner that had run down on them. He could not recall when it had been. One day was much like all the rest.

There had been no more letters from Catherine. He felt another touch of anxiety and concern. He could still hear her voice nonetheless. *Don't leave me . . .*

But all Avery saw was the vice-admiral.

It took another full day, even under all the sail *Valkyrie* could carry, before the small island of San Antonio was sighted by the masthead. Without the other ships in company it had been strangely lonely, and many times Bolitho had seen seamen pause in their work to stare at the sea as if they expected to sight another friendly vessel.

The island seemed to rise from the ocean itself as the *Valkyrie* tilted to the unwavering south-westerly. It was, as Tyacke had described, a bleak place. It could have been the remaining half of an extinct volcano, on the side of which Bolitho saw the crude monastery like an extension of the terrain it was built on.

With the coming of dawn every available glass was trained on it while the sailing master and his mates studied the chart, which they had mounted near the wheel itself.

Avery joined Bolitho by the quarterdeck rail, his jaw still moving discreetly on a piece of salt pork which was too tough to swallow.

'How long, sir?'

Bolitho rested his hands on the rail, feeling the rising heat that would soon engulf the whole ship.

'Two hours. More or less.' He rubbed his eye and trained the telescope once again. There was some smoke rising from a saddle in the land which he had taken earlier for haze. There was life here. He had heard that the monastery had had many changes of occupant during the course of its long life. Disease had taken a toll, and once, Tyacke had told him, all the monks had died of starvation simply because the sea had been too rough to launch any of their boats. What sort of men would give up the real world for such a demanding life, and, some would say, pointless sacrifice?

He heard Trevenen snapping out orders to his lieutenants. He was very much on edge, for the safety of his command, perhaps?

The sailing master called, 'Steady on nor' nor' east, sir!'

Trevenen folded his hands behind his back. 'Leadsman in the chains, Mr Urquhart, lively now!'

The first lieutenant was with the master. 'But there's no bottom hereabouts, sir.'

'Damn it, do I have to repeat everything I say? Do as I tell you!'

Bolitho could understand any captain's anxiety for his ship. But this place was known for its isolation, and for the impossibility of landing here without the use of boats.

Avery thought the same but said nothing. He watched

226

Urquhart hurry past, his face flushed with humiliation at being upbraided in front of the hands.

The leadsman's cry echoed aft. 'No bottom, sir!'

Bolitho raised the telescope and studied the hard landscape as it continued to grow and reach out on either bow. There was a patch of green below the monastery, a possible kitchen garden.

The sea was deep, and he watched a big swell at the foot of some fallen rocks. According to Tyacke and the chart there was a tiny cluster of huts used by visiting fishermen when their favourite catch was in season.

Bolitho saw Allday lounging against an eighteen-pounder, his new cutlass already in his belt. Urquhart might resent having Avery and Allday with him, especially as he was in charge. Trevenen would see to that.

Ozzard appeared at his side. 'Shall I bring your coat, Sir Richard?'

Bolitho shook his head. 'No. Someone may be watching *us*. It is better this way.' He saw Ozzard's expression as he stared at the island. As if he loathed what he saw. What had done this to him?

'No bottom, sir!'

Trevenen said, 'Shorten sail, Mr Urquhart! Take in the t'gallants and stays'ls. We are moving too fast over the water!'

Men swarmed to the ratlines. With their captain on deck they needed no urging.

Bolitho stiffened. There was the landing place, and he could see one of the wooden huts beyond it. Even a castaway would feel wretched here.

He said 'You may assemble the landing party, Captain.'

Trevenen touched his hat but did not look at him.

Bolitho watched one of the cutters being swayed up from the boat tier. The chosen party of men looked capable enough. They were all armed, and he saw the gunner getting ready to supervise the mounting of a swivel in the boat's bows once it was in the water.

Urquhart had donned his sword, and looked vaguely ill at ease as he handed over his duties to the second lieutenant.

Bolitho watched the courses being brailed up to the yards

and felt the way go off the ship as she rolled heavily in the offshore swell.

He said, 'Just make certain that all is well, Mr Urquhart. These are men of peace, and any unnecessary show of force would be resented. Discover what you can.' He glanced at Allday. 'And be careful.'

Urquhart nodded stiffly, very aware of his captain standing nearby with a sardonic smile on his lips.

Trevenen said, 'Stand by to wear ship. We shall heave-to!'

It would be a hard pull for the oarsmen, Bolitho thought. Nevertheless, he sensed that the sailors who were remaining on board envied the landing party.

'Sway out the boat!' As *Valkyrie* came up into the wind with all remaining sails flapping in confusion, the selected men clambered down into the cutter alongside. The last to board were the two lieutenants. Bolitho noticed that Urquhart was careful to climb down last, as if he needed to prove that, on this occasion at least, he was the senior officer.

'Bear off! Out oars!'

The cutter looked deceptively small in the great glassy swell, but was soon under command and cleaving through the steep water like a dolphin.

Bolitho said, 'You may get under way again, Captain. But stand no further offshore.'

Valkyrie steadied again as the courses and topsails were reset, and with neither Allday nor Avery to talk to he felt strangely depressed. Instinctively he reached up to his damp shirt and touched the locket inside. *I am here. You are never alone.*

He rubbed his left eye and winced. It must be getting worse. They must never know.

He took up the telescope again and looked for the boat but it was merging with the shore, moving briskly towards the landing-place, possibly aided by an undertow.

He went down into the cabin and dabbed his eye with water.

Yovell said gently, 'Is there anything I can do, Sir Richard?'

He dropped the cloth, angry with himself. He had told others to delegate and to trust those they commanded, so what was the matter with him?

228

He answered, 'I think everyone believes I am wasting time.'

Yovell smiled inwardly. Bolitho meant the captain. 'Never mind, Sir Richard. Mr Avery and Allday will get a warm welcome. Fresh faces must be more precious than Christianity in this place!' He was surprised as Bolitho turned to stare at him, his eyes wild in the reflected light. Then without a word he snatched the old hanger from the bulkhead, and was still buckling it around himself as he ran to the companionway.

'Captain Trevenen!' He swung round blindly, unable to see him, caught off-guard by the sun's power. 'Heave-to immediately!' He saw the others looking at him as if they thought him mad. Dyer, the second lieutenant, was turning to the captain, not knowing what to do.

Trevenen sounded very calm, almost defiant. 'You ask me to perform some strange things, Sir Richard!'

'I am not asking you. Just do it!' He could not resist adding, 'Do I have to repeat everything I say?' It was petty, and later he might regret it. But there was no time. Above the squeal of blocks and the boom of canvas he shouted, 'I want two boats, a squad of marines in each one!' Men seemed to be scampering in all directions, dodging the hands at the braces and halliards as they brought the ship into the wind again.

Bolitho saw Plummer, the sergeant of marines, near the nettings and called, 'Your best marksman and lively with it!' There was no time to seek out the debonair Captain Loftus. It might already be too late.

Why did I not think?

'I demand to know what is happening, Sir Richard! As officer appointed to command . . .' Trevenen got no further.

'Damn your eyes, sir! Stand closer inshore and watch for signals!' Then he was over the side and scrambling over the tumblehome into the nearest boat.

'Let me, Sir Richard!' It was Captain Loftus of the marines. He was actually grinning. 'I guessed something was up!'

Bolitho stared round, barely aware that the boats were away from the frigate's side, the oars thrashing at the water until they found the stroke.

It seemed so wrong without Allday at his side. *I should never have sent him.*

'Can you tell me, Sir Richard? I appear to be the only officer present.'

Boitho gripped his arm. *They will think me insane.*

But thank goodness Loftus was keeping his head. He peeked over the oarsmen as they dipped then rose above him, their eyes grim and intent. The shore seemed no nearer.

He said, 'My secretary saw it. I did not. It was a feeling and nothing more. *Because I had nothing left.*'

'Sir?' He was trying to understand.

Bolitho asked sharply, 'Is the marksman with us?'

Loftus nodded. 'Behenna, Sir Richard. From your part of the world, I understand.' He smiled. 'A poacher, in fact. It was a choice between the Corps or the rope. I am not sure if he believes he made the right decision!'

The casual humour did more than anything to steady Bolitho's racing thoughts.

'Tell your poacher to load his piece now. If ordered to shoot I fear there may be blood on my hands.'

The word ran through the boat and then the other one, so that men tightened their grip on the looms while others reached down in the bottom boards for their weapons.

The marksman in the bows turned and stared along the length of the boat at the vice-admiral in his flapping shirt, with the old blade between his knees.

Bolitho lifted one hand towards him. The poacher was trying to tell him something with a glance. Like the young seaman that day with the bruise of a starter on his bare shoulder.

Suppose things went badly wrong? He touched the locket again and knew Loftus was watching him. *Don't leave me . . .*

It seemed so wrong that Yovell, the most peaceful and unwarlike person he knew, should have seen it, and pondered on the island's total lack of welcome.

In his heart he answered her. *Never.* What he had said when they had abandoned the *Golden Plover.* And had lived to tell of it.

He heard the boom of water in some cave below the cliff and knew they were closer. He gripped his sword with all his strength and whispered, *I'm coming*, but he spoke only to himself.

'It all seems quiet enough.' Lieutenant Urquhart looked at the others, his frown deepening. 'Well, we're here, so I suppose we shall have to search the place, though it is God's truth I know not for what!' He glanced around for a boatswain's mate and snapped, 'Protheroe, take your party to the huts yonder. Find out what you can!' He pointed at a young midshipman. 'You go with them, Mr Powys, and *take charge!*'

Avery murmured to Allday, 'What were you saying to Sir Richard?'

Allday grinned, but his eyes were on the rocks. 'I says a lot o' things to Sir Richard.'

'About the place where you were so badly wounded.'

'Oh, when we were in Old Katie together?' He watched the little midshipman strutting away with the party of seamen. He was the one who had caused the man Jacobs to be flogged until he had eventually died under the lash. Little toad, he thought.

Then he said, 'At San Felipe, it was. Just after you were released from a French prison, I reckon.' He saw the shot strike home. *Always the pain.*

Surprisingly Avery gave a rueful smile. 'Even prison was better than this god-forsaken place!'

Urquhart seemed rather desperate. 'I shall go up to the monastery, if that's what they call it!'

Avery watched him. The first lieutenant was seeing all the pitfalls, and the end of it when Trevenen would vent his temper on him.

'No need, sir.' Allday eased his cutlass very slightly in his belt. 'The old fellow himself is coming down to *us.*'

Avery wondered if he would ever get used to Allday's humour. But there was awareness too, like a fox on the prowl when a hunter is near. They all looked up the path that led from the monastery's crumbling outer wall. It was so steep in places that here and there crude stairs had been hacked out to give access.

Avery watched the slow-moving figure in the brown robe, the hood pulled up over his head to keep out the wet, salty breeze. Each stair, like the stones of the building itself, had doubtless been cut by hand. He turned to seek out the frigate, but she had moved or drifted around the out-thrust spur of land. To see the water so empty sent an unexpected chill up his spine.

He shook himself angrily and looked at Urquhart. It was obvious he did not know what to do.

The figure was nearer now, still moving at the same steady pace. In one hand he carried a long, polished staff on which he leaned occasionally as if to get his breath. When he drew nearer Avery could see the fine carved crucifix on the top of the staff, below which was a plain gold band. It was probably the most valuable object in this dismal hole, he thought.

Urquhart said urgently, 'He must be the abbot! You see, I was right. There's nothing to worry about!' When Avery said nothing he insisted, 'He will demand to know what we're doing on this – this sacred land!'

Allday spat in the sand but Urquhart was too agitated to notice it.

Avery said, 'Tell him, then. If he becomes unreasonable, we can give him some ship's stores. Can we not?'

Urquhart nodded, relieved. 'Yes, I shall.'

Allday grunted. In ten minutes Urquhart would imagine it was all his idea. He knew that Bolitho thought the first lieutenant would be a good officer. He chuckled. But not this week.

The abbot stopped on one of the last stairs and held up the staff so that the crucifix faced Urquhart and his companions. Then he shook his head firmly while he held the staff. It all took place in complete silence, but he might have been denying them entry into the monastery with a voice like thunder.

Urquhart had removed his hat and now gave a brief bow.

He said, 'I come in the name of King George of England . . .'

The abbot stared down at him, his eyes expressionless. Then he shook his head several times.

Urquhart tried again. 'We mean no harm. We will leave you in peace.' He turned helplessly and exclaimed, 'He speaks no English!'

Avery felt the wildness surging through him. Something he thought he had lost or learned to contain.

232

The others stared at him as he said quietly, '*Duncere Classem Regem Sequi.*'

The abbot could only gape at him, and he added in a harsher tone, 'Nor Latin either, it would seem!' He knew Urquhart was unable to understand, and he shouted, '*Take this man!*'

A seaman seized the man's robe but he was too strong for him.

Allday pushed past them. 'Sorry, Father!' Then he smashed his fist into the man's face and sent him reeling down the steps.

Someone yelled, 'There be boats comin', sir!'

Allday straightened up and allowed the imposter's hand to fall on the stones. 'See the tar, sir! If he's a cleric, I'd be the Queen of England!' Then he seemed to realise what had been shouted and said with relief, 'Sir Richard, then. I knew it somehow!'

They all stared around as two shots cracked out, their sharp echoes repeating and ringing around the narrow landing-place as if twenty marksmen were firing.

Someone gave a shrill scream, and even as their ears cringed to that a corpse fell from the rocks overhead, still clinging to a smoking musket until he hit the ground and rolled off into the water below.

'Who was hit?' Urquhart stared round, his eyes wild.

A seaman called, 'Mr Powys, sir! He's dead!'

Somebody else said, 'He's no bloody loss.'

'Silence!' Urquhart was trying to assert himself.

Bolitho and the captain of marines appeared at the landing place, and a squad of scarlet coats fanned out amongst the rocks, their bayonets very bright in the sunshine.

Bolitho climbed up beside them and nodded to Allday. 'Well, old friend?'

Allday grinned, but the pain in his chest had been awakened and he had to speak carefully.

'This fellow must be one of them, Sir Richard.' He held up a pistol. 'Not quite right an' proper for a man of the cloth, eh?'

Bolitho looked at the abbot who was trying to recover his senses. Then he said, 'We've much to do here.'

Protheroe, who had been with the unpopular midshipman,

233

appeared on the slope, his eyes dull with shock. As a boatswain's mate he was one of those required to carry out a flogging, and yet by the navy's own code he was not blamed for what he must do. Especially under Trevenen's command.

'What is it, man?'

Protheroe wiped his mouth. 'Two women we found, sir. Raped several times is my guess, then cut about somethin' terrible!' He was shaking despite everything he had seen in his service.

Bolitho glanced at the figure in the brown robe and saw his eyes move. He said calmly, 'There appear to be no trees here. Take this man to the water's edge. Captain Loftus, you will detail a firing party. At once!'

Captain Loftus looked so grim that it was likely he would shoot the man himself. As he stepped forward the imposter flung himself forward, and would have gripped Bolitho's shoes but for Allday's heavy foot across his neck.

'Down, you scum! Butchering women – is that all you're good for?'

'Please! *Please!*' The man's earlier composure, which had so convinced Urquhart, had vanished like smoke. 'It wasn't me! It was some of the others!'

'Strange how often it's the others!'

Avery felt his hand trembling on his sword hilt but managed to say, 'Speaks English now well enough!'

'How many of you are there here?' Bolitho turned away. He was beyond pity. The women were probably fishermen's wives, daughters even. What a terrible way to end. Later he would see the corpses for himself, and tend to them. But now . . . his voice hardened. 'Speak out, man!'

The man did not struggle as a marine dragged off the robe and took the fine staff from him as if it might break.

The cowering figure sobbed, 'We was ordered to stay here, sir! I speak the truth! The monks are safe enough, sir! I'm a religious man – I was against what happened. Have mercy, sir!'

Bolitho snapped, 'Get a flag of truce for this creature, Mr Urquhart, and go with him to the door. His friends will know they cannot be rescued while we are here. If they resist I will have the door broken down, and there will be no quarter.'

Urquhart was staring at him as if he had never seen him before.

Bolitho watched as the man was dragged to his feet and a white rag produced from somewhere. He did not notice at the time, but it had blood on it. It was probably the hated midshipman's shirt.

'How many men? I did not hear a reply!'

But the prisoner was gaping at something beyond him, and without turning Bolitho knew it was the *Valkyrie* moving past the entrance. She more than anything would convince the pirates, or whatever they were.

Avery whispered, 'I'll go, Sir Richard. If they recognise you . . .'

Bolitho tried to smile. 'Like this?' He plucked at his grubby shirt. Had that hidden marksman seen him in uniform, he and not Midshipman Powys would be lying dead. He noticed that Avery had used his title despite what he had told him. It revealed that he was not as calm as he appeared.

He walked up the steps and asked, 'What of the Abbot? Did you murder him too?'

The man tried to turn but two marines gripped him fast. He whined, 'No, sir! A man of God?' He sounded almost shocked at the suggestion. 'He's locked in a room with the other prisoner!'

It was as if someone had spoken in his ear. 'You had better not be lying.'

The door was already opening when they reached it. There were ten of them. Had they wanted to they could have held the place against an army. But they were throwing down their weapons and getting a few blows from the marines as they drove them into a corner.

Bolitho saw the marksman swoop up an expensive-looking pistol from the floor, his eyes gleaming. Despite his smart uniform he still looked like a poacher in the guise of a ferret.

Their voices rang and echoed around the walls, which were dripping with moisture. The sound of chanting in this place must be like the cries of the damned.

His heart was beating so painfully that he had to pause on the stairs to recover his breath.

'Captain Loftus, search the building, though I doubt if you'll find anything. Have the prisoners taken to the beach. Tie them up if need be.' He was speaking in a harsh, clipped tone he barely recognised as his own, and his mouth was as dry as dust.

Allday said, 'This is the place, I think, Sir Richard.' He sounded very wary.

Avery lifted a large key from a hook beside the door and after a slight hesitation he opened it.

There was bright sunshine streaming in through a window, alien in this place, which was without furniture. The floor was strewn with loose straw. A man with a white beard was leaning against the wall, his leg chained to a ringbolt, his breathing laboured and shallow.

Bolitho said softly, 'Send word to the ship and have the surgeon attend here.'

He bent and then knelt beside the other man who was propped against the wall, one hand in filthy bandages. For a moment longer Bolitho thought he was dead.

He said, 'Thomas. Can you hear me?'

Herrick lifted his chin, then very slowly opened his eyes. Blue in the sunlight, they seemed the only living thing about him.

A marine handed Bolitho his water flask, and Herrick stared at the man's bright uniform as if he could not believe it was real.

Bolitho held the flask to his lips and saw Herrick's pathetic attempt to swallow some water.

Herrick said suddenly, 'Allday! It's you, you rascal!' Then he coughed and water ran down his chin.

Allday watched, his face like stone. 'Aye, sir. You can't get rid o' me that easy!'

Bolitho looked round and noticed Herrick's best uniform coat hanging on a wall, carefully protected from dust and damp by a piece of linen.

Herrick must have seen his eyes move toward it, and said, 'They wanted to parade us together, so they had to keep my

236

clothing nice and clean.' He almost laughed, but he groaned with the pain.

Bolitho took the bandaged hand very carefully and prayed that the surgeon would soon come.

'Who did this to you, Thomas? Was it Baratte?'

'He was here, but I did not see him. It was another man.'

'American or French?'

Herrick stared at the crude bandage. 'Neither. A bloody Englishman!'

'Save your strength, Thomas. I think I know the man now.'

But Herrick was staring past him again, at the prisoner who had taken the abbot's place. 'Whoever he was, he knew he was wasting his time when he questioned me about the squadron.' His body shook with silent laughter. 'Not that I had anything to tell. Remember, I was on my way to the great country.' Then he became very calm. 'So this renegade, or whoever he is, made me a promise before he left. That I would never hold a sword for the King again.' He gestured with his head to a stone block in the corner. 'They held my arm and smashed my hand with that!' He held up the bandage and Bolitho could imagine the damage and the agony. 'But they even made a mistake there, eh, Richard?'

Bolitho looked down, his eyes blurring. 'Yes, Thomas, you are left-handed.'

Herrick was fighting to stay conscious. 'That prisoner by the door. He did it.'

Then he fainted. Bolitho held him in his arms and waited while a marine prized open the leg-iron with his bayonet.

He looked round, thinking that Herrick had called him by name; and that while he had been struggling to speak, something had stopped, like a clock.

Sergeant Plummer said quietly, 'The old gentleman has died, sir.'

It was rare for a man to look dignified in death, Bolitho thought. He said, 'Remove his leg-iron, Sergeant, then take him to where the others lie dead.' He walked to the door as more men with Lieutenant Urquhart hurried in.

Avery asked, 'And what about this man, sir?'

The prisoner's eyes watched him like bright stones.

237

'We'll leave him with the others. Dead.'

The man's protests filled the barred room so that Herrick seemed to stir as if in a bad dream.

'I will not take him to the ship. The people have had enough examples of authority to witness.' He watched the horror and disbelief on the man's face. 'The only witnesses will be the women you destroyed!'

Outside the door Bolitho leaned against the wall, the stones surprisingly cold through his shirt. He listened to the man's screams and pleading cries as he was dragged down the steep stairs.

Avery waited with Allday as some sailors carried Herrick's limp body carefully through the door.

Avery asked bluntly, 'What does it mean? You can tell me, man!'

Allday looked at him sadly. 'It means he's found his friend again.'

They fell in step to follow the others, then Allday asked, 'What *did* you say to that rat, sir?'

'Well, I was not certain, you see. But all priests speak Latin. I was answering the question he should have asked. I said, To Lead the Fleet, to Follow the King.'

A single shot echoed over the monastery and Allday spat on the ground.

'Hope he said his prayers!'

16

Captains All

Yovell leaned slightly to one side as Bolitho ran his eyes over the orders he had just completed. Around them the big frigate groaned uneasily as she lay hove-to while *Laertes*'s captain came over in his gig.

Two days had passed since the landing party had entered the monastery and had rescued Herrick.

There had been others found there in the same spartan captivity. Apart from the remainder of the monks they had discovered some twenty masters and other officers from the many prizes taken by Baratte and his ships.

Bolitho had listened with great care to each of the prisoners and had built up a much clearer picture in his mind of the enemy's strength. Baratte had employed many small vessels for his attacks, and had fitted out some of his captures as privateers and for spying on ships sailing alone.

Baratte was both well-informed and prepared for any attempt by the military to deploy their transports, without which they would be beaten before they had even started.

Major-General Drummond's force was the obvious target. Baratte would know the strength of the Cape Town squadron, which even with Keen's support would be at great risk.

Bolitho had already dispatched the brig *Orcadia* with all the information he could muster, and had told Jenour to tell Keen to press the army to hold fast until Baratte's ships could be dealt with.

Jenour had seemed listless and tired, and Bolitho had wished

239

that he had had more time to speak with him. But time was slipping away, and with *Thruster* gone and Jenour sent to find Keen's ships he was well aware of the need for action. James Tyacke had come aboard only briefly at Bolitho's request, and had confirmed that the unknown English captain had to be a former sea-officer, who had commanded a small frigate in the King's navy until he had been court-martialled for cruelty to enemy prisoners-of-war. He was exactly the kind of unscrupulous character who would fit Baratte's requirements. A man who had recruited a company of scum, most of whom would hang if brought to justice. His name was Simon Hannay: privateer, pirate and murderer, who had for too long struck fear into the hearts of ship masters who sailed alone on the great ocean.

Tyacke had come up against him when he had been controlling a large flotilla of vessels which had preyed regularly along the African coastline. When slavery had been outlawed and the patrols had been strengthened Hannay had discovered that the Arab slave-traders were more frightened of *the Devil with half a face* than they were of him. Not for the first time he had offered his services to the French, and according to one of the freed prisoners he had been given a thirty-two gun frigate appropriately named *Le Corsaire*. Baratte flew his flag in another frigate, *Chacal*. She was new, but little was known about her. Baratte had many other small vessels, brigs, brigantines and former coastal schooners.

Bolitho walked away from the table and stared thoughtfully at the shimmering ocean. It was noon, and by now Tyacke would have clawed his way up to windward, ready to dash down on the two frigates if any strange sail was sighted.

He heard the stamp of feet and the shrill twitter of calls as Captain Dawes of the *Laertes* was piped aboard. Avery was up there to welcome him with Captain Trevenen.

Bolitho thought of the powerful emotions he had seen on Avery's introspective face when they had buried the two women and the elderly abbot among the wild flowers on the hillside. He himself had been shocked when he had seen the murdered women. Both were young, the wives of fishermen. They had been spared nothing, even the mercy of a quick

240

death. One of the released sailors had told him about the night when the guards had been mad with drink, and their wild cries had mingled with the screams of the women. Simon Hannay had not been there, but he might as well have been. And he would pay for it.

The monks had been almost harder to understand, Bolitho thought. They had displayed neither gratitude nor anger, and had shown little grief at the death of their abbot. Perhaps life on that pitiless islet had destroyed their capacity to feel the normal, worldly emotions of ordinary men.

He thought of Herrick down below in the sickbay, watched over by George Minchin the surgeon. Herrick had suffered greatly, and Minchin had insisted that he be left alone until some progress had been made.

Bolitho could still hear him calling him by name in that filthy cell.

There was a tap at the door and Trevenen, followed by Avery and Captain Dawes, came into the cabin. Dawes was young, about Adam's age, but had the severe deportment of a much older man. Perhaps he already saw himself as an admiral like his father.

Yovell moved to a corner where he could make notes if required, and Ozzard stood with a napkin over his arm while he waited to serve refreshments.

Trevenen sat down heavily. He had almost shown surprise when he had seen the man who had posed as the abbot and who had broken Herrick's hand with a rock shot to death by the captain of marines.

He had said in his harsh voice, 'It was quite unexpected, Sir Richard.'

Bolitho had faced him calmly, the dead women's contorted features still clear in his mind.

'I do not enjoy seeing a man die, even scum like that one. I simply could not think of a reason for allowing him to live.'

While Avery held the chart, Bolitho discussed the despatch he had sent with Jenour.

'Although it depletes our strength still further, it may prevent a greater loss of life.'

Dawes peered at the chart. 'Two frigates, Sir Richard?' His

241

eyes sharpened. He was already seeing fame and prize money. 'We can manage to dish *them* up!'

Trevenen said doubtfully, 'The renegade, Simon Hannay – what do we know of him?'

'Commander Tyacke knows him as well as anyone, but stories of his bloody career are legion.'

Why was Trevenen so unwilling to take Tyacke's word? He seemed to sift every event as if looking for flaws. Or what he considered to be a waste. Like the rescued mariners and the prisoners, for instance. Bolitho had seen him complaining to the purser about the extra mouths he would have to feed. It was as if it would all come out of his own pocket.

He said quietly, 'The real puzzle remains the role of the American, *Unity*. Without her interference we can tackle Baratte, and win.'

Trevenen interrupted, 'He'd not risk war, Sir Richard!' He sounded outraged.

'He might have a plan.' Bolitho studied them, and wished Adam were present. 'His government did not send their most experienced captain in their greatest frigate merely to *show the flag*. In his place I know what I would do. I would provoke an argument. It is nothing new in war, or in peace either, for that matter.'

Trevenen was unconvinced. 'Suppose Baratte has more men-of-war than we know of?'

'I'm sure he has. But the main force sailing from India will be heavily escorted. There will even be some of John Company's ships taking part. My guess is that Baratte will deploy his strength in their direction.' He looked at Dawes. 'Remember, your ship was once his, and I am his most hated enemy. Both good reasons for engaging *us*, eh?'

He heard the sentry murmuring outside the screen door and saw Ozzard scurry over to open it.

Bolitho's heart sank. It was Minchin, the surgeon. He said, 'If you will excuse me, gentlemen. Take some wine before we eat.' He spoke so easily that neither of the captains would have recognised his anxiety.

Minchin waited for the door to close. 'I'd not disturb you, Sir Richard, but . . .'

242

'Is it Rear-Admiral Herrick?'

The surgeon ran his fingers through his untidy grey hair.

'I'm troubled about him. He's in great pain. I'm only a ship's surgeon – *butchers* they call the likes of us . . .'

Bolitho touched his arm. 'Have you forgotten *Hyperion* so soon? But for you, many more would have died that day.'

Minchin shook his head. 'Some would have been better off if they had.'

They walked to the lower companionway and Bolitho saw Allday sitting on an upturned water cask working on one of his carvings. He glanced across, his eyes full of understanding, as if he had spoken aloud.

Deeper into *Valkyrie*'s great hull to the orlop deck below the waterline. Here all sounds of sea and wind were muted, with only the timbers murmuring like voices in the depths of the ocean itself. Here were stores, cordage, tar and paint, the canvas lockers and the hanging magazine. The very stuff of the ship herself.

They entered the sickbay, spacious and well-lit in contrast to most of those Bolitho had seen. The surgeon's mate closed a book he had been reading and glided past.

Herrick was staring at the door as they entered, as if he had known they were coming.

Bolitho leaned over the cot. 'How are you, Thomas?'

He was afraid that Herrick might forget what they had shared, that he might turn against him again.

Herrick studied him, his eyes very blue in the fixed lanterns. 'It plagues me, Richard, but I have had a lot of time to think. About you, about us.' He tried to smile but his face was stiff with agony. He said, 'You look tired, Richard . . .' He made as if to reach out, then suddenly screwed his eyes tightly shut and said quietly, 'I'll lose my hand, won't I?'

Bolitho saw the surgeon nod. It was almost curt, as if he had already decided. He looked at Minchin. 'Well?'

The surgeon sat down on a chest. 'It has to be done, sir.' He faltered. 'To the elbow.'

Herrick gasped. 'Oh, my God!'

'Are you certain?' Bolitho glanced at the surgeon's reddened features.

Minchin nodded. 'As soon as possible, sir. Otherwise . . .'
He did not need to continue.

Bolitho put his hand gently on Herrick's shoulder. 'Is there anything I can do?'

Herrick opened his eyes and said, 'I have failed you.'

Bolitho tried to smile. 'No, Thomas. Think of yourself. Try to hold on.'

Herrick stared up at him. He had been washed and shaved and to a stranger would appear quite normal. He peered at the blood-stained bandages on his broken hand.

'Send the telescope to my sister . . . if I can't fight it, Richard.'

Bolitho looked back from the door. 'You *will* fight it. And win, too.'

The walk to the cabin seemed endless. To Allday he said, 'I have a favour to ask, old friend.'

Allday nodded his shaggy head, and rolled up the leather cloth in which he carried his knives and the sailmaker's twine he used for rigging his ship models.

'Never fear, Sir Richard, I'll stay with him.' He watched the pain in Bolitho's eyes. 'I'll tell you if anything happens.'

'Thank you.' He touched his powerful arm but was unable to say more.

Allday watched him approach the door, where the sentry was already as stiff as a rammer in spite of the heavy motion.

Once through the door, face to face with his assembled captains, he would show nothing of his private despair. Allday was certain of it. What did they know? All they wanted was glory and someone to lead and protect them.

Ozzard came through the door and Allday said roughly, 'You got some brandy, Tom? The best stuff?'

Ozzard studied him. Not for himself then. This was different.

'I'll fetch it for you, John.'

'I'll have a wet meself, afterwards.'

Afterwards. The finality of the word seemed to linger long after Allday had gone below.

Captain Adam Bolitho glanced at his reflection in the cabin

mirror and frowned as he tugged his waistcoat into place and adjusted the sword at his hip. *Anemone* was plunging badly in the quarter-sea, and the cabin's heavy humidity warned of rain quite soon. Not rain as over the fields and villages of Cornwall, but heavy, mind-dulling deluges which could often pass away from a ship before any worthwhile drinking water had been saved. But he could leave that to his first lieutenant.

Adam Bolitho hated the ritual of a flogging, although to most sailors it was something that could never be permanently avoided. Perhaps this one had been the result of the endless patrols, sighting nothing unless it was a courier-brig or some trader trying to stay friendly with both sides in a war he did not understand. Boredom, disappointment after losing their prizes to the enemy when before they had cheered, a close company at least until the news had been passed to them by a naval cutter on the anti-slavery patrol: *Anemone*'s people were restless and surly. Sail and gun drills could no longer contain their frustration, and their eager expectation of close combat with the real enemy had given way to a sullen resentment.

The man in question had struck a petty officer after an argument about a change of duties. At other times Adam would have demanded an enquiry into the incident, but in this case the petty officer was an experienced and unusually patient seaman. Adam had known the reverse many times, when authority was abused even by officers, and the resulting discipline was unjust although administered in the name of duty.

The sailor was a landman, one of those pressed off Portsmouth Point who, despite several threats, had remained a rebel, a lower-deck lawyer as Adam had heard his uncle describe such men.

There was a tap at the door and the first lieutenant looked into the cabin, his expression vaguely surprised, as if he had almost forgotten what his captain looked like in full uniform.

'Yes, Aubrey, what is it?' He regretted his curtness immediately. 'Are you ready?'

Martin said uncertainly, 'I believe this was my fault, sir. As the senior aboard I should have foreseen it. Nipped it in the bud.'

As if to mock his words they heard the trill of calls, the sudden scamper of bare feet.

'All hands! All hands lay aft to witness punishment!'

Adam answered, 'In a way I can understand how they feel, but empathy is a luxury in which no captain should indulge for long. We are always at risk, Aubrey, even with those we think we know. I have heard of it many times. When the ship is a tinderbox for whatever reason, even understanding can be mistaken for weakness.'

Martin nodded, and guessed the captain had learned much of what he said from Richard Bolitho.

He asked, 'Any further orders, sir?'

Adam looked away. He was showing that same weakness even by discussing it. He said, 'Both watches at six bells this afternoon. We will alter course again, the next leg of our patrol.' He tried to smile but the effort was too much. 'In two days, maybe three, we should sight the commodore's convoy. There will be plenty to do for all of us then!' He was conscious that he had not mentioned Keen by name. Was that all part of his guilt?

They went on deck together, the sun high overhead making each set sail appear transparent against the taut black rigging.

The Royal Marines were lined up across the quarterdeck with their lieutenant, Montague Baldwin. The curved sabre he favoured was already drawn and resting across his shoulder. Lieutenant Dacre was the officer-of-the-watch and stood beside Partridge the sailing master, youth and old age together. The midshipmen and other warrant ranks stood by the quarter-deck rail, while on the gun deck, the gangways, and clinging to the shrouds the bulk of *Anemone*'s company watched in silence.

Martin saw the captain nod and give his own signal for the ritual to begin. The prisoner was brought up, a tall erect figure, head upheld like some well-known felon going to the gallows, flanked by Gwynne the boatswain and one of his mates, and followed by McKillop the surgeon and by the master-at-arms. Then there was complete silence, and even the bellying canvas seemed still.

'Uncover!' The few present wearing hats removed them.

Some men watched the prisoner, who had been generally disliked until now; the rest kept their eyes on the slim, dark-haired figure with the gleaming epaulettes, surrounded by his officers, protected by the double rank of marines, and yet completely alone.

Adam removed his hat and tugged the Articles of War from his coat. As he did so he looked at the prisoner. Of one company, he thought, yet a thousand miles apart.

His voice was steady and without emotion, so that many of the assembled seamen and marines barely heard him. Not that it mattered: the old Jacks at least knew the relevant articles by heart. Adam even imagined that he saw the carpenter nudge one of his mates when he reached the last line. ' . . . Or shall suffer death as is hereinafter mentioned.' He shut the folder and added, 'Given under my hand in His Britannic Majesty's Ship *Anemone*.' He replaced his cocked hat. 'Carry out the sentence.'

The grating had already been rigged against the gangway, and before he could resist the prisoner was stripped to the waist and seized up, arms apart, with further lashings to hold his legs so that he was spreadeagled.

Adam saw the youngest midshipman closing and opening his fists, but not out of pity. His eyes were fixed on the man's muscular back with the expression of a stag-hound approaching a kill.

Adam snapped, 'Carry on, Mr Gwynne.'

Somebody shouted, 'You show 'em, Toby!'

Lieutenant Baldwin said calmly, 'Steady, marines.'

It reminded Adam of Keen when he had served under him. He had used the same tone in moments of great tension, like a groom calming a nervous mount.

'Take that man's name!'

Gwynne the boatswain, who was completely deaf in one ear after close action with a French man-of-war, called, 'How many, sir?'

Adam moved up to the rail and looked at the prisoner, who had twisted his head around so that he could see him.

'Three dozen!'

247

The prisoner yelled, 'You bloody bastard, you said two dozen!'

Adam said, 'I changed my mind.'

The drums rolled, and down came the lash across his shoulders. The master-at-arms called, 'One!'

The first half dozen lashes made a criss-cross of bloody stripes like the claw marks of a savage beast.

The prisoner began to gasp as the punishment continued, his face almost purple when the boatswain handed the cat-of-nine-tails to his mate.

The master-at-arms counted hoarsely, 'Twenty-six!'

The surgeon held up his hand. 'He has fainted, sir!'

'Cut him down!' Adam watched as the man fell to the deck into his own blood. He was picked up and carried below to the sickbay. A man of his obvious strength would soon recover after he had had his back cleansed with salt water and his stomach lined with as much rum as he could swallow. But the marks of the cat he would carry to his grave.

The first lieutenant watched him warily. This was a mood he did not recognise.

Adam said, 'There will be no martyrs in my ship, Mr Martin.' He gave a tired smile as the men dispersed to their duties or their messes. 'There is more to command than prize money, believe me!'

He had scarcely gone below to change out of his uniform when the rain tore into the ship like a waterfall.

Adam glanced at himself in that same mirror. *What would she think of me now, if she saw me?*

He walked to the stern windows and thrust one open to stare at the horizon. The rain was already passing over: it would leave the decks cool, the sails hardened to receive the next wind. He looked at his coat, lying on a chair with its epaulettes glinting dully. He had been so proud when he had been posted. Now he held out his hands and felt something like sickness in his throat.

Three dozen lashes. Was that all? *As captain I could have run him up to the main yard for striking a petty officer.* The realisation of his power over these men had never failed to shock and awe him. But not now. It was his right.

He must have come a long, long way . . .

In the afternoon while he sat at his table with a plate of tasteless salt-beef barely touched nearby, he thought again about the letter, and wondered if she had received it, or even read it if she had.

If only they might meet as if by accident, on some winding track like the place where he had given her the wild roses. And she had kissed him . . .

He sat bolt upright as the lookout's voice pealed down from the masthead.

'Deck there! Sail on th' lee bow!'

Adam jumped to his feet. That was more like it. There was nothing between *Anemone* and his uncle's ships. The prospect of action would make all the difference and bring them together again. Cleansing, like the rain that had washed the blood from the grating.

The quarterdeck was crowded when he reached it.

Lieutenant Dacre touched his forehead, then pushed the wet hair from his eyes.

'I'm not yet certain, sir. The lookout says there's some mist to lee'rd – might be more rain.'

'We'd not find him if that happened.' He hurried to the chart as the master's mates uncovered it.

Partridge said, 'Might be a slaver, sir. Can't think o' nothing else this far out.'

'My thoughts, Mr Partridge! Call both watches and get the t'gallants on her. She'll likely show her heels when she sights us!'

Men poured on deck to the shrill of calls. Adam assessed their mood as they hurried past and below him. Some would still be thinking of the flogging, but by now others would be accepting it. *He had brought it on himself.* Or, *what can you expect from a bloody officer?* They could hate him when they felt like it; or perhaps when he deserved it. But fear him? That must never happen.

He saw Midshipman Dunwoody staring at him. 'Aloft with a glass. I can use your eyes today!' He watched him swarming up the ratlines, a long telescope bouncing across his buttocks with every step.

249

Martin had joined him now, his face eager and excited. As I once was, Adam thought.

'Set the main course, Aubrey. I want her to fly before they can lose us!'

They grinned at one another, all else forgotten.

Anemone was riding it well. With the wind across the quarter she was taking each long trough and roller like a thoroughbred horse jumping hedges. Spray was bursting over the figurehead in solid sheets, and as each sail was set and sheeted home it hardened as if being squeezed by giants, with the rain that had soaked the canvas flying over the struggling seamen to rush into the scuppers like small brooks.

Dunwoody's voice was practically muffled by the din of canvas and clattering rigging.

'Deck, there! Two masts, sir! I think she's seen us!'

Adam wiped his face with his shirt sleeve and realised he was soaked to the skin.

'If the rain holds off it will do them no good!'

He walked across the deck, at times barely able to prevent himself from being flung against the guns as his ship pointed her jib-boom at the sky, catching the returning sunlight like a golden lance. Then down again, the hull crashing into another trough, the timbers jolting as if they had hit a sandbar.

It was the lookout again. Perhaps Dunwoody was too choked by spray to call out.

'Deck there! She's a brig, sir! Can't make it out!'

Adam said, 'Use your speaking trumpet, Aubrey. Bring Dunwoody down. None of this is making any sense!'

Dunwoody arrived on deck, shivering badly in spite of the steam that was rising from his dripping shirt.

Adam asked, 'What ails you, Mr Dunwoody?' He was surprised that he could sound so calm, yet feel only apprehension.

Dunwoody stared down at the deck and would have fallen in the next wild plunge but for Bond, a master's mate, catching his arm. The boy turned his head to gaze across the water as if he could still see it.

'She's no slaver, sir. She is one of ours, the brig *Orcadia*.'

Adam turned to Martin.

250

'Is she mauled?' He squeezed the boy's arm very gently. 'Tell me. *I need to know!*'

Dunwoody shook his head, unable to accept it. 'She is out of command, sir, but she has not a mark on her!'

Martin persisted, 'Adrift? Abandoned? Speak out, man!'

Adam swung into the lee shrouds and began to climb, each ratline scraping at his fingers while the ship rolled from side to side.

He had to wait a long time for the ship to steady herself enough on one crested roller, and for the glass to clear while he rested against the shrouds.

Orcadia was pitching and rolling very badly, the sunlight sweeping across her stern windows and gilded gingerbread so that the cabin looked as if it were on fire. The quarter boat was still in place, but another was dangling from some loose tackles alongside, upended and smashing against the brig's side.

Not abandoned then. He waited for the next upthrust beneath the keel and tried again. *Orcadia*'s ensign was tangled in the rigging. Adam could feel the upturned faces below him willing him to tell them, just as he could sense the apprehension which had banished their sudden excitement. Another look through the dripping telescope, although he knew what he had seen. He lowered himself more quickly. Very soon everybody else would see it.

He found his lieutenant and Partridge waiting together. There was no sense in delaying it.

He faced them and said simply, 'Muster the afterguard, and then arm yourselves, gentlemen.' He held up his hand as Lieutenant Lewis began to hurry away. 'She is *Orcadia*.' He wanted to lick his dry lips but dared not. 'She flies the Yellow Jack.'

Lewis croaked, 'Fever!'

'As you say, Mr Lewis.' His voice hardened. 'Feared and hated by sailors even more than fire.'

Lieutenant Baldwin came on deck, his eyes everywhere as he buttoned his scarlet coat.

Adam said, 'We will bear up to wind'rd of her and lower a

251

boat.' He saw the quick exchange of glances. 'I shall call for volunteers and go across myself.'

'You'll not put aboard her, sir?' Dacre was staring around as if he could see the horror of it already in this crowded frigate.

'I will decide later.'

Marines were emerging from below deck, all armed, ready to fight and kill if necessary to retain order.

Martin watched the realisation running through the ship as the fear became a certainty.

He said, 'Her commander is a friend of Sir Richard's, I believe?'

'Mine too.' He was thinking of the Jenour he had known, trusting, loyal and likeable. Adam had thought him dead with all the others when he had gone to the memorial service at Falmouth. When his first lieutenant, Sargeant, and this same Aubrey Martin had galloped all the way from Plymouth to tell him the people most dear to him had survived. When he had lost Zenoria for all time.

'Will you take her in tow, sir?'

When Adam faced him again Martin was shocked to see tears in his eyes, running uncontrollably down his face to mingle with the spray.

'In God's name, Aubrey, you know I dare not!' It was another captain whom Martin had never seen.

Adam turned to Dunwoody, oblivious to those nearby. 'But Jenour comes from my uncle. It must be important.' He stared hard at the distant brig until his eyes were too blurred to see.

He heard Martin call, 'Hands aloft! Shorten sail, Mr Lewis!'

But only Dunwoody heard his captain's voice as he whispered, 'Dear God, forgive me for what I must do.'

Closer, and closer still to the stricken *Orcadia* until every telescope on the *Anemone*'s quarterdeck would recognise the vessel's absolute desolation: the double wheel untended and jerking this way and that while the brig drifted and rolled to the pressure of sea and wind. Near the compass box Adam saw two men lying as if asleep, their bodies moving only to the brig's violent motion. There was another corpse trapped

252

by a line against the splintered boat alongside, and as *Anemone* worked nearer, her yards braced almost fore-and-aft as close-hauled as she could respond, he saw the other spray-soaked bundles who had once been *Orcadia*'s company.

He heard the surgeon say, 'It must have been of the worst kind, sir. In a small vessel like her it would spread like wild-fire.'

Adam did not reply. He had heard of such virulent plagues in these waters, but had never seen them. Men falling at their stations, some dying before they had realised what was happening. The infection could have begun anywhere, in a vessel suspected of slavery perhaps. It had not been unknown for such ships, crammed to the deck beams with human cargo by captains who had put numbers before all else, to arrive at their destinations with most of the slaves dead and many of the crew soon to follow.

He said, 'Near enough, Mr Martin.' He sounded clipped and, to those who did not know him, without emotion.

Both watches were standing-to, some staring at the deserted brig as if it had harboured some kind of destructive force. A ghost-ship returned to avenge some past horror.

Several faces turned aft as Adam called, 'I want volunteers to crew the gig.'

He watched the mixed expressions: fearful, hostile, some filled with an overriding dread.

Nobody moved as he continued, 'She is one of us, as was the *Thruster*. *Orcadia* is a victim of war as much as any who fall to the enemy's iron. I have to know if anybody is left alive.' He saw McKillop the surgeon give a brief shake of his head. It only added to his sense of hopelessness, and his own profound foreboding.

'*Orcadia* was sailing with despatches for the squadron. They must be vital or my unc . . . or Sir Richard would not have spared her. Her captain was a friend to all of us. Must this suffering be for nothing?'

His coxswain George Starr said bluntly, 'I won't leave you, sir.'

Another shouted, 'Put me down!' It was Tom Richie,

253

Eaglet's boatswain, who had changed sides despite the risk to himself.

Adam said coolly, 'Still with us, Richie?'

A seaman whose name he could not remember banged his big hands together and even managed to grin. 'Never volunteer, they said! Look where it got me!'

Nervously, defiantly, one by one they came aft until Starr whispered, 'Full crew, sir.'

Adam turned as Dunwoody said, 'I'll come, sir.' He lifted his chin but it made him appear even younger.

Adam said gently, 'No. Stay with the first lieutenant. He'll need your loyalty.'

He looked over to Martin. 'Still want a command, Aubrey?' He smiled, but it did not reach his eyes.

My ship. My lovely Anemone . . . and I am leaving you.

He watched the gig being lowered and brought alongside under the frigate's lee.

Several men gasped at the sound of a single shot. Others flung their heads up as if expecting to see a hold punched in the reefed topsails.

Adam remarked to no one in particular, 'Yes, I think I would end it like that.' He touched the pistol in his belt, wondering how it would be.

Starr called, 'Ready, sir!'

Adam left the quarterdeck and walked to the port. He stopped as some sailors reached out to touch him. As if they were seeing him for the last time.

'Good luck, sir!'

'Watch out if they tries to board you, sir!' That from an older seaman, who could judge the real danger of close contact. He had made *Orcadia* seem like one of the enemy in just a few simple words.

'Out oars, shove off forrard! Give way all!'

Adam thought of Allday as the boat turned away and came under command. There was another shot, and the stroke was momentarily lost as one of the oarsmen peered nervously over his shoulder.

But the man Richie called between pulls, 'They tells me you're a pretty good shot with a pistol, Cap'n?'

254

Adam looked at him. Glad he had thrown the cutlass, the evidence, into the sea. It felt like a thousand years ago.

He said, 'When provoked!'

Then he gripped Starr's sleeve. 'Under her stern, but don't stand in too close. We could be dragged against her rudder by the undertow.' All the while he had the feeling that *Anemone* was close by, watching their progress, and when he turned in the sternsheets he was shocked to see that when she dipped into a deep trough she appeared to be a great distance away, the sea rising to her gunports as if to swallow her.

He took a speaking trumpet. '*Orcadia*, ahoy! This is Captain Bolitho of the *Anemone*!' He felt sick as he cried out, as if he were betraying them by offering hope when there was none.

Starr muttered, 'No use, sir. You done your best.'

'Round again.' He did not even try to conceal his distress. 'Then we'll go back.'

He saw two of the oarsmen glance uneasily at one another. The fire of volunteering was sifting away. His words had given them the relief they needed.

Starr thrust over the tiller bar, then exclaimed, 'Look, sir! In the cabin!'

The gig rose and fell in deep, nauseating swoops, the oars barely able to keep steerage way.

But Adam forgot the danger as he stared at the open stern window. The cabin was probably a twin of the one in his first command, the fourteen-gun *Firefly*.

There was someone there, a shadow more than any human form, and Adam felt something like fear as it moved very slowly towards the salt-caked glass. Whoever it was, he must have heard his voice through the speaking trumpet, and the sound had penetrated the mists of agony and disgust enough to rouse him to consciousness.

Adam knew it was Jenour without understanding why he did. Dying even as he sheltered there, dying as his little brig had battled on while men dropped until the last helmsman abandoned the wheel. Some must have tried to get away in the capsized boat: there may even have been a last attempt to restore order when it was already too late.

A seaman gasped, 'A bag, sir!' His eyes were almost starting from his head as he stared at the small leather satchel suddenly dangling from the cabin.

It must have taken all his strength: maybe his last, and if it fell now it would be lost forever.

'Hold on, Starr!'

Adam clambered forward over the looms, gripping a shoulder here and there to prevent himself from being hurled outboard. He could feel their fear at even so brief a contact.

As he reached the bows he seized the bag and tugged it over the gunwale.

'Back water! *Together!*' Starr was watching the bag, the brig's counter rising over the boat ready to smash it to fragments in the next trough. He thought afterwards that it was fortunate the boat's crew had their backs to the stricken vessel. Whoever it was must have tied the bag to his wrist, and the force of Adam's grip on the line had dragged him almost over the sill.

Like Adam, he could only stare at it. A commander's single epaulette, but surely nothing human and still alive?

Like something rotten. A face from the grave.

Adam cut the line and saw the figure vanish into the cabin.

He called out, '*God be with you, Stephen!*' But only the scream of gulls came back to mock him.

Starr swung over the tiller bar once more and breathed out very slowly as *Anemone*'s topsails rose to greet him.

But Adam was staring at the *Orcadia*, and said brokenly, '*God?* What does he care for the likes of us?'

He barely remembered their return to *Anemone*'s lee. Many hands reached out to help him, and someone raised a cheer for him, or for the volunteers, he did not know.

And then it was dark, and the deck was steady again under the pressure of more canvas.

Lieutenant Martin sat with him in the cabin, watching his captain drink glass after glass of brandy without any apparent effect. The leather satchel still lay on the table unopened, like something evil.

The second lieutenant entered the cabin and after a questioning glance at Martin said, 'We've lost her, sir. In these waters she could be adrift for months, years even.'

Adam said, 'Open the despatches.' He stared at his empty glass but could barely remember drinking from it. Like that time when she had come to him in the night at Falmouth. And had stayed with him.

Martin unfolded the crisp despatch, and Adam recognised Yovell's familiar round handwriting.

'This was for Commodore Keen, sir. He was to find you and to tell the squadron to delay sailing. Sir Richard believes that Baratte is on the move.'

'Jenour found us after all.' He tried to thrust the memory from his mind. 'And there is no time to make contact with the commodore.' He stared at the stern windows, at the swirling phosphorescence from the rudder and the beginning of a moon on the water.

Perhaps there never had been enough time.

He said, 'We will rejoin Sir Richard. Instruct Mr Partridge to lay off a new course and have the hands change tack.' He said nothing more, and eventually his head lolled, and he did not feel the others lift his legs on to the bench seat. Nor did he hear Martin murmur, 'I will deal with that, my captain. Just this once, *you* come first.'

17

All Is Not Lost

Bolitho took a mug of coffee from Ozzard and returned once again to his chart. Avery and Yovell watched him in silence, each knowing that he was thinking of Herrick below in the sickbay.

Bolitho sipped the hot coffee. Catherine had sent it to the ship for him. There could not be much more of it left.

He tapped the chart with his dividers and said, 'At least we have more time now that Commodore Keen knows what we are about. Major-General Drummond will have enough to trouble him with seasick soldiers and horses that can barely stand, without the threat of a sea-attack.'

As the others suspected his thoughts were of Herrick. He had visited him several times in spite of the need to remain in close contact with his little group of ships, and he had been shocked by what he had found. As Minchin the surgeon had said from the start, 'Rear-Admiral Herrick is too strong in character to submit. Most men either faint from the pain or drink themselves into a stupor. Not him, Sir Richard. Even under the knife he was fighting me.'

Herrick had seemed somehow defenceless and vulnerable on the last visit, his normally weathered features already like death. In between periods of insensibility he had been elsewhere, in other ships, shouting orders and demanding answers to questions nobody had been able to understand. Once he had called out the name of their first ship together, *Phalarope*,

258

and several times he had spoken in an almost matter-of-fact tone of his beloved Dulcie.

Bolitho's mind came back with a jolt as Avery said, 'Baratte will not know about your despatches, sir. But he will not wish to wait too long before he moves.'

Bolitho agreed. 'To the north of Mauritius there is an area littered with smaller islands, Gunners Quoin, for instance. It would take a whole squadron to search amongst them.' He rapped the chart again. 'It is my belief that Baratte and his murderous friend will bide their time there until he can gain intelligence of the first convoy.'

Avery held out his mug to Ozzard. 'It is our only advantage.'

'You sound troubled.'

Avery shrugged. 'It is beyond my experience, sir.'

Bolitho would have questioned him further but at that moment there were voices at the door. He turned, his spine like ice as Ozzard opened the screen and he saw Minchin's grey head in the entrance.

'What . . . ?'

Minchin came in rubbing his hands on his apron. He almost grinned as he said, 'Into safe waters, Sir Richard. A very close-run thing.'

'You mean he is all right?' He had been prepared, but not for this.

Minchin nodded. 'It'll take a while, but the fever is falling away. I'm quite surprised.'

'May I see him?'

Minchin stood aside. 'He was asking for you in actual fact, Sir Richard.' He beamed, and there was a strong odour of rum. 'My surgeon's mate must take all the credit. He reads medicine and surgery, morning, noon an' night. He'll make as good a surgeon as many an' better than most, in my opinion!'

Bolitho hurried down the two ladders to the sickbay. After all that had happened it was the best news he could have hoped for.

Herrick looked up at him from his cot and tried to smile.

'You told me we would win,' he said faintly, and closed his eyes.

Allday was grinning, a glass of brandy in his fist; and the

surgeon's mate, Lovelace, a pale, rather effeminate young man who had an almost prison pallor as if he rarely left the sickbay, said, 'The ship held steady, Sir Richard, so I used the double skin-flap method. It is more severe, but lessens the chances of gangrene.'

Bolitho eyed him gravely. 'I an indebted to you, and I shall see that you receive mention in my next despatches.'

They waited for Lovelace to leave, then Herrick said, 'Enjoys his trade, that one.' He winced as he moved, but he seemed lucid and composed, as if he had accepted it. As an afterthought he asked, 'What of the enemy and that bloody renegade Englishman? I heard that Commodore Keen's convoy has been ordered to stand fast – is that true?'

Bolitho said lightly, 'Are there no secrets in a ship, Thomas? But you are correct. I thought it best.'

He turned as shoes clattered on the companion ladder, and a midshipman's pale breeches seemed to glow in the orlop deck's poor light.

'The captain's respects, Sir Richard . . .' His eyes moved unwillingly to the cot and the bandages where Herrick's fore-arm had once been.

'We are all agog, Mr Harris.'

The youth flushed under his admiral's gaze and blurted out, 'The masthead has reported gunfire, he thinks to the south'rd.'

Bolitho controlled his instinct to hurry to the quarterdeck. It was common enough for masthead lookouts to hear far-off sounds, just as they would see another sail before anybody else. But this was from the wrong direction. Otherwise Tyacke's *Larne* would have reported it.

'I shall come up.' He looked at Herrick. 'I cannot say what this means to me.'

Herrick watched him thoughtfully, as if he were still grap-pling with something. But he said, 'Is this something unex-pected, Richard? Are we a match for them?'

Herrick's *we* warmed him more than he could have believed possible. He rested one hand on Herrick's uninjured arm. 'I have often been a flag officer with only two ships to command. This is the first time I have had one ship with two admirals in charge!'

Allday said anxiously, 'I'd best go, sir.'

Herrick was becoming drowsy: something Minchin had given him, or perhaps it was due more to Allday's brandy. He said quietly, 'I'll not forget, you rogue!'

Allday grinned. 'There, sir, your old self already!'

Bolitho found Trevenen and his lieutenants at the quarter-deck rail, each with a telescope as they stared at the eye-watering horizon.

'Deck there! Sail to the south'rd!'

Trevenen looked grim. 'We had better clear for action, Sir Richard.'

Bolitho wiped his eye with his fingers. Clear for action so soon? Why was he so on edge? *Laertes*'s pale canvas made the tiniest mark on the horizon, with *Larne* staying well up to windward. In contact, within sight of each vigilant lookout.

Trevenen continued, 'A broadside, I think, Sir Richard.' He was puzzled, and he could not hide it. 'Only one.'

'Well, this stranger must have sighted us, Captain Trevenen. She seems to hold her course.' He trained his telescope very carefully by resting it on Midshipman Harris's shoulder. It would make a good story for the dog watches, he thought.

'Deck there! She's a frigate, sir!'

Avery said, 'But which one?'

Someone murmured, 'By God, her captain knows how to make a ship take wings!'

Trevenen barked, 'Mr Monteith, I'd be more than obliged if you would keep such empty observations to yourself!'

The young lieutenant seemed to cringe, but swung away when he saw Avery watching.

Bolitho had heard the exchange. The frigate could be none other than *Anemone*. In such a short while he had proved what he could do, and he had the confidence to use his initiative whenever he got a chance.

But why Adam? Perhaps Keen had thought it prudent to send him. They were like extensions of himself, his ears and eyes, and the steel in his grip.

Bolitho said, 'We will not clear for action, Captain Trevenen.' He took a chance. 'Let me know when *Anemone* is within range of our signals. Mr Avery, come aft with me.'

261

In the cabin Yovell was already leaving, while Ozzard was mixing something to carry to the sickbay. Like Allday, each knew Bolitho's moods, and recognised in him now the need for private conversation with his flag lieutenant.

Avery said, 'I am delighted to hear of Rear-Admiral Herrick's recovery.'

Bolitho strode to the stern windows and shaded his eyes to look for *Larne*'s topsails.

'When you came to me and I accepted you as my flag lieutenant, we had a wary agreement with each other. Would you see it that way?'

He stared out at the sea and waited for his vision to blur. He could feel Avery watching him, could sense his unwillingness to speak of what troubled him.

Avery said, 'You have my complete loyalty as a King's officer, sir.'

Bolitho turned but could see very little in the shadows of the cabin.

'And friendship too, I would hope?'

'I value it more than I can express, sir. But after my experiences, and carrying the stigma of an unjust court-martial, I have been careful in what I say and do.'

'In case you lose your position, that rung on the ladder we all envy at times, and which was denied you by the very navy you so obviously love.'

Avery heard more cries from the lookout, some bare feet padding overhead as the sails were re-trimmed yet again. When he answered his voice was faraway.

'To keep silent and to do only my duty . . . I thought it was enough. I had no way of understanding the greater power of Admiralty.'

As if from another world, Bolitho recalled Catherine's warning that Sir Paul Sillitoe might be using Avery for his own ends. It hurt him more than he thought possible.

Avery said flatly, 'I wrote to my uncle. From Gibraltar, as a matter of fact. He told me things.'

'About me?'

Avery stared at him, shocked. 'Never, sir! I was merely

curious as to why a ship like *Valkyrie* should be given to Captain Trevenen.'

'Then you acted wrongly and improperly.'

Bolitho wished he could see his face, but after the ocean's mirrored surface the cabin's darkness was like being in a cave.

'I still require an explanation, Mr Avery.'

Avery replied, 'I did it because of you, sir, not in spite of you. I had seen how you hated the floggings and privations set upon the people, and you felt helpless to interfere.'

Bolitho waited. You saw a man every day, shared a meal or a memory, and all the while you did not know him. Perhaps until now.

'My uncle was well-informed. I suspect he knew when their lordships insisted upon your appointment to Good Hope.' He spoke with such anger he could not conceal it. 'This ship was Trevenen's reward for false evidence at a court of enquiry. He once served in the frigate *Priam*, an unhappy ship according to my uncle, with a captain who twice allowed men to die under punishment. Trevenen gave evidence to refute this, and the court of enquiry was only too eager to dismiss the complaints.'

'Can I guess the name of *Priam*'s captain?'

'I think you know, sir. It was Hamett-Parker, now Admiral Sir James Hamett-Parker. The one who instigated your appointment here.' He sounded out of breath.

Bolitho gripped the edge of the bench seat. 'He once made a point of telling me he had never served in frigates.'

Avery said quietly, 'The admiral is aware of Trevenen's hatred of your family, sir. A simple but cruelly effective weapon.' He was speaking more quickly, as if he might regret the impulse if he hesitated. 'Trevenen comes of lowly stock, sir.'

'All to his good, I'd have thought.' Even as he spoke Bolitho recalled Trevenen's endless discussions with the purser and his clerk about ship's stores and the fresh fruit which was so necessary in these demanding climates.

Avery said, 'This is not how I meant it to end, sir. You have my word on it.' He sounded as if he had turned away to look

263

around the cabin. 'It has been my great fortune to serve with you, and I know I have dismissed my chances for good.'

'There is something else?'

Avery said, 'I feel in my bones that we are intended to fight. I am not new to it, nor will I fail you when it begins.'

Bolitho heard the squeal of halliards from above in that other world, probably an acknowledgement to the other frigate's signal.

He tried to remain calm. 'I never doubted your ability.'

Avery said, 'When you know a secret . . .'

'Tell me only if you wish. You have said enough to destroy you already.'

'Captain Trevenen is a coward, sir. I have watched him. I am a good judge of men, I think.'

Heavy feet pounded on the ladder and Trevenen's knuckles rapped impatiently on the door.

For a moment they stood staring at one another. Then Bolitho said, 'That took courage too.' He paused. 'It is still a secret, Mr Avery.' He said sharply, 'Enter!'

Trevenen almost burst into the cabin, 'She is *Anemone*, Sir Richard!' It sounded like an accusation. 'Her captain is coming aboard!'

'Is that all, Captain?'

Trevenen took a grip on himself, his massive figure swaying about as if he had forgotten where he was.

'*Orcadia*'s lost! Yellow Jack!'

Bolitho caught his breath. Without asking he knew what must have happened. In the time available Adam had not been able to report to Keen, which probably meant that Keen's ships had already sailed.

'I shall come up directly.'

As the door slammed shut Allday came in by the other entrance.

Bolitho said quietly, 'Poor Stephen Jenour. He did not want a command, you know. I forced it on him. I might as well have shot him.'

Avery was disconcerted, uncertain what to say. 'I'm sure it's what any officer would want, sir.'

'I doubt that.' He reached out for Avery's arm but missed it in the shadows.

'We have a war to fight, Mr Avery. Put other thoughts from your mind. You did it for me and you acted rightly. Every commander must know his weakness as well as his strength.'

Allday placed a glass by his hand, 'Wet, Sir Richard.' He could not say more.

'We shall wait on deck, sir.' Avery followed the burly coxswain into the filtered sunlight. It seemed incredible that *Anemone* had already changed tack and run down under their lee. Avery could even make out individual figures, men dashing past the guns to haul on the boat-hoisting tackles.

Then he turned and was astonished to see the intensity of Allday's stare.

'What is it?'

Allday said steadily, 'I've not known you that long, sir, but I happen to believe you've come to belong to Sir Richard's little crew as he calls us.' He did not smile. 'Otherwise I'd not be saying a word, see?'

'I was sorry to hear about Jenour, though I scarcely knew him.'

Allday brushed it aside. 'He was a good man. We all trusted him, I mean.' Then he made up his mind. 'I think you should know, sir, because I've seen the way he's taken to you . . .' He hesitated and then blurted out, 'If you speaks of it to anybody but us, I shall know.'

Avery waited, knowing that it was not merely important, but vital.

'He's going blind, sir. Left eye. He was badly wounded. We have to watch him, like.'

'I thank you for your trust. I mean that most sincerely.'

Allday did not seem to hear. 'Sir Richard used to have a flag lieutenant, the Honourable Oliver Browne, he was. A real gentleman, an' I means that in the only true way. Always spoke of *We Happy Few*, he did. Then he got himself killed.' His eyes hardened. 'Not in any sea-fight, neither.'

He moved away as *Anemone*'s sails were backed and the gig dropped smartly alongside. Over his shoulder he said, 'Now you're one of the *few*, sir!'

265

Valkyrie came up into the wind, her sails like thunder in the fresh breeze. Avery stood by the hammock nettings while the side-party prepared to receive *Anemone*'s captain.

'So there you are!' Bolitho strode from the companion hatch and glanced at the compass before acknowledging the officer-of-the-watch.

Avery watched him, and was moved by the easy way he could bridge the distance from quarterdeck to forecastle, from naval hero to ordinary pressed seaman; and something of his admiration and his sadness must have revealed itself on his face. Bolitho looked first at *Anemone* and then toward Allday, who was standing by one of the guns.

Then he said quietly, 'He told you, didn't he?'

'A little, sir. You can trust me.' He hesitated. 'Can nothing be done?'

'I believe not.' He smiled. 'Let us receive my nephew and find out what he knows!'

It was astonishing. *I believe not*, he had said. But his tone implied the opposite.

Avery looked at Allday and saw him give the briefest of nods. He was accepted.

Bolitho stood just outside the door of the sickbay. Beyond the hull the sea would be in total darkness, with only the occasional glow of phosphorescence or a breaking crest to betray movement. The ship felt even quieter than usual, but for reasons other than fear of punishment.

Just before darkness had closed in to conceal one ship from another, *Larne* had made one last signal. Tyacke had sighted several sail to the north-east. They could only be the enemy.

Bolitho thought of Adam's brief visit to receive his orders and to describe the horror he had seen in the drifting *Orcadia*. He had the strongest feeling that, bad though it was, Adam had spared him the worst part. He had described how he felt about leaving his patrol area to join them, and how he had announced his approach by the single broadside the lookout had heard. He had sighted an Arab topsail-schooner, which must have been tracking the *Anemone* after she had left the *Orcadia*: one of Baratte's scouts, or a slaver who was still willing to risk capture. Either way there had been too little time to give chase with the added risk of losing her in an approaching rain squall. Adam had fired a broadside at extreme range and had left the vessel dismasted and adrift to fend for herself.

The enemy's strength was unknown, but their own numbers were probably already listed in Baratte's mind like a plan of action.

Whatever they were, they would not proceed further in the darkness. They would hold as close together as possible until first light.

Bolitho could picture the *Valkyrie*'s watch below, brooding over what they would perceive as inevitable, the landmen and the youngsters asking the old Jacks what to expect. *What is it like?*

He heard Avery walking very softly behind him. Leaving him to his thoughts, instantly ready if he was needed.

How did he know Trevenen was a coward? There had certainly been no doubt in his voice. Something Sillitoe had told him, or had it been his father, who had died in battle?

Trevenen's reward for lying under oath to save his captain from disgrace was no small thing. Just to be *Valkyrie*'s captain now was privilege enough to ensure his promotion to flag rank, if he could stand clear of trouble or causing offence to Hamett-Parker. It was not cowardice in that case, but just as dangerous.

Minchin loomed out of the shadows. 'Yes, Sir Richard?'

'How is he?'

Minchin scratched his head. 'Sleeping now. Been fretting a mite, but that's usual enough.'

He grinned as Herrick called, 'Who is that?'

Bolitho stepped into the light of a solitary lantern. 'I am here, Thomas.'

Herrick gasped with pain as he tried to drag himself into a sitting position. Between his clenched teeth he exclaimed, 'Hell's teeth! One arm is more trouble than two!' Then he lay still again, his eyes glowing in the flickering light.

'We're to fight then?'

'We have to *win*, Thomas.'

267

Herrick sipped from a mug which Lovelace held for him. 'Always the same. Not enough ships where you need 'em. We've known it a few times, eh? They never learn, because they don't have to see it. To do it!'

'Easy, Thomas.'

'I know, I know.' He moved his head from side to side. 'And I'm no use to you either!'

Herrick saw Avery for the first time. 'I abused you at Freetown, Mr Avery.' He looked away. 'I heard about Jenour as well. No age to go.'

Bolitho paused by the door again. 'Try to sleep. I shall see that you are looked after if . . .'

Herrick raised his left arm. '*If*. That has a chilling ring too.'

Outside the sickbay the ship seemed at peace. Some midshipmen were crouched in a tight circle, their expressions revealed only by the light of their glims. Like some strict religious sect; but Bolitho knew they were asking one another questions on seamanship and navigation. Preparing like all 'young gentlemen' throughout the fleet for that magic day when they would be examined for lieutenant. To midshipmen it was the first, impossible rung on the ladder, and few could see any further beyond it.

Lovelace left the sickbay carrying two books, and Bolitho recalled what the surgeon had told him.

He asked, 'Have you ever thought of taking the big step, Lovelace? To the College of Surgeons? Mr Minchin speaks very highly of you.'

It was the first time he had seen him smile.

'I too would like to own a carriage and pair, Sir Richard!' The smile vanished. 'I beg your pardon, sir. I meant no offence.'

Avery watched, leaning against the curved timbers at his back. He saw Bolitho reach out for the young man's arm, heard him say quietly, 'If we can break the enemy tomorrow, I will sponsor you.'

Avery almost held his breath, unwilling to miss any of it.

Bolitho said, 'My late flag lieutenant should have studied medicine, not war, like his father and uncle before him.

Instead . . .' He turned aside. 'But Fate decided otherwise, God bless him!'

Lovelace was still staring after them as they climbed the companion ladder together.

'That was a generous thing to have done, sir.'

'You reap only what you sow.' He gripped a rope hand rail as the hull dipped heavily in a cross-swell. Then he said, 'Sup with me tonight. I wish to discuss the signals for tomorrow. There may be little enough time later on.'

The meal was a simple one, washed down with some of Catherine's claret from St James's Street. In Ozzard's capable hands it made a fitting end to the day.

Even as, encouraged by the flag lieutenant, he reminisced, and spoke of men and campaigns he had known, Avery was aware that Bolitho was speaking of others like Jenour, who would be remembered only by the few who had shared those experiences.

He saw Bolitho touch the locket beneath his shirt, his gaze faraway as he said, 'I shall add a little more to my letter to Lady Catherine before I sleep. She was very fond of Stephen. He used to sketch her, like the daily scenes he saw around him.'

He would not have to tell her what to do when she received the news. She would go to Southampton herself and see Jenour's parents, to spare them at least the brutal formality of an Admiralty letter.

The Secretary of the Admiralty regrets to inform you . . .

Nobody should have to suffer that.

He said almost abruptly, 'If anything should happen . . .' He looked at Avery directly. 'There is a letter in my strongbox which you may deliver to . . .'

'I would prefer that it never need be read, Sir Richard.'

Bolitho smiled. 'That was well said.' Without realising what he was doing he touched his eye with his fingertips, so he did not see the concern on the lieutenant's face. 'Baratte is a devious man, a trickster who will use every ruse to overthrow us. Whoever loses will be a scapegoat, something too well known to you already. His father was denounced as a hated *aristo* during the Terror and was beheaded before those

269

howling murderers. He was an honourable officer, and France has had cause to regret his death and the blood on their hands of so many others like him. Baratte has done all in his power to prove his skill and his worth to his country, perhaps to protect himself. It is a weakness that may make him reckless enough to play one trick too often.'

'And what of the Englishman Hannay, sir?'

'He will fight as never before.'

'No weakness then?' Avery was fascinated as he watched the inner power of this man, the grey eyes full of intensity and emotions as he spoke of his enemies so lucidly that Avery could almost see them. It was impossible to know from his appearance that the vice-admiral was almost blind in one eye. Another secret.

'Only that he is unused to taking orders.' Bolitho shrugged. 'Especially from a Frenchman!' It seemed to amuse him.

He looked at Avery's serious face. 'Mr Yovell thought well of you from the start, that day in Falmouth. He was particularly impressed with your knowledge of Latin, although at the time I had no idea it would prove so useful!'

'A good deal will depend on your nephew tomorrow, sir.'

'Yes. I am very proud of him. He is like a son to me.'

Avery did not press the point. 'Mr Yovell tells me that he met Nelson, who spoke warmly of him.' He hesitated. 'Did you never meet him, sir?'

Bolitho shook his head, suddenly depressed. The same people who now sang the little admiral's praises had been the same ones who had tried to destroy him before he had fallen aboard *Victory*. And what of his dear Emma? What had become of her? How did those who had made promises to Nelson even as he lay dying manage to face themselves, he wondered?

And Catherine. Who would care for her if the worst happened?

He said, 'Go and speak with the first lieutenant. He needs to be reassured.'

Avery stood up and felt the ship around him, shivering repeatedly as she thrust the ocean contemptuously from her flanks.

270

'Tomorrow then, sir.'

Bolitho nodded, then said, 'What did you want to know about Nelson?'

Avery rested his hand on the screen door. 'Men who never knew or even saw him shed tears like women when they heard of his death.' He opened the door. 'I never thought to see it myself until I became your flag lieutenant, sir.' Then he was gone.

Bolitho smiled. Avery would think very differently if the day went against them.

After Ozzard had tidied the cabin and had departed thoughtfully to his pantry, Bolitho took a small book from his trunk and turned it over in his hands: not one of Catherine's gifts of Shakespearean sonnets in their immaculate green leather binding, but a much older book, stained by salt air and much handling, one of his few possessions which had actually been carried by his father. It was *Paradise Lost*. Like Captain James Bolitho, he had read it beneath the scorching tropical sun, or riding out a storm on blockade duty off Brest and Lorient, and in the calm of some unspoiled anchorage.

With great care he covered his left eye with his hand and held the page close to a cabin lantern.

> *What though the field be lost?*
> *All is not lost; the unconquerable will,*
> *And study of revenge, immortal hate,*
> *And courage never to submit or yield.*

Bolitho closed the book and walked across the cabin to the table where his chart still lay.

Perhaps it had already been decided, and there was nothing he could do to change what Fate had decreed.

The ship swayed again and the lantern's yellow glare touched momentarily on the sword that hung on the bulkhead. It seemed to bring the steel to life.

Aloud he said, '*All is not lost.*'

He stared at the stern windows, but saw only his reflection against the darkness of the sea. Like a ghost, or the portraits on the walls at Falmouth.

271

He felt suddenly calm, as if something had been resolved. It had so often been like this in the past when all that had stood between a victory and disaster had been the courage of individuals on either side or beneath different flags.

He sat down again and took the unfinished letter from a drawer. It would be summer in Cornwall, the air full of farm noises, sheep and cattle, the bustle of bees. The scent of roses. Her roses . . .

He touched the locket as he read the last lines of this lengthy letter. She might never see it.

I have some unhappy news to tell you about Stephen Jenour . . .

He wrote with great care, as if he were talking with her, or she were watching him at this table.

I feel certain that we shall fight tomorrow. He looked up at the deckhead as feet moved purposefully aft. The middle watch was about to begin. He smiled gravely and crossed out the last word and replaced it with *today*.

He pictured his few captains lost out there in the darkness, each as different as one man could be from the others. Young Adam, who might be thinking of the girl who could never be his. Peter Dawes, the admiral's son, who thought a little too much of taking prizes and making certain that he was never found wanting when it came to a fight: a keen young officer, who was not hampered by either imagination or doubt. James Tyacke, totally alone and yet so much a part of all that had happened. And of course the senior captain, Aaron Trevenen, hostile, resentful and in matters of discipline, completely unbending.

He heard some of the hands being dismissed to their messes. There would be little sleep for many of them.

He thought too of Nelson and Avery's surprising comparison. Nelson had written a letter to his beloved Emma even as the combined enemy fleets had left port.

He had ended it by saying, 'I hope that I shall live to finish my letter after the battle.'

Bolitho folded the letter but did not seal it. *I shall finish it later.*

18

The Most Dangerous Frenchman

Lieutenant George Avery peered around the confines of his small, hutch-like cabin. Soon now, the cabin would be torn down and the various screens that partitioned many parts of the hull to offer a small privacy would follow to be stowed in the frigate's hold. Sea-chests, clothing, souvenirs, portraits of loved ones, all would be gathered into *Valkyrie*'s belly. This was a ship of war, and it would be cleared from bow to stern so that every gun could work unhindered until the fight was won. The alternative was rarely considered.

Avery dressed with care, knowing that Bolitho would expect it. His stomach had shied away from the thought of food, and the smell of grease from the galley funnel had been enough to make him retch. He looked at his face in the small mirror propped on his chest. He had shaved and put on a clean shirt and stockings. He watched the face smile back at him. *The last rites*. He never doubted that there would be a battle: Bolitho had convinced him.

Avery had known other sea officers who had this gift, if it could be called that, but none like him. Avery, still unsure of himself with the vice-admiral, had thought he had gone too far when he had spoken of Nelson. If anything, Bolitho had seemed amused by his sincerity, as if he himself thought it absurd that he should be compared to his hero.

He tugged out his watch, all that had survived from his father's possessions after Copenhagen, and held it beside the lantern. He would call the admiral. How quiet the ship was, and there was no light when he walked past the companion ladder that led to the quarterdeck.

He heard Trevenen's harsh voice berating somebody up there. A man who had been unable to sleep like most of his crew. Avery smiled wryly. *Like me.*

The ship's corporal was speaking with the marine sentry; both of them looked grim, Avery thought. The sentry would be receiving his orders. If battle was joined, he would prevent any man from running below to hide, on pain of death.

The screen door opened and Allday came out carrying a jug of used shaving water.

Avery stared at him. 'Is Sir Richard about so soon?'

Allday eyed him curiously and replied, 'We thought you was goin' to lie abed till after the fight, sir!'

Avery shook his head. The humour was more unnerving than the grim preparations all around him.

It was very bright in the cabin, with several lanterns swinging from their brackets, and shutters across the stern windows to make it unusually private. He glanced at an eighteen-pounder, still tethered by its breeching rope and covered with canvas to make the cabin seem less war-like. Even this place would not be spared.

Bolitho came out of the sleeping compartment, pulling on a clean shirt while Ozzard trotted impatiently behind him to make adjustments to his belt.

'Good morning, Mr Avery.' Bolitho sat down to look at his chart while Ozzard struggled to arrange his stock. 'Wind's steady enough, but not much strength in it.' He moved away to look in his desk and Avery saw him tuck a letter into his waistcoat. One of hers. To have with him, like the locket which would be resting against his skin.

Bolitho said, 'We will clear for action presently. I am told that the people have been fed, watch by watch.' He seemed to think that amusing too. Perhaps he had had to overrule Trevenen once again. The captain might have wanted to feed his company *after* the battle: less food to waste, fewer mouths to fill.

He jabbed at the chart. 'We shall continue to steer north'rd. If the wind holds we should be on a converging tack with the enemy. If so, he will have to remain very much close-hauled, while we shall have the wind-gage. For a while.'

Yovell yawned hugely and continued to write in his folio. He looked so out of place here, Avery thought. An educated man who apparently preferred the dangers of the sea and the risk of sudden death to the easier life more appropriate to someone of his profession ashore.

Allday came back into the cabin and strode to the bulkhead where Bolitho's swords were usually displayed. Avery noted that the beautiful presentation blade from the people of Falmouth had already gone below. He watched Allday pull out the other blade, the old one he had seen in the portraits at Falmouth.

Bolitho looked fresh and calm, and gave no sign of doubt or anxiety. Avery tried to take comfort from the fact.

Heavy feet sounded across the deck. The captain.

Bolitho merely glanced up and commented, 'I have yet to convince that one.'

The footsteps faded and then moved on to the ladder. Trevenen looked surprised when he entered the cabin. Perhaps he had expected to find them all in a desperate conference, Avery thought coldly, or finding courage in a bottle of cognac?

'Galley fire is doused, Sir Richard. Both watches standing-to.'

His eyes were sunken, and his normally aggressive confidence was lacking. Bolitho looked away. It was a bad sign.

'You may beat to quarters, Captain Trevenen, then clear for action. In ten minutes, do you propose?'

Trevenen retorted angrily, 'In *eight*, Sir Richard!'

Bolitho nodded slowly. 'This will be quite a day for many of your people. Do not drive them too far. They are not the enemy.' He let his words sink in, then added softly, 'Not yet.'

Trevenen turned by the door. 'May I speak, Sir Richard?'

'Of course.'

'I think we are making a mistake. We lack the ships for any running battle . . .'

Bolitho met his gaze steadily. 'We will not run, Captain, while my flag flies from the foremast truck.'

275

After Trevenen left he looked at the closed door, feeling the other man's defiance and anger hanging in the air.

He said to Avery, 'If anything happens . . .' He lifted one hand to silence Avery's protests. 'Do what I asked you to do.'

Calls shrilled through the ship, and from overhead came the insistent rattle of drums.

'All hands! All hands! Beat to quarters an' clear for action!'

The decks seemed to tremble as the seamen and marines ran to their stations. Screens were already being pulled down. There was not much more time.

Avery watched as Allday fastened the old sword around his admiral's waist, and saw Ozzard carrying the dress uniform coat with the gleaming epaulettes, not the faded sea-going coat Bolitho usually wore. It made a chill fasten to his spine like ice. The same uniform that had drawn the French marksmen's fire to Nelson. To provoke Baratte even at such a terrible risk, or was it to show the people he was amongst them, to give all that he had for them?

Yovell had picked up his satchel, and said, 'I shall be giving a hand on the orlop, Sir Richard.' He offered a shy smile. 'Death to the French!'

Allday muttered, 'An' that's no error!'

Ozzard spoke nervously as the crash and scrape of furniture being taken below moved swiftly towards the cabin.

'Shall you need me, Sir Richard?'

'Go below. Keep Rear-Admiral Herrick company if you wish.' But Ozzard had already gone.

Bolitho adjusted his coat and said, 'Well, old friend, it gets no easier, does it?'

Allday grinned. 'I sometimes wonders what it's all for.'

Bolitho heard men running above and beneath him. 'I expect they do also.' He looked at Avery and said firmly, 'So they must be told, eh?'

Then the three of them left the cabin, while another party of men hurried past to remove the last obstacles.

Lieutenant Urquhart called, 'Cleared for action, sir!'

Trevenen glanced at his watch. 'Nine minutes. I expected better, Mr Urquhart!'

Allday saw Bolitho's face. It was easy to read his thoughts.

Trevenen never praised anyone, even in the face of danger. The only thing he could inspire was fear.

It was dark and remarkably cool on deck after the heat of the day preceding. But dawn came quickly out here, and sunset would arrive with haste to cover the pain and disperse the fury of battle.

Bolitho glanced around. The master and his mates were near the wheel where extra men stood by the spokes. Chain-slings had been rigged to hold the great yards in place if all the rigging was shot away. And nets, although Bolitho could not yet see them, to protect the gun-crews from falling spars and blocks. It was something he knew so well, had known all his life from the age of twelve when he had first gone to sea in the forbidding and unfamiliar world of the old eighty-gun *Manxman*.

Herrick would be down there in the comparative safety of the orlop deck below the waterline: fretting over his lost arm and his helplessness, but most of all, remembering.

He moved towards the tightly-packed hammock nettings and almost slipped on a stretch of spray-soaked planking.

He said, 'This part of the deck is not sanded, Captain.' He kept his tone level but was inwardly angry at somebody's carelessness. A man or men could slip and fall in the heat of a sea-fight. Just one gun left unfired could make all the difference.

Trevenen's answer was even more surprising. 'None of the deck is sanded, Sir Richard. If the enemy fails to appear, we would have used good sand to no effect.'

'Then do it *now*, if you please. I am sure that in an ocean of this vastness we could find some more sand!'

He heard a lieutenant passing the order and the immediate response of the ship's boys, who scuttled amongst the guns like terriers.

Allday had heard the sharp exchange and was glad Trevenen had felt the edge of Bolitho's tongue. He stared up at the rigging and said, 'I can see the masthead pendant, Sir Richard.'

Bolitho peered up at the dark sky, and imagined he could see the long red and white pendant curling out from the truck.

'As soon as the sun is up, they will see *us*.'

277

Avery glanced at the shadows around him. Listening, trying to gauge their own chances of seeing another sunset.

It was uncanny not to see or know the enemy's strength. Bolitho said, 'Tell your signals party to be ready, Mr Avery. As soon as it is light enough, make *Take stations as ordered* and tell *Larne* to *Close on Flag.*'

Avery could now see the white patches on the collars of his two signals midshipmen, but some of the flags already strewn by the halliards were still colourless in the lingering gloom.

Bolitho spoke as though almost disinterested. 'I feel certain that they will already have made it ready, Mr Avery, but the next signal will be *Prepare for battle.*'

He heard Trevenen ask, 'Suppose the enemy is not there, Sir Richard?' And Avery could feel the presence of the man he served like a force.

Bolitho answered coldly, 'Then I have failed, and by tomorrow Baratte will have found Commodore Keen's convoy. The rest you can imagine for yourself.'

Trevenen muttered thickly, 'Nobody can blame *Valkyrie!*'

'You and I both know where the blame will lie, Captain! So let us all be patient a moment longer!'

Angry with himself for being so easily drawn, Bolitho said, 'I see the masthead.'

He strained his eyes upwards through the taut rigging, the web of ratlines glistening in the darkness from moisture and spray alike. Men he had not seen earlier stood out against the pale hammock nettings, or crouching like athletes as they waited to run and seize hold of braces and halliards when the next order came.

Bolitho looked over the weather quarter: there was light, a mere hint of it. It would soon lift above the invisible horizon to lay them bare for all to see.

Trevenen rasped, 'What is that masthead lookout *about*, Mr Urquhart? Does he stand watch asleep?'

Urquhart was about to raise his speaking trumpet when Bolitho said, 'You go aloft, Mr Avery. You are my eyes this morning.'

Avery lingered, his mind hanging on to the remark, and

278

wondering if Bolitho had intended him to draw another meaning from it.

Bolitho smiled. 'No head for heights?'

Avery was strangely moved. 'Good enough, sir.' He took a signals telescope from the rack and swung himself out on the shrouds while two seamen opened the protective net for him. Bolitho could see the sailors' eyes now very white in the gloom as they watched the flag lieutenant swarm up the ratlines, his sword slapping against his thigh.

Avery climbed steadily, feeling the shrouds vibrating beneath his shoes, the very strength of the ship as she opened up beneath him. The black guns, each with its crew, barebacked and waiting to load and run out, were clearly visible. He climbed out and around the mizzen-top where some marines stared at him with surprise and interest as they tended a swivel gun on the thick barricade.

He stopped and looked down again, at the yellow shoulder of the figurehead and the flapping jib and staysails, pure white against the undulating water below. He turned slightly and was in time to see the sun's rim rise slowly from the sea itself, saw it spill over the horizon and reach out in either direction to sharpen its edge with pale gold. He unslung the telescope and entwined his leg around a stay. *You are my eyes this morning.* The words still lingered like something written.

For an instant he felt stiffness in his shoulder, the wound which had struck him down on that terrible day. He had often probed it with his fingers, but had never actually seen it until he had used a looking-glass. The French surgeon had probably made it worse, but the wound had left a deep gouge in his body, as if someone had done it with a huge spoon. He was ashamed of it. It made him feel unclean.

He peered at the mainmast as the lookout yelled, 'Deck there! Ships on the lee bow!'

Below on the quarterdeck Bolitho thrust his hands under his coat to contain and hide his impatience.

Trevenen bawled, 'What are they, man?'

There was no hesitation this time. 'Ship-of-the-line, sir! And smaller ones!'

279

Trevenen's nostrils seemed to flare. 'Even my ship cannot match guns with a liner, Sir Richard!'

Bolitho watched him and heard the triumph in his voice, as if he were addressing the whole ship. Baratte had saved this unknown card for today. Trevenen was right about one thing: a frigate could not survive close action against a ship used to the line of battle and built to withstand its massive broadsides.

He thought of Adam and the other frigate, Baratte's own flagship when he had been taken prisoner. It was over before it had begun.

He looked around: at the guns, their crews staring aft to discover what was happening, the scarlet-coated marines with their muskets by the protective nettings. Even they could do nothing if the ship's company refused to fight or, as they would see it, to be killed for nothing.

There were footsteps across the deck and Bolitho saw Avery walking unhurriedly towards him.

'I did not order you down, Mr Avery!' Something on the lieutenant's face steadied him. 'What is it?'

Avery glanced briefly at Trevenen, but barely saw him. 'She's no ship-of-the-line, sir. She is the U.S.S. *Unity*, exactly as your nephew described her, spar by spar.'

He had heard Trevenen's words as he had climbed to the deck, the relief in his tone as the bright sunlight which was opening up the ocean all around them had shown him a possibility of escape.

All that had changed. Trevenen seemed unable to close his jaws, and was staring at him as if he were an apparition from hell.

'I did not wish to call out from up there, sir.' He pointed although the eastern horizon was still curtained by sun-filled haze. 'There are several small vessels with her, ahead and astern, merchantmen by the cut of them.'

Bolitho said quietly, 'A convoy then?'

Avery looked at the captain, but it was as if he had been turned to stone.

'Far up to the nor'east there are other sails – they are clearly visible from the mizzen topmast. You were right, sir. They are Baratte's frigates, I feel certain of it.'

Bolitho reached out and touched his shoulder. 'So now we know how the game is set. The American ships will do nothing but sail between us and our own two frigates. Divide and weaken us while the "convoy" is allowed to proceed in peace.'

He turned to Trevenen. 'Well, Captain, here is the ship you doubted. The most powerful frigate in the world.'

'We must discontinue, Sir Richard. Before it is too late!'

'It was already too late when Baratte was released from prison.' He moved to the chart, feeling men step aside to let him pass. 'Hoist the signal, *Prepare for Battle.*'

'Already bent on, sir.'

Bolitho heard the halliards sing through the blocks as the flags broke out to the breeze.

'Signal *Larne* to repeat the signal if neither *Anemone* nor *Laertes* is yet in sight. They know what to do.'

Trevenen stared at him angrily. 'They cannot engage without support, Sir Richard!' He looked around as if to convince those nearest to him.

'At last we agree, Captain.' Bolitho took a telescope and scanned the brightening horizon. The enemy were only a few pale flaws like tiny leaves drifting on glass. 'We shall pass through the convoy. Continue on the same tack. In the meantime, have the boats put overboard.' He was going to add, *for the victors*, but refrained. Most of the officers and all the older hands would know what the order implied. It was to protect the men on deck from flying splinters if shots smashed through a boat tier; but to the landmen and other new men it was the last chance to escape or be saved if the worst happened.

Lieutenant Urquhart called, 'I can see the Yankee, sir!'

Avery said, '*Larne* has acknowledged, sir.'

Bolitho said, 'The ships are close-hauled as tight as they'll come. *Unity*'s captain will not wish to fall off down wind and seem to be running away.'

He considered Captain Nathan Beer. Strong, determined and a veteran of frigate warfare. His ship was so well-armed that she could probably outshoot a seventy-four. No wonder the lookout had been confused.

He would hold to his course, steadily converging with *Valkyrie.*

Avery asked, 'Will they not attempt to prevent us, sir?' There was no anxiety in his voice. It was merely a technical detail, a part of the inevitable.

Bolitho felt his skin becoming damp with sweat under his heavy coat.

'Captain Beer will have little choice but to warn us off. He is no fool – Baratte's unwilling and unofficial ally perhaps, but too concerned with his duty to tolerate interference.'

Trevenen said, 'I must note this in my log, Sir Richard.'

'Please do, Captain. But I intend to break through the convoy at its weakest part while we still have the wind on our side.' He saw some of the seamen staring astern as the ship's boats drifted away, held together by loose lines so that they would not smash into one another.

Trevenen said, 'The weakest part, Sir Richard?'

'Astern of the *Unity, directly!*'

He saw no understanding on Trevenen's heavy features, and said curtly, 'I shall wish to speak with the gunner and your lieutenants.' He raised his glass again. Perhaps Baratte had even foreseen this move. Surely he would not expect the English ships to retreat?

The white marks on the horizon seemed as before, but the embrace would begin within two hours. He heard himself say, 'Plenty of time before we load and run out.'

He studied Trevenen as the captain snapped out his orders. Unwilling to see his ship badly mauled and perhaps his own future in ruins? Or was he as Avery had described, a coward?

'Will you have the people lay aft, Captain? You will wish to speak with them before . . .'

Trevenen shook his fist violently, 'They will have to learn, Sir Richard, learn and obey!'

'I see. Then have them piped aft, Mr Urquhart. I will demand much of them this day. I owe them an explanation at least.'

The calls shrilled and the hands came stampeding aft. Those from forward who had seen and heard nothing of the exchanges on the quarterdeck peered almost fearfully at the larboard gangway as if expecting to see a grating rigged for a flogging, even in the face of an enemy they did not know.

They looked first to Trevenen and then, when it was apparent that he was not to speak to them, they fixed their attention on the vice-admiral who had taken their lives into his hands, and could just as easily dispose of them.

There was silence but for the sea and shipboard noises, and even those seemed muted.

Bolitho rested his palms on the quarterdeck rail and looked over and amongst them.

'Valkyries, I thought I should tell you something of what we are about on this fine morning. My Cox'n remarked just before we cleared for action that he sometimes wonders what it is all for.' He saw several heads turn towards Allday's powerful figure. 'Many of you were taken from your homes and villages and some from honest merchant ships, against your will, to face a life which has never been an easy one. But we must never give in to tyranny no matter how difficult it is to see any value in our sacrifice, even though it be in the name of King and country.' He had all their attention now. Some of the warrant officers and older seamen were probably thinking that had such comments been made on the messdeck or in a barrack room they would be branded as treasonable.

'England must seem far away to many of you.' He looked at them steadily, wanting them to understand, needing them to do so. 'Because I stand here with my two bright stars and a flag at the masthead it does not mean that I feel this any less. I miss my home and the woman I love. But without us, our dear ones, our homes and our countryside will be as nothing if the enemy is allowed to win!'

Avery saw his hands holding the rail until the tanned skin was pale from the force of his grip. Whatever happened, he knew he would never forget this moment. He thought of Stephen Jenour, and understood now more than ever why he had loved this man.

Bolitho said quietly, so that many men further forward pressed into their companions to hear his words:

'This ship that blocks our way is not at war with us, but any flag which is raised to help an enemy is our enemy too! When we fight, do not think of causes and the justice of things, which is the way of my Cox'n.' He guessed Allday was grinning

283

behind him, and saw several of the assembled sailors smile at his words. 'Think of one another, and the ship around us! Will you do that for me, lads?'

He turned away, his hat in the air as the cheering swept across the ship as loudly as any rainfall.

Allday saw the pain in his eyes, the emotion at what he had just done, but when he reached Trevenen his voice was without mercy.

'Do you see, Captain? Leadership is all they ask, not bloody backs simply to satisfy you!'

He turned again, and looked out at the cheering seamen until in groups they went back to their stations and the guns.

Lieutenant Urquhart, his eyes blazing with excitement, said, 'They'll follow you now, Sir Richard!'

Bolitho said nothing. Urquhart did not understand. None of them did. He had betrayed these same men as he had Jenour when he had forced him to take a command.

When he spoke once more he was surprised at the normality of his own voice.

'Very well, Captain, you may load, but do not run out.' Trevenen touched his hat, his eyes red-rimmed with strain and despair. 'And have other flags bent on, Mr Avery. The Colours must be kept flying, no matter what!' Then he spoke again, although whether to himself or to Avery the flag lieutenant was never certain.

'To think that Captain Beere once knew my brother. I sometimes think I never knew him at all.'

Bolitho stood loosely near the wheel and looked around at the lieutenants and senior warrant officers he had sent for. Young faces, tense expressions, and pathetic determination. The warrant officers, the professionals, had all seen action in one ship or another, but apart from Urquhart and of course Avery, the lieutenants had not.

He recalled all the wild, reckless times he had sailed into battle: sometimes with the drums and fifes playing a lively jig to ease the strain of waiting. But not so on this morning.

The breeze had freshened very slightly, enough to harden each sail, but not so that it could break the great undulating expanse of ocean. A few gulls and other seabirds circled the top-gallant masts, undisturbed by the sullen purpose of the ship below them.

If he turned his gaze very slightly Bolitho could see the other ships, brigs and brigantines for the most part, with the *Unity* sailing amongst them like a fortress.

He said, 'We will remain on this converging tack. *Unity*'s captain will believe we intend to pass through his charges ahead of him. If we can get close enough without taking a few of *Unity*'s broadsides I intend that we should alter course at the last moment and pass astern of her. It will be a hard thing to do. It is the only course of action open to us if we are not to leave our ships unaided. All officers will ensure that topmen and all spare hands are ready to make more sail immediately. We have the wind across the quarter – when we turn we will have it astern of us.' He smiled. 'A soldier's wind!'

He glanced along the crowded deck where men crouched by the guns or waited by each mast with their midshipmen and petty officers.

Every gun was loaded, but he had not ordered any of them to be double-shotted. Some of the new hands might lose their nerve, and there was every chance of a gun exploding and killing all the men around it if improperly handled. Worse, it could start a fire right inside the ship.

When he had explained to Trevenen what he intended, to keep all gunports closed and then engage with the weapons which now faced only an empty sea, he had exclaimed, 'They will see we are cleared for action, Sir Richard! They will guess your plan of action!'

'If we run out a single gun, Captain Beer will feel justified in firing into us at extreme range. *Valkyrie* could be dismasted before a single gun could bear. Beer's neutrality is one-sided. To gather this rabble of American vessels under the pretence of escorting them through the scene of a possible battle tells me everything. It is typical of Baratte. He must win this fight.'

Urquhart asked, 'Is this in breach of our rights, Sir Richard?'

'That will be for others to decide.'

He wanted to rub his eye to clear it but controlled the impulse. 'Good luck, gentlemen. Keep the gun crews out of

285

sight until ordered. When you run out it will be an all-time record!'

Surprisingly, some of them grinned. Bolitho turned to Trevenen. 'Do you wish to add anything, Captain? They will be looking to you today.'

But Trevenen did not answer, or maybe he had not even heard. He was staring at the advancing, uneven line of vessels. To a seabird it might resemble a giant arrowhead.

To Avery Bolitho said, 'Two more good lookouts aloft. I must see when, or if, our ships are about to engage.'

He turned as Allday commented grimly, 'Now there's an ugly sight if ever I saw one!'

Unity's gunports had opened as one. They had been well-drilled: it looked as if a single hand had done it.

Then the guns, squealing up to show themselves in the frail sunshine like jagged teeth. It would need a lot of men to move them up the deck, which was sloping slightly away from the wind.

In his heart Beer probably wanted to avoid a fight, no matter how one-sided it might now appear. Such an incident as this would have serious repercussions, no matter which flag flew at the end of the day.

It would surprise the American captain to see all of *Valkyrie*'s ports tightly sealed. It would merely appear that they intended to pass through the ships, to defy the accepted rights of neutral vessels but nothing more.

Bolitho heard Urquhart say quietly, 'How long, d'you reckon?' And Avery's calm response.

'Half an hour if it works, almost immediately if it doesn't.'

It was strange how the wardroom had shunned him because of rumour and the cruel half-truths told about *Jolie*'s surrender and capture. That, too, had all changed.

Bolitho tore his eyes from the ships and the threatening sight and size of the big American frigate, and watched Bob Fasken the gunner as he strolled along the deck, pausing to speak to each crew with no more fuss than a countryman walking with his dog.

Bolitho took a telescope. 'Over here, Mr Harris!' He rested

the glass on the midshipman's shoulder and thought he could feel him trembling. A mere boy. *As we all were once.*

He held his breath as the glass dragged the frigate into full perspective, the huge ensigns curling from gaff and masthead, the red stripes and circle of bright stars very clearly visible.

He saw the towering figure on the quarterdeck near one of the smaller guns there. Probably nine-pounders, he thought. He saw the man take a telescope and train it towards *Valkyrie*, moving it slowly until he could almost feel the American staring directly at him.

Captain Nathan Beer raised his cocked hat in a mock salute, and held it in the air until Bolitho acknowledged it with his own.

He smiled and looked at Urquhart. 'Re-set the courses and t'gallants, Mr Urquhart!'

It was what they would do if they intended to overreach the *Unity* before altering course to cross ahead of her.

There was a sharp bang, and a second later a waterspout shot from the sea before the ball richochetted across the surface like a flying fish.

A seaman said derisively, 'I could do better'n that!'

Bolitho said, 'As before. Steer due north!'

'Due north she be, sir!'

There was a puff of smoke from the most forward gun, followed by the whine of a massive ball tearing overhead.

Urquhart called, 'Stand fast, lads! The next one is ours!'

Men crouched at the guns or behind anything they believed might protect them.

Bolitho could see *Unity*'s tapering jib-boom reaching out as if to impale *Valkyrie*'s figurehead. It was a delusion: there were still seven or eight cables between them.

The second gun fired and this time it smashed into the lower hull with the force of a rock. Several men cried out; others stared at the masts as if they expected to see them fall.

Trevenen seemed to come out of his trance. 'Get all spare men on the pumps! The prisoners too – they'll soon see that they are in the most danger!'

Bolitho called sharply, 'Alter course, Captain!'

But Trevenen was staring at the other ship, his eyes wild.

287

Only two things could happen. *Unity* would have to fall off down wind to avoid collision if she maintained her present course and speed. Beer would not allow that, as it would expose his stern to attack. If he shortened sail, it would still be too late.

It was now or never.

'Alter course, *now*, three points to starboard!'

The breaking of the suspense seemed to make the waiting seamen fly to their stations even as the big double wheel went over.

'Braces, there! More men on the weather braces, Mr Jones!'

Above the deck each sail strained and cracked to its yard, and as more were set to build her into a great pyramid of canvas, Bolitho watched as the American appeared to forge across the bows.

'Steady she goes, sir! Nor'east by north!'

'Open the ports! *Run out!*'

With almost every sail set and hard-filled *Valkyrie* seemed to be charging towards the other ship. The bowsprit passed like a marker across *Unity*'s mainmast, and still further until Bolitho saw the same quarterdeck as they steered for the American's high poop and glittering scrollwork.

Then the whole of the *Unity*'s side seemed to explode in long angry flames, the gunsmoke fanning through the rigging like fog.

The weight of iron smashed into *Valkyrie*'s bows and fore-castle, up-ending some of the guns but causing few casualties, as most of the gun crews had been ordered to the larboard side ready to engage. Had she not altered course so quickly, more of the twenty-four pound balls would have found their mark.

But it was bad enough. Men ran dazed and bleeding, while others lay where they had been smashed down. Blood, corpses, pieces of men were scattered like gruel, while petty officers and lieutenants tried to restore order. Some shots had been aimed high, and already seamen were swarming aloft to repair the dangling tangles of severed rigging.

And there was *Unity*'s high stern, the windows of her cabin shining brightly above *Valkyrie*'s larboard bow like an ornate cliff.

Dyer the second lieutenant yelled, 'Ready, lads! Fire as you bear!' Then he clapped his hands to his face and fell, and his place was taken by a terrified midshipman. The Americans were shooting from the taffrail, and great splinters rose like quills on the quarterdeck as the unseen marksmen saw the admiral's epaulettes.

Unity's maindeck guns were already being run out again, but if Beer could come around with the English frigate he would have to use his starboard guns. There would be no mercy from those great guns next time.

The jib-boom was already passing the American's stern. Bolitho could see the gilded lettering of her name on the counter, could almost hear Adam's voice describing it despite Trevenen's contemptuous doubt.

The great carronade, laid and prepared by the gunner himself, lurched back on its slide, and for what must have been only a split second Bolitho thought it had misfired. And then he saw the *Unity*'s stern seem to open like a jagged cave. The carronade's great ball would explode within, releasing a hail of grape-shot to scythe throughout the full length of the ship.

'As you bear! *Fire!*'

Gun by gun down the *Valkyrie*'s side each eighteen-pounder hurled itself inboard on its tackles. Not even a blind man could miss at this range. Almost every carefully supervised shot would rip through the other vessel's hull, which, like their own, would be cleared and open from stern to bow.

'*Stop your vents! Sponge out! Load! Run out!*'

Despite the fear and the pitiful screams of badly wounded men, the many hours of gun-drill and discipline held them all together.

A white-faced midshipman came to a halt, his feet slipping in blood as he saw Avery by the rail.

'Pardon, sir!' He winced as a ball slapped into the driver overhead. 'The lookouts have sighted our ships! They are engaging the enemy!'

Avery said, 'I shall tell the admiral. Thank you, Mr Warren. *Walk*, if you please!'

Urquhart yelled, 'The Yankee is not under command, sir!' His voice was cracking with disbelief.

'But she's still fighting!' Even as Avery spoke another ball smashed through some hammock nettings and tossed three marines aside like bloody bundles. One of *Unity*'s nine-pounders, probably packed with grape and cannister shot.

The sailing master was down and one of his mates staggered to his place, his white trousers splashed with the master's own blood.

He called shakily, 'Steady as she goes, sir!'

But Avery could see nothing but Allday, who was holding Bolitho against his own body as if to protect him.

Avery ran over to them. 'What is it?'

He saw Allday's face twisted in anguish. 'Splinters, sir! Send for the surgeon!'

They carried Bolitho gently to the foot of the mizzen mast.

He said hoarsely, 'Splinters . . . in my face!' He gripped Avery's arm with terrible force. '*I can't see!*'

He lowered his face into his hands. His eyes were tightly closed. Avery touched his cheek and could feel some of them, like tiny fish bones protruding from the skin.

The hull shook again to the roar of a full broadside, although few of *Valkyrie*'s guns would still bear on their opponent. Avery barely noticed it. He looked up and saw Trevenen peering at them through the smoke.

'Is it bad?'

'He can't see, sir!'

Bolitho tried to get up but Allday held him firmly. '*Get closer*, Captain! Don't give him time . . .' He broke off, gasping with pain as he tried to open his eyes.

Trevenen snapped, 'Sir Richard is wounded! Mr Urquhart, stand by to disengage. That's an order!'

Avery stared at him. 'You'd *run*?'

Trevenen's confidence was flooding back.

'I command here! I said it would fail! Now Sir Richard has only himself to blame!'

A figure in a bloodied apron hurried across the deck. It was not Minchin but his assistant, Lovelace.

Trevenen shouted, 'Take Sir Richard below. He has no place here!'

'*Who says so, damn you!*'

Avery stared as another figure came through the companion hatch, teeth bared against the pain of his severed arm. From a distance it might appear that Herrick was grinning. He stared slowly around at the litter of battle, the dead and dying, and lastly at the corpses of the marines, lying in disorder like the ones who had fought to the end aboard his old flagship.

His eyes took in the American frigate, which was drifting further and further downwind, while some of the small vessels she had been escorting headed away as if *Unity* contained something evil.

Then he said, 'The Yankee will not trouble us again, not this time in any case. We will rejoin our ships without further delay.' He closed his eyes tightly as if to control the pain.

Trevenen was staring at him, wild with disbelief.

'What are you saying? I am in command . . .' He got no further.

Herrick took a pace towards him. 'You command *nothing*. You are relieved, and I'll send you to hell for your bloody treachery! Now get off this deck!'

Trevenen hesitated as if to protest, then, almost blindly, he turned and walked to the companion hatch. He had to push and thrust his way through his men, the same men who had once been afraid even to meet his eyes. Now they watched him in silence, without fear, only contempt.

Herrick ignored him. '*You*, Urquhart or whatever your bloody name is – can you sail this ship?'

The first lieutenant nodded like a puppet, his face blanched but determined after what he had witnessed.

'I can, sir.'

'Then do it. We shall rejoin our ships. They will be hard put just now!'

One of the surgeon's loblolly boys came to support Herrick but he shook him away angrily and tugged his dress coat more firmly around his shoulders. 'See to the others, damn you!'

Bolitho lay stiffly across Allday's knees, and almost cried out as Lovelace's strong fingers prised open his eye and applied

291

a soft dressing and some stinging ointment, while the other battle raged on in the distance as if it were not real.

What he had always dreaded had happened. With neither warning nor mercy, as it had happened to the men who were even now being dragged below to the hell of Minchin's surgery. How could he go to Catherine now? How could he even consider it?

Lovelace said, 'Hold him firmly, Allday.' Then he carefully turned Bolitho's face towards the strengthening sunlight and stared into his eye with fierce concentration. He said, 'Look up, Sir Richard.'

Bolitho opened his eye and felt Allday tense as he stared past him. For an instant there was only mist and drifting flecks of blood. Then things stood out in separate, unmatched images. Herrick in his shining rear-admiral's epaulettes, gripping the rail with his hand while he peered at something beyond the torn and bloodied hammock nettings. The boy-midshipman on whose shoulder he had steadied the telescope, staring down at him, sobbing noiselessly as the guns fell silent. Further still, to the severed rigging and punctured sails, a marine in the maintop waving his hat in the air. To whom, he wondered vaguely.

He hardly dared to say it. 'I can see again.' He did not resist as Lovelace lifted the lid of his left eye. For an instant Bolitho saw surprise, even shock on his face, but he said calmly, 'I do not think this one will change, Sir Richard.'

'Help me up.'

Bolitho stood between them while Lovelace removed tiny splinters from around his eyes. Each one was so small that it could barely be seen in the smoky sunshine. But just one would have been enough.

Lovelace smiled gravely. 'There were paint-flecks as well, Sir Richard.' He looked away as somebody screamed out in agony. 'I must go, sir. I am needed.' He looked at Bolitho, and Avery thought that it was as if he were searching for something. 'And yes, I will be glad to accept your offer!'

Urquhart yelled, 'Baratte's *Chacal* has struck to *Anemone*, sir!' He was wild with excitement.

292

Bolitho strode to the quarterdeck rail with Allday's shadow covering him like a cloak.

'What of *Laertes*?' He took a telescope and winced as the sunlight lanced into his eyes.

Before they blurred again he saw *Anemone* almost alongside the French frigate, her foremast shot away and lying across Baratte's deck like a crude bridge. Two cables away, *Laertes* had grappled with the renegade's ship *Le Corsair*. It would be a double blow to Baratte that his ship should be taken by Adam. He saw it all until the brightness forced him to lower the glass. *Anemone*'s sails were in tatters, her rigging like tangled creeper, but he thought he heard cheering. Adam was safe. No other captain could have fought his ship like that.

He felt Herrick beside him and knew Allday was grinning despite the death and destruction which lay around them.

Herrick said quietly, 'They didn't need us after all. But if the Yankee had really had his say there's no telling what might have happened.'

Urquhart called, 'No signals yet, sir.'

Bolitho nodded. 'The most dangerous Frenchman afloat, and they did it. And I saw none of it.'

Herrick swayed and looked at the spots of blood which were falling from his bandaged stump.

'And he wanted to parade us together as his prisoners, eh? God rot him!'

Avery asked, 'What orders, Sir Richard?'

'We must assist the others with their prizes. After that . . .' He swung round and asked, 'No signals, Mr Urquhart? No wonder Captain Hannay gave up the fight. Baratte was playing another old trick!' They stared at him as if the fear for his sight had deranged him. Bolitho shouted, 'Where is that brig?'

'Standing well away to lee'rd, sir!'

Herrick stood steadily as a warrant officer tried to retie the reddening bandage, but suddenly the pain was too much. He gasped, 'We did it, Richard, like those other times . . .'

Then he fainted.

'Take good care of him.' Bolitho laid Herrick's coat over him as some seamen carried him on to a grating. 'But for him . . .'

Then he said, 'Baratte was directing the fight from the brig but flew his flag from *Chacal*. Just in case *Unity* could not frighten us off.'

Avery said quietly, 'If Captain Trevenen had had his way . . .' He shrugged. It already seemed like history. Only the grim reminders were real.

Bolitho said, 'Make all sail, Mr Urquhart.' He glanced down at the sailing master's corpse as if he might still respond. But his face was stiff, frozen at the moment of impact. 'Baratte shall not get away this time.'

Allday watched him grimly as he touched his eyelid. 'You had me fair troubled, Sir Richard.'

Bolitho turned to look at him, his eyes very clear. 'I know, old friend.' He fingered the locket through his smoke-stained shirt. 'Now Commodore Keen's convoy will be safe. It is up to the military from this point.' He seemed to see it in his mind. Too many men, too many ships. The price was always unbearable.

The depression lifted slightly. 'I expect I shall be unemployed for a while.'

A voice called, 'The brig has set more sail, sir!'

Bolitho clenched his hands. 'Too late. Tell the master gunner to lay aft.'

Bob Fasken appeared below the rail and knuckled his forehead. 'I'm ready, Sir Richard.' His eyes seemed to ask, *how did you know?*

Bolitho stared past him as the brig seemed to drift into *Valkyrie*'s mesh of rigging.

'Fire when you are ready, Mr Fasken.' He smiled briefly. 'Your crews did well this day.'

It seemed to take an eternity to overhaul the enemy brig. Corpses were dropped overboard, and the protesting wounded vanished from the darkly stained decks.

Trucks squealed as one of the big eighteen-pounder bow-chasers was manhandled into position. The gunner watching with his arms folded. Handspikes were used to train the gun round, and some of the unemployed men stood on the gangway to watch, a few still searching for friends, a familiar face, which would never be seen again.

The bow-chaser banged out and the smoke was cleared away even as the crew were sponging out and reloading.

Bolitho saw the shot fall short of the brig's counter, and heard some of the seamen laying bets with one another, when only moments earlier they had been staring death in the face.

'Ready, sir!'

'Fire!'

This time Bolitho thought he saw the actual fall of shot. A dark blur, then wood splinters and rigging flying from the brig's hull to drift along her side.

Urquhart said in a whisper, 'He must strike, damn him!'

Avery pointed. 'Look, sir! He's running up his flag!'

Bolitho lowered the telescope. Like an answer to Urquhart's remark. He would never surrender.

'Fire!'

It was another hit, and men could be seen running like mad creatures as spars and rigging smashed down amongst them.

Fasken shaded his eyes to peer aft. When no order was given he took the trigger-line from the gun-captain and balanced himself in a crouching position inboard of the black breech, something which he had probably not done since he had been part of a gun crew.

Bolitho felt the deck rise and then settle, saw the trigger line go taut and then jerk to Fasken's strong pull.

For a moment longer it seemed that the gunner had missed. Then there was a mingled gasp of surprise and horror as the forepart of the brig exploded into a great tower of fire. Driven gleefully by the wind, the sails and tarred rigging were consumed in minutes, the fires reaching out along the hull and spitting through the open ports like tongues of bright sparks.

The explosion, when it came, was like a single clap of thunder. Perhaps a magazine had been ignited, or maybe the brig was carrying extra powder for Baratte's privateers.

As the sound rolled away the vessel's death pall was smeared across the sky like a black stain.

Bolitho watched the sea's face easing away the violent disturbances. For what, he wondered? So that Baratte could further prove he was a better man than his father and loyal to his country's cause? A vanity, then?

He heard himself say, 'Rejoin the others, Mr Urquhart. Then tell the purser to break out the rum.' He looked at the men who had once been too cowed even to speak. 'They are all heroes today.'

Avery ventured, 'After this, Sir Richard?'

'Home, if there is still justice in the world.' He let his mind linger on it.

The mood changed just as swiftly. 'Besides, we have a wedding to attend!' He slapped Allday's shoulder. 'Keep this one up to his word!'

Surprisingly, Allday did not respond as he had expected.

He said quietly, 'Would you really do that, Sir Richard?'

The men in the other ships were all cheering now, the fear and pain held at bay. Until the next time.

But Bolitho heard only the words of his old friend. His oak.

Somewhere in the past he could recall a signal he had once made. It seemed very apt for this moment, for this special man.

'I will be honoured,' he said.

Epilogue

Richard Bolitho gripped the tasselled strap as the carriage swayed and shuddered into some deep ruts like a small boat in a choppy sea. He felt drained, and every bone in his body was aching from this endless journey. In his tired mind it all seemed to overlay in vague, blurred pictures, from the moment he had stepped ashore at Portsmouth to be whisked immediately to London to make his report.

All the while he had been yearning to get away, to begin the long, long drive from that world to his own West Country. Surrey, Hampshire, Dorset, Devon. He could not remember how many times they had stopped to change horses, how many inns they had visited. Even when he had broken the journey to spend a night in one of the coaching inns the images seemed confused. People who had stared at him, wondering what business was taking him westward but too nervous or polite to ask. The smells of meat puddings and mulled ale, saucy-eyed servant girls, jovial landlords who lived off the coaching trade with far more success than the highwaymen.

Opposite him Allday sprawled across his seat, his bronzed face rested and untroubled in sleep. Like most sailors he could sleep anywhere, if an opportunity offered itself.

It was hard to accept that he was in England after all that happened. Baratte was dead, and even Tyacke, who had searched the whole area in his *Larne*, had found no living soul to survive the terrible explosion.

Under jury-rig and nursing their injuries and damage, the

ships, including the two French prizes, had crawled back to Cape Town. There, to his astonishment, Bolitho had found fresh orders requiring him to hand over his command to Commodore Keen and return home. They had passed Keen's convoy on passage but not close enough to communicate. Bolitho's flag at the fore would tell Keen all he needed to know. The way ahead was clear, and the first military landings on the islands adjoining the main objective, Mauritius, could go ahead.

Bolitho wiped the window with his sleeve. They had made an early start, as they had on most mornings when the road had been a good one. Bare, black trees, wet from overnight mist or rain, the rolling fields and hills beyond. He shivered, and not only with excitement. It was November and the air was bitter.

He thought of the good-byes and the unexpected partings. Lieutenant Urquhart had been left in charge of *Valkyrie*, supervising the repairs until a new captain was appointed. That was the strangest thing of all, Bolitho thought. Trevenen had vanished on the final night before making their landfall at Good Hope. A twist of fate? Or had he been unable to face the consequences of what he had done when Bolitho had been wounded? He had left no letter, no declaration. The ship had been searched from cable tier to orlop: it had been just as if he had been spirited away.

Or it might have been murder. Either way, the part played by Hamett-Parker in getting Trevenen such an important command might be reopened because of it.

Farewells. Tyacke, grave and strangely sad, able to forget his disfigurement while they had shaken hands: friends or brothers, they were both.

And Adam, whose *Anemone* had seen the worst of the fighting and had suffered the most casualties. Adam had spoken of them with pride and with a deep sense of loss. Two of his lieutenants had been killed. His voice had been full of unashamed emotion when he had described how they had grappled with the *Chacal*, which had been flying Baratte's own flag, and one of his midshipmen, called Dunwoody, had fallen.

'I had recommended him for early promotion. He will be greatly missed.'

Bolitho had felt his pain. It was often like that when a battle was permitted to have personality, faces and names: when the cost was so high, and so personal.

Bolitho had been glad to leave. He had been offered passage in a rakish little sixth-rate of twenty-six guns named *Argyll*. Her young captain was very aware of the importance of his passenger and the despatches he carried, and doubtless wondered why an officer of such seniority did not wait for a more comfortable vessel.

There had also been a letter at Cape Town from Catherine. On the speedy journey from the Cape he had re-read it many times. He had experienced a powerful jealousy and apprehension when she had written of her visit to Sillitoe; even fear for her personal safety and reputation.

I had to do it, for our sakes, yours and mine. I could never allow what has happened in my past to hurt you more than many have done already. You can always trust me, dearest of men, and there was nobody else I myself could trust, for whatever reason, to keep my secrets. There were times when I questioned my actions, but I need not have doubted. In some ways I believe that Sir Paul Sillitoe was surprised at his own sense of decency.

At London Herrick left him to have further treatment for his amputation. So different from that other Herrick. Still gruff and afraid of showing his innermost feelings, he had said, 'They might offer me something else, Richard.' His bright blue eyes had dropped to his empty sleeve. 'I'd have given a lot more that day if need be, just to regain your respect.'

'And friendship, Thomas.'

'Aye. I'll never forget that. Not again.' He had given a slow grin. 'I'll put things right. Somehow.'

Bolitho eased his position on the seat and pulled his boat-cloak closer around his body. The change from the Indian Ocean to an English winter had been harsher than he had expected. Getting older? He thought of his face in the looking-glass when Allday had shaved him only this morning at an inn in St Austell. His hair was still black except for the hated lock over the scar above his right eye where the cutlass had hacked him down all those years ago.

How would she see him? Might she have regretted her decision to stay with him?

He thought of Yovell and Ozzard, who were travelling at a more leisurely pace in a second carriage with all their belongings. He glanced at the slumbering figure opposite. The 'little crew' had diminished still further when the carriage had stopped overnight in Dorset. Avery, his companion through so much, would be staying in Dorchester with his married sister. It had been a strangely awkward parting, and Bolitho guessed that his flag lieutenant was considering the promotion which he had offered him. It was not certain if he could be tempted to remain with a vice-admiral who might be unemployed for some time.

Bolitho felt the carriage pause on the crest of a hill, the horses panting and stamping their feet.

All those weeks at sea, re-living past ships and lost faces, then days on the road. He dropped the window and looked at the nearest field, the slate wall heavy with moss and damp. There was a hint of ice at the side of the road but there was hard sunshine too, and no sign of snow.

He knew that Allday had awakened and was on the edge of his seat, watching him. Big and powerful he might be, but when required he could move like a cat.

He faced him, remembering the despair in his voice when he had prevented him from pushing the surgeon's mate Lovelace aside.

'Hear that, old friend?'

A slow understanding crossed Allday's weathered features and he nodded.

Bolitho said quietly, 'Church bells. Falmouth!'

Everything else seemed so distant here. Mauritius would be in English hands by now, with relief and gratitude on the part of the Honourable East India Company. Baratte's privateers and pirates like Simon Hannay would have nowhere now to hide and seek shelter from the English frigates.

300

He himself was so eager to get home, and yet his doubts rendered him uncertain. He touched his eye, unaware of Allday's sudden apprehension, recalling Portsmouth Point where he had been pulled ashore from the little *Argyll*. In the sternsheets he had turned and looked back at the frigate as she rode at anchor, her passengers and responsibilities gone.

It had been a clear morning like this one, with the frigate bright and sharp against the Isle of Wight and the cruising ranks of cats' paws.

Then he had covered his uninjured eye with his hand, the eye he had feared had been blinded by splinters, and had looked again.

The ship had appeared to be covered with mist and the sea much darker.

Allday leaned towards him. 'Beggin' your pardon, Sir Richard, I think I'll not be wed after all!'

Bolitho stared at him. 'How so?'

Allday gave his lazy grin. 'Because I think mebbe you've too many worries to be left alone!'

Bolitho looked at his hands.'I don't know what I shall do, old friend.' He felt a new elation running through him. 'But wed you shall be!' He thrust his head out of the window and called, 'Guard! Sound your horn when you see Carrick Roads!'

The horses roused themselves and the brake went down as the carriage rolled on to the sloping road.

At the echoing blast of the horn, clouds of rooks rose squawking from the fields and a few gulls flapped angrily overhead.

Some farm workers repairing one of the low walls turned to stare at the unfamiliar carriage with its coachwork caked in dried mud, until one of them pointed and called out something to his companions.

A Bolitho is back. A Bolitho is back. As men of Falmouth had been saying for generations.

Bolitho leaned out of the window, heedless of the sting in his injured eye, all else forgotten while the cold air drove away his fatigue.

Then he saw her: the fine mare Tamara which he had given

her coming along the last mile of the coach-road at a gallop. Bolitho called, 'Stop the carriage!'

Catherine wheeled the horse around until her face was almost touching his as he leaned from the window.

She was breathless, her hair broken free and whipping in the breeze as the fur-lined hood of her cloak fell away.

He was on the road, and felt her waist in his grasp as she dropped easily from the stirrup.

'I *knew*, Richard! I knew you were coming to me!'

He tasted the tears on her cold skin, felt the welcome and the longing in her arms while they clung to one another, oblivious to the coachman and guard. To everything but this moment.

A Bolitho is back.

John Allday and Unis Polin were married in the tiny parish church at Fallowfield just a week before Christmas 1810.

Ozzard had proclaimed many times that it was a good thing, if only to stop Allday from getting on everybody's nerves with his anxiety and constant worrying.

The day was fine, clear and bright, and many who came to wish the couple well were able to walk in the pale sunshine to the church, well wrapped up against the sharp south-westerly from Falmouth Bay.

The little church had never known such a gathering, and the young preacher was obviously more nervous than the couple he was about to marry. It was not merely the number of people, for Allday was a popular man and always welcomed whenever he returned from sea, but their variety, from England's naval hero and Falmouth's favourite son and his lovely lady, to the people who lived and worked in the port and on the farms. There were few sailors present, but most of the estate workers, local coastguards and excisemen, farmers, coachmen and probably a poacher or two filled the place to overflowing.

Fallowfield lay on Lewis Roxby's estate, and although he did not attend the wedding he arranged to have a huge barn decorated with garlands and flags so Allday and his bride could entertain all and sundry with room to spare.

Roxby also provided enough geese and beef out of his own pocket to, as Allday described it, 'Feed the whole of the Iron Duke's army!'

Bolitho had felt the eyes upon himself and Catherine as the packed pews had roared out another hymn. Unis Polin had been given away by her brother, proud and straight-backed, striding along the aisle with hardly a limp despite his wooden leg. Allday, supported by Bryan Ferguson, was outwardly composed, and very smart in a new jacket which Bolitho had made certain he had had fitted in good time. He wore gilt buttons, with a white silk neckerchief to mark this very special occasion.

There would be a few women in Falmouth who might still have hoped Allday would choose differently.

There had been one other sea-officer present. Lieutenant George Avery had come from Dorset as promised to witness the marriage, and to remember how Allday's courage and strength, and his total independence had helped to change his own life. Like James Tyacke when Val Keen had married his Zenoria, Avery had slipped into the church even as the small organ had creaked into life. Withdrawn, even remote as he struggled with his own doubts and loyalties, Avery was still very much aware that he was one of them. *The Few*.

Once during a lull in the service Bolitho had seen Catherine brush her fingers against her eyes. She had been looking at Avery, his features hidden in the shadow of a pillar.

'What is it?'

She had shaken her head. 'For a second only, I thought of Stephen Jenour.'

There had been humour too, when the preacher had asked the all-important question, 'Do you, John Allday, take this woman . . .' His words had almost been drowned by Allday's loud, '*Aye*, Reverend, an' that's . . .'

There had been a ripple of laughter and a frown of disapproval from the preacher. Bolitho had guessed that but for his bronzed face Allday would have been seen to blush.

And then it was done, and Allday with his smiling bride were towed in style in a carriage, not by seamen and marines, but by the men employed on the Bolitho estate. Many of them

303

had been thrown on the beach after being disabled or crippled in one of Bolitho's own ships. There could have been no escort more fitting, and Allday's face was a pleasure to see.

Bolitho had used Ferguson's little trap for the journey to the church. He had wanted it to be a day for Allday, one he would always remember. *Their day.* Young Matthew and the Bolitho carriage had been put at the disposal of the bride and groom.

Catherine had said quietly, 'It is so typical, Richard, and you do not even notice. To step down, to avoid the bows and the curtsies . . . nobody else would do it.'

They went to the barn to share in a toast to the bride and her man of the sea.

Bolitho thought now of the cheerful simplicity of the wedding, and wondered if Catherine resented that they could never be married.

As was so often the case she seemed to read his thoughts, just as she had known he was coming into Falmouth in that unfamiliar carriage.

She pulled off her glove and laid her hand on his cuff so that the rubies and diamonds he had given her in the church after Keen's marriage flashed in the filtered sunlight. 'This is *my* wedding ring, Richard. I am your woman, no matter who or what may try to come between us. And you are mine. It will always be so.'

Bolitho saw the men preparing to serve the food and drink, a group of fiddlers waiting to strike up for the dancing. It was time to leave. His presence here was like that of a senior officer visiting a wardroom: they were polite, friendly, curious, but unable to be themselves until after the great man had gone.

It was a moment he knew he would remember, and he could feel Catherine watching as he said his farewell to Allday and his wife. But Catherine knew that he was speaking only to his coxswain, the man she had grown to know and respect, even to love for his care and his qualities of courage and loyalty, which he had given her man for over twenty years.

'Good-bye, old friend. Don't be a stranger from now on.'

Allday gripped his hand, his eyes suddenly troubled. 'But you'll be *needing* me soon, Sir Richard?'

Bolitho nodded slowly. All those lost faces. Battles and ships he would never be allowed to forget. He had tried not to become too closely involved, to guard against the pain of loss when in his heart he knew there was no such defence. Like the midshipman Dunwoody, whom Adam had wanted to help, and who had died with all the others.

'I shall always do that, old friend. Be certain of it.' The handclasp broke. It was done.

Outside in the keen air Catherine said, 'Now we are alone.' She allowed him to help her into the little trap. Then she shook the reins and waved to some people who were still walking down from the church.

She said, 'I am so *happy*, Richard. When you left, the parting almost broke my heart. An eternity, and yet I had expected far worse. Now you are with me. I am yours, and soon it will be Christmas. I remember you once told me when you shared Christmas with me that it was the first you had had ashore since you were a midshipman. And the New Year – we can face that together too. The country still at war, the King insane . . . nothing makes any reason or sense but ourselves.'

He put his arm around her and felt his longing for her, as in the dreams he had shared with her even though they had been apart.

She threw back her head and allowed her long dark hair to be free. When she looked towards the sea beyond Rosemullion Point she said softly, 'All our friends are out there somewhere. Val, poor Adam, James Tyacke and the rest, and others who will never come back.' She looked at him, her eyes flashing. 'But we can remember them!'

The mood changed, and she pulled at the reins to turn the pony on to a narrow side-track.

She said, 'I have visited Unis Polin several times. She is a good woman, right for him. He needs love as much as we do.'

Bolitho held her arm. 'You are all mystery, Kate!'

She tossed her head but did not look at him. 'But for this icy wind I would take you to our private cove. And I would give you mystery which would shock you!'

They turned a corner where the small inn stood, strangely deserted, and Bolitho guessed that most of the local folk were celebrating in Roxby's barn.

The Stag's Head would be waiting for Allday from now on.

He stared at the inn sign moving very gently in the breeze. Except that it was no longer called the Stag's Head. It was a perfect painting of a ship-of-the-line in half a gale, her gunports almost awash, and he knew Catherine must have arranged it. The inn's name had become The Old Hyperion.

She said, 'I heard John Allday speak of your old ship so often. She was, after all, a very special one for some of us. She brought you to me at Antigua when I thought I had lost you.' All the time she was watching his face. 'Through her, Unis met her previous husband, and because of her Allday discovered the love of his life.'

Bolitho watched the swaying sign, as if the old ship were really alive.

He said, 'The ship that refused to die, they used to say.'

She nodded, satisfied. 'Now she never will.' She handed him the reins and nestled against him. 'Now take us home, please. Where we belong.'

KU-755-616

PLAYING FOR
CELTIC No.3

Overleaf:
—Another game . . . another roar of welcome from the crowd as
Tom Callaghan runs on to Celtic Park, closely followed by Jimmy
Johnstone and Willie Wallace

PLAYING FOR
CELTIC No.3
EDITED BY RODGER BAILLIE

STANLEY PAUL
LONDON

STANLEY PAUL & CO LTD
3 Fitzroy Square, London W1

AN IMPRINT OF THE HUTCHINSON GROUP

London Melbourne Sydney
Auckland Johannesburg Cape Town
and agencies throughout the world
First published 1971

© Stanley Paul and Company Ltd. 1971

*This book has been set in Imprint, printed in Great Britain
by offset litho by Flarepath Printers Ltd., Colney Street, St. Albans, Herts.
and bound by William Brendon, at Tiptree, Essex*

ISBN 0 09 108300 1

Contents

The Best moments of the Season

JOCK STEIN

I BELIEVE in the future of Scottish football . . . and I think it is time someone stood up to say that.

Admittedly a season such as the last one which included the almost total failure of the international team, a lack of impact by clubs in the European competitions, a drop in attendances and the grim memory of the Ibrox disaster, means there are vital problems which must be solved.

As a manager of a Scottish club I am concerned with the state of football generally in the country, and I want to tell you of some ideas which I think might help.

But first of all, looking at last season from purely a Celtic point of view, I find a lot to be cheerful about.

How could it be any other way? I have only to walk the short distance from my office to the board-room next door to see up there among the silverware, the Scottish Cup and the league championship trophy.

And I don't forget the three reserve league trophies that are there as well, the guarantee that we have young players who have already got into the way of winning awards.

It is hard for me to split my best moment of the season between winning the Scottish Cup or the league championship.

I have always felt that the players' greatest achievement since I went to Parkhead has been to change the image of the club who were always favourites for the Scottish Cup, but a bit short of consistency to win the league championship.

That has changed. You really cannot do much better than collect six championships. In fact, it's almost difficult to remember when we were not consistent in the league.

The history books show that our achievement equals the record set up by the Celtic side between 1904 and 1911 . . . I think it is a thousand times greater!

I mean no disrespect to those Parkhead predecessors of ours at the beginning of the century, it was a magnificent feat for its time.

But you cannot begin to compare the pressures on players then to

Flash-back . . . to Jock Stein, player! As, in his familiar role as
Celtic centre-half, he clears from Hibs forward Bobby Combe, in a
match at Parkhead, anxiously watched by colleagues Mike
Haughney and John McPhail

the stress which faces a team today. There was no European Cup competition then, no League Cup, and an extended close season which would be looked on as a luxury today.

I know there was criticism last season that Celtic had lost their edge of excitement, the sort of urge for glory which pushes a team forward to win trophies.

I must admit I've wondered at times myself about it. I dropped players, I freshened up the side from time to time, I tried every trick in the book to keep them on a winning course.

And I got my answer that Thursday night at Hampden when we clinched the league championship against Ayr United.

My mind flashed back to a May afternoon in 1966 when at Fir Park, Motherwell, we wrapped up the first championship, and I remembered so well the jubilation the players showed that day.

Yet at Hampden they were just as excited about the latest win, and some of them had been around to celebrate all six victories.

But no player on our staff, no fan on the terraces, was more pleased about the championship victory than our president, Sir Robert Kelly.

I went to visit him at his home after the game, for he was unable to attend the matches at the end of last season, and his words pleased me more than I could ever say.

For there I was talking to a man who was a living link with the Celtic past and the Celtic present. A man who remembered the Parkhead team which won the six championships away back in the early nineteen-hundreds.

And he told me he always hoped the record would be equalled, but he had come to think it was an impossible dream.

Yes, I was proud of the team's feat. But I never doubted that we would win the championship, not even when Aberdeen led the league for so long.

I always felt that, at the end of the day, the experience we have gained during all these previous campaigns would swing it for us.

And I think that was proved when Aberdeen fell at the last hurdle against Falkirk at Brockville. I'm not knocking them. It was a magnificent achievement to chase the title for so long, and I salute them.

But no team can afford to let up in the championship run-in, and that's where our previous knowledge worked so well for us.

I thought the vital match at Aberdeen, in which we drew 1–1 was one of the best League games I have seen anywhere for a long time. And at a time when so many clashes of such importance are marred by players getting involved in punch-ups, it was a pleasure to record it was such a sporting encounter.

Along with the league victory we also took the Scottish Cup. And

Pre-season chat . . . between Jock Stein and Newcastle manager Joe Harvey. But whatever they were talking about Newcastle's veteran director, Stan Seymour, keeps his eyes firmly fixed on the training

in its own way, this triumph was just as important as any match we played last season.

It's always important, a match against Rangers—just as important for them as for us. But we had started to lose too many Cup Finals, we had strung together a succession of defeats which included the Scottish Cup Final against Aberdeen, the European Cup Final against Feyenoord, and the League Cup Final against Rangers.

And we had lost another knock-out competition with the defeat from Ajax of Amsterdam in the European Cup quarter-finals.

The old sharpness had not disappeared completely, but the pattern was starting to look ominous, so what better opportunity to change it than against Rangers ?

An 'Old Firm' final is a match in which, perhaps more than any other, you take out of the game what your team has put into it.

We were far too careless in the League Cup Final when some of our players obviously considered it would be too easy, and surrendered the initiative.

And the same mistake was nearly repeated at the start of the Cup Final, but we overcame it, scored with a Bobby Lennox goal, and should never have been in the position where just one goal separated the teams with only three minutes to go.

If it was Evan Williams who had the blunder which led to Rangers equaliser, then as I say, we should not have to depend on that one goal, for we should have scored more.

Goalkeeper was one of my major headaches last season. It is always natural for any player to ease off slightly, he might not even be aware of it himself, if there is no one to pressure him.

And this was the worry about Williams. For when John Fallon took ill it meant that Evan's biggest rival for the position temporarily disappeared from the scene.

So he lost the edge on his play a little, and tended to mix some very good saves with some mistakes during a game.

But Williams, along with the rest of the team, played so well in the Cup Final replay. I was delighted that he was one of the players who got his first ever Cup medal for the club . . . along with David Hay, Lou Macari, Harry Hood and Tommy Callaghan, who had already won a winner's award with Dunfermline.

I think the winning of these medals will do a great deal of good for Hood and Callaghan especially. Both of them have a great deal of talent. They showed it last season, but both were transferred to the club and it takes time for players to adjust.

Maybe they were trying too hard to justify the transfers, with all the publicity that surrounds these moves, but I consider they overcame all the hurdles in that Cup Final replay.

The big laugh-in . . . between Celtic boss Jock Stein and Rangers manager Willie Waddell at the official opening of tha new Rangers social club

I could have made drastic changes for that replay, but I decided against it. Generally I think that if players have slipped up in the first game then they are the ones who should pull the club through in any second match.

I worked on that principle at Dunfermline in an earlier round, although I admit it was only the dreadful ground conditions that saved a few heads, and I followed it in the Cup Final.

These were sweet moments for everyone connected with the club, fans, players and officials. But naturally, no season is made up of just victories. And I had two major headaches during the season, one concerned a player, the other a Cup tie.

The player was Bobby Murdoch, whose form zig-zagged dramatic-allly ast season. Just when it seemed he was on his way back, he received a bad shoulder injury in the league game against Dunfermline and never really recovered his form for the rest of the season.

I still believe that a fit, on-form Murdoch can contribute a great deal to Celtic. He did not earn the title of the best wing-half in Europe for nothing. But his future is in his own hands.

The other problem was the defeat from Ajax in the European Cup. That alone was a big enough blow, but I had to worry about the effects it would have on the team's morale in the domestic competitions, the league and the Scottish Cup.

Players know when they have not done well in a game. You don't need to emphasise it to them . . . and Celtic had not played well in Amsterdam against Ajax.

So I consider it is even more to their credit that they lifted themselves off the floor, and went on to capture the double.

I do not usually like to pick out one player above the others, but this time I must break my rule, for there is one man to whom a pat on the back must be given for last season's efforts.

That player is Jimmy Johnstone. The little man struggled as badly as anyone in Amsterdam. It's the sort of situation in which too often in the past he would have retreated into his shell and perhaps faded out of the picture for the rest of the season.

But he was superb. He was our most consistent player for the last three months of the season, and you have no idea the pleasure it gives me to say that!

He achieved the consistency of which I always felt he was capable, but so rarely produced over any length of time.

His Cup Final replay display was as great a parade of a player's individual skills as I have ever seen, but the great thing was he did not just turn it on for one game.

I reckon that Jimmy Johnstone, an on-form Johnstone, gives Celtic an advantage over every other club in Scotland—yes, and Britain

It's Jock Stein, golfer . . . as he strides up to a putt during a game at Celtic's favourite seaside course at West Kilbride

too—for there is no one who can touch him at his peak.

Celtic are a club whose future is always connected with their past. By that, I simply mean that no matter how high we aim, I don't think we ever forget our roots.

That is why the 1967 European Cup winning team will always hold a special place in the memory of every Celtic fan ... I know it certainly does in mine.

But we can't go on living as a club on the memory of that achievement for ever. We have to aim at equalling the '67 team ... and even going farther than they did.

I was delighted everyone was able to have one last look at them together, in the final league game against Clyde, when they added another wonderful chapter to their glorious era.

But there are youngsters who are pushing through now, and they will get their chance. I have carefully guarded them from too many first team matches, for I have tried to strike a balance.

It is no use pushing youngsters into the side if things are going against the club, if they fail it would only retard their progress.

Yet they can also be held back too long, and the time has come to see if they have the ability to move into the league side.

Left: It's Jock Stein, bowler . . . as watched by Bobby Murdoch he relaxes on a trip to the North of Scotland by playing a game of bowls

Above: Eyes left . . . and trainer Neil Mochan, manager Stein, Jimmy Johnstone and Jim Craig keep a careful eye on golfers as they return to their hotel after a training session

I have a dream of achieving a transition in the team and still staying at the top. I cannot promise it will succeed, but it is certainly the aim of everyone at Celtic.

But Celtic's problems are not as great—thank goodness—as the ones which face the legislators of Scottish football.

I do not see many original ideas coming forward to help solve the headaches which face soccer.

One solution has been sponsored football. I am not against it, I think that football should get its share of any money which is going about the same as any other sport.

However I am against too many tournaments springing up to clutter up the fixture calendar. There is room for sponsored football within the present competitions, but legislators who imagine that the public will turn up twice a week right through the season to see matches are wrong . . . it will only throttle football.

15

It's the familiar airport scene, the welcome home smiles for the
camera. But this time the welcoming party was not for the head of
the house, it was for George Stein, met by his mother and father,
after he returned with Celtic Boys' Club from a trip to North
America

One new idea which is going to be looked at very closely this season is the juniors experiment of Sunday football. They are the guinea pigs. If it works, some of the senior clubs will climb on the bandwagon.

But we sadly lack new thought. I put forward an idea at the start of this year, and I make no apology for repeating it, for despite the official silence on it, I still think it had merits.

I wanted all the First Division reserve sides to join the Second Division to pep up that league, and also give reserve team football a boost.

I think it would be simple to operate. The present Second Division would be split into two sections, East and West. They would be joined by the reserve sides of the First Division clubs from both areas to make up two leagues.

There would be no question of any First Division reserve side if they topped the league, actually accepting promotion. The top two Second Division sides from the East and West sections would play off at the end of the season to see who won promotion.

People in football are so suspicious. They think that because I suggest a scheme, as manager of Celtic, then it is only to help my club.

Sure it would help my youngsters—there is a tremendous gap for babes to bridge from the reserve side to the top league—but it would help the youngsters of every First Division side.

And it would give a real boost to the Second Division. It can't go on forever as the Cinderella league.

Celtic play a series of friendlies every season against Second Division sides, and I know there is a market for these fixtures.

Our team is mostly composed of reserve players, and a few from the first team pool. Yet I was told by Raith Rovers last season that the attendance when we played a friendly there was greater than at any of their league games.

There are many ideas coming from outside football just now, business firms, management consultants, are all having their say.

Some of them are good, some others I am not so sure about. We should at least listen to them, for they may have some merit.

But people inside football cannot simply sit back and not come up with ideas. I think my plan would go a long way to getting rid of the boredom which hangs over far too many fixtures in the Second Division and Reserve Leagues.

Don't forget this has been largely cured in the First Division. There are so many extra competitions most teams have something at which they can aim in the league.

It's not the same in these other leagues. We should do something about it, and not wait until its too late for a rescue act for some of our clubs who will surely die unless the legislators act.

17

No Greater Challenge

THE news that the Celtic fans, players and officials, had waited anxiously to hear was told, fittingly enough, first of all to the team!

It was a simple enough statement from manager Jock Stein, not a carefully rehearsed speech, but thrown into his team talk before the vital league match against Aberdeen at Pittodrie.

And so, in the hotel at Stonehaven, as the cold North Sea breakers pounded on the beach only a few hundred yards from their hotel, his team were told . . . 'I want to be in that European Cup next season, with Celtic'.

It can surely not have been coincidence that in the match against Aberdeen, one in which their dreams for the championship could have vanished entirely, Celtic rose superbly to the challenge to come away with a 1–1 draw which made them favourites for their sixth title.

For months, ever since Manchester United had sacked their team manager Wilf McGuinness, and Sir Matt Busby had returned to take charge of operations again at Old Trafford, the guessing game had started about the name of the manager who would eventually take over.

Sir Matt had made it clear that his return was only temporary, a breathing space to make sure Manchester United had time to consider the position.

One man, with his vast knowledge of European football, rivalled only by Sir Matt's himself, obviously stood out . . . the manager of the first British team to win the European Cup, Jock Stein of Celtic.

For months newspaper columnists speculated about a possible Stein move to Old Trafford, some of it was informed, some of it bordered on the ludicrous.

A few days before his Celtic boss confirmed that he would not be leaving Parkhead one paper breathtakingly informed its readers that he had decided to sell up everything in Glasgow.

Stein resolutely refused to confirm or deny that United had made a positive move to secure him, and he contented himself eventually only with the statement that: 'I will stay with Celtic as long as I am needed. There is no place that holds a greater challenge.'

18

A stand for the seventies . . . and this is the architect's final plans
on the massive new Parkhead stand with three views (*top*) looking
down on the roof and rear entrance (*centre*) as it will look from the
playing field and the enclosure opposite and (*bottom*) how it will
appear as the fans approach from London Road

But, some day perhaps the whole story will be told, a script which even Hitchcock could not have dreamed up.

It was a happy ending that pleased everyone—apart from Manchester United whose search eventually became more difficult than they could have ever thought when the job first became available.

Celtic without Stein would have been difficult to imagine. For ever since his appointment in 1965, he and his team together had soared to a position of supremacy in Scottish football which only a few sides have ever enjoyed.

They had added Europe to their list of battle honours, the Scottish side who had changed the image of our country abroad from losers to winners, and others helped to take up the challenge.

No less an authority than Leeds United manager Don Revie publicly rated them as one of the six best-ever club teams.

But there was no doubt, and none knew it better than Jock Stein, that there was a job of reshaping to be done with Celtic.

Sadly no one has yet found a way to preserve age from taking its toll of a team. Already out of the side who beat Inter-Milan had slipped away 'keeper Ronnie Simpson into retirement, that marvellous little sweeper John Clark was no longer a first team player and Bertie Auld appeared only in odd games, most of them towards the end of the season.

But there was a mystery about the team, of why the players who were left, whose average age was still only in the mid-twenties, could escalate up and down so violently in their form.

For there were occasions last season when they failed to hit the standard which so many had come to accept as normal Celtic soccer.

There were words of warning from the manager, rumbles occasionally from the terracing. But it is worth recording that at the end of the season for all its problems, they could still justly claim the title . . . the best in Scotland.

And I do not mean by winning the Scottish Cup. For much as it is still a prized possession, and a great deal of prestige attaches itself to an 'Old Firm' final, the trophy that every manager still wants his team to win is the league.

Both Rangers manager Willie Waddell and Aberdeen boss Eddie Turnbull, told me during the season how they put the league championship above every other domestic honour.

For that reason then Celtic's feat of winning it for the sixth successive time is a super soccer effort.

Perhaps we are all too close to it, perhaps it has become almost accepted as a fact that Celtic will win the championship, but I believe that ten, twenty, thirty years from now people will look back and wonder at how any team could squeeze such an achievement into the crowded soccer fixture list of today.

Can Celtic make it seven, and go one better than those Parkhead predecessors of theirs who captured the six championships between 1904 and 1910?

The odds may be in their favour, but it takes a lot of skill to blend into a side of players who have won everything the youngsters whose enthusiasm every club needs.

That is Jock Stein's avowed aim, to build a new team and keep them at the top. It is something which has never really been success-fully achieved by any other side.

All of them, the great Spurs side of the early sixties, Rangers of the Jim Baxter era, Manchester United's European Cup-winning team, have had to step down before they could pick up the pieces again.

Yet, looking at the roll of honour since Stein went to Parkhead, who would honestly bet against it?

For there were players last season who rose to the heights to give hope for Celtic fans that this rare feat can be carried out successfully.

One was in defence, one in attack! And if you took two players from a team you could not imagine anyone more unlike each other in styles than Jim Brogan and Jimmy Johnstone. Yet each, in his own way, contributed a valuable part to the Celtic success.

Brogan had been one of the first of the new faces brought in after Lisbon, although he had hovered on the fringe of the first team for some seasons before that.

His trademark was enthusiasm, a hurry-scurry style of soccer which made him a valuable player for any side to have, yet his play earned the phrase 'a good club man' which can too often mean a case of damning someone with faint praise.

But last season, when Celtic's hopes were wavering it was Brogan who emerged as one of the giant stars of the team, a player who put a gloss on his play without losing any of his attributes of enthusiasm and tenacity, a player whose displays earned him recognition as runner-up in the Scottish Football Writers' 'Player of the Year' poll, and also a place in the international squad.

And then there was Johnstone. A star who in the last three months of the season lived up magnificently to all the wonderful tributes that had ever been paid to him in the past.

From the time of the defeat by Ajax of Amsterdam in the European Cup until the Scottish Cup and league championship were safely parcelled up for Parkhead, it was Johnstone who shone consistently in the attack.

And there can be no doubt that the fans of today will be boring their grandchildren, just as the grandfathers of today reminisce about the stars of the twenties, with the phrase . . . 'But if only you had seen Jimmy Johnstone'.

Fortunately TV films can be used to repeat the Johnstone magic, for at his best he is probably the last exponent in top-class British soccer of the real value of a touch line winger creating panic in an opposition defence.

It was a season where the team form fluctuated as I have said, and probably that is best illustrated by the fact that not one member of the team was an ever-present, and 24 players were used in the league championship alone, much more than the manager would have wanted.

It was a season where it took so long for the players to overcome the total shock of the European Cup Final defeat from Feyenoord.

The state of shock had lasted through the American and Canadian tour which followed soon after, when not one victory was recorded against the major opposition, and they had to wait until the holiday matches in Bermuda to win.

But there were better results from later friendly games, even if the score line was not tilted in Celtic's favour.

There was a 3–3 draw with West Ham at Upton Park, Celtic's first visit to London under Jock Stein. It was a memorable match to celebrate a memorable occasion, the benefit match for West Ham and England captain, Bobby Moore, and a unique offer that from all the clubs he could have chosen, he picked Celtic.

If the tag was officially a friendly, it carried with it the prestige of an England v Scotland match, yet retained the best spirit of these games to make it a showpiece occasion to remember.

And worth it alone to see the sight of actor Sean Connery, alias James Bond—or should it be the other way round ?—leaping up from his front row directors' box seat to cheer the Celtic goals.

The other notable friendly was a 1–1 draw with Feyenoord at Hampden, a game in which Celtic failed to gain revenge for their European Cup Final defeat but posed more problems for the Dutch side than they had ever managed the previous May in Milan.

These were the games that come to any team who is at the top, just part of the invitations which pour in from all round the world.

The close season work and play tour, with one match against Hapoel in Tel Aviv, a 1–0 victory and a short holiday, broke new ground with the highly successful visit to Israel.

But these invitations spring from the basic fact that promoters of these games gauge a team's drawing power on their domestic record, and their success in Europe.

Europe remains to be conquered anew! The youngsters who will soon have to try to follow in the footsteps of their marvellous predecessors started the trophy-hunting trail successfully with the clean sweep of the Reserve League trophies.

But there is a vast gulf to jump between the atmosphere of reserve team football and the cauldron of European soccer, they will have the chance to achieve it . . . the rest is up to them.

They saw what they have to aim at when they stood on the terrace steps, the stand had been pulled down as part of the reconstruction, and watched the Lisbon Lions roar for the last time as a complete unit, when they beat Clyde 6–1 in the final league game of the season.

It was another reminder to every fan of just how great that team at their peak had been. But now they are broken up finally, some of them have left the club.

There is a new generation of starlets poised on the threshold of stardom, the 1967 team has given them a wonderful target to aim at for the future.

But the sixth successive league championship flag flutters from the Parkhead flagpole as a reminder that there is nothing in football which cannot be equalled.

My Fight for a Place

TOM CALLAGHAN

THE Hampden roar was as loud as I have ever heard it . . . and as sweet as I have ever heard it as I walked down the gangway in front of the directors' box at Hampden clutching my Cup Winners' medal.

I suppose every player reckons there can be no greater thrill than receiving his first Cup Winners' medal. Believe me, it's better the second time around.

I already had one medal, when I played for Dunfermline in the 1968 final against Hearts, the year we put out Celtic on our way to Hampden.

I was proud of that medal, naturally. But I have to say that my second medal really means more to me . . . for it is the visible significance that I have won the battle of my football life.

It was a battle to win a first team place with Celtic, and last season was the first time I had felt I was settling down comfortably in the league side.

Maybe it was because I had a long spell before I adjusted to the fact that I was a Celtic player. . . for the transfer in December 1968, I can honestly say, was the biggest shock of my football career.

I had asked Dunfermline for a transfer six weeks before, and the request had been granted. It was at the same time as my brother, Willie, also asked to get away. But the club decided to keep him, and I got my wish . . . I don't think there's much doubt about who got the better part of the deal.

Willie and I had set up a few records together, we were the first brothers to appear together in a Cup Final since Celtic's Willie and Jimmy McStay in the 1928 match against Rangers. That was when we were in the 1965 Dunfermline side beaten by Celtic 3–2, the first honour the club won under Jock Stein.

And we were the first brothers in post-war years to be capped for Scotland, when we played in a league international against the League of Ireland in 1968.

It was the climax of our football careers together which had started as boys at St. Columba's School in Cowdenbeath. There must be something in the football air about the place, for it is still one of the

See how it fits . . . Willie Callaghan tries on a Scottish jersey on his brother, Tom, for size. They were the first brothers to appear together in a Scottish league side for many years

great strongholds which seems to produce young stars on conveyor belts.

One of the local laddies who stayed near our home and made his name just before us, was Jim Baxter.

Willie moved to Dunfermline first of all, then I followed, signed by Jock Stein when he was boss at East End Park.

That man Stein! How he has figured in my football career. I have been signed twice by him and the Scottish Cup medal with Celtic meant that under his management I had won every domestic honour in Scottish football.

I think Dunfermline's record in these years in the sixties was a fantastic achievement for a team outside a big city. Twice cup-winners, a team who came to be well known in Europe and a team who were feared in Scotland.

I was pleased to have had a share in these honours. But there are problems for a local boy playing for his local team. Everyone knew me in Dunfermline, and I have always considered that a local crowd are much harder on the players they know well than the ones who come from outside.

However, that was not the main reason for wanting to move. It was simply that George Farm, then the manager at Dunfermline, had dropped me into the reserves. I just could not see any future for me at East End Park, so I asked for a move.

Frankly the thought that Celtic would bid for me was the farthest thought from my mind. I had always fancied the club as a kid, but I had never really imagined I would be considered good enough to play for them.

Some people thought it was a good idea that I should be separated from my brother Willie. But I don't really know if it was a very valid theory.

Certainly if he was injured during a game I was naturally concerned, as he was when I got a knock. But I don't think we spared each other in criticising the other's play . . . at least Willie certainly did not where I was concerned.

But I had no regrets about leaving Dunfermline, and my big brother. I was overjoyed at the move to Celtic, I was only told about it by Dunfermline less than 24 hours before I signed.

I will never forget my début against Partick Thistle at Firhill. It brought home to me, perhaps more than a game at Parkhead where there are always crowds, just what it meant to be a Celtic player.

For as the team bus nosed up to the players' entrance, I looked around me and there were more fans than I had ever seen in that street in my life.

Normally when I had been there with Dunfermline, there would be

At home with the Callaghan family . . . as Tom and his wife, Kathy, pose with their two children, Marie and Tommy junior

CHE 4531

a few groups hanging around, but this time it was packed with fans.

I was lucky enough to score a goal in my début, and I could only look back on the few weeks previous to that, and marvel at my luck.

For Dunfermline had turned down Celtic's original offer, and I was really sick. I thought the chance had gone, and it was a move I wanted more than anything.

But I soon discovered the differences playing for Celtic and Dunfermline. You know a player can oppose Celtic and realise they are a good team, but playing for them is fantastic. It's like fitting into a machine.

Maybe that was the trouble. I seemed to be the piece of machinery that did not fit too well. My troubles started when I had a slight car crash and I had to drop out to substitute.

But mainly it was because I could not adjust to my new life. I still lived in Fife, and travelled through to Parkhead every day. But I found the journey boring and the best move I made was to buy a house in Glasgow.

That cut out the travelling time; it had meant nearly two hours' driving every day. I must admit I'm a bit disorganised in the morning, and the rush to get through from Fife had not been helping me.

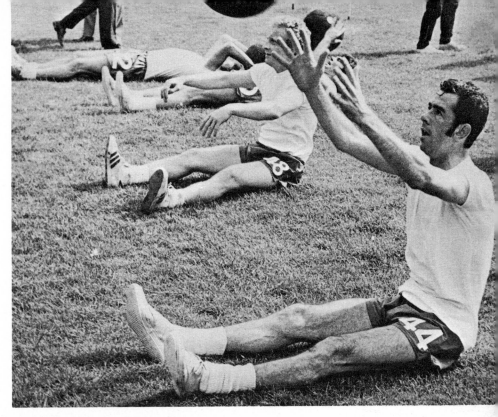

Left: A moment of anguish for Tom Callaghan . . . as he is
stretchered off Parkhead during the game against St. Johnstone
with a badly-gashed leg

Above: The sweat and strain of pre-season training for
Tom Callaghan and Jimmy Johnstone. But it's this training that
Tom considers so vital to the team's chances of success

But I was still too much on the fringe of the first team pool, although I won a League Cup winners' badge in the match against St. Johnstone two years ago.

And it did not look too good for me last season, when I was stretchered off during the league game against St. Johnstone with my leg split open. I honestly began to wonder if I would ever command a first team place at Parkhead.

Fortunately things did improve, and I ended up the season with a Cup Winners' medal and a League Championship medal.

A great deal of the credit for my improvement must go to the training at Parkhead. I used to find the training routine for much of my time at Dunfermline boring. But there is never any question of that with Celtic, it is always varied.

In fact, I reckon the pre-season training at Parkhead is so good that the players only have to keep a certain level of fitness for the rest of the season, because it sets them up so well.

One thing, of course, which training cannot really cure, is nerves. Fortunately I don't suffer much from them, but I defy any player who has appeared in an 'Old Firm' final, not to admit he did not have a few butterflies.

I had played in league games against Rangers, but never a Cup Final, and I must admit I was nervous for that first game at Hampden.

Remember the situation . . . Celtic had won the championship, Rangers the League Cup, and the Ibrox club had staked everything on winning the Cup.

That championship victory had been a really hard fight, especially in the closing stages with Aberdeen. The trouble was that every time they dropped a point, we seemed to do the same.

I think our worst moment was at Perth when St. Johnstone defeated us 3–2, but the loss of these two points was even harder to bear when we got back to the dressing-room and found that Aberdeen had also lost at Dunfermline.

Still, it worked out well for us in the end and we went to Hampden as winners of our sixth championship. I had been a spectator at the last game against Clyde, along with my teammates such as Harry Hood, Davie Hay and Jim Brogan, for Mr. Stein played the Lisbon Lions for the last time, and I would not mind watching that team any time.

But it was back to the team who had taken part in the final stages of the championship for the Cup Final.

As I say, I must admit I was a bit nervous. I think no one who has not played in that match, especially a Cup Final, can ever truly imagine what an experience it is.

I remember telling Jim Craig on the team bus coming up from Troon to the game how I felt. And my nerves just did not disappear immediately, I never felt I was getting properly into the game the whole of the first half.

I'm glad to say it all disappeared in the second half, but it was the end of these 45 minutes which gave me my worst moment of the season.

I was mentally getting ready to mount the steps to collect my medal, when Derek Johnstone grabbed the equaliser for Rangers. I really began to wonder if that medal was slipping away from me.

Somehow we clung on to the end of the game, but I don't think I have ever been so disappointed at the result of a match in which I had played.

But it was a different Celtic in the replay. Who can ever forget that display by Jimmy Johnstone? I can't speak for my teammates, but I know my tension had gone.

30

I hope that medal means I have won my fight for a first team place. I'm not complacent about it, you can't live on last season's medals, and there are plenty of bright youngsters about Parkhead.

Mr. Stein has often told me I should believe more in my play, and I think I am realising now just what he means. My role in the team has settled down as well, going forward as a link man but not forgetting the defence.

I have been able to do that because I have speeded up since I went to Parkhead, a tribute to the training I was talking about.

It has been a hard fight, but it has been worth every minute. I don't think most people imagine the pressures that surround a Celtic player which most other teams never have to face.

We are expected to win every game, we can never be permitted to fall below a certain standard on the pitch or our critics will shout we are on the slide.

But I don't mind. My dream was achieved when I signed for Celtic. Thousands of kids hope they will achieve such an ambition . . . I was fortunate enough to be one of the lucky ones.

And I've got these medals to prove it!

The League Cup

THE words were in the biggest and boldest type the club newspaper 'The Celtic View' could find. For right across Page One their banner headline read . . . 'This was the right result.'

But they were not looking back on yet another match of Celtic triumphant, there were no winners' medals, no Cup to take home to Parkhead from this match.

The heading was as unique as if Liverpool boss Bill Shankly had praised an Everton victory, or Sir Alf Ramsay conceded that a foreign international side were actually as good as England's.

For the match was the 1970 League Cup Final, which had ended with a score-line of Rangers 1; Celtic 0.

Yet not even the most rabid, green-and-white scarved supporter could quibble at the honesty of the heading, for Rangers had deserved to win.

That Hampden display by the Ibrox side shifted the League Cup from the spot where it had seemed to have become a permanent part of the furniture, in the Parkhead board-room.

Yet few would have bet on the result before the game, when it seemed as certain as one ever can be in these 'Old Firm' matches that it would tilt Celtic's way.

Only a week before the Final, thousands of Rangers fans had left Ibrox long before the end when their team tumbled to a 2–0 defeat from an Aberdeen side showing the first real hint of their league championship challenge.

Then only a few hours before the kick-off in the final, the injury which had dogged Rangers skipper John Greig all the early part of the season, forced him to call-off.

Not even his closest friends could ever call John Greig a polished player, but there can be no doubt of his value to Rangers.

Celtic players in the dressing-room when they heard the news that he was out felt they had got an extra bonus. Too often, Rangers without Greig have been like a ship without proper steering equipment.

And to add spice to a match which is never short of that commodity

Rangers had also taken a gamble in their team selection.

For, even before he knew about the Greig injury, their manager Willie Waddell had decided to include 16-year-old centre-forward Derek Johnstone, who had played only a handful of First Division games, in the side.

Certainly Celtic lined up without three of their injured stars, Tommy Gemmell, John Hughes and Jim Brogan, but their team still looked formidable enough for the task.

It was: Williams; Craig, Quinn; Murdoch, McNeill, Hay, Johnstone, Connelly, Wallace, Hood, Macari . . . Sub: Lennox.

And Rangers were: McCloy; Jardine, Miller; Conn, McKinnon,

Crash ! As the mighty figure of John Hughes tumbles to the Parkhead turf against Dundee United as he heads for goal during the League Cup tie

Jackson; Henderson, MacDonald, Johnstone, Stein, Johnston . . .
Sub: Fyfe.

Maybe all this kidded on Celtic players it would be too easy, but they were soon to learn otherwise.

For it was Johnstone who was to be the hero of the match, when in 40 minutes he soared above the Celtic defence to head home a cross from Willie Johnston, who had switched to the right-wing.

The script seemed too far-fetched—sixteen-year-olds are only supposed to score in Cup Finals in the pages of children's comic serials, not in real-life football fact.

But it was all too real for Celtic who went in at half-time after a tremendous buffeting, lucky to be trailing by only one goal.

They had one glorious chance in the second half, and their rain-soaked fans must surely have thought the equaliser was coming up in 67 minutes when Bobby Murdoch expertly eased his way through a maze of Rangers defenders to slip the ball to Willie Wallace, but the little centre blasted the ball over.

Every eye on the ball . . . as friend and foe follow the flight of the ball. But this shot from David Hay, extreme right, who got in his shot despite a posse of Dundee defenders was deflected by 'keeper Donaldson

Who knows what effect a score then might have had on the game, but with its failure Celtic were never to get as good a chance again, and the advantage slipped back to Rangers.

There was a needless incident near the end when Willie Johnston provocatively sat on the ball, almost goading the Celtic defence into lunging at him. Generally however the match was free of the more fierce scenes which marred the Scottish Cup encounter the season before.

So Rangers, after 1,641 days had won a major honour, their first since they had beaten Celtic in the 1966 Scottish Cup Final replay.

Manager Jock Stein summed it up when he said: 'We lacked determination, and we just could not get back into the game after Rangers early onslaught.

As hard to bear as a Cup Final defeat from Rangers is for management, players and fans of Celtic, it might, for once, have been easier to take with the knowledge that their departure from the League Cup could have come earlier . . . with a shock tumble to Second

Division Dumbarton.

That would have given them the reddest faces of any side in Celtic history, and wherever football is talked about they would have joined the elite band of clubs—who could well have done without it— such as Leeds United, beaten by Colchester, or Rangers, defeated by Berwick Rangers, who have been overcome by smaller teams.

Certainly the semi-final against Dumbarton seemed a mere formality for Celtic, they were to know different long before the end of the marathon tie.

For in the first match, forced into extra time after a goal-less first ninety minutes, the shock of it all seemed to affect Willie Wallace so much that he missed a penalty, and so the match was pushed to a replay.

The feeling of most of the soccer world that the first match had been a freak result was reinforced after only 17 minutes of the second match, for by then Bobby Lennox had skipped through the Dumbarton defence to score twice, and that seemed to have safely locked up the place in the final.

But that comfortable attitude was in ruins by the end of ninety minutes when ex-Celt Charlie Gallagher had scored from a penalty and inside-forward Kenny Wilson equalised for the Second Division side.

The angry look on manager Stein's face as he talked to his team at the quick break before extra time, was an obvious guide to his feelings on his team's display.

Celtic quickly stepped back into the lead when Willie Wallace scored in the fourth minute of extra time, and they got a fourth when Dumbarton 'keeper Lawrie Williams boobed when he forgot to play to the whistle.

The gallant 'keeper, who had heroically defied the Celtic attack over the two games, made no attempt to go for a David Hay cross which he obviously thought was going past.

However the ball changed flight and landed right in front of an empty goal for Lou Macari to put it into the net.

Maybe it was just as well they did get that goal, for Celtic conceded another just on time when wing-half Johnny Graham scored to make the final tally . . . Celtic 4; Dumbarton 3.

The fact that it was Dumbarton's high-spot of the season was emphasised by their failure to make any impact on the Second Division promotion race.

But for these 240 minutes on Hampden, they worried Celtic too much for comfort. It was the classic case of the under-dogs upsetting a top team, and for Dumbarton it lacked only the magic ending of a victory. However they could look back on spells in both of the

The power of Harry Hood . . . as he eludes the Dundee defence
to brilliantly steer a cross past 'keeper Donaldson in the League
Cup quarter-final at Parkhead

The power of Bobby Lennox . . . as eye firmly on the ball he
follows his header into the net for Celtic's second goal against
Clyde

matches when such a result had come perilously close for Celtic.

And the Second Division side paid Celtic the generous tribute that at least they had been allowed to play football by their famous opponents.

Celtic had earlier comfortably topped their League Cup section. They won the first match of the season 2–1 against Hearts at Tynecastle with goals from John Hughes and Jimmy Johnstone.

Then they defeated Clyde 5–3 at Parkhead, with those inseparable pals Bobby Lennox and Johnstone grabbing all the goals . . . Bobby scored a hat-trick and the wee winger got the others.

Still there was a hint of casualness about the display, for although they were leading 4–0 at one stage, they let Clyde creep back into the game.

Up, up go Willie Wallace, Harry Hood, and Rangers centre-half
Ronnie McKinnon . . . but away went the ball as this cross eludes
them all in the League Cup Final.

That was followed up by a 2–2 draw with Dundee United at Parkhead, the goals came from Tom Callaghan and Lennox.

Then there was almost a stalemate return match with Clyde at Shawfield, broken by two penalty goals from Tommy Gemmell, but marred by an ordering-off for Willie Wallace.

They wrapped up the section with a 4–2 victory at Parkhead against Hearts. It included a 25-second goal for John Hughes, who also scored another, and the remaining two came from George Connelly and Lou Macari.

The final match was a 2–2 draw with Dundee United at Tannadice, when Celtic twice trailed but David Hay equalised in 83 minutes, and when United snatched back the lead in 89 minutes, it took a Macari goal in injury time to snatch a draw.

Duel in the Cup . . . between Celtic centre   Willie Wallace
and Rangers 'keeper Peter McCloy as they battle it out for a cross
in the League Cup Final

The strain of it all . . . shown in the expressions of manager Jock Stein and his players as they prepare for an extra thirty minutes in the League Cup semi-final against Second Division, Dumbarton, at Hampden

Possibly the most satisfying games of the entire League Cup campaign were the quarter-final matches against Dundee.

The first, at Dens Park, when Celtic turned on one of their best displays of the season with all the formidable blend of power and skill which makes them one of Europe's top club teams.

But yet again there was a nagging doubt about the match, for although Jimmy Johnstone gave them a two-goal lead they let Dundee back into the game and it finished 2–2.

However they made no mistake in the second leg with a convincing

5–1 win at Parkhead, and the parade of scorers were Macari (2), Hughes, Hood and Paul Wilson.

But over the 11-match programme to retain the League Cup, which eventually was to end in failure, it was evident that the European Cup flop against Feyenoord in Milan the previous May still affected Celtic.

Admittedly some key players were injured, but there was a lack of consistency about too many of the others . . . the hangover from Milan went on too long!

The Double Dutch

THE eerie sound of the Dutch fans' klaxon horns wailed out over a cold and silent Hampden as the Celtic fans slowly made their way to the exits.

And for the second time in less than a year these horns sounded a requiem for Celtic's European Cup hopes.

Ten months separated these defeats, but the message was the same, Holland was again celebrating a European Cup victory over the team who had made themselves one of the most feared names in the competition.

It was perhaps a measure of Celtic's down-grading in Europe that in May 1970, when the team from Rotterdam, Feyenoord, had beaten the Scots 2–1 in the European Cup Final in Milan, it was rated one of the greatest soccer upsets of the decade.

Yet in March 1971, after Celtic's vain attempt to pull back the massive three-goal lead the team from Amsterdam, Ajax, had built up in the first leg of their quarter-final tie everyone accepted that it had been almost inevitable.

This was Celtic's fifth European Cup campaign—one which took them past Rangers to give them the honour of playing more matches in the tourney than any other Scottish side.

And in many ways it was the strangest. The first, of course, had been glorious . . . the year of '67 when Celtic swept to victory with a magnificent Final display against the defensive-based Inter-Milan which must rank as one of the great soccer memories of all time.

The next year had been an anti-climax, when they were beaten in the first round by Dynamo Kiev of Russia, but no team should have been asked to squeeze that match in, plus the world championship in South America in the same spell. They could justly claim that season that the authorities had done nothing to aid their passage.

The next season saw them bow out in the quarter-finals, but it had been an honourable defeat.

They had lost by only a single goal to the eventual holders, A.C. Milan whose passage to the title was studded with such names as Celtic, Manchester United and Ajax . . . no one could really be upset

Who would believe that Ajax flew into Scotland holding a three-goal lead . . . certainly ace scorer Johann Cruyff, accompanied by his attractive wife, Dany, does not look so happy as he arrives at Glasgow Airport. But with an aggregate score of 3–1 surely he must have smiled on the way out

by defeat from a team of that calibre.

Then came 1970, and another fabulous season soured only at the end by defeat from Feyenoord, but for thousands and thousands of fans at least partially compensated by the double defeat of the English champions Leeds, United, in the semi-finals.

But how could you sum up 1971? Certainly Celtic had made the quarter-finals and only once in their five years in the competition had they failed to make that exalted company.

But it was the year the competition never seemed to get off the ground for Celtic. They were like airline passengers who had checked in for their flight, received their tickets, boarded the plane but some-

Jam-up in the Ajax goalmouth, as Celtic desperately try to score
another goal . . . and Ajax just as desperately try to keep them out

how had never got any further than the end of the runway.

The first round was ideally tailored for Celtic's purpose during the
hectic domestic start-of-the-season programme.

They were drawn against Kokkola of Finland, a name which
sounded more familiar as a drink, than a football team.

And Celtic efficiently disposed of them by the massive score of
9–0 at Parkhead and then 5–0 in Finland.

Then in the next round they again dodged all the formidable
opposition around, to be drawn against the champions of Eire,
Waterford.

They moved the tie from their own city to the headquarters of

Irish Rugby, Lansdowne Road, Dublin, to squeeze in the crowd who wanted to see the match.

And Celtic romped to a 5–0 victory in the first leg in Dublin, in a match marred by a fight on the terraces which seemed to be between two sets of fans who both supported the club.

They had it a little harder in the second leg, but they still won 3–2, for an 8–2 victory aggregate.

These games had taken Celtic smoothly through to the quarter-finals without a problem, yet it was no disrespect to the opposition they had played, but a fact of football life, that somehow the magic had been missing from the European Cup.

The big teams, the teams with the great stars of Europe had not been in Glasgow. The frantic scramble for tickets, the ballyhoo which wraps itself all round these ties, had been absent.

Sadly, by the time Ajax came, a team who certainly generated excitement, Celtic were more than half-way out of the competition.

Yet it is a tribute to the pulling power of the European Cup, the reason why it is still the greatest club competition of them all, that more than 83,000 fans turned up at Hampden to see the game.

It was away back in November that Celtic were drawn against Ajax, and the time between the draw and the ties is more than three months, perhaps too long!

The spy game is played at full force during that time. Celtic manager Jock Stein and his assistant Sean Fallon, found their first attempt wrecked by fog over Amsterdam, but before Christmas they had managed to see their new opponents, in a 1–1 draw with the Parkhead side's old rivals, Feyenoord.

Ajax coach, Rinus Michels, had also seen Celtic draw 1–1 in the New Year fixture at Ibrox which was to end so tragically with the crowd disaster.

Yet when I visited Amsterdam in February and talked to Michels, he revealed to me he had made a secret visit to see Celtic against Morton on Boxing Day, and he also flew over unexpectedly to see the Scots in a friendly match against Feyenoord.

He told me then: 'I know Celtic's domestic form has been up and down, but that does not concern me.

'Great teams react to the European Cup, and they are a great European side. We certainly wished for an easier draw.'

Celtic had a pre-match headache—a transfer request from John Hughes, almost on the eve of the match, which was granted and then the player withdrew it a week later, but he did not travel to Holland.

Because the flight from Glasgow to Amsterdam was so short, only an hour—and as manager Stein pointed out they arrived in Holland quicker than the time it had taken them to travel to Leeds by train

46

The start of another European Cup campaign . . . as captain Billy
McNeill and the captain of Finnish champions Kokkola exchange
pennants before the start of the game at Parkhead

the season before—Celtic scrapped their usual European Cup pattern and arrived in Amsterdam only the day before the match.

They flew into a kidnap scare. A political extremist group in Holland had made a threat to kidnap the two star players of Ajax, Johann Cruyff and left-winger Piet Keiser.

So fourteen plain-clothes policemen guarded Celtic in the luxury Amsterdam Hilton Hotel, and players were not allowed to leave the hotel alone.

Even when they went out in groups, they had to inform the desk clerk . . . no one was taking any chances.

Manager Jock Stein had planned to use as a prototype the tactics which had served them so well in Italy two seasons ago when they drew 0–0 with A.C. Milan.

That meant simply winning the vital battle of the midfield. If they became the bosses there they could dictate everything, and even use it as a launching pad for their own attacks.

There was a problem that they were without Bobby Murdoch, a key-man for such a role to dominate the mid-field, and there was the headache of the team's erratic domestic form.

Maybe Jock Stein saw it more clearly than he wanted to publicly admit when he said: 'I am anxious about this tie, but I am hopeful too'.

And for sixty-two minutes, on a night when a vicious weather cocktail of rain and wind made it mighty unpleasant in the Olympic Stadium, Celtic had reason to hope that their tactics would work.

Certainly they had lived dangerously right at the end of the first half, when it seemed they might crack, but the fans on the terraces in the green and white scarves had reason to hope that they might fly back to Scotland after watching their team get a result.

The game itself was not memorable, but at such a late stage in the European Cup it is an indisputable fact that results matter more than performances.

However there was an alarming lack of pressure on the Ajax defence, the moves designed to take the weight off the Celtic defence were just not coming off.

Then, just when it seemed Ajax might be getting fed up with no reward for so much effort, they struck.

The man who did the damage was Johann Cruyff, the forward who lurked like a shark waiting his chance to pounce.

Suddenly he streaked on to a long ball out of his own defence which caught out Celtic and before they could recover he had flashed it into the net.

Now the question for Celtic was to see if they could contain the score to only one goal, and still give themselves a chance in the second leg in Glasgow.

48

Another attack . . . another occasion when the Ajax attack foiled
Celtic. This time the men up waiting for a slip were Willie Wallace
and Billy McNeill

Celtic protested rightly about the free-kick which led to the second
Ajax goal, but it made no difference to a fussy Portuguese referee.

And when centre-forward Muhren fought his way into the Celtic
line-up, and then nipped out to leave a gap for wing-half Huulshoff
to shoot through, the Scots were suddenly two down.

But the final blow, the one which made it as virtually certain as
anything can be in football, that Celtic were out, came almost on the
final whistle.

That was when left-winger Keizer, off his beat on the right, shot home the third goal to make the chance of pulling back such a lead almost a superhuman task.

Celtic had played an extremely defensive line-up, with right-back Jim Craig listed at inside-right as an extra defender, and there were murmurings that the tactics had been wrong.

Only a few weeks before Amsterdam the manager of the Scotland international team, Bobby Brown, had faced a national outcry because of defensive tactics in the European Nations Cup tie against Belgium.

A European Cup goal for Jimmy Johnstone . . . as he drives in his side's third goal in the game against Waterford at Parkhead

Manager Jock Stein talked to me frankly about it afterwards: 'We were defensive because we were pushed into it.

'I had three forwards, Johnstone, Wallace and Lennox, and two attacking midfield men, Callaghan and Connelly. I played the game to suit the players I have at the moment, and it was to make chances from the midfield.'

So what went wrong with the tactics? Stein stated simply: 'A lack of concentration after half time and our failure to put any pressure on them.'

Certainly there was only one course open to Celtic to save the tie,

The goal that could have been a life-saver . . . Jimmy Johnstone
and Harry Hood, and 'keeper Stuy (*left*) watch as his shot goes
into the net for Celtic's only goal against Ajax at Hampden

and that was to put pressure on Ajax in the hope the Dutch defence would split.

One player, perhaps, was more disappointed at the result than any other, outside-right Jimmy Johnstone.

For weeks before the tie a succession of Dutch journalists had flown to Scotland to interview the litte red-head, and the fans in Holland were warned that their team would face one of the most dangerous forwards in Europe.

Sadly it had been a night of failure in Amsterdam for Johnstone, and no one knew it better than the wee man himself.

'I simply felt I had let everyone down. I had such an ordinary game, anyone who read the pre-match stuff must have wondered what all the fuss was about.'

But he had vowed: 'I've never been so determined to do so well, and we really have put in a lot of work into our training.'

And it was Johnstone who was to carry the attacking torch for Celtic, a torch which was never to burn more brightly than in the twenty-seventh minute of the second leg at Hampden.

That was when the hopes of the fans soared, when one of the three goals was cut back, thanks to Johnstone, who popped up in the middle to punish a Dutch defensive muddle. But there were hints that Ajax could be just as lethal with swift breakaways, one of which smacked

No need to ask the Ajax players
what they think about the Scottish
weather . . . their expressions betray
exactly their feelings about Scotland's
mad March days as they leave
their Troon training headquarters for a
limber-up

the ball against the post just before half time.

Despite all the flurries of the second half, and a header by Billy McNeill, which was just tipped over, time became Celtic's implacable enemy.

And the longer it went, it almost seemed the less chance they had of scoring. Maybe the Celtic side of one, two or three seasons ago would have achieved the break-through, but that is only speculation, three goals is a mountain which is almost impossible to climb.

Were they finished as a great side in Europe ? Certainly the evidence pointed that night at Hampden to a need for a reorganisation, but it was too early then to assess what changes should be made.

But sadly the overwhelming memory of the game was of Celtic punching forward with furious pressure, but too often adopting the battering tactics which had been the trade-mark of Scotland in Europe until Stein's green machine had come along to revolutionise it all.

There was a dreadful lack of guile, the unexpected flair which made it such a pleasure to watch them at their peak.

I wonder if any of the fans, as they filed out of Hampden remembered the last European Cup game at the stadium . . . the victory against Leeds the previous season.

That had been a marvellous night . . . the contrast less than a year later could hardly have been greater.

The Night I was Booed

By DAVID HAY

As a Celtic player I naturally know the way to Parkhead as well as any fan. Yet there is the odd occasion as I am driving to the ground, when I almost have to stop to wonder if I am going to the right place.

There's nothing wrong with my sense of direction. The simple reason is that since I moved into the Celtic first-team pool we have played so many games at Hampden—so many matches of such vital importance—that it has come to be our second home.

Start of season friendlies, middle of season challenge matches, Scottish Cup games, League Cup tussles, European Cup games, even league matches when our ground improvements were being made . . .

You name it, and I've played the lot at Hampden, so it is no wonder perhaps that some of my best, and worst, football memories have centred around Britain's biggest stadium.

The best of them . . . well, I can only hope there's more to come, but I'll settle for the moment for the European Cup semi-final against Leeds United two seasons ago.

This was the game where, according to the English critics, we were going to be shown that we had really no right to be challenging against the might of the Football League champions for a place in the European Cup Final.

After all, we were always told, everyone realised how poor the standard of the Scottish League was, compared to the English First Division.

I don't know what the writers of all those pre-match jibes thought they were trying to achieve.

But if they imagined it would scare us, they had the wrong idea entirely. I think it gave us that little bit extra incentive, made everyone from manager Jock Stein down to the youngest player on the staff, determined to do better.

Straightaway let me say that I consider Leeds a very good team, just about the best club side I have ever played against.

They are a really great side, and a team who did not need some of the excuses that were put out for them after their defeat by Celtic.

I know they must have been tired, and I realise that in their final

Eyes firmly on the ball . . . David Hay shows all the concentration
of a top-class soccer star as he starts up a move in the match
against Falkirk at Parkhead

league games, when that long, long programme is dragging to a close, they must have felt the effects of the season.

But I don't believe you can be tired in a European Cup semi-final. The adrenalin is pumped through a team, somehow you summon up that last bit of additional effort to pull you through.

The fact is that over those two games, we did prove to be the better side. The scorelines, a 1–0 victory at Elland Road, and a 2–1 victory at Hampden barely reflects the superiority we showed in the ties.

And the marvellous excitement of it all poured from the fans at the end of the Hampden game . . . I don't think I have ever seen a crowd get so worked up about a result.

I heard later that although the official attendance was only supposed to be 134,000, an extra 2,000 actually squeezed into the ground.

But whatever the crowd limit was, they certainly made the most wonderful noise after the game was over.

As I listened that May night in 1970, to the fans chanting out my team's name again and again, I could hardly have imagined that, just six months later, I would hear from the same Hampden terraces the sound of booing . . . and it would be directed at me!

That was the night of the Scotland-Denmark European Nations Cup tie, when a section of the crowd at the traditional Rangers end of the ground, kept chanting for the Ibrox right-back Sandy Jardine to take my place.

I must admit I don't often pay a lot of attention to what a crowd is shouting during a game. Naturally if they are bellowing encouragement I hear it, but I have learned to shut my ears to most of the other variety of terracing expressions.

I had been doubtful with 'flu before the Denmark game, but I have always considered it an honour to play for Scotland—and that is not a ritual quote every player gives when he is selected—I mean it, so I made an extra effort to be fit.

But it was impossible that night not to have heard the fans chanting for my substitution. I would have needed to have stuffed my ears with cotton-wool for the whole match.

It was a game Scotland had been expected to win, but it was a match in which the entire team struggled to get a grip on the game.

I don't know whether it was frustration by the fans, and I happened to be the most convenient target, but as the chanting went on and on I could not help thinking back to the time I had heard it directed at my team-mate, Jimmy Johnstone.

I had been sitting in the Hampden stand that night as the Rangers fans roared for him to be brought off, and Willie Henderson brought on instead.

58

I thought then how unfair it was to any player, but I never expected to be the fall-guy in the same position.

Eventually I was substituted near the end and the Scotland team manager Bobby Brown told me it was because he felt my illness before the game had taken away some of my strength.

A tremendous controversy went on about it. Manager Jock Stein made it very plain that he was not happy about any of his players receiving such treatment.

Feet up! And a rare picture of David Hay, an all-action star for Celtic for once taking it easy as he relaxes at home

The best in Britain! And Celtic stars David Hay (*left*) and Jimmy
Johnstone show off their awards after a presentation ceremony,
when both had been voted into an all-Britain side by a panel of
sportswriters

As the man in the middle I have kept silent about it until now!

But my feelings are simply this . . . as a professional player I still want to play for Scotland, and if I am picked I will give it all the effort I can.

However, I must admit something has gone from the honour, it has been slightly devalued since that November night.

Two months later Mr. Brown described the treatment I received as 'nauseating'.

Perhaps the saddest aspect is that it is doubtful if any amount of words from any team boss, or legislator, can change the situation much.

Yet any hopes Scotland has of becoming a world power at international level will always be sunk if the fans cannot give us their support.

I know there are team-mates of mine at Celtic who just do not want to know about playing for Scotland.

They are entitled to their viewpoint. Mine, as I have said, is that I would still like to be picked.

The whole business about the fans' emnity towards players is pointless. If they only knew, some of the best friendship in the Scotland party is between Celtic and Rangers players, you should just see how well Ronnie McKinnon and Jimmy Johnstone get on together.

But, of course, while Hampden has been important to me it can never truly take the place of Parkhead in my affections.

One of the highlights of my career was the goal I scored in the 1969–70 Scottish Cup game against Rangers at Parkhead.

Although I have occasionally worn one of the forwards' numbers even then I am not used in an attacking role, so naturally I was delighted when I scored the goal—a long-range shot from 25 yards— which put us ahead 2–1, and a couple of minutes later Jimmy Johnstone scored another to really make certain.

Talking of that wee man, Johnstone, I am always delighted when I see him skipping past defenders, that he is in the same team as I am . . . he really must be the most difficult forward of them all to pin down.

Yet, in one time in my Celtic career, I thought the chances of playing with Jimmy or any of the rest of the Parkhead first-team would only be a dream.

I started my career with St. Mirin's Boys' Guild team in Paisley and then when I signed provisionally for Celtic and even when I joined the club properly, I was still a part-timer.

I was studying to be a chartered accountant and looking back on it now I think I got the worst of both worlds.

61

I was not making much headway at either job, in fact I used to count myself lucky when I got a reserve game.

I had not been in Lisbon in 1967—like thousands of other fans I had watched the game on television—and I was beginning to wonder if that was the nearest I would ever get to the first team.

It is tremendously hard for youngsters to break into a side that is as successful as Celtic. When I was attempting to get into the first team there were three experienced full-backs ahead of me, Jim Craig and Tommy Gemmell, who had played in the European Cup winning side, and also Willie O'Neil in the reserves.

It got to the stage that while I never actually sat down to write a transfer request, I privately gave myself another season and I felt if I had not made any progress by then, I would have to think of a move.

Yet all the time, and even when I was playing regularly in the reserve side, I realise now I was working my football apprenticeship.

It's manager Jock Stein's way of doing things. I would get an odd game as substitute in the first-team. I went on a few foreign trips and although I knew I had no hope of playing, I learned all about the atmosphere of these European Cup ties.

So that when my chance did come—and it's the same with any kid who makes the Celtic team—it is not just an untried youngster who is going into the side.

It is a gradual process. I must admit sometimes I was hardly aware it was going on, but I can only say in my case it prepared me well for the team.

I suppose I was the first of the reserves to break through after Lisbon, Jim Brogan was the other player who made the team but he had already appeared in the first-team before the European Cup Final.

And it is to the credit of the other players, a tightly-knit bunch, because of all they had gone through together, that I never encountered any jealousy . . . in fact, I got a great deal of help.

I have varied between the mid-field and full-back, and frankly I have no particular preference for either position, I look on it simply that I am lucky to get a place in the team.

However, I do object to the belief some people have that all you need to do at full-back is crunch in the tackle and boot the ball up the park.

That's not the way any modern full-back would want to play, and not the way we play it at Celtic Park . . . or, for that matter, Hampden!

Swop! And two iron men of soccer, England's Nobby Stiles, with blood streaming from a cut eye-brow, and Scotland's David Hay exchange jerseys after a Scotland - England international at Hampden

The Fans Chorus

By HARRY HOOD

I DON'T know what secret sign starts the chant—for it can begin even when I have not scored—but as sure as there are fans on the Parkhead terraces, I could bet my bonus that they will start up a chorus with that familiar refrain . . . 'Harry, Harry . . . Harry Hood!'

It's highly flattering to be singled out for special attention, but I have never been able really to work out why the fans have always awarded me this special accolade.

The only reason I can think of is that when I first arrived at Celtic from Clyde one of the top favourites in the hit parade of the time was the song 'Hare Krishna' and my name happened to fit the music of that chorus.

I appreciate the support from the fans, but I don't suppose they know the jokes it sparks off against me from my team-mates. It's all right if I've scored a goal . . . but it's a different matter if things have not been going too well for me.

Even the boss joins in! I think Mr. Stein sometimes imagines I pay for the choir to begin that chorus.

But if I am the object of praise from the Celtic fans, the chant is slightly twisted into another meaning by the Rangers fans . . . and I've had to sit and listen to it.

I don't very often go to matches involving the Ibrox team, but one game I did watch last season was their Scottish Cup semi-final replay against Hibs at Hampden.

Over it came, loud and clear, just what they thought about Harry Hood. I wonder what the reaction would have been if they had known that the man about whom they were singing—or should I say jeering?—was sitting a few yards away from them in the Hampden stand.

Maybe the only response would have been the noise would have got a bit louder. I reckon the only answer is to form a club with my team-mate Tommy Gemmell, and Hibs manager Dave Ewing . . . the other constant targets for the Rangers fans.

Yet strangely enough, the chant did not start at Parkhead, but at Sunderland—my second senior club—and a place where I ex-

64

It's another autograph by Harry Hood, but this was for no kid's book, it's one of the most important of his life . . . the signature that took him to Celtic as he signs in the office of manager Jock Stein (*right*) and watched by Clyde boss, Archie Robertson perienced some of the real heart-breaks of the game.

I often wonder what the fans down there who began it all must think when reports filter south of anything I achieve at Celtic.

Yet it is one of the twists of my career that if things had worked out I would have gone straight from Clyde, my first senior club, to Parkhead, instead of that somewhat roundabout route which involved my spell with Sunderland and then back to Shawfield before I arrived finally at Parkhead.

I want to tell you about these three clubs, for in my comparatively short career, I think they covered the whole range of how teams are run—from good to bad.

And let's start with the bad news, for I reckon that's what Sunderland was to my football career.

I moved there in November 1964, and I really imagined that the gates had swung open on the road to soccer success.

Remember they were still a First Division club at the time, still rated as one of the teams who, given just a few breaks, would be back to their old glory days . . .

And they had some of the most loyal and faithful fans in the entire country. I'll always remember that about my time there.

I liked Sunderland a great deal, we had a nice house, pleasant neighbours, everything for a happy life except for one major snag . . . my football career almost came to a complete stop.

One of the myths about English football is how thorough they are in all their preparations, how much more professional they are in their attitude to the game compared to Scottish clubs.

Perhaps this is true of some English clubs, but I regret to say it was not true of Sunderland in my time there as a player.

I was there in the years which I consider the most important in any player's life. First of all, of course, he has to get a club, but once he has made the grade the late teens and early twenties are the most vital times of all his career.

For it is then he polishes up his basic knowledge of the game, the years when the framework for his future career is forged.

These were the two years I spent at Sunderland . . . and I am sorry to say I learned nothing!

Why should such a great club spin into an apparently unstoppable decline? It is not for me to put forward all the answers, the blame must lie at various levels, from the board downwards.

Maybe they suffered from having so many managers. I was signed by George Hardwick but towards the end of that first season he was fired, and his place was taken by Ian McColl, who only a couple of weeks before he moved to Roker Park had lost the Scotland team manager's job.

Meet the swinging Hood family . . . as Harry and his wife,
Kathleen, line up with their children, Lisa, Siobhan and baby
Nicholas, in a moment of relaxation during last year's busy season

Stopped! As a superb Ajax
tackle foils Harry Hood as he
attempts to dash through the
defence in the game at
Hampden .

Maybe it was a case of the new manager not fancying the old manager's buys. It has happened before and it will happen again—I don't know the real reason—all I know is that Mr. McColl and I did not get along together.

I thought I had played reasonably well in my first season with Sunderland, and I was in the team for the opening pre-season game, the one in which Jim Baxter made his début for them after his transfer from Rangers.

The opposition was a team called Celtic, who had certainly never heard of the tag friendly, for they trounced us, and it was goodbye Harry Hood.

I hardly played in the first team again for that entire season. Whatever I had done wrong against Celtic, I was not going to be lightly forgiven.

But my real grievance was that nothing much was done to put it right! Mr. McColl concentrated a great deal on the older and more experienced players, the younger ones were left to fend for themselves.

And when we did play in the first team, the manager's criticism after the game was always reserved for the youngsters, the big stars escaped any after-match censures.

I remember one game particularly for that, against Southampton, when the coach at the time, Jim Mortimore, praised my performance but a difficult effort I had missed was criticised by the manager although one of the regular forwards had messed up a perfect chance.

So, as you can gather, it was with no regrets that I moved back to Shawfield, twenty-three months after I had gone south to Sunderland.

And I was back in time to help them to one of their most successful seasons ever in the First Division, and I think one of the greatest feats for a part-time team.

For that season we finished third in the league behind Celtic—it was the year of their grand slam and they lost only two games to Dundee United—and Rangers.

I suppose some people looked on us as a freak side, but it was the result of a lot of hard planning to get to that position.

The simple answer is that we operated as a full-time team, from manager Davie White downwards, even if we did not have all the resources of the big-time outfits.

You see, we talked about the game an awful lot. And if that sounds too simple to be true, you must understand that not every club in the country works on these lines.

Naturally we did not win by just talking. I had a very good understanding with Stan Anderson, now one of Rangers' coaches, in mid-field, and with the engine-room of the side working efficiently, the rest followed as everyone worked at their game to make up for the

The footballer's favourite relaxation . . . and Harry Hood gives a
bunker shot at Seamill the same careful concentration as he does a
shot on the soccer field

The goal that helped to win the League . . . as Harry Hood
(*extreme left*) rounds an Aberdeen player to score the vital first
goal in the key match at Pittodrie

deficiencies of being just part-timers.

I always used to say that there was no real difference between part-timers and full-timers. I could never work out much distinction between the set-up at Shawfield and the one at Sunderland.

But there was a difference, and I soon found that out when I moved to Celtic!

Players must really work at the game, you can't have just a few hours boring track work and call yourself a full-timer.

The first problem I had at Parkhead was simply to last the pace with the rest of the team. I found myself becoming dreadfully tired in the last twenty minutes, as my team-mates, used to the training routines, just swept on regardless.

There are other differences as well. I could adjust eventually to the physical pressure, but there is the mental pressure as well.

Above them all . . . soars Harry Hood as he scores the first goal for Celtic against Hearts at Tynecastle

There is no such thing as anyone sitting back complacently imagining that they will be in the team regardless . . . I think that was made pretty clear last season.

Quite simply we are expected to win every game. That was not the case at Sunderland, and if it had been, it had long since gone, and Clyde could hardly set their sights so high.

Full-time is certainly beneficial to any player, but only if the time is used properly, and I had to wait until I joined Celtic before I found out the right way a team should be run.

I know some fans interpret the meaning of full-time as players training continuously morning and afternoon.

But, with modern training methods, most of the work can be packed into the morning. The advantages lie in a different direction . . . a player has time to go back to the ground in the afternoon if he

Back home . . . another trip is over, another success. This time it was to Finland, to play Kokkola in the European Cup, and just look at the joy on Lisa Hood's face as she greets her father at Glasgow Airport wants to improve some particular part of his game, and he is spared the bug-bear of all part-time clubs, trying to get off work for mid-week fixtures.

It also means that he can usually spare the time for another job which can be fitted into his football life.

I know there has been a lot of controversy about the outside interests of Celtic players, with the allegations that it has taken the edge off our play.

Well, I can't speak for all of my colleagues, but I do know how it has affected me. . . and I feel it has benefited my game.

I remember how I used to feel at Sunderland, when we were finished by lunch-time, and I had no other way of filling in most of my days. Now I have a business, a restaurant and pub near Uddingston, but it does not affect my football life in the slightest.

I spend some time there every week, enough to give me an added interest, and a bit of extra security for myself and my family.

But I am never very far away from football. You would go a long way in the West of Scotland to find a pub where the customers don't talk about the game, and mine is no exception.

However, I must emphasise that my business is completely secondary to my football, I hope to go on playing for a long time yet.

They say that every goaikeeper secretly wants to be a goalkeeper. I don't visualise any change as dramatic as that.

But maybe a move to the midfield would suit me at some future date. Some strikers, such as Bobby Charlton, have made the move successfully, and, although Celtic have converted me to striker, I did play in a deeper role at Shawfield.

Certainly the move up front paid off last season, when I was fortunate enough to finish as top scorer not just for my club, but also in Scotland.

Yet the difference between success and failure for any forward is wafer thin. I finished the season before last in the doldrums, so I know what a player such as John Hughes must have been going through last season. No matter how hard you try, nothing seems to come right.

People said to me how upset I must have been to have missed games such as the Leeds match.

But I believe every footballer has to be honest with himself and I was disappointed naturally at not playing a part in these epic matches, yet I knew I was not playing well enough at the time.

My disappointment deepens when I think of the few European Cup games I have played for Celtic, and that's something I aim to remedy.

One critic suggested I did not have enough class apparently for a place in the Scotland team. He's entitled to his opinion but I would not say every forward who had been picked for the international side had this elusive quality called class.

So I aim for the Scotland team, and I know there's only one way to make sure of both my targets . . . by putting the ball in the back of the net!

Yet of all the goals I scored last season I suppose there were two which were the most significant, one affected the destiny of the league championship, the other the Scottish Cup.

And, as befits different competitions they were entirely different types of goals. The league one at Aberdeen, which helped us gain a 1–1 draw there and foil the Pittodrie side's championship hopes, was scored with a low flick from a Jimmy Johnstone on the left, and the Cup Final goal was a penalty.

I suppose there can be few more nerve-wracking moments for any player than a penalty in an 'Old Firm' Cup Final. As soon as Ronnie McKinnon went to tackle wee Jimmy I knew it was going to be a penalty . . . and I had to stop a thousand thoughts flooding through my mind.

Celtic had just scored two minutes before, another goal would surely seal the fate of the match. A miss . . . and Rangers would undoubtedly take renewed heart for the rest of the match.

But I had to wipe out all these thoughts. I just could not afford to think how important it was, for that would have been a sure way to have missed the spot-kick completely.

Many people must have wondered what Billy McNeill said to me when he ran up and we had a quick chat before the kick was taken.

He was simply giving me a few words of encouragement. Earlier in the season, in a league game against Rangers at Parkhead, Tommy Gemmell had been off injured and Jim Brogan felt he was in a better frame of mind to take the kick, but sadly he missed it.

Sure, I was nervous, but I tried not to show it. Once I betrayed any nerves I would have handed the advantage to 'keeper Peter McCloy and given him a giant vote of confidence. So I concentrated on taking it steady and not to take a wild kick at it, but hit the ball low.

Fortunately I did score, and helped my side to collect the Cup. I got my winner's medal, and later on a massive black eye in a collision with the big Rangers 'keeper. Later on I could see so little out of it that I was substituted in the second-half.

I looked like a refugee from a terracing punch-up as I walked up to collect my medal. But I didn't care . . . if I had to have hobbled up on crutches I would have been there to collect that award.

The New Chairman

CELTIC'S new chairman thoughtfully fingered a scar on his eyebrow and smiled as he told me . . . 'I got that in a match playing for Queen's Park against Celtic, when I clashed with Jimmy Delaney'.

It was a recollection for Desmond White of the pre-war days when he was Queen's Park's first-team goalkeeper, and getting an entirely different football view from his elevated position today as chairman of Celtic Football Club.

That was the position his father, Tom White, held before him for a record 33 years—and to which he was elected last April when ill-health finally forced the retirement of Sir Robert Kelly.

Sir Robert, Scotland's most honoured football legislator, was a man whose powerful views often created controversy, but a man who was as familiar to the fans as many star players.

Desmond White, by the fact that for 31 years he was club secretary, has been more in the background, but that does not mean he is a man who is merely a juggler with accountancy figures.

Yet, if he remained until he took over the chairmanship as a slightly unknown figure to the public, he has not been an anonymous figure at Parkhead.

He is the man whose importance, for example, on trips abroad is as high as anyone's in the party, responsible as he is for the organisation of these frequently large groups.

There can be problems with players, who can be occasionally careless with such vital, but loseable pieces of paper as aircraft boarding passes. And not only players . . . at least two distinguished members of the Press who did not keep a careful check had to ruefully report to Mr. White on one trip the loss of their tickets.

To Desmond White falls the task of leading Celtic into the seventies, and the job of overseeing the work to make sure that the club's ground at Parkhead lives up to their stature on the field as one of Europe's major clubs.

At a lunch-time talk the week of his appointment, he elaborated to me some of the details of the new plans for Parkhead.

The face is familiar, but this is one role the Celtic fans will not see their new chairman in again. For in this flashback to the thirties Desmond White, in his role at that time as the last line of defence for Queens' Park keeps an anxious eye on an opposition attack

The immediate improvement, of course, is the doubling of the stand accommodation from 4,000 to around 9,000, a long over-due improvement in this age when more and more fans have come to want a seat in comfort to watch a game.

Mr. White told me: 'We have not had fans who were stand conscious. Many of them seemed to prefer to stand on the terracing,

82

but I am convinced that was merely because of lack of accommodation in the stand.

'People would arrive hoping to get a seat, and find the place was filled, so they got more used to the terraces'.

The main feature of the new stand is that there is no obstructing pillars, surely a welcome innovation. For which football fan has not been delighted at obtaining a seat in the stand, perhaps at an all-ticket match, and then arriving to find his goal-mouth view blocked by a huge pillar.

The new chairman explained: 'This new concept in design makes it the most modern in Europe. The idea for it has been copied from the hangers built for the Jumbo jets.

'Obviously you cannot have obstructions for these giant planes, they need a space uncluttered by any obstacles, and the same principle will be applied for the stand'.

And by 1973, it is hoped that there will be new amenities to complete the building into the most modern stand in the country.

This will include new facilities for both fans and players. For the fans more modern snack-bars—something in which most clubs have been lamentably behind the times—and places for light meals.

For the players, there will be new dressing-rooms, new office accommodation, everything to bring the ground up to the standard a club of Celtic's prestige deserves.

For those who scoffed that such improvements were only pipe-dreams that would never get beyond the planning stage the answer came—coincidentally the week of Mr. White's new appointment—when the demolition men moved in to start taking the roof off the old stand.

What else does he visualise to improve the ground, and which will send the bill for such major surgery to the place to the breath-taking figure of over one million pounds?

A minor, but important, change will be an improvement in the exits into London Road to make them as safe as possible, and this is scheduled for next close-season.

And eventually Mr. White forecasts another new stand, on the site of the original 'Jungle' enclosure which was replaced by a new enclosure with concreted steps a few years ago.

Celtic have often switched matches especially showpiece fixtures to Hampden, such as important start-of-the-season friendlies, their World Club championship game with Racing Club, the European Cup clashes with Leeds and with Ajax.

And towards the end of last year they helped to prop up the desperately ailing finances of amateur Queen's Park, owners of Hampden, with a £10,000 donation.

Why then did they not go the whole way, and purchase Hampden to pour the reconstruction money into the giant stadium which so badly needs it?

Mr. White explained to me the answers, and it shows that even in this finance-conscious, budget-balancing soccer world of the seventies, there can still be room for sentiment to go with the money game which football has become.

'For a start our roots are in the East End of Glasgow. They have been ever since we started, and I think it is very vital for a club to maintain these links, even in today's more sophisticated set-up.

'But Hampden is so vast it is almost impossible, unless you get a huge crowd, to inject any atmosphere into it.

'It is like going to the theatre. If the place is full, there is a touch of excitement about it all, if it is half-empty then it is a struggle for the actors to whip up interest.

'Football players are no different. They respond to the roar of the crowd, and that's difficult to get at Hampden for ordinary matches.

'A crowd of 30,000 to 40,000, round about our average gate for an ordinary League match, is just lost in such vast surroundings.

They strive for soccer safety . . . and outside Parkhead Desmond White (*left*) talks to former England team boss Walter Winterbottom (*centre*) now a member of the Government panel on safety at football grounds

'We can take 80,000 at Parkhead, and even with all the improvements we will not be going above that limit. Our aim is more comfort for the fans, not to increase the capacity at the expense of the fans.'

But a super stadium without a team to match is as hard to take as Bacardi without coke, Laurel without Hardy—the two are absolutely inseparable.

That's why the chairman was delighted at the decision of the manager to stay with the club . . . Stein without Celtic would have seemed just as strange.

'I was very pleased at Mr. Stein's decision. From a personal point of view, and from the club's as well.

'It means that the established, and successful set-up will carry on. And I am sure Mr. Stein will create a new team which can match the triumph of Lisbon.

'Obviously it would have caused a lot of problems for me if we had faced complete changes as soon as I had taken over.'

The fact that finance and football are so bound together today was shown in his remark when I asked him about the future in Europe.

'Well of course, we want to be in Europe as much as possible. A great deal of a season's income can come from a successful run in the major European tournaments.

'But at the same time we must be realistic. We have enjoyed football at a very high level for the last six years—that will always be the club's aim—but we must allow for the human element, we may not hit these peaks every season.'

The Celtic chairman perhaps nurtures one dream more than any other, to have a tilt again at the World Club championship.

'That is the Everest of club football. It is something which we can aim at, for it is no use taking part in the competitions that lead up to it, the League championship, the European Cup, and then stepping back when you reach it.

'Our experience the last time in South America was regrettable, but some good even came out of that. The governing bodies of the game made new rules, and took over the running of the tournament.

'I know it has not completely cleared up the trouble, and some of the incidents which happen in South America make frightening reading. But we have just got to go on till we break down the barriers.'

Desmond White, like many other old players, looks slightly longingly at the money made by present-day players, and perhaps wishes his playing career had been thirty years later.

'Players today earn their money, and they have increased in stature in the community, partly because of that.

'It's a good thing too. In my youth, as an apprentice chartered accountant, it was unheard of to join a professional club, and I never gave it a thought.

'Today of course, it would be quite a natural thing to do. I think that's what affected Queen's Park recruitment more than anything else, there is no stigma attached to being a professional and that's the way it should be.'

His soccer career was as a goalkeeper, but he nurtured a secret desire to be a centre-forward, and it was only when he earned a representative honour as a 'keeper that he decided to stick between the sticks.

Not that it kept him entirely out of controversy, he was one of the few Queen's Park players of those days to be sent off after a clash with a forward.

He had a spell with the now defunct Edinburgh City, before he joined Queens—he was their regular League 'keeper—but he retired in 1938 and soon after became the Celtic secretary in succession to the legendary Willie Maley, who had combined the job with his manager's post.

'It was nothing then compared to the volume of work today which is almost full-time,' he said.

He injured his right arm in a war time flying accident, he was a Flight Lieutenant, which has resulted in a partial disablement.

But you would never guess it from his tales of mountaineering, or another of his sporting loves, under-water swimming.

Maybe it was at swimming he had one of his few failures, an unsuccessful attempt to teach this writer how to swim on Celtic's close-season trip to Bermuda last year.

I asked him before I left him that lunch-time, if he had ever thought there would be a time when he would be chairman of Celtic.

'I never really imagined it. I had worked so well with Sir Robert Kelly, and especially in those last six marvellous years I had been far too busy as club secretary.

'I am pleased to have been given such a high honour, my one regret about it is that it came about because of Sir Robert's illness,' he said.

So now the club have a new chairman for the new challenges of the seventies, but Celtic's history has been one of continuity—Mr. White's father as chairman, Jock Stein's time as the club captain—and many others.

I believe that the best of that old tradition will still be kept, not in tangible assets—the old buildings must make way for new ones—but in the heart of a great club, and that still counts . . . even in today's fiercely competitive soccer world.

The Sixth Championship

THEY stood there in the centre of the ground where their soccer style had been born, arms raised high in salute to the fans . . . and in return the roar of the crowd washed over them, sound wave crashing on sound wave.

It was a sun-bathed May afternoon, so similar to that other day in May—could it really have been four years ago ?—when this team had joined the soccer immortals with their European Cup winning achievement.

Now it was the last hurrah for the Lions of Lisbon, and it would have taken a very hard man indeed not to have watched these final, farewell scenes without a trace of a lump in his throat.

It was a superb piece of soccer showmanship by manager Jock Stein to parade his most famous side—Simpson, Craig, Gemmell, Murdoch, McNeill, Clark, Johnstone, Wallace, Chalmers, Lennox, Auld—on the last Saturday of the season.

This was, as the old theatre bills used to say, positively their last appearance. Even then, Ronnie Simpson, one year retired, only took part in the shoot-in. And it was a last look in a Celtic jersey at Bertie Auld, freed the day before by the club, and destined to sign for Hibs the next week.

Yes, it was a day for nostalgia, and not just because 1971 happened to be the year when the current theme was a longing to look back, but it was also a day to be grateful.

Grateful for the reminder of how great this team really had been, grateful that it had not been brought together again for some charity match when the years had rounded their stomachs, thinned their hair and slowed their legs.

This was a living Hall of Fame, some of the legends might be showing slight cracks, but there was enough vigour in the rest of the side to conceal the cracks.

It was a day to show the kids, who might have been too young to understand it, the first-ever British team to win the European Cup, so that years from now they might tell their kids they had seen this Celtic side . . . and so legends are born.

88

The last hurrah . . . for Bertie Auld, as hoisted high on the shoulders of his team-mates, he is carried off Parkhead at the end of his final game for Celtic

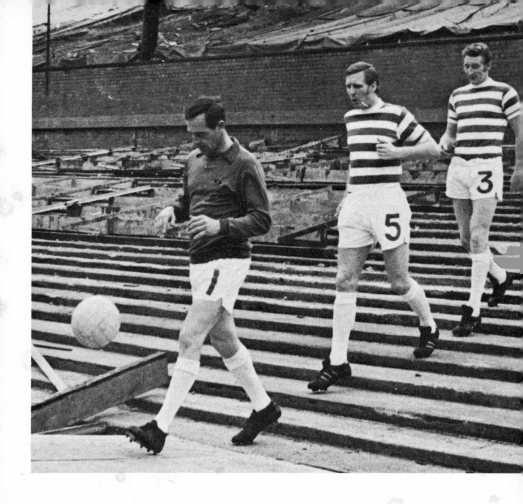

One eminent football columnist, who in late-night liquid football discussions has sometimes seemed to be addicted to the memory of the Hearts trio of Conn, Bauld and Wardhaugh, brought along his son . . . 'I thought he should see this team,' he said simply.

The backcloth to the game was as strange a setting as soccer could ever devise, a Parkhead where the stand had been partially demolished and only a handful of seats were available.

It reminded me of a school sports day. The sun shone, the V.I.P's —the directors and their friends sat on a few rows of hastily arranged chairs—the 35,000 fans packed on to the terraces, and the rest of us took up position where we could.

The press parked themselves on the concrete enclosure steps, high above them the remnants of the old press-box, which almost qualified for a historical monument certificate, was just a crazy fret-work of a few iron girders and bits of plaster-board.

But no one cared, right from the moment when the team appeared, picking their way gingerly down the enclosure steps and led by Ronnie Simpson.

After the shoot-in he went off to a personal chant from the crowd, to be replaced for the actual match by Evan Williams.

It was the thirty-fourth league game of the season, and despite the carnival atmosphere there was a bit of football business to be completed.

Celtic's last match should have been against Ayr United but, due to a switch-around because of postponed games, in the hurry to finish the season their final league opponents were Clyde.

The title had already been won two nights before against Ayr United, but they still had the same points total as Aberdeen . . . Celtic had never won any of their previous five titles simply on the old goal average or the new goal difference system.

They wanted to win the championship on points, not just pip Aberdeen by statistics, only a fairground score of 12-0 against Celtic

What a team! The lions of Lisbon roar for the last time! As led by their former 'keeper, Ronnie Simpson, they march on to Parkhead for the final appearance together in a competitive match, against Clyde. The line-up of Scotland's most famous club side is, *left to right*, Simpson, McNeill, Gemmell, Clark, Auld, Lennox, Chalmers, Johnstone, Wallace, Craig and Murdoch would have robbed them, and as so often in the past—this team made no mistake.

For if it was a day to remember all their soccer yesterdays, it was also a day when they magnificently accomplished their target, as they bowed out with a memory of the superb soccer which was always their trademark.

There was the trickery of Jimmy Johnstone, the dash of centre Steve Chalmers—the man who scored the winning goal against Inter-Milan in the final in Lisbon—and whose goal brought the loudest cheer of the afternoon.

And, at the back, there was an impeccable performance of efficient sweeping by John Clark, the little man who had slipped into the shadows, but whose presence many felt always made the Celtic defence more solid.

All the moves were strung together as they raced to a 6-1 victory, with a hat-trick from Bobby Lennox, two by Willie Wallace, and that one, the last goal of the afternoon, by Chalmers.

Maybe at times they turned on the style too much, one moment in the second-half when Bertie Auld sat on the ball, to taunt his opponents, brought manager Jock Stein out of his temporary dug-out to angrily wave to his team to get on with the game.

Then, a final blast from referee Jim Callaghan's whistle and it was over, not just ninety minutes of a match, but an era.

Back they went into the centre circle for the last time together, and as they left it they suddenly stopped and hoisted Bertie Auld up on the shoulders of his team-mates.

Incredibly the crowd somehow managed to summon up enough lung-power to let loose another deafening roar—a final vocal salute to this team of all the talents who had done so much, not just for Celtic, but the whole of Scottish football.

Yet one game, and I have devoted space to it because it was such a unique soccer spectacle, does not win a league championship.

The slog is in every game, and even if the only two rivals for the 1970–71 championship, Celtic and Aberdeen, seemed to approach the finish looking like marathon runners who could hardly dredge up the strength to reach the finishing post, the statistics for the Parkhead side were impressive.

It was their sixth successive title, a fantastic feat, they totted up 56 points, one fewer than the previous season, and their scoring rate was slightly less, 89 to the year before's 96.

But their goals tally was still an incredible 21 more than Aberdeen's. They dropped only three points at home, a defeat by Aberdeen and a draw with Dundee United, and they lost twice away from home, to Hibs and St. Johnstone, and they had draws with Rangers, Hearts,

92

Falkirk, St. Mirren and Aberdeen.

In many ways it was the strangest season of them all. For a start the challenge of Rangers, who had finished second to Celtic in the previous five seasons, had fizzled out feebly as early as the New Year.

And there were stretches when it would be wrong to say Celtic's form had showed all their old flair. But credit their players, and not one of them was an ever-present right through the championship, with an amazing resilience.

Like an old-time champion craftily absorbing all the punishment they still managed to hit back and prevent one defeat turning into a losing streak to lose them all chance of the championship.

Perhaps the biggest crisis points from that point of view was the League Cup Final defeat by Rangers, they wobbled in the next game against Hearts, and the home defeat from Aberdeen at Parkhead in early December.

The congratulations are warm, sincere and mutual . . . as Jim Brogan and Martin Buchan meet at the end of the league 'decider' at Pittodrie. Celtic finished ahead of Aberdeen in the league, but Martin had one consolation, he was voted Scotland's 'Player of the Year', with Jim as runner-up

The strangest Parkhead picture of them all! For the old stand,
halfway to demolition, makes an odd setting as Bobby Lennox,
with a typical goal-snatching effort, scores the first of his side's
six against Clyde

That was a victory which sent the Dons to the top of the table, a position they were to keep until the very last week of the title race.

And again the February defeat by St. Johnstone at Perth when faced also with the Scottish Cup survival bid and the coming European Cup clash, it would have been so easy to have slid slightly, but fatally.

So let's take a look, with the aid of a month-by-month guide at the thirty-four steps which took Celtic to yet another league championship.

AUGUST: The first league game—after the opening flourish of the League Cup—and the first victory, a 2–0 win against Morton at Parkhead, with both goals by Bobby Lennox.

However, this win was marred by an injury to left-back Tommy Gemmell, which was to keep him out for nearly four months.

SEPTEMBER: A 5–0 win against Clyde at Shawfield, something of a hoodoo ground for Celtic, and a ground where manager Stein once said he could not remember a good game between the teams. Scorers were Lou Macari, with two, David Hay, John McHugh, own goal, and Vic Davidson.

That was followed by a convincing win against Rangers at Parkhead, with a goal in the first half from John Hughes, and a superb Bobby Murdoch goal in the second, one that was a reminder of all his old skill and power. They even missed a penalty, with Jim Brogan taking over in the absence of Gemmell and blasting it over the bar.

A week later, it was the same score, 2–0, but this time Celtic were on the receiving end when they were deservedly dumped by Hibs at Easter Road . . . and both goals were brilliantly scored by ex-Celt Joe McBride.

The last game of the month, and the third time they had met Dundee in three weeks. The clubs had already contested the League Cup quarter-finals, a draw at Dens Park, and a victory at Parkhead for Celtic.

Three days after the second League Cup game, Dundee were back at Parkhead on league business. The result was another victory for Celtic, by 3–0, with two goals from Jimmy Johnstone and one from Lou Macari. Not surprisingly in view of so many meetings in so short a time, there was trouble on the park, Dundee's Ron Selway was ordered off, and team-mate Jim Steele booked.

OCTOBER: And it started with a 2–0 win at Dunfermline, never an easy place for Celtic to pick up the points, the scorers were Macari and Willie Wallace (penalty).

Willie Wallace again, when a 1–0 win narrowly gave them victory against St. Johnstone. But there was some concern about the team's form . . . there was a warning from the manager to them about lack of consistency in the club's match programme.

The injury problem struck again in this game, when Tommy Callaghan was stretchered off.

A good 3–1 away win against Airdrie at Broomfield, again a ground where it has been so difficult in the past. The goals came from Harry Hood, with two, and Lennox.

It's interesting to note that although Hood finished Scotland's top scorer, he had to wait until the middle of October to get his first league goals.

One Saturday in October went to the League Cup Final, when Celtic were beaten 1–0 by Rangers, and there seemed to be a hangover in the next game against Hearts at Parkhead, when they trailed by 2–0.

But, inspired by Bobby Murdoch at his best in mid-field, Willie Wallace cracked in two goals against his old team, and then Harry Hood stunned Hearts when he notched the winner to make it 3–2.

Shake . . . as Tommy Gemmell, captain for the day, meets Rangers skipper John Greig before the start of the New Year fixture at Ibrox. Wonder what they were talking about

Six to one against! But these odds, made up of a blanket Falkirk defence, cannot stop Willie Wallace powerfully heading in a goal for Celtic at Parkhead

NOVEMBER: The league pattern was now taking shape, with Celtic first, Aberdeen second and Rangers third.

And on a dreadfully wet day at Fir Park, with pools of water spread all over the pitch, Celtic raced to an impressive 5–0 victory against Motherwell, with goals from Hood (3, one penalty), George Connelly and Johnstone.

Two first half goals by Fifer George Connelly helped to dump one of his county teams, Cowdenbeath in a 3–0 victory at Parkhead . . . Wallace got the other goal.

Then came a 3–0 victory against Kilmarnock at Parkhead with goals from Murdoch, Wallace and Johnstone.

There was a grim fight at Brockville where Falkirk held Celtic to a no-scoring draw, even although referee John Paterson amazingly stretched the match out for 95 minutes.

It was the first of a hat-trick of excellent results Falkirk had at home against top opposition, later in the season they beat both Rangers and Aberdeen at Brockville.

The last victory of the month was a 3–0 win against St. Mirren at Parkhead, with goals from Tommy Gemmell—back again after injury—and two by Vic Davidson.

DECEMBER: A crazy sequence of own goals against Dundee United at Tannadice, but it still gave Celtic a 2–1 victory. Billy McNeill scored United's goal, Stewart Markland for his side against Celtic, and Davidson got the only one for the right team.

Then one of the season's highlights, the game against Aberdeen at Parkhead. And the Dons kept up their amazing sequence against Celtic when they rang up their third successive victory, thanks to a second half goal by Joe Harper, then the most dangerous goal snatcher in Scotland.

But Celtic bounced back with a 2–1 victory against Ayr at Somerset Park, with goals from John Hughes and Harry Hood.

One of the season's biggest bombshells exploded the following week, when both captain Billy McNeill and right-winger Jimmy Johnstone were dropped for the game against Morton at Cappielow.

And Celtic won 3–0, the goals were scored by Steve Chalmers Lennox and Wallace.

JANUARY: And a start which seemed so bright, but which turned so very, very sour . . . and not because a point was dropped.

It was the traditional New Year 'Old Firm' fixture, and it seemed to be Celtic's match when Jimmy Johnstone snapped a goal only a minute from time.

But a minute later, Colin Stein equalised, and as thousands of Rangers fans, delighted at their team's 1–1 draw made their way from the ground, there was an accident on the ill-starred passageway 13 . . .

Another goal for Harry Hood! But this time, even with super scorer Hood's help it was not enough to save Celtic. For they lost the match against St. Johnstone by 3–2

h has its fling . . . as Vic Davidson, promoted to the league
dashes into the St. Mirren penalty area, but this time he was
d by 'keeper Denis Connaghan

Hit the deck ! But it's worth it for Willie Wallace as he heads
home a goal against Airdrie at Parkhead

and sixty-six fans died in Britain's worst ever soccer disaster.

A week later, after the funerals and seven days of near-national mourning, the football world was still filled with gloom.

Celtic players joined Rangers and civic officials in a memorial service in Glasgow Cathedral for the victims. Then in the afternoon they played Hibs at Parkhead, and it was hardly surprising that with the morning service, a two minute silence before the start and black armbands, it should have been a sombre occasion.

For the record, Celtic won 2-1 with goals by Callaghan and Hood.

But the team really roared into its stride the following week, with one of the high-spots of the season . . . an 8-1 victory against Dundee at Dens Park.

The goal-scorers in this romp were Hood, 2, Wallace, 2, Callaghan, Johnstone, 2, and Dave Johnston of Dundee, an own goal.

The last game of the month was a 1-0 victory against Dunfermline at Parkhead, and the scorer was Wallace.

FEBRUARY: There was no shining bright start to this month. A smart display of attacking soccer put Celtic right off their stride at Muirton against St. Johnstone.

Saints took the lead, Hood equalised, and then when they went 3-1 ahead, Wallace could only pull one back for a final 3-2 score.

After a break for the Scottish Cup, Celtic crushed Airdrie 4-1 at Parkhead with two goals from Willie Wallace, Hood, and Macari.

And there was the unusual sight of Celtic fans cheering a Rangers result . . . after the Ibrox side had drawn 0-0 with league leaders Aberdeen at Pittodrie.

However, it was Celtic's turn to drop a point the following week when Harry Hood's goal gave them the lead against Hearts at Tynecastle . . . but the match ended in a 1-1 draw.

MARCH: Relegation candidates Cowdenbeath were trounced 5-1 at Central Park, and the goals came from Hughes, McNeill, Hood, (one penalty) 2, and Lennox.

Then came a boost for the European Cup match against Ajax with an emphatic 4-1 victory over Kilmarnock at Rugby Park, and the scorers, all in the second half were Hood, 2, Hughes and Davidson.

Sadly there was no reproduction of that score against Ajax, however the team picked themselves up after they had been knocked out of the European Cup with a 4-0 fighting win against Falkirk at Parkhead.

This was potentially a difficult fixture, with the threat of a European Cup hangover over it, but Celtic won well with goals from Wallace, Hughes and Hood, 2.

APRIL: And the start was as chilling as a series of April showers, with a 1–1 draw against Dundee United at Parkhead on Easter Saturday, and one of Celtic's worst performances of the season.

It was a game in which they never managed to take command, but Willie Wallace grabbed a second half life-saving point.

Two days later, against Motherwell—and helped by team changes —they roared back with a 3–0 victory at Parkhead, and goals from Wallace, Johnstone and Hood.

Then the scene moved to the crunch game of the season, the 35,000 all-ticket clash between Aberdeen, top of the League, and Celtic, the second top, at Pittodrie.

The stage was set for an epic clash, an Aberdeen victory would virtually have made sure of the championship for them.

However, Celtic needed only a draw, and with a quick two-minute goal by Harry Hood, that man again, it seemed they would go even a step further and take two points.

But a defensive slip towards the end of the first half let Aberdeen snatch the equaliser, and that's the way it stayed, 1–1, until the end.

Celtic's next match, against Ayr United at Hampden, because Parkhead was under reconstruction, was cancelled because of a freak weatherstorm.

But on the same Saturday, Aberdeen lost their last league game, against Falkirk at Brockville, and left a clear run to the championship for Celtic.

It also meant a swift fixture change-round, and because Hampden was not available the following Saturday, the last game had to go back to Parkhead.

They stumbled slightly, with a 2–2 draw against St. Mirren at Paisley, although the point did not save the Love Street side from relegation. The goals came from Hood and Lennox.

Two nights later, at Hampden, Celtic sealed the championship with a 2–0 victory against Ayr United, and goals from Lennox and Wallace.

It was the sixth successive championship, strangely enough not one of them had been clinched on their own ground . . . the previous five had all been settled at spots as far apart as Fir Park, Ibrox, Dunfermline, Kilmarnock and Tynecastle.

Now it was at Hampden, and as the players took a bow in the middle of the park they waved for manager Jock Stein to join them in the centre of the park.

MAY: The end of a long, long campaign . . . and that fabulous finale to the league season, the 6–1 victory against Clyde, a performance for which every spectator could only say . . . 'Thanks for the Memory'.

The
Jimmy Johnstone
Show

EVERY fan on the terraces, every observer in the press-box has his own private set of standards he uses to mark up the ability of a player in a game.

And because one person's judgement can vary so widely from his neighbour's, it is the fuel which sets alight so many arguments on football, and gives the game its spice.

I suppose in a massive crowd of 103,000 you would get just as many opinions as people on how the game went, and on how the stars played.

But on the night of Wednesday, 12, May I don't think you would have found many fans—Rangers supporters just as much as Celtic—to disagree with the choice of man of the match in the Scottish Cup Final replay.

For that honour went to the smallest man on the pitch, Celtic right winger Jimmy Johnstone, showing yet again that his giant soccer skills far outweigh his tiny frame.

It takes a great player to rise above the performance of his team-mates and opponents in a soccer show-piece such as the Cup Final, to put his imprint so conclusively on a game of that stature that it is known for ever more, not just as the Cup Final of that year, but as the game that belonged to him.

Perhaps the most famous example was the 1953 English Cup Final, officially a contest between Blackpool and Bolton Wanderers, but enshrined forever in the hearts of football fans as The Stanley Matthews Final.

Maybe there could be no greater tribute to Jimmy Johnstone than that he should follow a man in his own right-wing position . . . and claim a Cup Final for himself!

For it was in this game that Johnstone truly demonstrated that he is probably the only Scottish domestic player who could match the towering talents of the world-class giants, the Peles, the Eusebios, the Moores.

Yet a stranger looking at wee Jimmy lined up on the right-wing spot before a game might wonder if someone had not made a mistake.

The joy of it all . . . skipper Billy McNeill (*right*) adds his congratulations to Jimmy Johnstone (*second from left*) after the wee winger had helped set up a goal for his captain against Queen of the South

For the little Celt looks as if he should be occupying the front spot on the terraces, to make sure he sees all the action on the park, instead of taking on defenders to whose shoulders he barely reaches.

But when that whistle goes it pumps life into Johnstone. As Arsenal and Ireland full-back Sammy Newton neatly summed up: 'I've seen him on television, and it looked as if the film was speeded up. Johnstone was running like those horses in the old cowboy films. He's fantastic.'

Certainly Rangers players, officials and fans must have wished the wee man had been anywhere but that Hampden pitch on the night of the replay.

For Rangers, the team who had gone into the Cup Final as under-

A victory salute . . . from the so-dangerous Lou Macari as he pops in a goal against Rangers Reserves at Parkhead, with Kenny Dalglish shouting encouragement dogs had proved yet again to the bookies and the experts that form can be made to disappear so quickly in an 'Old Firm' match.

The men who face Celtic and Rangers week by week on the park were not any better. The jibes at the newspaper columnists, who almost unanimously tipped Celtic, could just as easily have been directed at the captains of Scotland's sixteen other First Division teams.

They split 14–2 in favour of a Celtic victory in a newspaper poll, just as they had plumped 13–3 for a Celtic victory in the League Cup. Even the experts can be wrong in an 'Old Firm' match!

Rangers fans had nursed hopes for four months—ever since their side had dramatically disappeared from the league race—that it was to be their season for the Scottish Cup.

As their team overcame such First Division opposition as Falkirk, St. Mirren, the holders, Aberdeen, and Hibs on their way to the final, the confidence of the Ibrox fans for a Cup double—the League Cup and the Scottish Cup—increased.

Then, within sight of the final, they suffered the loss of first of all Dave Smith, the most creative player in the Ibrox side, and then right-back Sandy Jardine, one of the most impressive players of the season.

The three most dangerous forwards in reserve
team football . . . Vic Davidson, Kenny Dalglish
and Lou Macari in the final of the Second
Eleven Cup against Falkirk at Brockville

But as the teams lined up on Saturday, 9 May before a 120,000 crowd at Hampden, it was still a strong-looking Rangers side . . . McCloy, Miller, Mathieson; Greig, McKinnon, Jackson; Henderson, Penman, Stein, MacDonald, Johnston . . . Sub Johnstone.

Celtic's side was: Williams, Craig, Brogan; Connelly, McNeill, Hay; Johnstone, Lennox, Wallace, Callaghan, Hood . . . Sub Macari.

It was a game that had not been without its share of pre-match troubles. A group of Glasgow Corporation councillors had protested because the S.F.A. had set the all-ticket limit for the ground as high as 134,000 and a furious controversy had raged about it.

But the fans who had got one of those precious tickets soon found they were going to get plenty to keep them excited. Some of them got too carried away . . . there were over 180 arrests.

And, at the start, most of the action was centred around the Celtic goal. For the second successive Cup Final against their old rivals, the Parkhead team, usually such explosive beginners in a game, were knocked out of their stride.

Rangers should have taken a quick lead, at least twice. Once Willie Johnston incredibly missed a low cross right in front of goal, and then he was foiled by a brave save from 'keeper Evan Williams.

The march to the final . . . and the Airdrie defence can only look as little Jimmy Johnstone somehow manages to climb above them to score in the semi-final at Hampden

The march to the final . . . there's no sign of a Celtic player in this
picture, but six Dunfermline defenders can do nothing to stop this
scoring effort from Willie Wallace, just out of camera range, going
into the net

The strain of it all . . . as Celtic and Rangers players walk off
Hampden at the end of the 1–1 Scottish Cup Final. Rangers Derek
Johnstone, the kid who grabbed the late equaliser is third from the
left

Still, Celtic cannily absorbed all the punishment, and then delivered
a lethal counter-punch of their own.

That came in 40 minutes, when they so simply swept into the lead.
A neat header from Willie Wallace was pushed on by Harry Hood to
little Bobby Lennox.

He shrugged aside a challenge from right-back Alex Miller, to
shove the ball into the net, and start a dance of joy from the Celtic
fans on the terraces.

That goal brought a gloss to Celtic's game. They should certainly
have stretched that so-narrow one goal margin to a more comfortable
two or three.

There were some misses that must have haunted them by the end
of the game. A Jimmy Johnstone shot which soared high over the bar
after a superb run by Tommy Callaghan down the right, and two
efforts by Lennox, one was saved by Peter McCloy, one hit the side
net.

Then, just as they must have been getting ready to tie the green-
and-white ribbons on to the Cup, disaster struck for Celtic.

Rangers were looking less and less likely to score. Their final effort,
and it had been so near to coming off, was a hooked shot by Colin
Stein after Willie Henderson had flicked the ball on to him.

110

But the ball slid past, and Henderson buried his head in the ground, as his disappointment was mirrored on the faces of the rest of his team-mates.

That was in 80 minutes, and for the next ten minutes it seemed only a question of Celtic coolly and carefully guarding their lead.

Then as thousands of fans sneaked a quick look at their watches, and with only three minutes to go, Rangers snatched an equaliser . . . thanks to a terrible mix-up in the Celtic defence.

A long ball from McCloy was punted down to Willie Johnston on the left. His cross, probably more in hope than anything else, was met by substitute Derek Johnstone, who had come on in 73 minutes for Andy Penman.

It should have been cleared by George Connelly, it should certainly have been cleared by 'keeper Even Williams.

But he was caught in the most vulnerable position for any 'keeper. He had left his line, and he had failed to beat the big Rangers teenager to the ball.

There was no one guarding the Celtic goal, as the ball floated down and rolled over the line into the empty net.

Celtic made frantic appeals for the goal to be chalked off, but referee Wharton rejected them, and my impression at the time was that Johnstone did not appear to be offside.

So Derek Johnstone, the kid whose goal earlier in the season had taken the League Cup to Ibrox, was the hero of Rangers again.

The tension of it all after the goal overcame Jim Brogan who had played Rangers danger-man Willie Henderson so magnificently. He was booked for a late tackle on the little winger, to join Tom Callaghan and Alex MacDonald who also had their names taken towards the end of the first half.

But perhaps, over the testing, nervy course of the 90 minutes of an 'Old Firm' final, a draw had been the right result, for both sides could look back and point to chances they had missed.

The history books showed that Rangers had not lost a Cup Final replay since 1905, but Celtic could point to two previous rounds against Dunfermline and Airdrie, where they had really overwhelmed the opposition in replays after a shaky first performance.

And manager Jock Stein had said forcibly—after the semi-final draw against Airdrie—"The team who defeats us in the Cup will have to do it at the first attempt."

Celtic made only one change for the replay, Lou Macari came in for Willie Wallace, but there was a shock Rangers selection at right-back.

Alex Miller had suffered a broken jaw in the first game, and his replacement had been kept a secret until almost the last minute. He

111

was the totally unknown Jim Denny.

It created a sensation, for young Denny had been signed only three months before from Yoker Juniors and had never played in the first team.

The rest of the Rangers team was the same as the previous Saturday, with Johnstone, the kid with the magic goal touch, again the substitute.

Again Rangers started powerfully, and managed to create two half-chances, with Brogan diverting a shot round the post, then having to slam another over his own bar for safety.

But these were brief Ibrox flurries, for it was quickly clear that there was going to be no repeat of the first game.

Celtic were out to take charge of the game, and they did it with some superb soccer, led by the ace in the pack, Jimmy Johnstone.

There is always a gnawing tension for both sides in these games as they strive for the vital first goal, and, as so often in the past, there was a tinge of desperation at times in the football of the teams.

Johnstone, with some incredible ball control, set up a chance for Billy McNeill which his captain, in any other game, would have slammed into the net. But the big Celtic skipper, no doubt hoping he would not give the Rangers defence time to re-group, hit the side netting.

But it was McNeill, up in attack, who helped with the first of the hammer blows—there were two in two minutes—which knocked out Rangers.

He dummied a Lennox corner in 24 minutes which had been fired low across the goal, and as the Rangers defence stood still, Lou Macari popped up in the heart of the goalmouth to slam the ball into the net.

The cheering for the goal among the Celtic fans had not ended, when it was revived again . . . thanks to Jimmy Johnstone.

He zipped on to a ball which had shuttled along the side of the Rangers penalty area, gathered it up and strode forward away from the Ibrox defence.

Centre-half Ronnie McKinnon, in no position to stop him legally, could only fling out both hands and tug at the winger's body to send him crashing to the ground.

There was a not split second's hesitation from referee Wharton as he pointed to the penalty spot. Harry Hood was the man who took the spot-kick, surely the most testing moment of any player's career—a penalty in an 'Old Firm' Cup Final.

But, without a trace of a flutter, he coolly walked up and tucked the ball away from McCloy and into the back of the net.

Celtic, with the boost from that two-goal lead, moved completely

How to send a goalkeeper the wrong way, and Harry Hood neatly
shows the right way to take a penalty as he coolly beats Rangers
'keeper Peter McCloy and ends the great Hampden hush as the
ball crashes into the net to start the Celtic fans' Hampden roar

into command. It was a command that was so superior it made them
careless.

They forgot again about the big boy Johnstone, again brought on
as a substitute at the start of the second-half in a desperate effort to
save the game for Rangers.

The Parkhead side started playing about with the ball, but there
was a casualness about their play which might have been permissible

if they had held a four-goal lead, it was certainly not so clever with only a two-goal margin.

And they paid the penalty in 57 minutes when Johnstone—what a jinx he is to the Celtic defence—headed the ball towards goal. Williams made a good save, but he only cleared to his own right-back Jim Craig, who, in his desperation to clear, could only boot it into the net.

But this time there was no Rangers revival, for Celtic steadied again and took a grip of the game . . . right until the final blast on referee Wharton's whistle which signalled not just the end of the match, but his own retirement.

Yet for once the fans of the beaten teams stayed to the end. Rangers fans chanted their team's name, as the delirious Celtic fans acclaimed their team's magnificent second-half of the League and Cup double.

Johnstone, clutching a bottle of champagne under each arm, said as he left Hampden, to a personal roar of triumph from the fans who

The goals that won the Cup . . . and not even a four-man Rangers iron curtain of Willie Mathieson, Peter McCloy, Colin Jackson and John Greig can stop Lou Macari piercing it as he slams home the ball for Celtic's first goal had waited to hail him. . . .

'I was delighted to have played the greatest game I ever have against Rangers on such an occasion.

'But I must praise the Rangers fans. I thought they took it so well, and I admired every one of the beaten Ibrox side.'

Later wee Jimmy, who had been such a giant star in the match, revealed to me: 'I've never been so keyed up before a match, and I was just the same after it.

'There was a time in the replay when I could not get a drop of moisture in my mouth. I was taking the sweat off my brow and putting it on my tongue.

'Then when Rangers trainer Tommy Craig ran on to attend to one of their players, I got some water from his sponge.

'I stayed up with my wife to three o'clock playing records after the game, and I still could not sleep, so I took the dog for a walk at five o'clock.'

And he praised the club's part-time masseur, Jim Steele, one of the backroom men at Parkhead.

'He was the man who helped to relieve the tension before the match. He's a great joker, it really helps the boys. You know I don't

The joy of it all . . . as his Celtic team-mates rush to congratulate Lou Macari after his goal against Rangers in the Scottish Cup Final replay. *Left to right:* Billy McNeill, Bobby Lennox, Tom Callaghan, David Hay, Macari and George Connelly, with Andy **Penman as the lone Ranger**

think any other team has a man like him, who can lift the strain before a game . . . it's a wonderful help.'

Yet Johnstone's Cup Final form was not just a one-game wonder, it was the climax to a marvellous end of the season for him. And it brought rare praise from his boss, Jock Stein, who said:

'For the last three months he has been Celtic's most consistent player, and you have no idea the pleasure it gave me to say that.

'He has produced the form I always wanted from him, and that in the past he has rarely been able to string together for more than a few games.'

The moment Johnstone changed from being one of soccer's headaches, a player who so often failed to match up to his potential, to become one of the great stars is traceable to the aftermath of the Ajax defeat in Amsterdam.

'I sat down then and wondered where I was going in my football career.

'Everyone at Celtic was down in the dumps after the Ajax defeat, and it suddenly struck me that we could just as easily be out of the European Cup next season.

'For me that is the supreme competition. I could not substitute it

Duel between two players . . . and it seems that Lou Macari and
Rangers' Ronnie McKinnon have almost the whole of Hampden to
themselves as they tangle for the ball in the Cup Final replay

for anything else. I want to win that trophy again. The first time we did it I don't think we were really aware of it, we could hardly believe it ourselves . . . next time, it will be different.'

Time alone can answer the question if the Johnstone who helped carry Celtic successfully over the last lap of the championship, and the Cup as well, is to take over permanently from the old Jimmy Johnstone.

But he has shown that he can stretch his form to more than a few games a season . . . he has a worth-while target to aim at!

Yet Cups, just like the league championship, are not won by the final alone. Manager Stein had looked at the football fates and decided that as his team had won the trophy in 1965, 1967 and 1969, it was their turn to do it again!

He turned out to be right . . . but Celtic doubled their own work-load, by involving themselves in three replays.

They also kept up their amazing sequence of being drawn at home in the competition. It started with a 5–1 victory against Second Division Queen of the South, and the goals came from Wallace, Hood, 2, Callaghan and McNeill.

And they were still at home in the next round to Dunfermline. They scored first, a brilliant header by Willie Wallace, but that man Joe McBride how he hammered his old team last season—snatched the equaliser to force a replay.

The score-line from the second game was Dunfermline 0, Celtic 1, but that does not tell the whole story of this match.

For this was one of Celtic's peaks of the season, although at the end they had to depend on a first-half Harry Hood goal to see them through.

Hood had been a surprise choice. He had been substituted on the Saturday, and it had been expected that he would be dropped from the side for the replay.

Mr. Stein later admitted: 'I had told Harry Hood that he would not be in the replay. I had intended to make changes, and then when I saw the dreadful weather conditions I decided to keep the same team.

'It was not the sort of night to put in youngsters. It was a situation that the senior players had put us in, and it was up to them to get us out of it.'

He revealed his anxieties at that stage of the season when he went on: 'I spoke as hard to these players before the match as I have ever spoken to them in all my time at Celtic Park.

'The players proved again that when they are firing on all cylinders that they are as good as ever.'

Celtic knocked out another Fife team in the next round, giant-killing Raith Rovers, who had already beaten St. Johnstone and Clyde

But they received a 7–1 spanking at Parkhead, with a hat-trick from Lennox, a penalty from Gemmell, and three other goals from Callaghan, Wallace and Davidson.

Then came a semi-final clash with Airdrie, a score-line that amazingly finished 3–3 and it had swung crazily during the game in Celtic's favour from 1–0, 2–0, 2–1, 3–1, and then Airdrie edged back to 3–2 and finally 3–3.

It was the second semi-final, it came after the dreadfully dull first clash between Rangers and Hibs, the match which sparked off Hibs manager Dave Ewing's notorious quote that the Ibrox side were 'rubbish'.

And for a neutral observer this Celtic v. Airdrie match swept away the memory of that first soccer yawn-in. There were some great

Champagne and Coca-Cola . . . the victory mixture for the Celtic babes, reinforced by Bobby Murdoch and Tommy Gemmell, after they had won their third reserve team trophy, the Second Eleven Cup at Falkirk

The joy of it all . . . they've just won the Cup, and the Celtic party
line up in front of their team coach with the precious trophy.
The line-up is top row (*left to right*) . . . George Connelly, Danny
McGrain, Bobby Murdoch, Billy McNeill, Jim Craig, manager
Jock Stein, Evan Williams, Kenny Dalglish, director James Farrell,
masseur Jim Steele, Tom Callaghan and assistant manager Sean
Fallon.

And in front . . . Jimmy Quinn, Jim Brogan, Bobby Lennox,
David Hay, Willie Wallace, Jimmy Johnstone, Lou Macari, Harry
Hood, trainers Bob Rooney and Neil Mochan

goals, Celtic's came from two by Harry Hood and one by Jimmy
Johnstone.

But there was a great fight-back by Airdrie, and some wonderful
goals from them from Whiteford, Wilson, and Busby to punish a
nervy Celtic defence.

Airdrie, although they hit the bar in the first minute of the replay,
never looked like pushing their way to the final, and a right-hook
from Johnstone and Hood finished their chances.

Rangers had already beaten Hibs in their replay, so that paved the
way to another 'Old Firm' Final . . . and the Jimmy Johnstone Show!

Sean Fallon's Story

THE accent—even after 20 years in Glasgow—still comes over with as strong an Irish brogue as any speaker in a St. Patrick's Day Parade.

But there is no doubt where the loyalties of Sean Fallon, the Celtic assistant manager have been for a very long time, firmly entrenched in Glasgow, S.E.

Celtic's connections with Ireland go back to the days of their founders—there has usually been at least one Irishman on their staff—but as Sean pointed out to me: 'In the south, there has always been a greater interest in teams from England.

'One of my earliest football heroes was the great Everton star, Dixie Dean, who played for my home town team, Sligo.'

Yet there was a thread running through his life, a connection which made him forget about his previous idols, Deans and Arsenal star Cliff Bastin, and turned him into a fervent Celtic fan.

When his young sister was involved in a swimming accident, one of three men who helped rescue her turned out to be Joe McMenemy, son of the legendary Jimmy McMenemy, the inside-forward who had been one of Celtic's greatest masters of soccer.

A friendship sprang up, and soon after his return to Scotland, Joe McMenemy sent a parcel to Sligo, which contained a copy of 'The Celtic Story' by Willie Maley, an autographed picture of the famous Empire Exhibition side, and a Celtic jersey.

Sean Fallon's father, who had been wounded serving with the British Army in the Dardanelles during the First World War, had also lived for a time in Glasgow. He had worked as a postman in Ibrox, but he had become a follower of Celtic, and when he returned to live in Ireland he founded a team in Sligo . . . and naturally called them 'Celtic'.

And to tie all the strings together another reason was the original founder of Celtic, Brother Walfrid, came from Sligo.

Yet if it had not been for the fact that the rulers of Gaelic football, the all-action game played in Ireland, frowned so much on soccer, Sean might never have realised his dream of playing at Parkhead.

120

Celtic assistant manager, Sean Fallon, framed by the old Parkhead stand, looks out over the pitch that he has known as player and coach for twenty-one years

For Sean played both codes, something which the Gaelic football authorities did not permit. He had progressed to play for his county, and in one match had scroed two goals against Dan O'Keefe, of Kerry, one of the great goalkeeping stars of the sport, who is still talked about in Ireland today.

However, just before the match, he had played for Junior Ireland against a Lanarkshire League select at Dalymount Park, Dublin.

The Gaelic football bosses employed vigilantes to make sure their players did not take part in soccer, and Sean's double sporting life was reported to them. It resulted in suspension for him, along with his friend, Angus McMorrow, who went on to be capped for Ireland at rugby.

So there was no alternative! It had to be soccer. It became his big interest, and eventually, in March 1950— it led to manager Jimmy McGrory signing him for Celtic.

As we sat in the Parkhead board-room, crowded with the trophies, the pennants and the presents from so many trips, he said simply: 'It was a dream for me that I would become a Celtic player. I've been fortunate. Very few people in life are lucky enough to see their dreams come true.'

His career as a defender earned him the title of the 'Iron Man'. And when you listen to him reel off his list of injuries as casually as if they were a shopping list, you get some idea of how he won the title.

His left arm was broken five times, he had a collar bone broken, his nose broken, repeated cartilage operations and a rib fractured.

Maybe it was the legacy of his days as a Gaelic footballer but he says: 'I played hard, and I respected opponents who did the same.

'I believe that tackling is part and parcel of the game, it can be as much an art as any other part of soccer.

'I respected players who could not match me physically, but tried to beat me with ability and agility.

The celebrations for the first trophy under a new regime . . . and Jock Stein (*right*) and his assistant Sean Fallon naturally look happy as they line up for this 1965 picture. The Scottish Cup stands bedecked in green-and-white ribbons after the victory against Dunfermline

'Defensive tackling has lost much of its snap in recent years, but it can be very effective. Maybe I should not praise our own players, but I think Danny McGrain and Jim Brogan are two of the best tacklers in the game today.'

Sean's Celtic career lasted for eight seasons and took in two of the club's greatest achievements in the pre-Stein era, the Cup and League double of 1953–54, and the 7–1 League Cup victory of 1957.

Almost all that time he played as a defender, apart from the controversial spells at centre, a position he admitted to me he did not really like.

He first played at centre in a tour game, one of those matches in which so often a club is forced into emergency switches. It was in America and because of an injury to John McPhail, he took over for a game in Philadelphia.

But he did not move to centre again until the later stages of the pre-season St. Mungo Cup tournament, a competition to celebrate the 'Festival of Britain' at the time, and he scored two goals in the final against Aberdeen, one of them which was wrapped in controversy . . . for it was started by a throw-in from Charlie Tully, hit against the body of Aberdeen full-back Davie Shaw and from the quick cross, Sean scored.

Then it was back to full-back, and a succession of injuries, including one he received against ex-Celt Jimmy Delaney, then playing with Falkirk.

'It was a most unusual injury. My arm seemed to get squeezed between our two bodies. At half time we thought it was muscular, but I finished the game with the sweat pouring off from the pain, and there was no doubt it was broken.'

Then came a broken collar-bone against Hearts, and it seemed that with the end of the season looming up he would be finished with football until the following August.

Let Sean tell the story . . . 'I was all set to go to recuperate in Ireland. I had the ticket for my flight arranged, I even went as far as putting my bags in the air terminal at St. Enoch Square to collect them after I had watched Celtic play that day.

'The fixture was against Hamilton and during it John McPhail got one of the worst groin injuries I have ever seen.

'The club were in a real spot for injuries at the time. I was standing in a corridor just before I left to catch my plane, and I could see some of our officials talking and always looking over at me.

'Eventually I was called over and they asked me if there was any chance that I might stay on, and make an effort to play.

'Of course I couldn't refuse the request, and I volunteered to have a go. I remember the first game after that so well, it was against

Airdrie . . . on St. Patrick's Day and I played centre.

'It was the start of my run in the position which went on and included the Cup Final, when I scored the winning goal.

'I didn't kid myself that I was heaven-sent in the position. But it was explained to me that I was there to balance up the front line. At that time we had some very skilful players in the attack, John Higgins, Willie Fernie, Jimmy Walsh, but they needed someone to take the weight off them.'

But it was at full-back that Fallon got his last, and one of his major honours with Celtic, a League Cup Winners' Medal after the 7–1 1957 victory against Rangers.

'We had a wonderful team, just at that time. Two forwards up front, Billy McPhail and Sammy Wilson, who really hit it off together. But great team as it was, I would not say it had the consistency of the side that won the double. That was really something.'

Yet the moments for Fallon to recall the past are rare, and something in which he does not dwell. For his part now is in the Celtic of the future . . . with his charge the second team and the starlets who could become the heroes of tomorrow.

A final flourish to the season took Celtic's babes to a clean sweep of the honours, the Reserve League, the Reserve League Cup, and Second Eleven Cup.

Yet the big factor for any reserve side is not just the trophies they win, important as they are to youngsters' morale, but how they will succeed when they step into the test of the league side's big-time.

Fallon told me: 'I am sure some of these boys will be a success. For they have become proficient in the basic skills, and that is something too many players neglect today.

'They have proved in their games in the league team that they will be capable of eventually commanding a place. Look at Lou Macari, with a goal in the Cup Final replay against Rangers.

'They have scored over a hundred goals in the reserve league in the last two seasons. I don't suppose there's a top team in Britain who can equal that.

'I was delighted we won these trophies. A club like ours must impress on our youngsters from the start that we want to win.

'But we have also made sure that we did not neglect their future just for the sake of winning. We've experimented with them in different roles, something you just can't afford to do in the big team.

'Take Kenny Dalglish. He's got a hunger for goals, but when he was at wing-half he showed a tendency to run ahead of his own attack in his enthusiasm. So we moved him up permanently, and he certainly cracked in the goals.

'Vic Davidson was moved slightly back, so that he struck more

The Celtic line-up on the first day of training . . . for season 1954–55. How many faces can you spot among the players talking to trainer Alex Dowdalls?

That's Sean Fallon, bottom row right, and Jock Stein, fifth from the
left in the top row. Other famous names include Alex Boden, Neil
Mochan, Charlie Tully, Jimmy Walsh, Mike Haughney, Frank
Meechan, Bobby Collins, Bertie Peacock, John Bonnar and coach
George Paterson

from deeper positions. I can't say if these will be their final positions, but they are gaining experience all the time.'

How do these kids today, some of whom were only infants when the 1953–54 team were sweeping to the double, compare with the players of Sean Fallon's time ?

'I think they have improved certainly in one aspect, in physical fitness. When I was a player you more or less decided yourself how much you trained.

'The players who wanted to shirk it could always find ways. Some of them could get by on natural ability so their lack of fitness was not noticed.

'That just does not work today. But in some teams the natural ability has been curbed, and not perhaps always for the good of the game.'

A major influence in the life of the Parkhead players of Sean Fallon's generation was the club chairman, later to be knighted as Sir Robert Kelly.

'I think we all admired his strength of character. Even the people who disagreed with him knew he really believed in what he said.

'It took a lot of courage to stand up for his youth policy at a time when the club was not getting success, and he was under fire from so many quarters.

'I can think of few men who would not have flinched, and perhaps made some alterations to bow to the clamour.

'But he never changed and it was a very proud moment for him when the youngsters he had pinned so much faith on won the European Cup.'

Now a new generation of Celtic youngsters are coming along the pipeline. Fresh-faced kids, as raw as the Jimmy Johnstones, Bobby Murdochs, and Billy McNeills—the household names of today—were ten years ago.

Those flashing Irish eyes of Sean Fallon have twinkled with delight at some of their performances for he can visualise the time when they will be the stars and a new crop of kids will be waiting to slot into the vacancies.

It is the continuing process of the Celtic story. As it has been since the club was founded . . . and will be as long as there is a club called Celtic.